JOINS THE RANKS OF
GORKY PARK
New York Times Book Review

RUSSIAN SPRING

"The author keeps the action reined in until the tension reaches the screaming point. Dennis Jones, who gave us the bestseller <u>Rubicon One</u>, has written a frighteningly realistic political thriller in a class with the best."

UPI

RUSSIAN SPRING

"Jones's superb plotting and attention to detail keep the reader totally involved in the fast-flowing narrative, which comes to an explosive conclusion. Highly recommended."

Library Journal

"a well-written and gripping story"
Winnipeg Free Press

RUSSIAN SPRING

"an intriguing read"
The Ottawa Citizen

"a well-researched and gripping work"
Booklist

RUSSIAN SPRING

"Frighteningly accurate, <u>Russian Spring</u> is a taut political thriller that will keep readers guessing until the chilling climax."

Mystery News

RUSSIAN SPRING

A NOVEL

DENNIS JONES

General
— PAPERBACKS —

A Division of General Publishing Co. Ltd.
Toronto, Canada

Stoddart Publishing edition
published in 1984

General Paperbacks edition
published in 1985

Cover design: Brant Cowie/Artplus

ISBN 0-7736-7096-3

Printed in Canada

Northeast Afghanistan
February 26 — 27

COLONEL ANDREI MIKHAILOV saw the bodies first. There were three of them, lying splayed in the road's frozen mud just around the last curve before the valley. Mikhailov focused his binoculars. The uniforms were mud-caked but unmistakably Russian. There were no helmets or weapons nearby; the men had been running away when they were cut down.

Their boots were gone, too, stolen by whoever had killed them.

The driver in the BMP armored troop carrier ahead had seen the bodies and the vehicle began to slow. Colonel Mikhailov clicked the transmit switch on his headset cable and said, "Point vehicle, speed up. Don't stop." Idiot, he thought, as he released the button. Stop and you politely give them a sitting target.

He turned in the hatch of his own BMP and looked back at the rest of the armored company as it clattered around the curve. The ten BMP armored carriers were bunching up around the four T62 tanks again. He cursed to himself; he had warned the company commander about this at least twice before the column left Faizabad.

"Captain Tyurin," Mikhailov said into his microphone. "Get your vehicles spread out. Fifty meters. Remember?"

An incoherent acknowledgment in his headset. The vehicles began to increase their spacing. The two self-propelled guns at the column's rear had to slow almost to a stop. Mikhailov fumed.

The mujahidin guerrillas had very few heavy weapons, and were poor shots, but a slowly moving vehicle was within their capabilities.

There was no firing from the rock slopes and crags above the road. Mikhailov relaxed slightly.

They had almost reached the bodies. Beyond the still forms the road narrowed again to no more than five or six meters across, then plunged between two ragged faces of rock down into the valley. Here, if anywhere before they reached the village, they would have to fight: one vehicle hit in the gap, another at the rear of the column, and they would be immobilized and cut to pieces. It had happened to others.

A clattering reached Mikhailov's ears despite the headset. Momentarily he left off sweeping the binoculars over the slopes above, and looked up. A Mil-24 helicopter gunship wop-wopped overhead. A thousand meters above it flew the silver-gray darts of Sukhoi ground-attack aircraft: air support from the Faizabad base. They had got up despite the overcast that lay halfway down the higher peaks. That will make things a little easier, thought Mikhailov. A little.

The BMP ground past the bodies. The road was so narrow that the vehicle's left tracks almost touched one of them. Mikhailov thought he saw the man's hand move, in supplication or in fear of the treads. He averted his eyes.

They were through the gap. In front of Mikhailov the road, rock-strewn and rutted with frozen mud, snaked down into the valley where the unit they were supporting had been ambushed an hour earlier during an antiguerrilla sweep. Half a kilometer away, across the stream that watered the valley, lay the village, grayish-white against the snow-streaked coppery earth. A few leafless plane trees poked above the flat roofs. Between the village and the stream lay a scattering of ruined tombs. Several columns of smoke were rising from among the houses. Two wrecked Russian trucks lay among the tombs, one on fire. Three BMPs stood, apparently deserted, at the village's edge.

The column debouched from the pass and deployed into battle line, the tanks moving abreast of each other ahead of the personnel carriers. Tyurin's doing this part all right, thought Mikhailov. He seems to like to work by the book.

"We've got the other unit on radio," said Tyurin's voice in the headset.

"What's the situation?" Mikhailov continued to scan the mountains' flanks above. They were gray-brown, a jumble of boulders and scree, cut with deep ravines.

"The infantry's pinned down in the village. The BMPs are giving them fire support. The commander's been killed."

"Who's in command?"

"Lieutenant Redin."

"All right. Where are the other BMPs?"

"Other side of the village. They're bottling up the bandits."

Not likely, thought Mikhailov. With our infantry stuck in the village the mujahidin will slip through our cordon like shit through a goose. "How many bandits?"

"Twenty or thirty."

"All right. Carry on."

What a screw up, Mikhailov thought. Above, the ground-attack aircraft circled impotently. The helicopter bobbed uncertainly along the ridge lines, searching.

We'll have to pry our people out somehow, he told himself. His stomach knotted. No air strikes, because they're mixed up with the mujahidin in the village. They shouldn't have come up here without air support, what were they thinking of?

Captain Tyurin's small force, spread out in the textbook order of a Russian infantry company on the attack, was now only a hundred meters from the stream. A figure wearing gray robes and carrying a bundle ran from one of the houses. Mikhailov couldn't tell whether it was a man or a woman. Ten meters from the shelter of a cairn of stones, a burst of gunfire knocked the figure into the snow. One of the tanks' guns banged. A plume of smoke rose from the slopes above the village.

Mikhailov's BMP splashed through the stream and halted on its far side, in line with the other infantry carriers. The four tanks had stopped abreast of each other, a hundred meters ahead. Soldiers tumbled out of the BMPs and shook themselves into a ragged line. Someone was shooting at them from the village. One of the tank machine guns replied and the firing stopped. The men broke into a trot. Mikhailov clambered out of his vehicle with the eight soldiers of his guard squad and followed them. Technically, as he wasn't supposed to be involved in combat, he should have stayed put, but he wanted to see at close hand how Tyurin's unit would deal with the situation.

They passed among the ruined tombs. Fragments of marble and alabaster, some incised with flowing Persian script, lay on the sandy earth. A few worn turban stones poked above ground level, betraying older monuments beneath. The village appeared as deserted as the graves. Without warning, somewhere in the mud-walled streets ahead, shooting began again. Mikhailov could hear the harsh, deep rattle of Russian weapons and then the characteristic scratch of an American M16. The firing stopped as abruptly as it had started. Mikhailov looked up at the ridge lines to see the helicopter, which he had forgotten about, swing back over the valley and dip toward the slopes above the village. Its guns began to fire. The sound reminded Mikhailov of tearing canvas.

They're breaking out of the village, he realized. Once they're up in the ravines we've lost them.

Tyurin trotted up. The line of soldiers had stopped, the men lying down with their weapons pointed at the village. "We've established contact in there," he said. "Everyone will be out in a couple of minutes."

"What about the bandits?"

"They're moving up onto the slopes. The planes are after them now. We'll have to pull back, the planes are going to hit the village too."

"All right."

Russian troops began to filter out of the maze of mud walls. Several were wounded, carried by other men. Everyone went back to the streambed and took up firing positions while the planes made two attack runs across the upper slopes. On the third run they bombed the village. Mikhailov stopped watching after the napalm had been dropped, the jellied gasoline burning and sending up thick gouts of black smoke streaked with red. This was the eighth village he had seen destroyed.

"They're coming out," said Captain Tyurin excitedly. Firing broke out up and down the Russian line.

Mikhailov looked through his binoculars. About a score of villagers were running for the line of trees and scrub southeast of the houses. As he watched, three of them went down.

"They're civilians," he said.

"So what?" said Tyurin, forgetting himself. "They let the bandits in there."

"Stop the shooting, Captain," said Mikhailov.

After a moment Tyurin shouted an order. The men stopped firing, but not before two more of the villagers had been hit. The remainder reached the scrub and disappeared.

A lieutenant hurried up. "Captain Tyurin, sir. The planes have to go back. Fuel."

"What about our air cover on the way back?"

"They're sending two more helicopters."

"Good. We'll pull out in an hour." Tyurin looked at the village. The flames were dying down; there was little to burn. "We'll do a body count up there first. Have everyone get ready to move."

Mikhailov got up stiffly. He dreaded entering the village, not because of the risk of being shot at — that was minimal now — but because of what he knew he would see there. There must have been civilians left for the napalm.

Tyurin and his company were already starting up the slope. To put off following them, Mikhailov walked a few dozen meters east, toward the edge of the tomb area. He looked at the inscriptions on the fragments of alabaster and wondered what they said and how old they were. Mikhailov could speak some Persian and Pashto — the major languages of the country — but could not read their complex scripts.

He found them around the corner of an empty marble tomb half sunk in the frozen earth. The woman had to be the figure he saw fleeing the village at the beginning of the attack. She must have crawled to the tomb for shelter after being hit near the rock cairn, dragging the child with her. Mikhailov couldn't understand how she had done it; the lower half of her *chadri* was drenched with blood and the white bones of a shattered foot protruded from beneath its hem. She was quite dead.

At first he thought the child was dead as well, with the great wound the bullets had torn across the left side of her face. The right side was unmarked; she looked to be five or six. He was about to turn away when he saw her undamaged eye follow him.

No, he thought.

He knelt beside her. The remnants of her mouth fluttered. She had been hit in the body, as well. She could not possibly live, not up here, with the rudimentary aid they could give her, even if Tyurin would bother to spare it.

She whimpered. The pain would start now, as the shock wore off.

Carefully, without letting her see, he unsnapped the flap of his holster and drew out the Makarov. He spoke to her gently in Pashto, then he put his left hand gently on her undamaged cheek, positioned the gun, and squeezed the trigger. Her head snapped momentarily to the right and then settled.

Mikhailov stood up, leaned against the tomb, and vomited. He was still leaning on the cold marble when Captain Tyurin came back from the village. The captain looked pale and sick. He glanced down at the child's body. "Cleaning up?"

Mikhailov nodded. "She wouldn't have lived."

"I would have done it myself," said Tyurin savagely. "We found one of the other company's sergeants up there. They cut his balls off and bayoneted him; likely the women did it. He's still alive."

Mikhailov wiped his mouth with the back of his hand. "Any prisoners?"

"No bandits, they all got away except for two the planes hit."

"Civilians?"

Tyurin waved his arm upslope. "A dozen."

Mikhailov looked in the direction of the wave. Most of the Russian soldiers were walking back to the BMPs, leaving six guards with a group of ragged villagers. The villagers stood between the soldiers and the wall of a shattered house; all of them had their hands clasped on their heads, even the children.

"Let's go back to the BMPs," said Captain Tyurin. Mikhailov wiped his mouth again and walked up the slope, leaving the captain behind. The lieutenant who had spoken to Tyurin earlier was standing with the guards, dragging nervously on a cigarette. The soldiers watched Mikhailov approach, their weapons cradled loosely in their arms.

"You're not planning to take them back, are you?" asked Mikhailov. "There's no room in the trucks, we've lost two of them."

The lieutenant's eyes were blank, yellow-brown, and slightly mad. He shook his head, looking away from Mikhailov toward the villagers. The Afghans watched dully.

"Have you searched them for weapons?" asked Mikhailov.

A nod.

"What?"

"Yes, Colonel. And the houses. There were no weapons."

"Then get your men back to the carriers. You've done everything you need to."

The soldiers fidgeted with their weapons. One of them stared hard at Mikhailov, insolent, murderous.

The lieutenant threw the half-smoked cigarette on the ground and said, "Back to the carriers. With your permission, Colonel."

Mikhailov nodded. He waited until the soldiers had started down the slope and then followed them. Despite the chill wind his back and armpits were wet. Behind him he heard the villagers scuttling back into their muddy ruins.

At the BMPs, Tyurin asked, "What did you stop them for? They might have shot you as well as the villagers."

"Did you want them to kill the children too?"

"They'll grow up to be bandits."

"Don't you listen to your political officers?" asked Mikhailov with more than a hint of sarcasm. "How are we going to have a socialist revolution if we execute all the peasants?"

"They were only black-asses, Colonel."

The racist term, which Russian soldiers used as well for Soviet troops of non-Russian stock, infuriated Mikhailov. "Shut up."

"Yes, Colonel."

On the way back to Faizabad the mutilated sergeant died.

Mikhailov was writing his reports. He sat at a wooden desk in a spartan office in the regimental headquarters, stabbing irritably at the keys of a badly maintained typewriter. The office had a dirty window overlooking the main street of the heavily defended firebase outside Faizabad. One of the last snowfalls of winter lay on the roofs of the barracks across the street; the morning sun was already melting the snow into ragged streaks. Beyond the roofs, across the Kochka River, Faizabad lay in the low hills among groves of plane trees and poplars.

Mikhailov stopped typing and looked out the window. He was a tall man, very thin from poor food. His eyebrows, like his hair, were a deep auburn. The eyebrows turned up slightly at the outer corners, giving his face a permanently quizzical expression. He had green eyes and a straight, thin nose, which was a little too long for his face. Women found him attractive.

The light off the snow hurt his eyes. He rubbed them with his fingertips and returned to his typing.

The "c" key jammed again and he freed it, cursing in a monotone. He was finishing the last page of his first report, which read:

> and attention should be paid to this. The captain of the Third Company is particularly at fault, consistently allowing vehicles to travel at less than the minimum separation required in hostile territory. In addition, this officer arranged his assault on the enemy position without allowing for the fluid nature of bandit tactics, which enabled all but two of them to withdraw successfully. I recommend that Captain Tyurin receive further instruction in the particulars of counterinsurgency operations.

He rolled the sheet of paper out of the typewriter, signed it, and clipped it to the other six pages of the first report. This report he would give to the commander of the Faizabad counterinsurgency headquarters, as a guide to improving Soviet effectiveness against the Afghan guerrillas; or bandits, rather. The mujahidin were never referred to as guerrillas, as it was thought that this would give the insurgents a legitimacy they did not deserve or which could not be admitted. Mikhailov usually thought of them as guerrillas, but this was a private indulgence. He was a counterinsurgency specialist based in Kabul at the general headquarters of the Soviet forces in Afghanistan, and was routinely assigned to various combat headquarters around the country to evaluate and suggest improvements in their tactics. He also reported to Kabul GHQ on the effectiveness of the combat units and their commanders, and as a result was not much liked, although his military skill was respected. At general headquarters, on the other hand, he wielded a good deal of influence, both because of his professional ability and the fact that his uncle was a powerful member of the Politburo.

He had one other set of responsibilities, which he would fulfil by writing the second report. These responsibilities were not common knowledge at all; in fact, there was only one other person in Afghanistan who knew that he had them. This person was Lieutenant-General Stepan Gordik, head of the KGB Third Directorate in Afghanistan, and the officer responsible for monitoring the loyalty of the Soviet forces in the country. Gordik possessed a comprehensive surveillance network comprising several dozen officers who reported on their men, their seniors, and each other. Only a tiny proportion of the officer corps worked with the Third Directorate, but their presence, although unadvertised, was known and served to restrain any but the mildest dissidence. Mikhailov was unusual in that he controlled no informants himself; Gordik used his mobility and rank to monitor the upper officer levels where unofficial Third Directorate recruits were harder to acquire. Mikhailov held colonel's rank in the KGB, and was paid well, and unofficially, for his extra duties.

He inserted another sheet of the rough army paper into the

typewriter, took a cigarette out of a flat metal case, and lit it. His hands shook as he did so. He had noticed that when he looked at blank areas, like walls or sheets of paper, the shattered features of the child up in the valley seemed to appear on the surfaces. He had never had to kill a child deliberately before.

We shouldn't be here, he thought, as he stared at the keys. We never should have come here. We're supposed to be here to protect the socialist revolution but the people are hungry and poor and we are killers of children. Even at home the food lines are long and there's starvation in the countryside. But I can eat. I can buy shoes. And I watch the Party's elite ride in Zil limousines and buy western shoes for their mistresses in the hard-currency stores where the average Russian is chased away if he so much as puts his nose in. Or is sent to Afghanistan to shoot children in the head.

He realized that he was shaking with fury. The cigarette had burned away to ash. I have to do something soon, he thought, hunching again over the typewriter. Something, soon.

Kabul
Monday, March 1

"*I* HAVE AN APPOINTMENT with Lieutenant-General Gordik," said Mikhailov.

Gordik's secretary, a pale young corporal wearing an ill-fitting uniform, nodded and consulted a list. He knew Mikhailov, but the ritual had to be followed, rather in the same way that Captain Tyurin laid out his textbook attack on the village, regardless of realities.

Mikhailov followed the secretary to Gordik's office, which was on the third floor of what once had been the Kabul Hilton and was now the center of Russian military power in Afghanistan. Gordik's cover was a straightforward one, that of head of the Operational Studies Bureau. The OSB had been established two years previously to develop improved counterinsurgency techniques and help units in the field to apply them. Mikhailov had been transferred from the GRU, Military Intelligence, into the OSB shortly after being posted to Afghanistan. He was fairly certain the Third Directorate had influenced the transfer, to allow him more mobility. Gordik, through the OSB, had access to all available information about mujahidin activities and intentions, and to confidential reports on the effectiveness and behavior of the Soviet troops fighting them. His position made him a very useful Third Directorate officer, and a very powerful influence in army-command circles.

Gordik looked up from his desk as the secretary announced

Mikhailov. He waited until the office door was closed again, studied Mikhailov over the tops of his spectacles, and said, "Sit down, Colonel."

Mikhailov sat down in a red, plushly upholstered chair. It was surprisingly hard. He waited.

Lieutenant-General Gordik took off his spectacles, polished them with a bit of green cloth, and replaced them on his nose. He was a small, sleepy-looking man of about fifty, with thinning blond hair worn a little longer than regulation. He picked up a sheaf of papers, which Mikhailov recognized as his report from Faizabad, and put it down again.

"So," he said. "You don't think much of Colonel Serov."

Serov was the commander of the 302nd Motorized Rifle Regiment, based at Faizabad. "He's politically very conscientious," said Mikhailov.

"That's clear from your report. But he doesn't look after his men."

"Politically, sir, as I said, he's irreproachable. He makes sure they attend all the education sessions."

"So that among political education, training, and fighting, they don't have time to sleep."

"Yes, General." Mikhailov paused momentarily. "Also, the food is very bad. In January the line troops were given nothing but *kasha* and macaroni. No meat, nothing fresh."

"What happened to the meat ration?"

"I think the commissariat people put it on the black market."

Gordik made a note. "I'll have the inspectorate look into that. Although what good it will do, I don't know, they're all running their own little schemes themselves. What's the state of morale up there? I don't think a report can give the real...ah, flavor of it, perhaps."

Mikhailov cleared his throat. He had kept the tone of the report moderate, on the principle that either praising or condemning too much could bring unwanted attention from Moscow. He decided to be straightforward with Gordik.

"It's very bad. The men are sullen." He recounted the incident of the captured villagers up in the valley. He left out the episode of the mutilated girl. "I think," he ended, "that if things had gone the other way, the men would have shot me. They wanted to kill those civilians."

Gordik considered this for some time. "It's happened," he said finally. "We have twenty-three verified accounts of disaffected troops shooting their officers in the past four years."

"I didn't know there were that many," said Mikhailov.

"Those are the ones we're certain of," Gordik replied. "The suicide rate in the ranks is also very high, I'm sure you're aware of that."

Mikhailov nodded.

"What do you think we should do about it?" asked Gordik.

"Well," answered Mikhailov carefully, "I would say the best response would be to improve the quality of the political education given the troops. To impress upon them more strongly their role in the advance of socialism. If they're well motivated, these problems will disappear."

Gordik studied him with an expression of faint amusement. That's the right answer, the general's face said, but it's a crock of shit.

"Improving their food and giving them more rest would help as well," muttered Mikhailov.

"Yes," said Gordik. "We'll see what we can stir up at GHQ." He picked up a brown envelope and opened it. "Now I have some good news for you. Two pieces of it, in fact." He extracted two sheets of paper. "First, your application for extraordinary leave has been approved. You have two weeks to spend at home. I've arranged air transport back to Moscow for you."

Mikhailov stared at the paper. He had applied for leave five weeks previously, when a cable from his sister arrived informing him that his daughter had contracted pneumonia and was in serious condition in a Moscow hospital. Two weeks ago, with the leave still not forthcoming, the child had gone home, largely recovered. He had been frantic with worry; she might have died with him away. And now they gave him the leave.

"Thank you, General Gordik," he managed.

"Also, when you come back, you'll be posted for the spring and summer to Herat. It's another step up the ladder for you, you'll be taking over the district OSB office there. They're going to need good counterinsurgency people over there, the Afghan National Liberation Front's supposed to be planning big things for the spring. You'll have lots to do."

"I hope so, General Gordik." Mikhailov barely heard what he was saying. Two weeks at home. And then, in the back of his head, like an echo from the shabby office at the firebase in Faizabad: *time to do something.*

"One last thing," said Gordik. "On your first day back, that's the eighth, you are to see General Tolbukhin at Dzerzhinsky Square, at ten in the morning. Don't be late."

Moscow
Monday, March 8

THE CITY was still in deep winter. Beyond the large double-glazed window of the apartment's living room, where Mikhailov stood eating toasted rye bread, fresh snow lay on the sidewalks connecting the sixteen-story towers of the apartment complex. From Mikhailov's vantage point twelve floors above the ground, he could just make out the domes of the Donskoi Monastery, and beyond them, fading into the gray sky, the latticework mast of the television tower. It was seven o'clock in the morning.

He heard a faint noise in the corridor that led to the two bedrooms. His sister, Nadia, came into the living room, rubbing her eyes and yawning. She was a slender woman, prematurely gray, unlike her brother. Mikhailov swallowed the last of his toast and put the plate on the television set. Nadia came over, gave him a long hug, and said, "You should have woken me. I'd have made you breakfast. Oh, it's good to see you again."

He squeezed her arm. "It's all right, I didn't want much. And I didn't want Valeria to get up before she has to."

"I'll make tea."

She disappeared into the tiny kitchen. It was one of the few things Mikhailov didn't like about the apartment, because it was too small to eat in. Russian kitchens were traditionally the center of the home, where everyone talked, ate, drank, and argued. To make up for the small kitchen, the apartment had two bedrooms as well as its own bathroom, which meant that nobody had to sleep in the living room. Mikhailov's KGB rank rather than his army one had got him the privilege of such accommodations and with them that most un-Russian luxury, privacy.

He heard Nadia pouring tea and took his empty plate back to the kitchen. His sister was two years older than he, and some eight years ago had made a bad marriage to a junior foreign-ministry official who had remained junior because of vodka. He blamed Nadia for his drinking, but wouldn't consent to a divorce because he might have to leave his apartment for a smaller one. When Mikhailov's wife, Kseni, died of a heart condition two years ago, Nadia moved in with Mikhailov, temporarily, to take care of four-year-old Valeria. With Mikhailov's posting to Afghanistan shortly thereafter the arrangement had become more or less permanent, to everyone's advantage. Valeria got better care than she would in a state crèche, Nadia's husband kept his apartment and drank in peace, and Nadia led a less troubled existence. She was a department supervisor in GLAVLIT, the state censorship bureau, and she and Mikhailov shared the costs of the household, which she ran with determined efficiency. When he was home she mothered him, which he understood; she had no children of her own.

They drank the tea at the dining table at the end of the living room. The apartment still felt strange to Mikhailov. Nadia had put up new curtains sometime since his last leave and he hadn't noticed them when he arrived late the previous night. He hadn't awakened Valeria, only looked in at her in the dim light from the hallway. He thought she had grown.

Nadia finished her tea. "I must get her up or she'll be late for school and I'll be late for work."

"I'll do it," said Mikhailov.

He went to his own bedroom and got the stuffed bear out of his kit. He had turned Kabul inside out to find her something when he heard that she was ill and he had still thought he would get his leave quickly. The bear was covered in soft brown plush and had round yellow eyes with black centers and wore a small blue satin jacket. It came from East Germany. Mikhailov had found it in the officers' special store at the Kabul firebase; why it was there was a mystery known only to the army commissariat. They couldn't ship in enough food for the troops, but they could stock the officers' stores with toy bears. He had been torn between anger and happiness when he found the little creature.

Valeria's room, where Nadia slept when Mikhailov was at home, was dim, the curtains closed. He opened them slightly and sat down on the narrow bed beside his daughter. In sleep she looked so much like her mother that his eyes stung. "Dumpling," he said, and rubbed her shoulders.

Valeria blinked mistily. He watched as the sleep cleared from her face. She had blue eyes, freckles on an upturned nose, fine reddish-gold hair.

"Daddy?"

"Hello, dumpling."

"Daddy, you came back." She struggled to sit up. "Oh, *daddy*." She threw her arms around his neck and clamped herself to him. After a full minute she sat back and looked at him. "I thought you were going to stay away for*ever*." Convulsed with emotion, she burst into tears.

"No, don't worry. I'll always come back. Look, I brought you something. From far away. A bear. A little Russian bear with a vest to keep him warm."

She sniffled and studied the bear, fingering its softness. "All the way from where you were?"

"All the way from there."

She was recovering.

"I love him. Aunt Nadia, Aunt Nadia. Daddy's home and I got a new bear!"

Nadia was at the door. "What a nice bear. Did you say thank you?"

"Thank you, daddy."

"You're very welcome, dumpling. Now, we'd better get you up for breakfast, so you won't be late for school. All right?"

"Do I *have* to go today?"

"Yes, but I'll take you there and come for you this afternoon when school's over."

"Are you going away again soon?"

"Not very soon. I'll be here fourteen whole days. Now go along with Aunt Nadia."

She went away to the bathroom. On her bedside table next to the little pottery lamp stood a picture of her mother, his dead wife. Kseni. Heart damaged by rheumatic fever, the doctors had said. She had been fine-featured, a beauty, with flawless skin and hair so blond it was almost silver. Valeria was going to look like her, but darker, because of Mikhailov's reddish-brown hair.

He got up and straightened her pillow, smoothing out the wrinkles. Without warning, the ruined face of the Afghan child superimposed itself on the white cloth. Mikhailov closed his eyes, opened them, and went to the window and pulled the curtains back all the way to let in the light.

This morning I have to see General Tolbukhin, he thought. And soon I am going to have to decide what I am going to do. And then, most difficult, I shall have to decide how to do it.

At half past eight he took Valeria to the *detsky sad*, the kindergarten in the shadow of the apartment towers. The *detsky sad*'s windows were tightly shut against drafts, and the air smelled of children's bodies, potato soup, garlic, and fried fish. The children were having skating lessons that day, and Valeria bounced excitedly. After promising that he and not Nadia would come for her after school, he left the building and walked to the Lenin subway station.

The train was packed with Muscovites on their way to work. All the way to Dzerzhinsky Square Mikhailov stood by the car doors, feeling alien. If he had said, "I've come from the war in Afghanistan" to the man or woman next to him, they would have stared at him with incomprehension. The newspapers published only economic news of the "glorious advance of the Marxist-Leninist revolution in Afghanistan," when they referred to it at all. Anyone who heard anything more by listening to western radio was careful not to mention it in public. No casualty lists were published; those who had lost sons or relatives were warned to keep their grief to themselves. In any case, no one was much interested; the effort of obtaining enough to eat and drink, clothes to wear, and a few luxuries was sufficient to absorb most people's energies.

He left the subway at Dzerzhinsky Station and walked out into the square. It had stopped snowing. Three old women were sweeping the snow off the sidewalk in front of the KGB headquarters.

He was expected. The reception clerk gave him a badge and assigned him an escort who took him up to the fourth floor and delivered him to Tolbukhin's secretary, a middle-aged doughy woman with untidy hair. The secretary verified his identity — again — and said, "Sit down and wait. The general will see you shortly."

In the Soviet bureaucracy that could mean any length of time. Mikhailov hung up his coat and composed himself to wait. After twenty minutes, the secretary's intercom buzzed.

"You may go in now, Colonel."

General Tolbukhin's office was large, as befitted the chief of the Third Directorate. On the wall behind him were portraits of Lenin and General Secretary Chernenko. An overstuffed green sofa stood along one wall, and there were two leather chairs in front of the desk. The walls were of highly polished pale wood. A pair of tall windows gave a view of the square and Vuchetich's statue of Felix Dzerzhinsky, capped now with new snow.

General Tolbukhin looked up from the file he was reading. He looked, to Mikhailov, to be in his middle sixties, with silver hair that formed itself into waves. His nose was small and neat above a salt-colored mustache; his pink cheeks gave him an air of openness and good cheer, like a favorite uncle.

"Ah, good morning, Colonel Mikhailov, right on time. I'm pleased to see you at last." He waved at one of the leather chairs. Mikhailov sat down in it, carefully. It squeaked and hissed as air escaped from its cushions. "I've been reading the file of reports you've made over the past year. We certainly picked the right man for the job."

"Thank you, Comrade General."

"Congratulations on your promotion to full colonel, by the way. January, wasn't it?"

"Yes, General. Thank you." Mikhailov had been promoted from lieutenant-colonel to colonel two years earlier than was usual. He still wondered how much the KGB had had to do with it, although combat officers did move up in the hierarchy more quickly than those without battlefield experience.

"I want to go over your personal file with you," said Tolbukhin, "to elaborate on a few matters. A sheaf of paper's no substitute for the real man, eh?"

"One can miss things by just reading a file," Mikhailov agreed.

"Exactly. Now let me see. You're thirty-eight. Born in Moscow. Young Pioneers, Komsomol, joined the Party, entered Frunze Military Academy on the four-year course. Graduated, were invited to work for us . . . good record as attaché in Prague, two years as military attaché in London. GRU work. Is your English still good?"

Taken aback by the change of subject, Mikhailov hesitated and said, "It could use some polishing."

"Good, as long as it's still serviceable." Tolbukhin closed the file and leaned back in his chair. "You have an excellent record indeed. Only to be expected, given the family you come from. I knew your father slightly."

"I think I heard him speak of you."

"A good soldier, Sergei Mikhailov. He knew everything there was to know about artillery. And rockets, later on. It was a loss to the Strategic Rocket Service when he died."

"My father lived for his work. I learned a great deal from him."

"It shows," said Tolbukhin. "Let's get down to work."

They went over the last year's worth of Mikhailov's reports. Mikhailov sensed that the older man was looking for something specific, but was intentionally keeping his questions obtuse. Not until they had talked for nearly an hour did Mikhailov realize that Tolbukhin was worried not so much about the morale of the soldiers but more about the attitudes to the war that the officers held. Mikhailov couldn't understand why this was so; some officers were more outspoken about it than others but instances of outright condemnation were unknown.

Excepting perhaps myself, Mikhailov thought. Or there may be others like me, who also don't speak, who have chosen other ways. But this is typical. All through its existence the KGB, Cheka, MGB, whatever they called it at the time, has been finding plots where none exist. They are so frightened, they believe in no one's innocence, they cannot believe that innocence exists, everyone is guilty of something.

Tolbukhin closed the folder. "Very good. I wish you a very pleasant leave. First, though, there's a matter you can provide some assistance with. You should enjoy what you're being asked to do, in fact."

"I'm at your disposal, General Tolbukhin."

"You knew an American named Eric Fowler while you were stationed in London?"

Mikhailov thought back for a moment. "Yes. He was a trade-relations counsellor at the US embassy. His wife and mine got along well, we sometimes had picnics together. They left London a few months before my wife and I did." Before we came home for her to die, he added in the back of his head.

"You were looking for weak points the GRU might use to gain his cooperation."

"That was my assignment. But it never resulted in anything. He was very careful."

"Did you ever correspond?"

"Once or twice. We stopped about the time my wife died."

"Yes, of course. I'm sorry. Fowler no doubt knew exactly why you were socializing with him, he's quite competent. However, my colleagues in the Second Directorate haven't given up on him yet. He was assigned to the US embassy here two months ago, still in trade relations. They want to take another crack at him."

"But I thought I was going back to Afghanistan," said Mikhailov, misunderstanding.

"Oh, you are. The Second Directorate people merely want you to introduce Fowler to the person who will try to bring him over. It's smoother that way, better than if a stranger struck up a conversation with him."

"Yes, General," said Mikhailov. He felt nauseated. He had liked Fowler.

"At any rate, you'll make the introductions this Friday. There's a reception for the new American ambassador at the Grand Kremlin Palace that evening. Fowler will be there. Report here at seven. Someone will take you to the Kremlin. Wear civilian clothes."

That evening, after Valeria had gone to bed, Mikhailov went for a walk. He walked a long way north, as far as the Moskva River. The sidewalks were rough with frozen snow and ruts of ice and the air was very cold and clear. The streetlights seemed to have halos of ice crystals; the stars were bright enough to be seen even against the city's glow.

Mikhailov trudged along the Moskva's embankments, his boots squeaking on the dry snow. The river was frozen from bank to bank, humped and hillocked where pressure had forced the ice into ridges. In a few weeks the thaw would begin and the ice would break up into great dirty yellow lumps leaving dark leads of water between them.

Mikhailov was thinking about Tolbukhin's instructions. He didn't want to go to the reception, he didn't want to see Fowler again, the meeting would raise too many memories of London, and of Kseni. Mikhailov sometimes even disliked returning to Moscow, for the same reason. Had it not been for Valeria and his sister, he might not have bothered to take leave at all.

I have to go, though, he thought, looking across the river to the rim of lights on its far bank. I don't have any choice in the matter. It's an order.

Why do we have to kill children? They don't even know why we are shooting at them. What sense does that make?

They've had their own way too long, he thought. Stalin, Beria, the camps, even after the worst of the terror went away they've kept the threat of it alive. Look at what happened to General Grigorenko when he spoke out against the invasion of Czechoslovakia in 1968, and what they did to him. They put him in a mental hospital. He wasn't crazy, they were. They can't stand the thought of anybody thinking for himself, he might see through the lies.

The worst of it is, they make the rest of us into liars too, just to get enough to eat, just to stay out of trouble.

He paused in the pool of light from one of the embankment streetlamps to light a cigarette. There was a slight wind and by the time he had the cigarette going his fingers were numb. He could taste sulphur from the matches.

I could make a contact with Fowler, he thought, trudging on. I don't know whether he's CIA but, if he isn't, he'd certainly put them onto me. They don't get a walk-in of my rank very often. Perhaps they could get me out. No, I don't want to leave. I don't know whether I'd like living in the west, and I'd never be able to get Valeria away.

I wonder how long I could last?

Probably a long time. Who'd suspect the nephew of Vasily Romanenko?

The cigarette had gone out. He tossed it into the gutter and turned for home, leaving the frozen river gray-blue under the embankment lights.

MIKHAILOV OWNED two decent western suits, which he had bought in London during his assignment there. He hadn't worn either of them for two years and he had lost weight in Afghanistan; the trousers of even the best-fitting suit were too loose in the waist. He waited nervously in the KGB headquarters foyer, his shabby Russian overcoat over one arm, while the guards studied his clothes suspiciously. After ten minutes of this, a man of about Mikhailov's age came out of the side hallway.

"Colonel Mikhailov?"

"Yes."

"I'm Pavel Deniskin. You're ready to go?"

"Yes, ah — "

"Pavel will do, forget ranks," Deniskin said. "There's a car outside."

They left the building and got into a black Moskvitch. Deniskin started the engine and pulled into the street with an easy familiarity that made Mikhailov envious. He had never owned a car, although with his political connections and the supplement to his army pay from the KGB he could have acquired one fairly easily; but doing so didn't make much sense while he spent so much time out of the country.

After a block Deniskin said, "You're related to Vasily Romanenko, aren't you? Isn't he one of the Central Committee secretaries?"

"Yes," Mikhailov said. He had begun to dislike Deniskin's patronizing tone of voice. "He's also on the Politburo."

"Seen him lately?"

"Earlier in the week."

"Did you mention you were coming to this reception?"

"No." He had paid a visit to Uncle Vasily at his apartment in the Lenin Hills on Wednesday evening, with Nadia and Valeria. Mikhailov made a point of seeing his uncle once or twice whenever he was in Moscow; not only because it was politic, but because he genuinely liked the man. Valeria adored her great-uncle, who in turn enjoyed standing in for the grandfather she could barely remember. Romanenko was not actually related to Mikhailov by blood; he had married Mikhailov's Aunt Ekaterina in 1943 when she was a nurse in Leningrad and he was an infantry lieutenant fighting the Nazis during the bitter siege of that city. They had had no children, which accounted for their affection for Mikhailov and his sister, and for Valeria.

Deniskin pondered for a moment. "Why didn't you tell him?"

"I had no orders to do so."

The KGB man glanced sharply at Mikhailov, as though suspicious of the tone, and then said, "You should show some initiative, Andrei Sergeyevitch. Suppose he were to turn up at the reception? Wouldn't he wonder why you didn't tell him you were coming? After all, this isn't the sort of affair that army officers usually attend."

"I assumed I'd be given cover for that."

Deniskin switched the windshield wipers on; it was beginning to snow. As he turned the car into Kuibyshev Street toward Red Square he said, "All right. You're present, as far as Fowler's concerned, because you're a nephew of a senior Central Committee member and you have the influence to get a free feed. And don't worry about meeting your uncle, he won't be there."

"Why — " said Mikhailov, and stopped.

"I don't know why he won't be there," said Deniskin. "Probably because it'll be mostly foreign-ministry bigwigs and American embassy people and a few hangers-on."

All the same, Mikhailov reflected, I would have thought Uncle Vasily would have gone. He's always made a point of meeting westerners. Maybe he's just too busy.

They turned into Red Square and drove along its edge to the Savior Tower of the Kremlin. At the gate that pierced the tower they stopped. Deniskin showed a pass to the guards and they waved the Moskvitch through. The interior of the Kremlin was dimly lit. On their left lay parkland dropping down to the southern wall, and on their right the porticoed facade of the Kremlin Theatre. The snow was heavier now, falling in large, wet flakes that collected slushily on the car's windshield. As they drove past the cathedrals of the Archangel and of the Annunciation, Mikhailov, peering out at the dim arches of the facades, asked, "What exactly am I to do?"

"The reception's in Saint George Hall in the palace. We'll wait out of sight until the formalities are over, then go in. Get yourself a drink, and then find Fowler. I'll be watching you. After you've talked for five minutes I'll wander up and you'll introduce me. I'm a department head in the Ministry of Overseas Trade. You are acquainted with me through your uncle, Vasily Romanenko. As far as Fowler's concerned, you're soldiering somewhere in the east, he won't press you for information. Shortly after the introductions you will say that you have an engagement elsewhere, and leave. Give this pass —" he handed Mikhailov a small envelope — "to one of the guards and you'll be escorted to the Red Square metro station. Have you got that?"

Mikhailov muttered some reply. He hoped desperately that the guards would not search him before he entered the palace; on a slip of paper in his right trousers pocket he carried what could become his own death warrant.

A good ninety minutes passed while Deniskin and Mikhailov waited at the back of the conference hall that ran along the south facade of the palace. The lighting was dim, and the pale statue of Lenin that stood above the podium at the front of the hall seemed translucent, like a suspended ghost. Neither man spoke much, except when Deniskin asked Mikhailov to repeat the cover story.

"All right," said Deniskin at last. "Let's go in."

They walked into the white vestibule of the main entrance and through the golden doors leading into Saint George Hall. It looked as though Mikhailov would escape being searched, if there had been any danger of it at all. Most of the security was outside the palace and in the hall itself, in which knots of diplomats and Soviet officials and their wives stood about in guarded or animated conversation, depending on mutual suspicion or lack of it. Mikhailov grabbed a glass of Georgian champagne from a passing waiter, who gave him a surly glance, and looked around, feeling ill at ease and conspicuous. He couldn't see Fowler, so he went and stood next to one of the helical white columns at the side of the hall. At the top of the column across from him stood an allegorical statue representing some czarist victory or other. Above it arched the ceiling with its intricate coffering, from which were suspended six enormous gilt chandeliers. He studied the ceiling for a moment and then caught sight of Deniskin watching him with irritation. Mikhailov moved quickly into the crowd; judging from the rising volume of talk, a good deal of alcohol had already been consumed. Several of the westerners were stealing guarded glances at the magnificence of their surroundings, as though they didn't want to be caught admiring anything Russian.

After five or six minutes, during which he began to worry that Fowler hadn't come, he rounded a group of Soviet trade officials and a clutch of westerners jabbering in a mixture of Russian, English, and French, and there was Fowler standing in an alcove. The American was as pale and slim as ever. He was with his wife, Emily, and another couple, western by their dress. Mikhailov gave a convincing start of surprise.

"Eric!"

Fowler looked taken aback for a moment, not recognizing Mikhailov.

"Good Lord. It's Andrei. Look, Emily, it's Andrei."

"My God, so it is." She was quite a pretty woman, with an upturned, slightly skewed nose and black hair that was showing signs of gray. "*What* a surprise. How are you? How is Kseni? I hope she's well now..." Her words trailed off as Mikhailov looked down at his champagne. The bubbles were very clear in the pale golden liquid.

"Oh, Andrei, I'm sorry," she said.

"It's all right," said Mikhailov. "I should have written and told you. It was just that... well, I was very busy. Valeria, that's our daughter, if you remember, she's six now. She's in kindergarten."

There was a pause. Then Fowler said, "I'm forgetting my manners. Andrei Mikhailov, I'd like you to meet Beth and Patrick Mason. They're with the Australian embassy. I dragged them along tonight for some company."

Everyone shook hands. Mikhailov was rigid with tension. He had hoped to find Fowler alone; passing the message would be difficult in these circumstances. He hadn't much time before Deniskin arrived on the scene.

After a moment he excused himself, found a waiter, and returned to the group with a full glass. As he did so he palmed the slip of paper he had been carrying in his trousers pocket. The small wad felt as though it were corroding a hole in his hand. He stood next to Fowler, who was now between Mikhailov and one of the great pilasters supporting the ceiling. Mason and his wife screened them from the main body of the hall.

"I've never been in here before," Mikhailov said. "I have a sore neck from looking up."

He sensed or imagined Fowler edging closer to him. "I was here once," said the American. "They had a special tour. You see the names on the tablets up on the pilasters? They're winners of the Order of Saint George. It was the highest military decoration under the czars."

Everyone obediently looked up.

Mikhailov slipped the wad of paper into Fowler's left pocket.

"There are so *many* of them," said Mrs. Mason, looking down from the tablets. "There must have been a great many brave Russians."

Everyone smiled. Fowler said, "No more than there are now. Right, Andrei?"

"You flatter us," said Mikhailov.

Deniskin's face appeared over Mason's left shoulder.

"Here's someone you should meet," said Mikhailov. For a terrible moment he thought he would forget Deniskin's first name. "Pavel, this is an old friend from London."

Deniskin smiled and said, "How do you do?" in moderately accented English.

Ten minutes later Mikhailov was on his way out of the hall. In his pocket were two cakes he had wrapped up to take home to Valeria.

Four kilometers to the south, Vasily Romanenko was sitting at his great oak desk in the study of his apartment in the Lenin Hills. He was a big man, so the desk did not overwhelm him. His face was reflected indistinctly in the polished surface of the desk, especially the white eyebrows and hair; the eyebrows were bushy and had caused some people to comment — out of Romanenko's hearing — that they made him look like Brezhnev. Unreasonably, this irritated Romanenko when he heard about it; he had considered Brezhnev hidebound and rigid. Romanenko's eyes were not good, and he wore thick spectacles with silver rims, which sat precariously on the bridge of his nose. The nose was prominent, separating intelligent blue eyes, which were now staring at the study's opposite wall without seeing it. The study itself was lavishly furnished, with russet walls and a thick burgundy-colored rug partly concealing a highly polished floor. The ceiling was ivory white, which lightened what would otherwise have been a dark room. There were several comfortable armchairs, a couch where Romanenko occasionally took naps, and a sideboard on which stood a clock, a samovar, and a number of bottles, decanters, and glasses. There were two telephones on the desk, one green, one black. The green one clashed badly with the decor.

Vasily Romanenko was a survivor. Born in 1923 in Smolensk, he had fled eastward at the age of eighteen before the tide of Nazi Wehrmacht engulfed his home city. He had spent a good deal of his army service in the dreadful siege of Leningrad, where the bodies lay in the winter streets for weeks on end because there was no one in the starving city strong enough to hack graves in the frozen ground. The experience had marked him with a horror of famine that went even beyond that of most Russians, who had seen more than one long starvation.

He had entered Berlin in the spring of 1945 with the

victorious Red Army, and joined the Communist Party of the Soviet Union later that year. By 1955 he had moved into full-time Party and government work, and by 1960 was deputy chief of the Leningrad Party Committee. He became a member of the Central Committee in 1961, but with the fall of Khrushchev he also went out of favor and spent three years as deputy chief of the main political administration of the armed forces, which oversaw the political indoctrination of the military. He made a number of useful friends in his years with the MPA. In the mid-seventies he got back into favor and rose steadily through the Party hierarchy until he was a full member of the Politburo, and a senior secretary of the Central Committee, responsible for the general supervision of the economy and the provincial Party organs. After General Secretary Chernenko, he was one of the three most powerful men in the Soviet Union. The others were Oleg Zarudin, chairman of the Council of Ministers and Central Committee secretary of the General Department, and Boris Lebedev, who supervised culture, education, science, and foreign policy. Neither of these men had Romanenko's degree of support in the Central Committee, which elected both the Politburo and the Secretariat; Romanenko was personally popular, competent, and politically very adroit.

At this particular moment Romanenko was writing in his journal. The clock ticked quietly, reached ten o'clock, and started to bong. Romanenko sighed, flipped back several pages, and began to reread what he had written in his fine, spidery handwriting. Keeping the journal could be dangerous in the wrong circumstances, but setting down his thoughts helped clarify them. He had been writing the journal for six years; this was the fourth volume. When he had finished reading, he closed the book and stared at its black cover.

Will we succeed? he thought. We have to. There is too much promise in us not to try.

There was a knock at the door. Romanenko put the journal back in its drawer. "Yes?"

"It's only me."

"Oh, come in. I thought you had gone to bed."

His wife, Ekaterina, closed the study door behind her. She was wearing a green robe and her gray hair was piled into a bun. She was Romanenko's age but looked younger; she was still an attractive woman. "I was in bed but I couldn't sleep. Writing?"

Only Ekaterina knew he kept the journal. "Yes."

"May I ask what about?"

"What we were discussing the other day."

"Oh." She sat down on the edge of one of the chairs and crossed her ankles. She was wearing furry white slippers. "Do you think you'll be able to do it?"

She sounded worried. An intelligent and perceptive woman, she had given Romanenko sound political advice on a good many occasions, and he trusted her judgment of people. She was aware, almost to the same extent as her husband, of the dimensions of the crisis facing Russia. She also knew what he wanted to do. He trusted her utterly.

He spread his palms. "I don't know. I think so. It depends on how long General Secretary Chernenko holds on. If he dies soon, Smilga and Zarudin..."

"Won't have everything to their liking yet," she finished, and grimaced. "I loathe that man. Smilga. He makes me think of a toad."

"He doesn't look like one."

"He reminds me of one. How is the general secretary?"

"He went to the hospital out at Kuntsevo yesterday. His heart is very bad."

She brooded over her fingernails. "It might not be long, then."

Romanenko shrugged. "Who knows? The doctors might try heart surgery. Chernenko's convalescence might go on for a· long time."

"Dmitri Smilga certainly would like that. He doesn't want you as general secretary any more than Oleg Zarudin does."

"Smilga made the arrangements to get the latest diagnostic equipment available."

She snorted. "He would. That's typical. Chernenko must have been asleep when Smilga grabbed the KGB."

"He was sick," said Romanenko defensively.

"There should be a way to handle sick leaders," Ekaterina said with some snappishness, as though she had read his thoughts. "Look what happened, or what didn't happen, when Andropov was dying. The country drifted for fifteen months. Nobody knew what to do. Now, when Chernenko dies, we'll have another scramble while everybody grabs as much as he can. And if Zarudin wins — "

"I'll be on my way out."

"Yes."

"You wouldn't like being married to the head of the Bratsk Hydroelectric Commission, or whatever they'd make me?"

"It's not something to joke about. You've said yourself we have to change the way we do things or there'll be chaos again."

Romanenko nodded somberly. No one outside the upper reaches of the Soviet hierarchy was fully aware of the dimensions of the crisis that was facing the Soviet Union. Food production was falling again, victim of a rigidly centralized bureaucracy that no one seemed willing to dismantle. There was periodic food rationing, which was supposed to be impossible in a socialist society. Most capital resources were committed to heavy industry and defense, penalizing consumer production and the development of technology. Despite the vast commitments to defense, however, everyone in the military command knew that the armed forces were in poor combat condition — whatever the Pentagon chose to believe — but finding out how poor was next to impossible, because of the cancerous patronage systems that had developed in the services. Everyone protected everyone else, falsifying readiness reports, bribing inspecting officers, exerting political influence, until the General Staff went nearly wild with frustration trying to decide how well, or even whether, the troops would fight if there were war. At the very bottom, the conscripted soldiers led a miserable existence, with alcoholism, suicide, and desertion in some units reaching epidemic proportions. Added to everything else was the constant problem of the non-Russian nationalities who didn't want to become Russianized and who, given a few more decades, would outnumber the Russians themselves.

The only real answer, or so Romanenko believed, was a decentralization of authority, which would allow more individual initiative and freedom of choice in both the military and the civilian sectors. It seemed the only method of clearing away the lethargy, self-interest, and unjust privilege that afflicted the Soviet Union. But it had its dangers, and dreadful ones. It could set off a landslide of long-repressed demands for better housing, more food, a few luxuries, less censorship, freedom of assembly and travel, and, most worrisome in some eyes, fewer privileges for the members of the Party. It could also lead to the fragmentation of the Warsaw Pact, and in the short term to disastrous consequences for the economy and agriculture.

But if we don't do something soon, Romanenko thought, the pressure will burst its container anyway and destroy us all. We must let it off bit by bit, with the most delicate care.

"Chaos again," he said. "None of us wants that."

"If you become general secretary," his wife asked him, "can you stop it? Can you stop Smilga?"

"I'll do everything I can." Smilga, he thought, that adder. Ironically, it was the army that wanted to go into Afghanistan in the first place, and Andropov's KGB that advised against it. Now the army agonizes over the stalemate there, and Smilga and his Stalinist allies like Oleg Zarudin intrigue against the withdrawal of a single man. But if Chernenko dies before those two entrench themselves too deeply... I have the greater strength just now. Zarudin will have a hard time getting the general secretaryship if the general secretary dies soon. And I have Konstantin Tsander and the MPA with me, as well as Defense Minister Yasev. Although Yasev will support whoever will extend the military's position in the government. That happens to be me, at the moment.

"I'll do everything I can," he repeated.

She stretched out in the chair, relaxing. "I know. Valeria's growing, isn't she?"

He was used to Ekaterina's abrupt changes of subject. "Yes. Andrei's very proud of her."

"I wish she hadn't lost her mother. Nadia's raising her well, but... why can't Andrei come home? He's been in Afghanistan nearly two years."

"I mentioned something about that to him last Wednesday. Offhandedly. I don't know whether he thought I was just making conversation or was suggesting a posting home. He didn't follow it up, anyway. He takes the army seriously."

"Does *he* think we should be fighting there?"

"I don't know. With his job, he'd have to say he did, anyway."

She looked at her slippered feet and wiggled them. "He's not the Andrei he was last time he was here. There's something troubling that young man."

"He's not that young. And he's seen a lot of fighting."

"Still . . . I thought this time he was different." She yawned. "I suppose I imagined it. But he should come home. For Valeria."

"I'll see what I can do," said Romanenko.

Mark Lasenby thoughtfully tapped the small rectangle of paper with his index finger. The finger was crooked where it had been mangled by a shell fragment outside Hue in 1968.

"What do you think?" he asked Fowler.

Fowler rubbed his eyes. He had waited for half an hour before the CIA station chief had reached the chancery building in the American embassy compound. It was nearly midnight, and he was tired. The two men were sitting in Lasenby's office in the secure area on the ninth floor of the chancery, where all sensitive material, verbal or otherwise, was handled. This was Lasenby's real office. He had another in the more public part of the chancery, where he worked under his cover of commercial attaché. Fowler was a first secretary in the same department.

"It's too early to tell," said Fowler. "I think."

"If Mikhailov's really trying to come over, he took an awful risk. You might have decided he was setting you up, pushed the note back in his face. That would have been the end of him. Why didn't you, by the way?"

"I didn't think the KGB would try to burn me in the Kremlin Palace." Fowler paused. "I knew Andrei in London, there was some talk then of trying to get him to come over. I scouted him, but he didn't seem interested."

"Not at that point," Lasenby observed.

"No."

"He was probably doing the same job on you," Lasenby added.

"Likely. We were pretty sure he was GRU under the attaché cover." Fowler yawned and then straightened suddenly. "They haven't found out I'm deputy station chief, for God's sake, have they?"

"I don't see how. You haven't been here long enough. Anyway, we tied that can to what's-his-name in the consular section."

"Patterson," supplied Fowler.

"Yes. The poor bastard can't hiccup without the KGB recording it."

"He's an ass, that man. He should have known better than to play cloak and dagger to impress people. He might have blown somebody for real."

"He won't, now."

Lasenby studied the note again. "Mikhailov's given us just enough to work up an appetite. One, that Deniskin is going to try to turn you. All right, that's useful to know, but not surprising. Two, that he can give us information on the Afghanistan situation, and that he's been posted to Herat. Three, that he'll be in the reptile pavilion in the Moscow Zoo on Sunday at one-thirty in the afternoon. With a six-year-old girl wearing a red coat and white boots. He wants a brush contact to pass further bona fides. And that you're not to be the contact. Then he gives the brush method."

"It doesn't look as though he's trying a burn," said Fowler. "In any case, there's nothing to retaliate for at the moment. And the KGB'd be more selective about a target than this."

"Yes." Lasenby prodded the note again. "He's probably a lieutenant-colonel by now, if he was a major in London. I think we'd better have a look at him."

"Have you got someone to handle it?"

"Oh, I think we can scrape up somebody or other," said Lasenby. "It's only for a week. When he goes back to Afghanistan it'll be Washington's problem."

Moscow
Sunday, March 14

*T*HE DAY WAS BRIGHT, windless, and cold. Mikhailov stopped momentarily at the entrance to the reptile pavilion, to make sure his timing was right. It was twenty minutes past one.

Valeria tugged at his sleeve. "Can we go in now? I'm getting cold."

"All right. Come on."

Inside the pavilion it was dark, humid, and very warm. Adults and children moved slowly about in the dimness. Set into the corridor walls were glass-fronted cages. This part of the pavilion housed snakes. Mikhailov and Valeria walked slowly along, looking at the coiled and sleeping creatures: rattlesnakes, kraits, vipers, boas. At the boa cage they stopped longer; it was a very large snake. As they watched, the creature awoke, raised its head, and seemed to look at them. Valeria involuntarily clutched at Mikhailov's hand.

"Would you like me to pick you up so you can see better?"

"Yes."

"Yes what?"

"Yes, please."

He picked her up and she watched in fascination as the boa poured itself off the branch where it had been sleeping and glided to its water container. The narrow head bent to the water, the forked tongue danced.

"Why does his tongue do that?"

"He's tasting and smelling all at once. With his tongue."

At the next cage, which housed a reticulated python, there were three adults and a child, all dressed in thick Russian coats, boots, and fur hats. Mikhailov cursed them mentally and willed them to move on. He was supposed to make the brush contact in front of the python cage. He studied the group with his peripheral vision. There were two women and a man, who was holding the child's hand. It was one twenty-nine.

"Can we see the next one?" Valeria asked.

"Just a minute." He put her down. "You're a heavy girl, did you know that?"

"Yes, I'm growing, Aunt Nadia said so."

The others were moving. But one of the women only shifted a little, and then remained, studying the python.

Shit, thought Mikhailov. Where is he, anyway? There was no one other than the woman in the immediate vicinity.

They've decided I'm a plant, Mikhailov thought dispiritedly. Now what am I going to do? Maybe I'll take Valeria back home and get drunk. But Nadia wouldn't like that.

"Daddy."

"All right."

The woman put both hands, which were gloveless, up to her fur hat. She took the hat off, shook it, and put it back on. In doing so she dropped the gloves. As she bent to pick them up, Mikhailov reached into his left pocket for the folded envelope. The woman now was standing motionless in front of the python's cage, her arms folded.

Mikhailov moved so that he stood a little to the woman's right and partly behind her.

"What's that one?" Valeria asked.

"A reticulated python, it says on the card," Mikhailov told her. "It's from Burma." He slipped the envelope into the woman's coat pocket. She made no sign or motion.

"Where's Burma?"

"A long way away."

"Pick me up. Please."

He did so. The woman moved on to the boa cage, toward

the pavilion doors. Mikhailov felt a rush of relief mixed with apprehension. He was committed. Valeria wriggled closer to him.

If they catch me, he thought, what will they do to you? Is anything worth the risk of losing you? What would they tell you about me, afterward?

He didn't put her down for the rest of their journey through the pavilion, though his arms ached fiercely all the way.

"She got away with it," said Lasenby. "He didn't burn her."

"Did you expect him to?" asked Fowler, sitting down. He and Lasenby were in the latter's secure office again; it was eight-thirty in the evening.

"No. I wouldn't have sent her otherwise. She's extremely valuable. A journalist. You'll have to meet her soon."

"Oh." Fowler hesitated. "They're usually off limits, too dangerous for them professionally if they got picked up for espionage. Wouldn't ever get into an East-Bloc country again, or a lot of others."

"This one's different. Journalism's her second career. It was still a little fast to make a contact, though. I always worry."

Fowler nodded. It would have been safer to develop the contact with Mikhailov through a "principal agent," someone he could associate with normally. The principal would be a person who could associate in turn with Mikhailov's case officer, or with someone in contact with the case officer.

"If we decide to take him on," said Fowler, "who'd be the principal? I don't think it could be me, although I know him. If they ever found out what I am, they'd suspect him automatically."

"I'm thinking about the journalist."

Fowler pursed his lips. "The KGB isn't keen on army officers hanging about with foreign journalists. They'd have to be very careful."

"It might have to be a clandestine contact. Or a very occasional social one. The trouble is, we don't have anyone at the moment who could be an out-in-the-open principal for him. He's been out of the country too much to be a part of the social scene where we could get at him."

"Has she ever been a principal?"

"Yes. In Berlin, before her magazine sent her here. She was good at it."

"But she's not one just now."

"I've been keeping her up my sleeve for something like this, where we can't use one of our Russians easily. If he's worth it." Lasenby was grinning.

"Is he?"

Lasenby fished an envelope out of his jacket and handed it to Fowler. "Judge for yourself."

The envelope was already open. Fowler took out several sheets of onionskin and smoothed them on his knee. "He must have written it with a magnifying glass, didn't want it too bulky — gives name, address, unit, rank — he's moving fast, he's a colonel, with the ... Operational Studies Bureau?"

"Read on."

"Counterinsurgency specialist," said Fowler. "Ah. I see. Useful. Gives command structure of headquarters in Kabul, casualty rates in January. They've been hurting, haven't they? Mostly disease, though, not combat." He broke off suddenly and looked up. Lasenby was still grinning.

"You're kidding," Fowler said. "He's kidding."

"I hope not," said Lasenby. "Because if he isn't we've fallen down a diamond mine. He's a goddamned colonel in the Third Directorate. We get the army *and* the KGB. Two for the price of one. We'll have to arrange a meeting with a principal. *And* we've got to find a way to keep in touch with him in Afghanistan. All in a week."

Moscow
Wednesday, March 17

THERE WAS AN EARLY THAW. Beyond Mikhailov's apartment window a light mist hung over the city, hiding the top of the television tower and obscuring the upper stories of the apartment blocks. Mikhailov stood at the window, watching the midmorning traffic flow along the short stretch of Vavilova Street that was visible between two other towers of the complex. The asphalt looked black and slick. He had put a Mozart recording on the West German-made stereo; the music always calmed him.

He wondered whether anyone else was listening to the Mozart. He didn't really think there were microphones in the apartment, since he was so rarely there, but there was always a chance that the Third Directorate might want to know whether he was discussing Afghanistan with friends or with his sister. But Mikhailov had found, during his first week back in Moscow, that the people he had once been close to had drifted away; Afghanistan had made him an outsider in his own city. He had no desire to talk about it with anyone who hadn't been there, and none of his friends had been. They were academics and engineers now, or Party bureaucrats, or rising career diplomats, with a few failed ones among them; he was the only one who had decided to make a career of the army and intelligence work. It ran in the family, his father had said. Your grandfather fought the Whites in the revolution; before that he fought the Germans at Tannenberg and the Austrians in

Marshal Brusilov's offensive. I fought the Nazis, who knows who you'll need to fight? But we must always be ready.

I'm the first Mikhailov to work for the Chekists, though, Mikhailov thought, using the old name for the organization that had become the KGB. And I'm certainly the first to work with — for? — the Americans. Will they think I want money? I didn't mention money in the documents I gave her.

He went to the stereo and turned the music up a little. There aren't any microphones, he told himself. I've never put a foot wrong as far as I know. Not that that's any guarantee of safety. What was the old joke out of the camps?

"What did they give you?"

"Twenty years. And I did nothing."

"You can't have done nothing. For nothing they only give you ten years."

Mikhailov grimaced. The one thing that bothered him, apart from his own safety and that of Nadia and Valeria, was what his uncle would think if he knew what Mikhailov was doing. Would Vasily Romanenko understand? Occasionally his uncle had let slip a phrase or sentence that showed his concern about the path Russia was following, but he would never countenance this. Treachery. Treason.

But it isn't treason, Mikhailov thought. The treason has been committed by the Party bureaucrats, the powermongers who took the Russian people's revolution away from them. Lenin should have got rid of Stalin, or maybe he tried but he failed. So the tyranny came back. It's no treason to betray a tyranny. Lenin used any means at hand, even took help from the Germans for his own purposes, back in 1917, to bring about the revolution. I'm no Lenin. But I can help weaken the men in the Kremlin, and the ones in the Lubianka. If they can be weakened enough, we can make them listen to us.

Will they listen? The czars never did, not until it was too late.

What we need is a second revolution.

He felt suddenly weak and ill. His forehead was clammy. He had never followed such a channel of thinking. It frightened him with its simplicity and inevitability.

He turned from the window. It was nearly time to go. The

telephone call had come late the previous afternoon. Every word of it was scored into his memory.

"Hello? I keep getting the wrong number. Is this one-three-five-one-one-eight-four?"

"Sorry," Mikhailov had said.

The caller had rung off without another word. Mikhailov had given them four possible places and times to meet him, with corresponding "wrong numbers." They had selected the third on his list.

The Mozart was drawing to a close. He let it finish, turned off the stereo, and got the copy of *Marshal Zhukov's Greatest Battles* and his coat and hat. The hat he pulled well down over his ears to hide his military haircut. He had no idea where they would take him but he wanted to be as inconspicuous as possible.

Out in the street the air was damp and raw. Mikhailov thought of Valeria, back in the *detsky sad*, and his fear for her, which had not really left him since the afternoon in the zoo, swept over him again. He tried to shake it off as the bus drew up to the curb, but it only retreated to the back of his mind and stayed there, waiting.

He got off the bus at the Leninsky Prospekt metro station and went down to the platform. He had made sure that no one was following him but he hadn't expected it, anyway; there was no reason for it to be done. On the train north toward the center of the city he tried to imagine how the Americans would arrange a meeting long enough and secure enough for their purposes. They would want to tape the conversation, of course. It couldn't be any place foreigners lived, because the militiamen guarding the entrance would ask him for identity papers and report him. Such apartments were always bugged, anyway. A Russian-occupied building would be much better, but there was always the risk of KGB informants among the residents.

He left the metro at Revolution Square Station, fifteen minutes too early to make the contact. He walked past the Lenin Museum, around the corner, and into the GUM store. As usual, it was jammed with people shopping while they should have been at work; after the first year or so of Andropov's rule, his attempts to prevent job-shirking had collapsed completely. Chernenko hadn't even bothered to try. Mikhailov went up to the upper level and walked along the mezzanines for ten minutes, window-shopping, after which he went back to the ground floor and made his way toward the fountain at the store's center. He was a minute early, but the contact was already there, leaning on the broad, chest-high rail that formed an octagon around the fountain.

He was sure it was the woman from the zoo. On the rail by her left elbow stood a cheap brown Russian carryall. The zipper was half undone and there was a long diagonal scratch across the carryall's plastic side. Mikhailov went to the rail beside the woman and leaned on it. If the bag had been completely unzipped, he would have kept going. He put the copy of *Marshal Zhukov's Greatest Battles* on the rail so that she could see the title on the spine.

She clasped her hands in front of her mouth and said, "Be at Kompositorskaya Street, number eighteen, apartment 305, in thirty minutes. Cough if you have that."

Mikhailov coughed. The woman picked up the bag, still unzipped, and went off into the crowd.

Kompositorskaya Street ran off the Smolenskaya embankment just north of the metro bridge over the Moskva River. Mikhailov walked along the embankment on the river side rather than going straight up Smolensky Street; he had a few minutes to waste. In daylight the river ice looked slushy and rotten, with occasional veins of black water. On his right, on the landward side, rose fourteen-story apartment blocks of pale-yellowish stone, their ornate Stalinist facades contrasting with the austere curve of the river wall and the trim glass towers of the SEV building beyond Kalinin Prospekt ahead. The sun had begun to reappear and watery light glinted off the puddles on the sidewalk.

At the intersection of the embankment and Kompositorskaya Street he stopped to light a cigarette, turning to shield the match from the wind and to look behind him. There was no one anywhere near except a fat *babushka* with an English-style baby carriage. What was it they called them, he thought. A perambulator. She hadn't been there when he walked under the metro bridge, so he leaned on the river wall and looked at the dirty ice until she had rolled the perambulator by. One of its wheels squeaked annoyingly.

There was no one else within two hundred meters. He hurried across the embankment, up into the shadows of Kompositorskaya Street. Number eighteen was the ninth building along, on the right, an apartment building like the ones facing the river, but smaller. Mikhailov threw his cigarette into the gutter and went inside. The empty foyer smelled of cooked cabbage and the walls needed paint. Several of the floor tiles were broken.

Mikhailov ignored the elevator and walked along the hall to the stairs at its end, hoping that apartment 305 was at this end of the building and that he wouldn't meet anyone on the stairs. He didn't, and the apartment was the second on the left. At the far end of the corridor a woman came out of her own apartment and glanced briefly in his direction. Mikhailov tested the door handle of 305. It was unlocked. He went in and closed the door quietly behind him.

The apartment was a shock. It was large, would have been bright except for the closed curtains, and it was luxuriously furnished. A thick green carpet covered the floor and the walls were painted a restful sandy-white. Two reproductions of classical paintings hung on the walls. A large stereo console dominated the space under the window, its western lines at odds with the ornate Russian lamp sitting on top of it. The sofa and chairs were Russian too, but of high quality. A big glass-fronted bookcase stood against the wall on Mikhailov's left. The titles were almost all Party literature, with a few approved classics interspersed. To the right a hallway went off toward what must be the kitchen and bedroom, or bedrooms. The apartment was even bigger than Mikhailov's.

The woman was sitting on the couch. She wore a white turtleneck sweater and gray slacks. Mikhailov hadn't gotten a good look at her either at the zoo or in the GUM, but he saw now that she was unusually good-looking. Her hair was glossy jet-black and she had very pale skin without a blemish. It looked like porcelain. She was also quite small, and very slight, with delicate features and a rosebud mouth. She reminded Mikhailov of nothing so much as the Dresden china figurines he had seen in shops in London.

Be careful, he thought. She looks like an innocent child. They are very clever.

"Come in and sit down," she said. "Make sure the door's locked."

She spoke excellent Russian. Mikhailov tested the door, took his boots off, and padded into the living room, feeling awkward. He sat down in the chair opposite her and said, "Hello."

There was a silence, while she studied him professionally. Her eyes were green. About the color of mine, thought Mikhailov. Her skin is absolutely flawless. Like Kseni's.

"Well," she said at last, "how do you feel, Colonel Mikhailov?"

"Nervous," he said bluntly. "This is the apartment of a senior Party worker. Exactly the sort of place I shouldn't be."

She smiled. "This is likely the only time we'll meet here, but I assure you it's safe. We have a couple of hours to get to know each other, so we'll have to work hard since we won't likely meet again before you go back to Afghanistan. We'll also make arrangements for you to see me next time you're on leave."

"Are you on the embassy staff?" he asked.

"Not exactly. I'm a journalist."

He stared at her. "They don't like army people being around journalists. How are you going to manage that?"

"I work for a Canadian newsmagazine called *Seven Days*. It's like *Time* or *Newsweek*. You've heard of those."

"I used to read them in London."

"*Seven Days* is somewhat leftish. Because of that, and its being Canadian, your government is more favorable to it than it is to American publications. Slightly more favorable. We're seen as more sympathetic to Soviet problems than the American press, so I've been able to develop a wider range of contacts than American journalists. They will be of some help."

"Your range of contacts includes the owner of this apartment?"

She smiled again. "My name is Chantal Mallory."

"You speak Russian very well for an…but you're not American."

"No. I'm Canadian."

"But you work for the Central Intelligence Agency."

She made a dismissive gesture. "It's a long story. But, basically, yes. Now we have to talk about you for a while."

"All right." Mikhailov stood up and took his coat off. As he was draping it over the back of his chair, with the book on top so he wouldn't forget it, she said, "Washington is very impressed with the information you've given them. But they aren't sure why you're doing it. You're part of the Soviet elite, an officer in the army and the KGB, and you have excellent political connections. There wouldn't seem to be any reason for you to jeopardize that."

Mikhailov sat down and stared into space for perhaps a minute, trying to bring order to his thoughts. Finally he said, "It was Afghanistan. Just before I came on leave I did something…" The words were difficult to get out. "I had to kill a child. A little girl. She was about my daughter's age. She was too badly hurt to live, we had no extra morphia….I shot her." Mikhailov passed a hand over his eyes. "I've seen worse things in Afghanistan. Both the guerrillas and we have committed atrocities. But this was too much."

"So you decided you had to do something constructive."

"Yes. It's been bothering me for a long time, the way Russia works. The privilege. The lies. Especially the lies. I've lived in the west, I know you have problems, serious ones, but at least you'll sometimes admit it to yourselves. And try to make changes. Here, it's get as much as you can, do whatever you have to to keep it, don't ever admit there might be something wrong."

"In some ways," she said, "the west isn't very much different from that."

"You have law," he said. "Here we have socialist justice. We even have a constitution. But they don't mean anything, the authorities do what they like anyway. Once, while I was in England, I went to see a criminal trial. He, the accused man, the police said he'd embezzled money. It was all very complicated. But in the end he was set free, because the authorities couldn't prove *beyond a doubt* that he'd committed the crime. Here he would have been considered guilty at the start of the trial, and the trial would be just a form, so the defense could try to get him a lighter sentence. If there's any doubt here, they decide against you. It showed me how things could work here, should work. So that the authorities have to obey the law too, so that they can't change it to suit themselves."

"That's perhaps a little idealized," she said, "but yes, that's how it's supposed to work."

"Don't misjudge me," said Mikhailov. "I'm not a western liberal democrat. I'm a communist, I think that communism will work, if it can become human. We all know our government admits, more or less, that true communism's a long way off. But they won't admit why. It's because of the leaders, the ones who betrayed the revolution in the twenties. Who locked us into this prison."

He realized that he was speaking very quickly, and that he was sitting up straight, his fists clenched on his knees. Chantal was staring at him intently. He gestured with both hands and sank back into the armchair. "I'm emotional about it, I'm Russian."

"That's all right," she said.

"I don't want to be paid for this," he went on more slowly. "You must also remember one other thing. I'm not doing this to help the United States gain supremacy over my country. I'm doing it so that the men in the Kremlin will be weakened enough to see that they have to change. They're insulated by everything, by the limousines, by the dachas, by the special stores. And especially by the KGB. If you take the power of the KGB away from them...that's one of the things I want to do, help break the power of the Chekists."

"That's rather a lot for one man."

"Somebody has to start somewhere."

"Tell me some more about Afghanistan."

It took him a long time. He began with the first weeks of his posting there, and went through as much as he could: the frustration of counterinsurgency work in a hostile country; the growing conviction that it was not the Marxist regime in Kabul that reflected the desires of the Afghan people, but the mujahidin themselves; the heat and the flies in summer; the ice and snow and numbing rains of fall and winter and spring; the sullen Soviet troops and even more sullen Afghan levies; and over all the sense of the utter impossibility of transforming the country into what its Marxist rulers thought it ought to be.

"It can't possibly be done," he finished. "Not without killing three-quarters of the population. Stalin might have succeeded, with his methods, but Chernenko can't."

"What does the Third Directorate — General Gordik — think of the situation?"

"I think they're all worried. The KGB didn't want to go into Afghanistan in the first place, but the army high command thought they could clean things up in three or four months, and get some useful combat experience as well. Now we've been there for years, with no end in sight. I believe General Gordik feels the army's morale and effectiveness are being badly damaged, like yours — the Americans' — were in Vietnam. We've got all the problems now that they had. Alcoholism, drugs — the mujahidin make sure the black market supplies plenty of hashish — and bad discipline. Some troops have refused combat, some've shot their officers, some have thrown grenades at them in combat, what was that called in Vietnam?"

"Fragging," Chantal said in English.

"Yes. I remember, when I first heard about that, I wondered how any army's morale could drop so low. Now I know. The men don't know why they're there, they don't believe the propaganda after they've been in the country for a week. They just have to go on fighting, with no prospect of winning, and with bad food and filthy living conditions. It's a wonder we haven't had a full-scale mutiny by now."

"That's one of the things you and Gordik and the Third Directorate are supposed to prevent, isn't it?"

"Yes. But when the security service starts sympathizing

with the prospective mutineers, *that's* when the situation turns really serious."

"Is that happening?"

"I think it's beginning to. Or that it soon will."

Chantal looked at her watch. "We're running out of time. I won't be seeing you before you leave Moscow, and there are a few other things we have to sort out. First, what thought have you given to coming over to the west?"

"Defecting?"

"Yes."

Mikhailov looked at his hands. "It's tempting. I could likely get out, either through Afghanistan or by using some political influence to get a posting to the west. But I wouldn't go if I had to leave Valeria."

"What if it were that or a question of being caught?"

He shrugged. "I don't know."

"Could you arrange to have Valeria go with you, if you got a posting to the west?"

"Possibly. That would be the only situation in which I'd defect." He paused again. "But that isn't what I want to do. As long as I can work in reasonable safety, I'll stay here."

"Let us know if you change your mind. If you can even get yourself and Valeria to one of the Warsaw Pact countries, we can almost certainly get you out."

"Almost."

"There's always risk."

"Yes."

"Now, for the next question." She leaned forward, elbows on knees and hands clasped under her chin. "About establishing contact in Herat, when you go back to Afghanistan. I'm told we will try to put somebody in, somebody who can get facilities from the mujahidin. How freely can you move about?"

"There's little danger from our own security people," Mikhailov said with a faint, wry smile. "Particularly since I'm one of them. However, it can be dangerous for Russians to wander about alone very much, even in the pacified areas. And Herat is not well pacified. In the daytime, however, I think I can manage. How long will it take for you to insert someone?"

"As late as the end of April or the beginning of May."

"That long?"

"Yes. I don't know why."

"I do. Six of your people in Kandahar and Herat were caught in February." Mikhailov took an envelope out of his jacket and handed it to her. "There's as much as I know about it in there, as well as other things. The KGB counterespionage people were very pleased."

She was obviously nonplussed. After a moment she said, "I imagine they were. How can we make contact, though?"

"In Bihzad Park. There's a ruined mosque there, with six minarets still standing. In the northernmost minaret, on its north side, there's a crack in the wall about two meters up. That's the best drop to start with: there won't be much danger in my going there in daylight, and it's normally pretty deserted. The first drop should tell me when and where to meet the contact and what the recognition signals are. I won't go there until I see two white chalk marks, each five centimeters long, on the lampost directly across from the old governor's mansion. I'll check the drop the next day, if I can. If the meeting place is no good, I'll add a third chalk mark to the other two. If it's all right, I won't signal."

"Good. If there's any problem with that you'll get a wrong-number phone call tomorrow afternoon at three. Otherwise this is the last contact until Herat. Is that satisfactory?"

"Yes." Mikhailov stood up and put on his coat, being careful not to forget the book. "Until next time," he said.

"Until then," she said. "Good luck."

When he had gone, she got down on her hands and knees, got the minirecorder out from under the sofa, and checked the sound quality, as she had before Mikhailov arrived. The words were clear, despite the modifications to the recorder that allowed three hours of taping without changing cassettes. Anything but a detailed electronic check would show it to be the sort of machine a journalist would carry as a matter of course.

She removed the cassette, sealed it in a small plastic bag, and sat down to wait out the fifteen minutes until she could leave for the drop.

Moscow
Friday, March 26

ON THIS DAY Konstantin U. Chernenko, long a member of the Central Committee and for the last few years of his life General Secretary of the Communist Party of the Soviet Union, died of sudden congestive heart failure.

His death took no one in the upper reaches of the Soviet government by surprise. There were only two real contenders for the now-vacant general secretaryship: the chairman of the Council of Ministers, Oleg Zarudin; and the senior secretary of the Central Committee, Vasily Romanenko. Both men moved quickly, but Romanenko more quickly than Zarudin.

Romanenko got the news at 7:53 A.M., as he was shaving. Ekaterina appeared at the bathroom door and said, "It's Konstantin Tsander. He says he has urgent information for you."

Tsander was Central Committee secretary for the military and the defense industry, and one of Romanenko's strongest allies in the Secretariat and Politburo. Romanenko dried his face hurriedly and went to the study.

"Hello? Konstantin?"

"Yes. Vasily, it's happened. The general secretary's dead."

Romanenko exhaled, a long, slow breath, and said, "I see. When?"

"Not fifteen minutes ago."

"When will the Central Committee be convened?"

"As soon as you can persuade Pripoltsev to do it. He'll try

to delay." Pripoltsev was the chairman of the Party control committee, a supporter of Zarudin's but without Romanenko's power base in the Secretariat, which was what mattered.

"Very well," said Romanenko. "Have you spoken to Defense Minister Yasev?"

"Not yet."

"I'll call him. I'll be at Staraya Square in an hour." The headquarters of the Central Committee and the Politburo were at the Party building in Staraya Square.

"Yes. Good. I'll see you there."

Romanenko pressed the cradle of the telephone, released it, and dialed. He got an answer on the first ring.

"Minister Yasev, please."

"Speaking."

"Konstantin was discussing a political situation of the gravest importance with you last Sunday. The situation is now present."

"Are you at home?"

"Yes."

"Fifteen minutes. I'll pick you up."

"Good." Romanenko hung up. Ekaterina was standing in the study doorway. There were fine lines around her mouth.

"Vasily. What's going on?"

"Chernenko's dead. I have to call Ignati Pripoltsev and get him to convene the Central Committee as soon as possible. Could you bring me a cup of tea, please?"

"Vasily — "

He was already dialing. Ekaterina hesitated, and then left.

In a large apartment on Kutuzovsky Prospekt, Oleg Zarudin and KGB Chairman Dmitri Smilga regarded each other with suppressed fury. The apartment belonged to Zarudin, the one above it to Smilga. The KGB chairman had come downstairs as soon as the news about Chernenko had reached him. Chernenko had been dead for twenty minutes.

"And what *exactly* do you propose we do?" Zarudin asked. He was a tall man, angular and slightly stooped, and was wearing a dressing gown that showed two inches of bare ankle above his slippers.

"Call Pripoltsev. Persuade him not to convene the Central Committee yet."

"I've already called him."

"And?"

"He was evasive. I think he's been talking to Romanenko."

"Pripoltsev's supposed to be on your side," Smilga pointed out.

"He knows where the power lies at the moment," snapped Zarudin. "And so do you. Chernenko died too soon."

"You can hardly blame me for *that*." Smilga laughed without humor, revealing unevenly spaced teeth flecked with gold fillings. He was a short man, thick with muscle partly transformed into fat. "*I* did everything I could."

"You haven't answered my question," Zarudin said.

"Which one?"

"What do we do now?" Zarudin wrapped his arms around his torso as if he were cold. "Defense Minister Yasev's in Romanenko's pocket, thanks to Konstantin Tsander and the MPA. The KGB can't take on the army."

"I'm going to move two companies of Ninth Directorate troops to Staraya Square anyway," said Smilga. He got up, preparing to leave. "If Yasev isn't serious about supporting Romanenko, this is the time to find out. I'll also try to persuade Yasev that the Ninth troops can guard the Central Committee just as well as the army. We may be able to befuddle some of the Committee members into thinking the KGB has the whip hand. That could turn the vote, if it's close. Let me use your phone."

"You'd better not make any mistakes," said Zarudin. "If Romanenko wins and decides on a purge, you and I will be on the first prison train east. The phone's over there."

It was a raw, chill morning, with a low cloud cover. Along Chernysevskovo Street, heading for the center of Moscow and Staraya Square, roared a column of light tanks and tracked BMP armored personnel carriers. There were three companies of them, a full battalion of the Second Guards Taman Motorized Rifle Division, one of the ceremonial divisions that were more usually seen in parades and May Day celebrations in Red Square. They were not well trained for combat, spending most of their time preparing for such displays, but then the KGB Ninth Directorate troops were not seasoned either. A second battalion was on its way to Staraya Square from the north, along Dzerzhinskovo Street.

Young Captain Ilitsev, who was riding in the turret of the lead tank, had no idea why they had been abruptly dragged away from their early-morning political classes and sent into the city from the barracks, and he suspected that the battalion major didn't know either. Their orders, however, were quite clear: take up positions in Staraya Square and guard the Central Committee building against all comers. And no, they were not to cooperate with the KGB. They were not to permit KGB troops, MVD militia, or anyone else to interfere with movement into and out of the building.

Ilitsev hunched himself deeper into his greatcoat against the wind of their passage and wondered what was going on, particularly because of the instructions regarding the KGB. Wouldn't it be nice, he daydreamed for a moment, if we could take a shot at those KGB buggers and get away with it.

He grimaced at the dangerous thought and dismissed it. Staraya Square was just ahead.

Romanenko, meanwhile, was riding with Yasev in the latter's Mercedes; they were just passing the north side of the Rossiya Hotel on Razina Street, only a block from the Central Committee building. In front of and behind the big — and bulletproof — vehicle rumbled armored cars, their commanders standing high in the turrets.

"You've sent the planes?" asked Romanenko. This was desperately important; Romanenko needed full attendance of the Central Committee to ensure his election as general secretary, and many of the members lived and worked far from Moscow. Yasev's support was essential to achieving the plenum, as he had the resources of the air-transport command at his disposal.

"The planes are on their way," said the defense minister. "Everyone will be here by noon."

Romanenko relaxed slightly. Smilga apparently hadn't

found out about the airlift plans, then. This was as it should be, since no one besides himself and Yasev had known about them, except for the Central Committee secretary for defense and industry, Konstantin Tsander. Romanenko knew that Tsander had had some unofficial contacts with Tolbukhin, head of the KGB Third Directorate, but they had made sure Tolbukhin had not found out about Romanenko's intentions, no matter what his sympathies.

The Mercedes rounded the corner and drove into Staraya Square.

"Buckets of shit," said Yasev. "Smilga's called out the Ninth."

A confrontation was shaping up in the square. The Ninth Directorate guards and several trucks were distributed across the front of the Central Committee building, weapons unslung. In front of them the Taman division's tanks and BMPs rumbled sullenly. The army troops must have just arrived; the soldiers were still dismounting from their vehicles. Next to the curb at the entrance to the building stood a large black Zil limousine.

That's Smilga, Romanenko thought as the Mercedes drew up to the line of troops and BMPs. He wants to see how far he can push before, or if, he's stopped. Always the opportunist. "I don't want any shooting," Romanenko said.

"We'll try to avoid it," Yasev answered. "What are you going to do?"

"Walk over and see what he wants, of course," Romanenko said. He got out of the Mercedes and started across the thirty meters of pavement separating the two lines of soldiers. Behind him he heard Yasev leave the car to find the officer commanding the army troops.

The Zil seemed to draw nearer very slowly. Romanenko was on edge; he did not really think that Smilga would resort to violence, but there was always a chance that the KGB chairman would decide to stake all on Romanenko's permanent removal. It could be put down to an accidental shooting by nervous soldiers.

Somebody was rolling down the rear window of the Zil. It was Smilga. Romanenko stopped a meter away from the car and said, "Good morning, Dmitri Alexeyevitch. I see your men are carrying out their responsibilities in their usual efficient manner."

"So are yours, Secretary," Smilga said. He got out of the car and leaned on it. "You needn't have concerned yourself with security, however. With all respect, that's my job."

"Minister Yasev wanted to ensure that there were no misunderstandings," said Romanenko. "He's kindly arranged for the army to be present during the Committee plenum. I suggest that your men be reassigned to less boring duties."

Smilga's eyes shifted rapidly from Romanenko to the Taman Division's soldiers out in the square, and then back to Romanenko. Both men could hear the clank and roar of heavy vehicles approaching from the north. From Smilga's expression, he knew they weren't his. "We need to display army-KGB solidarity," he said. "My men can maintain security within the building."

"Remove your guards," Romanenko said softly. "They are neither needed nor wanted."

Smilga hesitated. Then he said, "Certainly. As soon as the Central Committee delegates begin to arrive. I — "

"Now, Comrade Chairman," said Romanenko. "Not later. Now."

Smilga inclined his head slightly, smiled, and said formally, "At once, Comrade Secretary Romanenko. You need only ask." He turned and said into the car, "Order the Ninth guards to return to barracks. Security here is under control."

"Very good, Dmitri Alexeyevitch," said Romanenko. "I appreciate your cooperation very much." He turned and began to walk back toward Yasev, who was standing by the Mercedes. By the time he got there the KGB troops were climbing back into their trucks.

"They're returning to barracks," he told Yasev.

"Good," said the defense minister. "I'll send along an escort to make sure that's where they go."

A little farther along the square, Captain Ilitsev watched the KGB soliders break ranks. He felt an acute, and extremely illegal, disappointment.

The plenum of the Central Committee met at two that afternoon. By unanimous vote, Vasily Romanenko was chosen General Secretary of the Communist Party of the Soviet Union. Yasev's ring of troops remained around the Central Committee building all through the night, and well into the next day.

Herat, Afghanistan
April 10–13

SOVIET REGIONAL HEADQUARTERS in Herat was the old governor's mansion, which by some quirk of cultural diffusion had been constructed years before in imitation wedding-cake Stalinist architecture. It lay at the north edge of the New Town which, with its flat-roofed stores and villas and hotels built in the sixties for the tourist trade, looked like any other new town in Asia: nondescript, dusty, and mud-brown. Abutting the New Town on the west lay the Old City of Herat, a labyrinth of alleys and blank walls with inset doors, and the bazaar, which had once been covered but now lay open to the sun and dust, in its center. On the northeastern edge of the city, between the governor's mansion and the road to Maimana, lay the Soviet firebase. Its location had the disadvantage of being on the edge of the city opposite the small airport, but it was comfortably close to the regional HQ in the event of trouble.

General Bachinsky, commander of the Fifty-fourth Motorized Rifle Division, which was responsible for operations in the Herat region, had assigned Mikhailov an office in the east wing of the governor's mansion. The office was directly above the kitchen that served the headquarters officers' mess, so Mikhailov's office had cockroaches. His OSB regional staff, which he had found demoralized by a series of minor but real mujahidin successes in the mountains to the east, had greeted his arrival with something less than enthusiasm. The colonel whom

Mikhailov was replacing had been sent home with an unspecified ailment that Mikhailov, after interviewing a few of the staff, had concluded was a failure of nerve. Herat and its surroundings had been a problem area ever since the invasion. What little hard intelligence was available indicated that the ANLF had decided to make the problem even worse.

Despite the cockroaches, Mikhailov was having lunch in the officers' mess. The mess was on the ground floor and underfurnished to the point of austerity, with three long tables, a couple of decaying armchairs, and a portrait of Lenin on one smudged whitewashed wall. The food was just passable: today it was bean soup, bread, and lukewarm, greasy mutton with rice. There was plenty of vodka and Georgian brandy, however. A dozen headquarters officers were making inroads on both, noisily.

Major Leonid Rosseikin, Mikhailov's senior assistant, was sitting at the table with Mikhailov. He folded the last of his bread and wiped the last drops of the bean soup out of his bowl with the wad. Rosseikin came from a small village near Volgagrad and had poor table manners. Around the soggy mouthful he said, "I wonder how they're doing?"

Mikhailov looked up from a particularly fatty bit of mutton. "How who's doing?"

"Bachinsky sent a company up the road toward Karrukh this morning. Punishment duty. There was a black-marketing ring in the unit."

"They were *all* black marketing?"

"Enough to make Bachinsky shit on the whole company. They're maintenance troops. Filling in that cratered stretch. It won't hurt them."

"Where are they from?" A lot of Soviet service troops — the ones who built and repaired bridges and roads and did much of the heavy, dirty work — were drawn from non-Russian ethnic groups.

"Uzbeks. A few from Tadzikhstan."

Mikhailov put his fork down and frowned. When the Soviet army had entered Afghanistan in December 1979, it had done so with soldiers who were drawn largely from the southern republics of the Soviet Union. These troops were related by ancestry, culture, and Islam to the Afghans. The theory was that this would cause the Afghans to accept the invaders more readily, on the principle that they wouldn't be perceived as aliens. The principle was wrong. The Afghans had fought as bitterly as they would have if the invasion force had been composed exclusively of blond, blue-eyed Slavs. To make matters worse, some of the Soviet ethnic troops had refused to fight men who were closer in kind to them than were their Russian officers. In short order the Kremlin withdrew the initial invasion units, replacing them with divisions manned by Russians or other Slav nationalities. The only ethnic troops now left in the country were the service-and-maintenance units, like the company General Bachinsky had sent up the road that morning.

"What did you say they were supposed to do?"

"Fix the road. It's got some bomb craters in it."

"Oh." Mikhailov picked up his fork again. "There were reports of bandits up that way yesterday."

Major Rosseikin shrugged. "Do them good to get shot at. Then maybe they'll be a little keener on fighting back."

"Maybe," said Mikhailov. He was feeling extremely uneasy, for no obvious reason. He pushed his plate away.

"I can't eat any more of this shit either," Rosseikin said. "Do you want some brandy?"

"All right."

Rosseikin went away to the bar and came back with a bottle that was half-full and two badly washed glasses. He poured. Mikhailov picked up his glass and drank. The brandy cut the greasy coating in his mouth and felt comfortably warm on the way down. Rosseikin said, "Well — "

The mess door flew open with a crash. General Bachinsky stood there, his face purplish-red with fury. "Alferyev, Perchik, get your noses out of the vodka and come with me." Two officers at the next table hurriedly got up. Bachinsky's gaze shot around the room and settled on Mikhailov. "Colonel Mikhailov, you too. *Right now.*" He turned and disappeared around the door frame.

"What the devil's going on?" asked Rosseikin plaintively.

"Ask the general," said Mikhailov, already on his way. He grabbed his hat from the hook beside the door and set off after Bachinsky. Alferyev and Perchik were hot on his heels; the general had a rough tongue and disciplinary instincts to match.

In front of the governor's mansion Bachinsky was already getting into his BRDM-2U command vehicle. Alferyev and Perchik followed him into the large hatch on the vehicle's deck where the turret had been removed to make room for the command staff and communications equipment. After a moment's hesitation, Mikhailov followed. His presence made the command compartment a very tight fit for the four of them. Somebody, perhaps Bachinsky, had been eating onions.

The BRDM pulled away, exhaust roaring, in the bright spring sun. Over the racket Bachinsky yelled, "We've got a mutiny. Those fucking black-asses we sent up to repair the road near Karrukh."

"What happened?" This was Perchik, a colonel and Bachinsky's chief of staff.

"Somebody shot at them from the village. Major Svetanko told them to go in and clean it out. They got up to the outer houses. When they were ordered to open fire they refused. Svetanko tried to arrest one of them. Somebody shot him."

"Shit," said Alferyev.

"The other officers got away. The mutineers went into the village. They're still in there."

"What about the sniper who shot at them?"

"Don't know."

Mikhailov poked his head out of the hatch. The BRDM was nearing the firebase. Ahead, a column of trucks and personnel carriers was roaring out of the main gate toward Karrukh. Two self-propelled guns and a tank brought up the rear. Down in the BRDM's command compartment, Bachinsky had commandeered the radio: Mikhailov could hear him swearing at whoever was leading the column for not moving fast enough. There was a rattle of static as Bachinsky signed off. Mikhailov hunched back down into the vehicle.

"Stupid bastards wanted to wait for me," said Bachinsky.

"Can't they think for themselves? Colonel Alferyev, you're supposed to be in charge of operations. Start planning."

"We can do one of three things," Alferyev said. "Try to negotiate them out, starve them out, or blow them out."

"Never mind negotiations. I don't negotiate with monkeys. Most of them can hardly speak Russian anyway. And we aren't going to take time to starve them out."

"If they decide to fight," said Colonel Perchik, "we'll take casualties. Unless we simply flatten the village on top of them and pick up the pieces afterwards."

"I'm not going to have good Russian soldiers shot at by a bunch of fucking mutineers," said Bachinsky. He was seething with fury. "I want air and artillery on that village. Get on the radio," he told Alferyev.

Alferyev shrugged, put on the headset, and began patching himself through to the airbase. Mikhailov said, "With your permission, General, the civilians might be allowed to leave."

Bachinsky glared at him. "What are you going to do? Invite them politely to go away?"

"We should at least give them a chance, sir."

"You know they're too stupid to move."

And they probably won't, Mikhailov thought dispiritedly. They won't understand what's going on, and they'll be afraid to go out in the open where we might cut them down. It's happened often enough. Still.

"I'd like to try. With your permission."

A pause. "All right. You speak the language. You do it."

"Yes, sir."

They were overtaking the rear of the column. The driver kept the BRDM to one side of the road, to stay out of some of the dust. There was still more than enough to silt thickly on their uniforms and skin. Mikhailov's face felt caked. He put his head out the hatch again, for some air. It was a beautiful day, neither too hot nor too cold, and the fields on either side of the road were greening. Before long they would be browned and dessicated by the constant wind and the sun, but for now they were lush and bright.

The column reached Karrukh shortly after one o'clock.

The BRDM pulled up to the lead personnel carrier and Bachinsky and the others got out. A major Mikhailov did not know hurried up to Bachinsky.

"The village is surrounded, General. They're still in there."

Any sign of them coming out?"

"No, sir."

There was a mounting howl. Four Su-22 fighter-bombers shot overhead, banked over the village, and receded into the blue. Mikhailov looked southwest, toward Herat. There were four more specks against the sky, moving slowly: helicopter gunships.

Bachinsky turned to Mikhailov. "If you're going to try to get the civilians to leave, you might as well see what you can do with the monkeys. No promises. Just tell them that if they come out unarmed they'll be treated properly under military law; only the ringleaders will be held responsible. Remind them they haven't gone too far to stop. You've got ten minutes. After that they get hit. Tell the villagers whatever you want."

"Have you got a white cloth?" Mikhailov asked the major.

"One moment, Colonel. I'll see."

Bachinsky shifted impatiently from one foot to the other until the major came back with a bayonet and a square of canvas. It was more gray than white, but it would have to do. Mikhailov stuck it on the point of the bayonet and stepped out of the shelter of the BRDM, holding the bayonet at arm's length so the men in the town could see the parley flag.

It was perhaps five hundred meters from the BRDM to the edge of the village, which was perched a little way up the side of the valley, with terraced fields above and around it. Several of the larger mud-brick houses were serviceably fortified, with narrow windows and squat lookout towers. A few plane trees and poplars broke up the flat lines of the roofs.

Mikhailov stumbled into and then out of a dry ditch. He was now only two hundred meters from the closest building, a low affair that looked very much like a blockhouse. Three heads were visible at the edge of its roof. They wore helmets. There were no Afghans to be seen.

Someone shouted at him. The wind carried the words

away. Mikhailov cupped his free hand to his ear and walked another hundred meters.

The shout again. He thought it was one of the soldiers on the roof. Then the one on the right raised his rifle and fired a shot into the air. Mikhailov stopped.

"Who are you?" The shout was in badly accented Russian.

"Colonel Mikhailov," he called back. "I want to talk to whoever's in command."

"I am. What do you want?" The man who had fired stood up, cradling the rifle but keeping it pointed at Mikhailov.

"To talk. We haven't much time."

"Then talk, Russian." The man's voice was harsh but there was an edge of fear in it. The sixty or so mutineers by now would be realizing the implications of what they had done.

"Put down your weapons and come out. You'll be treated fairly."

"We know what that means. Twenty in the camps."

"It's better than being dead," called Mikhailov. He had no more than four minutes.

"What makes you think that, Russian? Ever been in one?"

"We know you have grievances. They'll be taken into account." Not likely, Mikhailov thought. Not for mutineers. "You haven't gone too far to stop. Come out peacefully and that will count in your favor." They really had no choice. They hadn't a chance of getting up into the mountains, and even if they did the mujahidin would kill them.

"Piss off, Russian. Come in and get us."

"Are you speaking for everybody? Why not let everyone who wants to come out do so? And let the civilians leave if you're determined to screw up."

He had three minutes, perhaps. There appeared to be a consultation going on on the roof. Then the spokesman yelled, "Everybody's staying here. If you bomb us, you bomb the civilians."

"You know that won't stop General Bachinsky."

"Tell General Bachinsky to pull the pin on a grenade and shove it up his ass. You can get us out but it'll cost you a lot of Russians."

It was no use. "At least let the women and children out."

"Get lost before I shoot your balls off."

Mikhailov turned and began to walk back the way he had come. His shoulders ached with tension. They might very well put a bullet in his back before he reached his own lines; they had nothing to lose now. The futility of the whole situation made him feel sick. A good many soldiers would be killed and the more-or-less innocent population of the village would be decimated, because Russian officers wouldn't or couldn't deal with the problems of the men they were supposed to be leading. Even a small mutiny like this one would cause reverberations all the way to the Kremlin. Bachinsky might be relieved of his command, along with his senior officers and the commanders of the mutinous unit. Ethnic troops would be trusted even less than before, and treated accordingly, which in turn would drive morale even lower, and make them even more likely to revolt. The cycle fed on itself.

He had almost reached the BRDM and the other vehicles and they still hadn't shot at him. He began to relax.

There was a spatter of automatic-weapons fire from the village. Mikhailov ran. He reached the BRDM and threw himself behind it, almost on top of Perchik, who was crouching behind one of the vehicle's wheels.

"They waited too long," said Mikhailov, light-headed with relief.

"They weren't shooting at you," Bachinsky said. He was on the ground, peering under the BRDM's body at the village. "Look."

Mikhailov looked. Half a dozen figures were running for the shelter of the trucks and armored personnel carriers. Three more men lay on the ground.

"Some of them decided to surrender," said Bachinsky. "The others don't want them to."

Mikhailov watched as the six men went down, two at once, then one, then another, then the last two. They had got nowhere near Bachinsky's troops.

Bachinsky got up. "Take up positions," he said. "Get the vehicles back farther. Alferyev, have the planes and the helicopters put all their ordnance on the village and then give it ten minutes of artillery, rapid, sustained, then rapid. Flatten the place and we'll dispose of what's left over."

"Wait," said Mikhailov. "Look."

People were running out of the village, up the slope to the northwest, to the terraces and the scattered poplars. They weren't soldiers.

"They let them go," said Mikhailov. "They said they wouldn't."

"I hope it makes you happy," Bachinsky said, and then to Alferyev: "Get those planes down here. I want to get this over with."

Twenty minutes later the village was a ruin. It had been blown apart so thoroughly that it wasn't even burning much, and there wasn't a wall left that stood more than a meter high. Most of the villagers seemed to have gotten away, but up on the terraced slopes where Bachinsky's troops had been spread thinly there were at least twenty dead or wounded mutineers. It was as though they had been trying to break out under covering fire from their comrades in the village.

"That's peculiar," said Alferyev, scanning the terraces through his field glasses. Bachinsky's troops were moving in on the village. Mikhailov and Alferyev were standing by the command BRDM, which was parked in a poplar grove. "Why would they try to get up into the mountains? I'd rather be bombed dead than be skinned alive by the bandits." He lowered the glasses and looked at Mikhailov.

"The mutineers were from the south," said Mikhailov. "They were Moslem long before they were Communist."

Alferyev whistled thoughtfully between his teeth. "You think they might have been trying to go over? Defect?"

Mikhailov shrugged. "I've never heard of it happening. It's not likely."

He was wrong.

They had been bringing the bodies out for an hour. Only twelve mutineers had survived to become prisoners. Fourteen Afghans were dead, and six injured. Five of the six were women, children, or old men. The sixth was a man in his mid-twenties, who had been discovered partly buried under a collapsed wall at the edge of the village nearest the terraces. He had a broken leg, a concussion, and severe bruises but seemed otherwise healthy. Next to him was lying an old but serviceable Lee-Enfield rifle. Perchik had him carried down to the poplar grove with the rifle and put on the ground next to the BRDM. Bachinsky came up from some unspecified business and said, "Who's that?"

Perchik told him.

"He must be the one who fired from the village at the start of all this," Bachinsky said. His rage had gone and he looked old. "Just a minute. That means he was up in the village at the same time the mutineers were. Why hadn't he buggered off long before?"

"Maybe he hid," said Alferyev, and then looked as though he wanted to bite his tongue off.

"Don't be an asshole," General Bachinsky said. "Colonel Mikhailov, do you speak whatever he speaks?"

"Possibly. It depends on the area he's from. Most of them speak Persian but some of the dialects are — "

"I don't want a language lecture. Get him back to the base and interrogate him. Find out what he was doing up there and why. I want answers by tonight. Do whatever you have to, just don't kill him."

They had put the Afghan guerrilla in the punishment building, an ugly cinder-block structure at the edge of the firebase. Mikhailov waited in the firebase headquarters building with Perchik while medical staff cleaned the man up. Perchik located a half-full bottle of vodka somewhere and he and Mikhailov drank it tepid and without water while they waited. Perchik was morose. After the fourth ounce of spirit he said, "That's it for me. One brilliant military career into the shit."

"They can't hold you responsible. The regimental political officers and the colonel will be the ones they'll skin," Mikhailov told him.

"Kabul will want somebody higher than that," said Per-

chik. "To make an example of. To keep everybody else in line."
He hiccuped. "I'm the one they'll nail. Skin a divisional chief of
staff, everybody jumps. You watch. Bachinsky will make sure
all the shit comes in my window."

"He's in trouble himself over this."

"You watch," Perchik said again. "He'll fix it so I carry the
can. He's good at that. And Alferyev will be wearing my hat
inside of a week."

"If he wants it."

"Oh, he wants it. He's ambitious, that one. Give me some
more."

Mikhailov poured the last of the vodka into Perchik's glass.

"As for me," said Perchik, "I'll be counting blankets in
Termez. Oh, well, I wanted to go home. But not to Termez,
shit, what a hole *that* is."

"Nobody will shoot at you, anyway," said Mikhailov.

"Shit," Perchik repeated. "Termez. Shit."

The door banged open and Bachinsky stormed in. "Perchik. What are you doing here? Drinking on duty. Asshole.
Get back to GHQ. Mikhailov — sorry, *Colonel* — the monkey's
back in one piece. Find out what he knows. There's a medic
outside, he'll show you the cell."

Perchik stood up, saluted with some lack of coordination,
and walked out. Mikhailov followed. A regimental medical
officer was standing on the porch. There were bloodstains on
his tunic.

"I'm the interrogating officer," said Mikhailov.

"Yes, Colonel." The MO turned and started toward the
edge of the firebase and the punishment block. Soldiers, almost
all Russians or Slavs, sat on the steps of the barracks that lined
the firebase's main street. They avoided looking at Mikhailov or
the medical officer.

"He's in the first cell on the left," said the MO as they
reached the punishment block. From the barracks behind them,
someone shouted, "Shoot the fucking monkeys."

The medical officer stiffened. Mikhailov said, "Where are
the others?"

"What?"

"The troops up in the village. There were twelve of them. About."

"They've been isolated. There were just enough cells."

"What shape is the Afghan in?"

"Adequate. He had some internal injuries, as well as the leg. We've done what we could."

"They may want him in Kabul," Mikhailov said.

"He ought to live that long."

"All right."

They went past the guards and into the punishment block. The guards were very alert. Inside the building it was cool, almost cold. The spring sun had not yet warmed the walls and roof.

"He's in there," the MO said.

Next to the steel door stood a guard, and next to the guard, peering through the door's slit, was Major Veshkin. Mikhailov had read over the assignment list for GHQ Herat; Veshkin had "general duties." He was actually an interrogation specialist. His methods, according to Rosseikin, were "creative."

"Major Veshkin?"

Veshkin turned from the slit and looked at Mikhailov. The face was pure Mongol.

"Ah, Colonel Mikhailov," said Veshkin. "Did General Bachinsky send you over?"

"Yes."

"You speak Persian." Veshkin seemed affronted at this.

"That's right."

"Most of my interrogation experience has been with Heratis," said Veshkin. "They've got a peculiar dialect."

"It's urban," said Mikhailov. "You don't find it outside Herat."

"I can't follow this one," Veshkin said. "I tried. You go ahead."

The cell door wasn't locked. Mikhailov and Veshkin went in and the steel slab clicked shut behind them. The guerrilla lay on a low bench against the wall. His leg was splinted, not in a cast. There was a smear of blood on his forehead and he was naked except for a dirty cloth around his waist. He appeared to be asleep or unconscious.

"Can he hear?" Mikhailov asked.

"He could a minute ago. I saw him through the slit. He was looking around."

Mikhailov looked down at the still figure on the bench. The man's face was drawn with pain, the skin over the cheekbones grayish-brown. He wasn't more than twenty-five.

"Get two chairs," Veshkin called to the guard.

"What is your name?" Mikhailov asked in Persian.

Silence.

"I am Colonel Mikhailov. I see from your weapon that you are one of the soldiers of God."

One eyelid flickered.

"It is written that those who die in battle against the unbelievers will find rest in paradise," Mikhailov said. "It is not so written of those who die in prison. If you do not tell us why you were in the village, you will most certainly die in prison."

The cell door clanked open and the guard appeared with two wooden stools. Mikhailov and Veshkin sat down on them. The door closed again.

"If you tell us what you were doing," Mikhailov said, "you will not die in prison. Someday you will be free. Then you will be able to take up the *jihad* again, the holy war. We are both soldiers, you will understand why I must know."

"*Rus,*" spat the man.

It wasn't enough to identify the dialect. Mikhailov hoped he was being understood. "Yes," he said. "Russian. Why were you in the village?"

The eyes closed again.

Veshkin leaned across Mikhailov and struck the splinted leg with the edge of his hand. The guerrilla's eyes flew open. He drew a great, sighing breath. Then he closed his eyes and mouth and lay as he had before, unmoving.

"Don't do that again," said Mikhailov. He had seen mujahidin endure the most appalling wounds without a sound. "It won't help, you'll only send him into shock."

"He has to talk," Veshkin said.

"That won't do it. You could cut his fingers off a joint at a time and he wouldn't tell us anything. This is a hill man, a Pushtu I think. He's not like one of your Heratis."

"General Bachinsky wants information."

"I know he wants information. It may take a long time to get it. He may not get it. Have you tried the mutineers yet?"

"That's going on now."

"You're more likely to get it out of them than this one." Mikhailov turned back to the bench. "This officer wishes to hurt you unless you answer my questions. I have told him that that will not make you speak, but he does not believe me. Our soldiers, the ones who were with you in the village, they have told us why you were there." Mikhailov paused, hoping that he was not about to make a serious tactical error. "You were to assist them in escaping from our army. They were to go into the mountains with you and fight in the *jihad*."

The guerrilla's eyes opened again. "God will smite you all," he said. "The believers who are in your army will cut your throats in the night." The Persian was heavily accented, but Mikhailov could follow it.

"And then they will join the *jihad*?" asked Mikhailov. But the man turned his face to the wall.

"What did he say?" asked Veshkin.

"I suggested that he was to bring the mutineers over to the mujahidin. He didn't deny it."

Veshkin looked stunned. "If that's true — "

"Were the men in the work party of Moslem descent?"

"A lot of them."

Mikhailov studied the man on the bench and then asked, "How did you establish contact with our soldiers in the beginning?"

There was no answer. They didn't get another word out of the man, although they tried until sunset, whereupon Veshkin went off to supervise the interrogation of the mutineers. Mikhailov stood for a moment at the cell door, looking at the guerrilla. The guerrilla turned his head and stared back.

"Go with God," Mikhailov said.

The mutineers were much more forthcoming. By noon the next

day Veshkin had what he wanted. Mikhailov's guess had been right; the ringleaders of the mutiny — all dead, unfortunately — had been in contact with the mujahidin for some weeks. There wasn't any single factor to account for the revolt; it resulted from various kinds of ill-treatment, racial prejudice, and, apparently, the conviction among the mutineers that they were the natural allies of the men they were supposed to be fighting. The bond seemed to be based on Islam; a couple of the mutineers had referred to their interrogators as unbelievers. The guerrilla had in fact shot at them from the village, but it was a signal. The plan was that this "attack" would cause the company officers to order the occupation of the village; once the men were inside their officers would be killed, and the guerrilla who fired the shot would lead the mutineers into the mountains. Things had gone wrong after they shot Major Svetanko too early, and the other officers had escaped. Otherwise the plan might very well have succeeded. If nothing else, it would have been a tremendous propaganda victory for the mujahidin.

That evening the headquarters shake-up began. Perchik was demoted two ranks and sent back to Russia. The political officers who had failed to identify the mood of the men were also recalled, for unspecified punishment. Alferyev became chief of staff; Bachinsky, who must have had influential friends in both Moscow and Kabul, wasn't touched.

The rot had to be cut out elsewhere, as well. On the morning of the second day after the revolt, the twelve surviving mutineers were taken out of the punishment block, paraded in front of selected units of the division, and shot.

The guerrilla was sent to Kabul by air, for more sophisticated interrogation.

Moscow
Wednesday, April 14

TWO REPORTS resulted from the Herat mutiny, and they followed two separate paths to Moscow.

The first, which glossed over the incident "pending further investigation," made its way from General Bachinsky to GHQ in Kabul, and from there to Moscow and Marshal Paul Osipov, chief of the General Staff. Osipov informed Defense Minister Yasev of the incident in a brief phone call on the morning of 14 April, along with some other matters concerning Soviet troops in Afghanistan. Yasev, after a little consideration, decided to let the matter rest; the mutineers had been dealt with and he felt it unlikely that attempts to defect to the mujahidin would occur again. He did, however, contact the head of the main political administration of the armed forces, which was responsible for the political reliability of the troops, and instruct him to take any indoctrination measures necessary to prevent a recurrence.

The other report, which included Mikhailov's account of the incident, originated with General Gordik in Kabul. Gordik sent the report to the chief of the Third Directorate, General Tolbukhin, who received it in Moscow shortly after lunch on 14 April. He read the report at first with disbelief and then with mounting consternation. Gordik had contacted him the day after the mutiny with some sparse information, but what was in the report was worse than Tolbukhin had expected. When he had finished the document he read it again, and then locked it in the safe built into the right-hand pedestal of his desk.

He disliked intensely the thought of bringing the incident to KGB Chairman Smilga's attention, but he could see no way of avoiding it. The matter reflected badly not only on the main political administration, for not ensuring the loyalty of the troops, and on the combat officers, for not controlling them, but also on Tolbukhin's Third Directorate personnel, who should have reported that something was brewing long before it erupted in the firefight at Karrukh. General Gordik had informers in Bachinsky's division, but they hadn't noticed a thing. More disturbing was that the Third Directorate agent in the mutinous company appeared to have joined the mutineers. Unfortunately the man could not be questioned, as he had died in the bombardment of the village.

Mikhailov, fortunately, would not suffer as a result of the mutiny, as he was not in the operational chain of command in Herat and had been there only a few days when the event occurred. It was Mikhailov's account of the incident that most disturbed Tolbukhin. Most of Gordik's report had been compiled from information provided by Third Directorate personnel in Herat, who were anxious to exonerate themselves for slipshod work, and were therefore likely slanting the truth. Gordik, in a covering letter to Tolbukhin, had had the courage to point this out, and had directed his superior to Mikhailov's analysis for an unbiased opinion. "Colonel Mikhailov," he had written, "considers the events leading to the mutiny as secondary to the causes underlying them. If he has made a correct evaluation of the conditions under which the troops of this unit lived and fought, and of the attitudes arising from these conditions, then this incident will not be an isolated one but is certain to repeat itself. I personally feel that Colonel Mikhailov is quite correct."

Unless, Tolbukhin thought, we withdraw all non-Slavs, or at least all the Moslem service troops, from Afghanistan and replace them with Russians or other Slavic nationalities. We had to do that with the combat elements back in 1980, when we found the mujahidin didn't care whether the men in the Red Army uniforms were from Tashkent or Leningrad. But that means either confessing we can't handle the problem, or diverting trustworthy units to noncombat duties. Much better to improve the attitudes of the men. How? More political education? There's so much already it's cutting into their training.

Tolbukhin, who had had his full share of political lectures and indoctrination courses, was cynical about their value in a combat environment. He had never been convinced that most soldiers fought better out of commitment to some higher cause or other, like communism, or even Mother Russia, whatever they might say; in his view they endured wounds, disease, intense discomfort, fear, and the risk of death because of the strong personal loyalties that formed among the members of small combat groups. What kept men in the firing line was more the fear of disgracing themselves in front of their comrades than a burning faith in the principles of Marxist-Leninism. Soviet army doctrine, however, actively discouraged such personal bonding, because it generated loyalties not directed to the regime, but outside it and therefore beyond its control.

That service company in Herat, thought Tolbukhin. Now there's a prime example of what we're afraid of. The loyalties turned inwards, instead of outwards to the Party. So you get rebellion. Worse, not only rebellion — we've had that before — but an attempt to go over to the enemy. Treason. Dmitri Smilga will go through the roof. When he comes back down heaven only knows what he'll do.

Sighing, Tolbukhin picked up the internal phone to make an appointment with Smilga.

He got his meeting too soon to suit him, an hour later. Smilga's office was on the top floor of the building, overlooking Dzerzhinsky Square. When Tolbukhin entered it, after a discreet tap on the polished oak door, Smilga was standing at the window, apparently looking down at the statue of Felix Dzerzhinsky. Tolbukhin noted that the portrait of Stalin still hung on the wall next to the windows. In a number of offices Tolbukhin knew about around Moscow, such pictures had come down. It was rumored that the new general secretary didn't care for Josef V. Stalin and the bloody footprints he had left through Russian history.

Time to start rewriting the history books again, thought Tolbukhin. But not for Smilga. He would have liked working for Old Mustache.

Smilga turned and said mildly, "I just finished reading the report. We'll wait a minute or two before we start. I want Volkov to join us."

Georgi Volkov was head of the Fifth Directorate, whose departments were responsible for control of political dissent, religion, unauthorized literature, the Jews, and ethnic nationalities. "May I ask —" began Tolbukhin.

"Why Volkov's coming? You may. You will also have to wait for your answer."

"Yes, Chairman," Tolbukhin said, smarting. He had worked under Smilga for two years and had loathed every minute of it. The man had a good share of the social graces, but rarely displayed them. He was, however, highly competent, quite ruthless, and convinced that the KGB was the spiritual — although he would not have used that word — guardian of Russia.

"Sit down, General Tolbukhin."

Tolbukhin did so, in a hard chair. The only comfortable one was behind Smilga's desk, on which resided half a dozen telephones of various colors. From that desk Smilga could talk to any senior KGB officer in the world, usually within minutes of placing the call.

Volkov came in looking worried, as he usually did. He was near-sighted and wore thick-lensed glasses, which magnified his eyes. Together with his receding chin and slightly protruberant teeth, the magnifying effect gave him a harmless, pet-rabbit look. In fact he was not at all harmless, as a good many purveyors of *samizdat* literature, Jews who tried to emigrate, and Ukrainians who wanted more recognition of their national culture had found out, usually unpleasantly. Without being asked, he sat on the chair next to Tolbukhin's.

Smilga left the window and slowly lowered himself into

the seat behind all the telephones. He folded his arms neatly on the report Tolbukhin had sent him and studied his two directorate heads in silence. Tolbukhin writhed internally.

"Well," said the KGB chairman quietly, "this is a pile of shit, isn't it?" He tapped the report with one forefinger and looked pointedly at Tolbukhin. "Isn't it?"

I better watch it, Tolbukhin thought. No point in blowing away my pension three years before I can start collecting it. "Yes, Chairman. It's extremely serious. We have had units and individuals refuse to obey orders before, but never with the intent of deserting to the, ah, bandits."

"That's all you have to say?"

"Chairman, the report has only been in this building for ninety minutes. I felt such a serious matter couldn't be acted upon without your participation."

"So now you want me to do your job too, eh?"

Tolbukhin had learned, through bitter experience, that it was best to say nothing in response to questions like these.

Smilga turned to Volkov. "What do *you* have to say for yourself?"

Volkov looked even more worried. "Chairman, I don't follow you. What's happened?"

"There's been another mutiny among Asiatic troops in Afghanistan. That's bad enough. But according to this Third Directorate officer — " Smilga flicked the report with disgust "— Mikhailov, the mutineers were planning to join the bandits."

"That's appalling, Chairman. But I don't see —"

"What this has to do with you? You think this is purely a Third Directorate and army matter?"

"Well —"

Smilga took a deep breath. "Might it not occur to you that such mutinies wouldn't occur if the men who mutinied weren't inclined that way *before* they were put into the army? Or were infected with disloyal thinking while on leave at home? Which leads us to the conclusion that your directorate isn't doing its job in the places these men come from. Why do you think we *have* a Fifth Directorate? Eh? Why?"

"To ruthlessly combat backwards-looking bourgeois nationalist tendencies," said Volkov, by the book. "To develop a unified social consciousness in all peoples of the union."

"Exactly. You're not doing very well, are you?"

Volkov remained silent. Smilga stared at him until he said, "No, Chairman. But there are many forces of reaction against us."

"If there weren't," Smilga barked, "we wouldn't need you. Also remember, both of you, that there are other people in this organization who feel they could do as good a job as you are. If you aren't careful, they may get a chance to try. In twenty-four hours I want an outline of the measures you propose to take in each of your organizations, to insure that this insurrection is the last. Twenty-four hours. Get to work."

The two directorate chiefs stood up. Tolbukhin paused. There was something he had to know.

"Chairman, both the head of the main political administration and Defense Secretary Tsander will be asking for our information about the mutiny. How far are we to accommodate them?"

"Refer any MPA queries, or any snooping from the secretary, to me. They'll be told as much as they need to know. Why are you still here?"

They left. Smilga got up and went and looked out the window again. Curse it, he thought, this will make Romanenko even more set on his so-called reforms. Tsander's his bedfellow, they both want to wet-nurse the soldiers, they think that easing up will make them fight better. Discipline is what will make them fight better. Iron discipline. Stalin knew that. He didn't save Russia from the Nazis by wiping the men's bums for them, he saved us by ordering them to fight naked with their bare hands and with empty stomachs if they had to, and by shooting them if they wouldn't.

As long as I'm in this office, the picture of Joseph Stalin stays on my wall.

Late that afternoon Konstantin Tsander, Central Committee secretary for the military, the defense industry, and the police, was preparing to leave his office in the Central Committee building in Staraya Square. To his annoyance, his assistant put his head in the door just as he was locking up his desk.

"Yes? What is it?"

"A package for you, Secretary. It was delivered by hand."

"Give it to me. Then you can go home."

"Thank you, Secretary."

Tsander looked at the package. It was a brown envelope with his name written neatly on it in black ink. He fingered it and then slit one end with his letter opener.

Inside was a copy of the documents Tolbukhin had received from Kabul that afternoon. On a slip of paper was written:

I believe you ought to see this.

T.

Tsander nodded to himself and began to read. When he had finished he locked the documents in his safe, burned Tolbukhin's note in his ashtray, and ground the ashes to powder with the letter opener.

London, England
Thursday, April 22

*T*HE SAFE HOUSE, which the London CIA station had arranged for Chantal Mallory, was actually a room in the President Hotel in Southampton Row. She was registered under her own name in the Mount Royal, a good distance away. She had managed to persuade *Seven Days* to allow her a few days' leave, on the strength of her coverage of the death of Chernenko and the accession of Romanenko, and the fact that little was happening in Moscow now that the new government, after nearly a month, appeared firmly in the saddle. She hoped fervently that nothing important would happen before she got back; she put a good deal of herself into her journalism.

She looked at her watch. Fowler should be arriving soon. She lit another cigarette. There were already four half-smoked butts in the pressed-metal ashtray.

I wish I had a cup of coffee, she thought. The words formed themselves in French. She had noted long ago that her thinking reverted to her mother's tongue whenever she was under stress.

She went to the window and peeped around the edge of the curtains, which were drawn. The gray fronts of the old buildings opposite stared back at her blindly. A figure moved in a window; carefully, slowly, Chantal let the curtain slide back into place.

Paranoia, she thought, stretching out on the bed again. No

one's watching. On the other hand, I'm still free and healthy. What's Fowler going to tell me to do about the Russian? Mikhailov's a cautious man, a professional, they wouldn't have had me come here unless they wanted him. Is Fowler going to ask me to be his principal?

That would be dangerous, she worried. More dangerous than Berlin. On the other hand, he's Romanenko's nephew. That will give him a certain immunity from the KGB he wouldn't otherwise have. And they'll trust him more.

It's a long way, she thought, from being a trainee surveillance operative in Montreal to hobnobbing with the nephew of the general secretary of the Communist Party. What would old McFee think of it? I wonder what he's doing now; probably out to grass. It nearly killed him when they wrapped up K Section.

She mused for a little while about K Section of the Royal Canadian Mounted Police. It no longer existed, and had never existed, officially. The RCMP table of organization started at A Section (security screening), went on to J (electronic surveillance), and then skipped K to end at L (informers). The omission of K in the series had led a number of journalists to speculate that K Section was either so minor it wasn't worth mentioning, or so important that it couldn't be.

The truth lay somewhere between the two views. K Section had been established in the middle sixties to provide an overseas intelligence arm, which the RCMP had never possessed, having always depended on the British MI6 and the American CIA to provide for its foreign-intelligence needs. The dozen or so operatives of K Section worked under deep cover, so deep that they were sometimes more successful in their cover professions than in their real ones. They were all Canadian citizens in various fields: journalism, science, international finance, and the like. Most spoke at least two languages: Chantal, child of an English-Canadian father and a French-Canadian mother, spoke both tongues fluently, and had added more after K Section recruited her in 1976. The CIA provided the training and technical resources for K Section's operations, and in return had access to agents who, not being Americans, were sometimes able to go places Americans weren't welcome.

In the course of time and human nature, CIA interests began to overpower those of the RCMP. K Section began to be more of an arm of Langley than of Ottawa. Then, in the late 1970s, shortly after Chantal joined K Section, evidence of RCMP illegal activities began to surface. K Section had had nothing to do with them, but its connection to the CIA made it a political landmine awaiting a careless governmental foot. It was quietly dissolved in 1981 and all records pertaining to it were hidden or destroyed. Its operatives were given the choice of becoming what they ostensibly were, or of transferring to the CIA. Only a few went to the Americans. The RCMP, with the relief of a paramilitary organization finally getting rid of a clutch of unruly civilians, washed its hands of them.

Chantal had been working for the CIA since the dissolution of K Section. She had been back to Canada and Montreal only half a dozen times since then, and had never regretted her decision.

She lit another cigarette and watched its smoke spiral toward the ceiling. It made her think of burning leaves in October, or mist rising off a lake in the morning. She yawned.

There was a knock at the door, two solid raps. Her eyes snapped open. She waited.

A second knock, this time the d-d-d-d of the Morse V, the first phrase of Beethoven's "Fifth Symphony." Americans, she thought, getting off the bed. They all think we knew Churchill personally. "Yes?" she said to the closed door.

"We have to be at the British Museum by noon."

The pass phrase was adequate, if uninspired. She opened the door. She had already seen Fowler once, at a press conference in the Moscow embassy. He looked paler than he had then, and tired.

"Hello," Fowler said.

"Come on in."

She closed the door behind him. Fowler sat down in the chair beside the diminutive desk.

"What's up?" she asked.

"Got a cigarette?" he asked. "I left mine at the hotel, dammit."

She passed him the pack and her lighter. He lit a cigarette and said, "How would you feel about dealing with the gentleman you met a while ago? On a more permanent basis?"

So she had been right. The meeting in London, away from the sensors and microphones of the KGB, had presaged it.

"Do I have a choice?"

"On this one you do. It's more dangerous than Berlin."

"What's involved?"

"Now that Romanenko is the general secretary, we feel that the gentleman would be more useful at home than where he is. They're going to try to get him to arrange a posting."

"At which point I deal with him."

"That's right."

"You have no native principals? Or Americans?"

"We don't want to use natives. This is too sensitive. You're a journalist. Your interest could be easily accounted for."

"If I could get near him. By default he's a prominent citizen now. There could be all sorts of barriers."

"You're our best bet at the moment."

She took one of her cigarettes but didn't light it, instead rolling it back and forth between her fingers. "What did headquarters think of the tape?"

"The psychologists took it apart. The consensus is that his dissatisfaction with the regime is real enough, but that what's triggered his current behavior is guilt."

"The child he...?"

"That's right. He doesn't see that, of course. The shrinks say he's rationalized his killing of the child as something the regime forced him to do, so he can justify his rebellion."

"What do you think?" Chantal asked. "You heard the tape, I presume."

"Yeah. But I also knew him. We were both working in London at the same time."

If the information surprised her she didn't show it. "Are the psychologists right?"

There was a gentle tapping at the window. It was beginning to rain. "Christ," Fowler said. "I don't know. They might be, about the guilt crystallizing his thinking, I mean. But I don't think it's just guilt. I think he's truly disgusted by what's going on around him. He makes me think of Penkovsky."

Chantal nodded. She knew the Penkovsky case well. Oleg Penkovsky was a colonel in Russian military intelligence, the GRU, who had approached the British Secret Service in the late 1950s and had been turned by them into a devastatingly effective double agent. He had been one of those rare operatives who were motivated by ethics rather than by ideology or material rewards, and had been liked and respected by his British controllers, which was an unusual achievement for a double agent. He was eventually caught by the KGB, and was executed in 1962. "So we may have another Penkovsky," she said. She lit her cigarette. "I don't want to lose him like the British did the original one. He sounded very naive on the tape. Will he be careful enough?"

"I know he sounded politically naive," said Fowler. "What he wants, emotionally, I think, is a regime that will do what was promised back in the revolution. He hasn't thought any further than that."

"It may make him hard to handle. What will you do if he decides he's had enough?"

"We'd bring him out, if we could."

Chantal sat in silence, listening to the rain.

"What do you think of him?" asked Fowler.

Instead of answering she asked, "How important is this?"

"Very. We have no one in a position remotely like his."

She became silent again.

"Miss Mallory?"

"Yes," she said. "I'll take the assignment. But if he gets carried away, I want you to pull me out. Immediately."

"That's understood," Fowler said.

Afghanistan
Monday, May 1

BEYOND THE COCKPIT'S WINDSHIELD the land was a ghostly silver. In the light of the half moon, ravines and ridges and stretches of open sand and gravel appeared, miragelike, and then swept by at two hundred knots beneath the helicopter's nose. The big machine was flying very low to avoid detection by Iranian radar; there was little to worry about from anyone on the ground seeing them, as this border area of Iran was a desert and almost unpopulated, and anyone who did hear them would be far from a telephone.

Richard Gray cleared his throat and said, "How much longer?"

The pilot's voice in the headphones was curt with fatigue. He had been flying the big machine close to the ground, in the near dark, for three hours. Even with the terrain-avoidance systems it was a strain.

"Fifteen minutes. We're just south of Duruh."

"Any sign of the beacon?"

"Not yet," said the relief pilot. "They're not due to turn it on for another five minutes."

"Okay," Gray said. He slipped his hands under the headset and rubbed his ears. With the headset off the drumbeat of the helicopter's engine and rotors was deafening. Surely they can hear us all the way to Tehran, Gray thought.

The helicopter was from the carrier *Nimitz*, which was cruising two hundred and fifty kilometers off the Iranian coast, out in the Gulf of Oman. Gray didn't know what exertions Langley had gone through to persuade the navy to fly him the six-hundred-odd kilometers over hostile territory, but he suspected they had been considerable. Langley CIA headquarters clearly wanted this Russian Mikhailov, and wanted him badly, even to the extent of putting Gray into Afghanistan despite the fact that he was six years past his last field operation. The deciding factor in using Gray was that he had worked in Kabul for some years prior to the Soviet invasion, and had become friends with a certain young Afghan named Mir Zafar. Mir had popped up some time after the Russians overran the country as the Afghan National Liberation Front leader in the Herat region. Under Mir the ANLF had inflicted a number of small but stinging defeats on the Russians, and he had a fairly secure network of bases in the northwest of the country. Arrangements had been made through the ANLF headquarters in Peshawar, Pakistan, to have Mir's people insert Gray into Herat.

Arrangements in this country have a habit of breaking down, Gray reminded himself, especially when they're made by a ramshackle organization like the ANLF. Oh, well, if nobody meets me I can try to walk out.

He rubbed his hook of a nose thoughtfully. The other reason Langley had decided to use him, although they had tactfully not mentioned it, was that Gray looked very much like an Afghan himself, courtesy of a Turkmen grandfather who had emigrated to the United States around the turn of the century.

"I have the beacon," the relief pilot said.

"Bearing?" asked the pilot.

Gray felt some of the tension dissipate. At least he was expected. He wondered whether Mir Zafar would be with the reception party.

The helicopter turned slightly, homing on the radio beacon. They were higher now, because the land was rising. Off to the north it clumped into jagged mountains, forming a natural barrier between the Dasht-i-Lut on the Iranian side of the border and the Khash Desert on the Afghan side. Off to the south lay the small Iranian settlement of Zabol and the swampy flats where the Helmand River petered out after its journey from the mountains of Afghanistan to the northeast. The helicopter was to set Gray down just outside Afghanistan, where a party of ANLF mujahidin were to meet him and take him over the border. Once inside the country they would travel the nearly four hundred kilometers to Herat and establish Gray there while he set up the contact with the Russian. That, at least, was the theory as it had been expressed back at CIA headquarters in Langley. How much of it could be borne out in practice remained to be seen. The land outside looked, and was, cold, inhospitable, and dangerous.

"We're nearly on top of them," said the pilot. "You ready?"

Gray's kit, equipment, and the two crates were by the starboard door. He was already dressed in Afghan clothes: loose, thick trousers, heavy robes, boots, the tightly wound turban, all dirty and down-at-the-heels. He also carried a Soviet Kalashnikov assault rifle as a present for Mir.

"Light," said the relief pilot.

A tiny yellow star had appeared ahead and below. It blinked three times, went out, then repeated the pattern and stayed on.

"Shit," said the pilot. "How far away is that damned light?"

The moonlight made distances deceiving. The helicopter was moving slowly now. Ahead there appeared a flat expanse of naked rock.

"I'm putting down here," said the pilot. "Good luck."

"Beacon's turned off," the relief said, getting out of his seat. Gray and he went back to the door and the relief pilot slid it open while Gray shouldered his pack and the Kalashnikov. They put the rest of Gray's equipment and the two wooden cases onto the ground. The rotor wash was blasting up sand and Gray had to shield his eyes as he trotted away from the helicopter, ducking although the scything blades were well over his head. Outside the circle of the rotor wash he turned and looked back. The pilot was peering at him from the cabin, his face a pale blur. Gray waved. The helicopter's engine revved and the machine lifted slowly, then faster. In a few seconds it was almost invisible against the stars. The beat of the engine faded steadily. After a minute Gray could hardly hear it, and then it was gone. The night was utterly still and the yellow light was nowhere to be seen. He thought it had been toward the northeast, and walked a few meters in that direction.

Something clinked, metal on stone, off to his right. He stopped.

"*Amrikan?*"

"Yes," said Gray, in Persian. Then he repeated the word in Pashto.

"Wait." The whisper was almost inaudible.

Gray waited. Cold bit at his lower calves, where the robes stopped. After a few minutes he squatted and drew the robes around his feet. He began to be thankful he had loaded the Kalashnikov.

After perhaps ten minutes he heard a dry scraping from the jumble of rocks in front of him. Then, in a low voice:

"American. Leave your weapon and walk toward me with your hands on your head. When I say stop, stop."

Gray stood up and held out his arms to show that his hands were empty. Then he clasped them on the rough cloth of his turban and began to walk.

"Stop."

Gray stopped.

"Remove your turban but keep your hands up when you have done so."

Gray complied. He was frightened. If the mujahidin had the slightest suspicion of him they would kill him immediately, if he were lucky. These were descendants of the men who had flayed captured British soldiers alive in the Afghan wars of the last century.

The turban was off. He stood with it dangling from one hand.

A light shone blindingly in his face. He closed his eyes. The light went out.

"This is the man," a voice said. "Richard. You may put your hands down now."

His night vision destroyed by the light, Gray peered at the rocks. He could dimly make out a figure in dark-gray robes emerging from the boulders. The westering moon shone into the man's face as he walked closer. It was Mir.

The two men embraced. Gray caught the sharp smell of

the other's unwashed body, felt the rough beard on his cheek. Then they broke apart and looked at each other. Mir had aged; even in the moonlight Gray could see the lines of strain.

"God has brought you back," said Mir. "Remember? I told you once that if you left you would never be able to stay away."

"God is magnanimous," said Gray, "to give me such a friend. I only wish he had returned me here sooner."

"We do as God wills," said Mir. "I am very glad to see you again."

"And I," said Gray.

Mir turned to the rocks and called out softly, "This man is to me my brother. Although he hasn't taken the faith, he thinks like a Musulman. You will treat him as one. Remember that he fights the *Rus*, and that our enemy's enemy is our brother."

Five more robed figures appeared from among the rocks and stood silently, like ghosts. Mir turned to Gray. "The sentries say no one is near, particularly not the godforsaken Russians." He spat. "We have to be over the border before dawn. We must move quickly. One of us will carry your pack. Is there anything fragile in it?"

"A camera and a radio."

"We'll be careful."

"There is something for you as well," Gray told him. Mir followed him to where the pack and the Kalashnikov lay on the stone. Gray picked up the big weapon and presented it to the Afghan leader. "Be careful," he said. "It's loaded."

Mir felt the weight of the gun. The moonlight lay gently along the dull barrel and silvered the edges of the big ammunition clip. "Perfect," he said. "A beautiful gun. A Russian gun to kill Russians. I thank you."

"I wish I could have brought you more," said Gray. "There are six more guns in the long case, and ammunition in the other."

"*Allah Akhbar*," said Mir reverently. "We'll leave the guns outside Farah until I can send the other trucks for them. Now we must go. In four days we will be in Herat, if God wills and the Russians don't catch us."

Moscow
Tuesday, May 11

THE MOOD OF MOSCOW, Chantal typed, *has changed in the past weeks. There is an air of expectancy, as though something unusual were in the wind. The*

"*Merde,*" she said, and leaned back from the typewriter. "What crap." She keyed the paper up three lines and stared at it with annoyance.

The trouble, she thought, is that there *is* something in the wind, but it's next to impossible to pin it down. It's got something to do with the new leadership, but I can't say anything about that without backup. Something's going to happen, and I'm damned if I can find out what it is. And to add insult to injury, I have to use this bloody typewriter. *Merde.*

She looked over at the corner of the living room, where the screen of her microcomputer stared blankly and glassily back at her. She had been editing copy on it for eighteen months, and the ease of doing so had spoiled her. The machine had mysteriously stopped working a week ago and she would have to take it back to the west on her next leave to have it repaired. In the meantime, it was back to the typewriter.

The clock on her desk said seven-thirty. She turned off the typewriter and got ready to leave. She was socializing tonight, and didn't take the minirecorder.

Outside the apartment complex, where a good proportion of the non-Soviet press lived, she walked along Sadovo-Sovotechnaya Street to the Mayakovskaya metro station. The traffic on this part of the ring road was heavy and noisy, as usual, but the evening was pleasant and warm and there was still enough sunlight to gild the upper parts of the buildings. In any case it was a relief to be out of her apartment, which was too small and was noisy, especially when the *New Statesman* correspondent upstairs was playing his stereo at what had to be nearly full volume. He probably thought he was fooling the microphones that way. The atmosphere in the apartment complex was never very good, either; one of the prices of living in Moscow was that you were suspicious of everyone, including other journalists. You were careful of Russians because you never knew who they might be working for, and you were careful of your colleagues because everyone was always on the lookout for Russian sources and might try to steal yours. Or, as bad, frighten them away altogether. Before she learned the ropes, Chantal had lost contact with a young Russian university teacher who, if not quite a friend, was more than an acquaintance. She had made the mistake of introducing the woman to an overly brash, recently arrived Australian correspondent. He had tried to pump her on some political question or other and she had taken flight. The Australian had got into trouble with the authorities shortly afterward and was ordered out of the country, but the Russian girl had never contacted Chantal again.

"One thing you have to know about Moscow," an old Russian hand had told her just before she left Berlin, "is that you won't have any close friends there. Not just Russians, no westerners either. Keep your guard up."

She had only let it down the once, when she was new, but she still regretted it.

At the Arbatskaya station she left the metro and at street level waited under the red-lit M. No one paid any attention to her; she wore no makeup and early in her work in Moscow she had adopted Russian clothes for most of her unofficial forays into the city's life. She had learned a good deal simply by being indistinguishable from a Muscovite.

"Hello."

He had come up while she was looking the other way. She turned. "Hello, Volodya. Couldn't Maya come?"

"She's back at the apartment, cooking. We'll *eat* this evening. Come on."

They took a trolley bus down Gogol Boulevard and then walked the block to Volodya's apartment building. As he opened the door Chantal could hear Maya singing off-key in the kitchen. The fragrance of roasting pork filled the air. Through the living-room window the last rays of the sun fell on the tan wallpaper and the overstuffed couch with its green upholstery. Most of one wall was devoted to crammed bookshelves and in one corner was a small desk on which stood a 1930s-style lamp with a green shade.

"I'm in the kitchen," Maya called unnecessarily.

"Give me your coat and go on in," Volodya said.

Maya was taking the pork out of the miniscule oven. "Sit, sit. Just a minute, and we'll be eating. Are you well?"

She was a solid, dark woman, with short legs and a broad face with the high cheekbones of a distant Mongol ancestry. Despite her stockiness there was an allure about her, and an earthiness that seemed to Chantal peculiarly Russian. Volodya was at the other end of the physical spectrum: tall, gangly, and blond, balding a little in front. Chantal had met them eighteen months ago, when she had happened to sit next to them at the Metropole Cinema. They were fascinated by westerners, although it could be risky for them to associate with her. For Chantal they provided an invaluable window into middle-class Moscow life. Most journalists cultivated Russian contacts, although Chantal was particularly careful not to be blatant about hers. But to have none at all would be almost as suspicious as to have too many.

Volodya came into the kitchen and said, "Well? Of course she's well. She looks well, doesn't she? As always," he added with a touch of awkward gallantry.

"She never eats enough," said Maya pragmatically. "Go ahead, start."

Chantal and Volodya sat down and began to eat the cabbage soup. Volodya hacked off thick slices of bread to go with it. The bread was dark and contained caraway seeds. Maya made gravy and joined them.

"News," said Volodya around a mouthful of bread.

"Oh?" said Chantal. Maya and Volodya were good friends, but she was still careful not to pry. Volodya held a junior position in the Moscow Institute of Language and Literature, and seemed to like the work. He also wrote short stories, "for recreation" as he put it. Chantal had read three or four; they were competent and bland. He had never tried to get any of them into print, although Chantal thought they would be acceptable to the Soviet publishing industry.

"I know somebody who knows somebody who works in GLAVLIT," he went on. "There are rumors." He waited expectantly.

"What about?" asked Chantal. Maya had stopped eating.

"That they're going to allow a new edition of Solzhenitsyn's *Cancer Ward*. And maybe one of *Dr. Zhivago.*"

Chantal ceased chewing, and then swallowed with difficulty. "You can't be serious."

"It's only rumors. But something's going on. I also heard that a new issue of the *Chronicle of Current Events* has appeared. But I haven't seen it, if there is one."

The *Chronicle* had been an underground publication that was the nearest thing to a free press in the Soviet Union. It had been suppressed in the mid-seventies.

"What was in it?"

"I don't know. I only heard about it. Also," he went on after another spoonful of soup, "there's a rumor they're going to do something about the food shortages. Again, I don't know what."

"I haven't heard any of this," Chantal said.

"The rumors only started a couple of days ago."

"What's going on?"

"*I* know," said Maya. "They're going to loosen up for a while to see who takes advantage of it. Then they'll know who to crack down on. They've done it before."

"Maybe not," said Volodya. "Maybe they've finally realized they have to treat us like human beings." He was getting excited, gesturing. "It was the war," he said portentously, imitating some Party official, "the war that has made it so difficult to realize all the fruits of true Communism. We must rebuild, then there will be more than enough for everyone. Well," he continued in his normal voice, "we've been rebuilding for more than forty years. How long can we go on blaming the war for everything?"

"Until the authorities decide to stop," Maya said snappishly. "That's how long. Eat. The pork will get cold."

They finished the meal with little conversation. Chantal knew that Maya was sometimes critical of the regime, but she kept it to herself much more than did her husband. In the first months of their acquaintance Chantal had thought Volodya might be a KGB provocateur, but had since concluded that he wasn't. He wasn't well enough off, for one thing. The meal they were eating probably constituted a month's luxuries for him and Maya.

"Let's smoke and drink," said Volodya after the dishes were cleared away. "To a new Russia."

There was vodka, Armenian brandy, and wine. Chantal and Maya drank wine. Volodya alternated between brandy and vodka, chasing them with gulps of mineral water. Chantal began to feel pleasantly mellow.

Toward ten o'clock Volodya, who had been talking at furious speed about Dostoevsky, fell silent. He was a little drunk. Maya looked at him with concern. "Are you all right?"

"Perfectly. Chantal, I've got something I want to show you."

"Volodya," his wife said warningly.

"It's all right," he said. "Chantal's a friend. A French-Canadian, too, an oppressed minority. Like us. Only we're an oppressed *majority*." He found this amusing, and laughed. "Just a minute," he said, and got up from the table.

"Volodya, please don't," Maya said. But he had already gone into the living room. Maya looked at Chantal imploringly. "Please understand. What he's got isn't really him, it's not important, you shouldn't take any notice."

"What do you mean, not important," Volodya said, reappearing in the kitchen. He sat down a little too abruptly, pushed glasses aside, and put a sheaf of typescript in front of Chantal. "It's more important than that drivel I write at the institute."

Maya got up and began to stack dishes unnecessarily loudly. Chantal felt acutely embarrassed. After a moment Maya stopped and sat down again. "It's all right," she said. "I'm sorry I insulted you by not trusting you. Please read it." She refilled her glass, this time with brandy, all the way to the top.

With relief Chantal looked down at the manuscript. It had been typed on a very old typewriter with a ribbon so worn that some of the letters were almost invisible. She mentally blocked out her companions and began to read. The manuscript was a short story called "The Execution" and was about a sixteen-year-old captured by the Germans during the war. They tortured him to make him reveal his companions' base. Instead of heroically keeping silent to the bitter end, however, he capitulated when the Germans promised him his life in return for the information. As a result his comrades were captured and shot. The Germans then executed the boy as well. The story, if it ever came to the attention of the authorities, would cause Volodya a great deal of trouble. To start with, the hero — if that were the word for him — failed to live up to the partisan mythology, and the story failed to condemn him for this. Quite the reverse; it demanded compassion for a human being driven past his breaking point, and for others whom he could not help betraying. It could also, without much difficulty, be seen as a parable of the relationship between the Russian people and the regime, with the Germans standing for the latter. The story was not far short of brilliant, and treasonable.

She finished the last page and looked up. Volodya was watching her shyly. He looked extremely vulnerable.

"It's good," she said. "It's very good."

"I have others. Another time you can read them, it's getting late." He was drawing back a little. She hoped he wouldn't regret what he had done when the alcohol wore off. "There's such a difference," she said, "between this one and the others I've read. They might have been written by different people."

"Oh, those," he said disdainfully. "People at the institute

know I write. When they want to see some of it, those are what I show them. They're nothing. Do you really like it?"

"Very much. Maybe if you're right about the rumors, you could have it published someday. Perhaps there'll be a thaw."

"A real Russian spring," said Volodya wistfully. "Then the world could see what we can really do." He shrugged. "Let's drink to writers."

When she left the apartment an hour later she was more than a little tipsy. She was also melancholy that someone with Volodya's talent should have to keep his best work in a desk drawer unread.

Perhaps, she thought, I could take them to the west, translate them, and get them published. Even if he's never read in his own country, it would be something.

Not a chance, she answered herself. If the Russians ever found out it was me behind the stories, I'd never get back in. I have to stay clean. Her thoughts turned to Mikhailov: Andrei will be expecting to see me when he comes back.

Moscow
Wednesday, March 12

KGB CHAIRMAN DMITRI SMILGA and Defense Minister Igor Yasev were having dinner together in one of the private rooms of a very inconspicuous restaurant in the northwest quarter of Moscow. It was so inconspicuous that it did not even have a name. It had been established by the KGB services directorate, which was responsible for the organization's physical facilities. Very senior KGB officials patronized it, and used it from time to time for discreet and comfortable meetings with useful people. The furnishings were baroque, the decor red and gold, and the food superb.

Defense Minister Yasev pushed his empty dessert plate away, leaned back, and sighed contentedly. He linked his fingers comfortably over his middle and said, "Very good, Chairman. The salmon especially." He looked sleepy, but Smilga didn't think he was. However, Yasev was not wearing uniform; Smilga took this as a good sign. The minister was being circumspect.

"Yes," he agreed. "It's a very good place to eat." He reached behind to the buffet. "We have some very old Armagnac to go with the coffee."

"Excellent."

While Smilga poured, Yasev looked around at the small, dim room. Theirs was the only table in it. The room was wainscoted with a dark shiny wood, above which the figured

red velvet began. On one wall hung a mirror in an ornate gold frame. Yasev studied it for a moment.

"It's only a mirror," Smilga said. "There's nothing behind it but wall." This in fact was quite true. KGB men had unofficial business to transact from time to time, and the restaurant was off-limits to microphones, one-way windows disguised as mirrors, recorders, and any sort of camera. It was one of the few places in Moscow that was.

Yasev shrugged to show he didn't care anyway, and said, "We didn't come here to discuss surveillance techniques. What's on your mind?"

Smilga warmed his glass gently at the alcohol lamp that whispered under the brass coffeepot. "I have some concerns for the new leadership. I wanted to share them with you."

"Oh," said Yasev. He sipped at his cognac. "What sort of concerns?"

"Like anyone else," Smilga said tranquilly, "I want General Secretary Romanenko and the Secretariat to succeed in carrying out the enormous tasks before them. In the past six weeks, though, it has occurred to me to wonder whether things are being done in *exactly* the right way."

Yasev's eyes were downcast and hooded in shadow. He may take all this back to Romanenko, Smilga thought, but I doubt it. Not if I have read him correctly. Before Romanenko's accession to the secretaryship he supported him, but that was because he didn't want a Party hack like Zarudin in power, and because he fears more KGB control of the military. Yasev does not really wish for change, except to strengthen the army's hand in the government. He already thinks he can use an alliance with me to control Romanenko's experiments. Or he would not be here.

"Do you remember a professor Yevsei Liberman?" Smilga asked.

"No."

"He proposed the elimination of central economic planning back in the late sixties. Khrushchev took him up, thought it was a good idea. Supply and demand would regulate agriculture and industry. There was even an allowance made for profit, and reinvestment of the profits into the organization that produced them. Sound familiar?"

"Capitalism," said Yasev.

This man is not an economic sophisticate, Smilga thought. "Precisely. Even Kosygin was tempted by the scheme, after Khrushchev...left power. It seemed an easy way out of the economic problems of the time. Fortunately, Secretary Brezhnev put a stop to it. Otherwise..."

"Otherwise what?" prompted Yasev.

"It would have jeopardized the Party's leading role in the guidance of the Soviet Union. It mocked the principles of Marxist-Leninism. The industrial managers would have become an independent force. They would have developed bourgeois capitalism all over again, and it would have had to be rooted out all over again. For example, your defense ministry would have to go cap in hand to the managers and ask them to make tanks and guns for you. You would have no control over the fulfilment of your needs. Enough of this, and the capitalist nations would be at our throats again. Perhaps even Germany."

The mention of that old nightmare plunged Yasev into thoughtful silence for a moment or two. Then he said, "What makes you think Romanenko intends to bring back Libermanism?"

"Oh, he wouldn't call it that. And he would do it much more slowly than Khrushchev tried to do. But he intends to do it. He's already talking about diverting resources from heavy industry to light, to produce what people want, rather than what they need."

"Like defense?" Yasev suggested.

"Among other things."

Yasev refilled his glass and drank a third of it. "There are enough balancing forces in the Party and the government to prevent such a thing."

"No doubt. I only refer to it so that your influence with Secretary Romanenko might help keep him to the Marxist-Leninist path. We should drink to that."

They did. Then Smilga said, idly, "I had a report some time ago. I gather there was some trouble with Asiatic troops in Herat."

Yasev drank again before he answered. "Minor. It was dealt with in hours by local forces."

"There were reports that the mutinous troops were trying to desert to the bandits."

"Rumors," snapped Yasev.

"Indeed?" Smilga allowed some of his power to show. "That's not the information I received. Apparently it was carefully planned, and it was only by luck that it didn't succeed."

"The matter is a *military* affair," said Yasev, with heavy emphasis.

"I have my responsibilities," Smilga told him, "as you have yours. I've always admired your abilities and those of your General Staff. But we're both responsible for the results our organizations achieve. The Third Directorate does all it can to insure the loyalty and commitment of our soldiers, but it can't do *everything*. I suppose Secretary Romanenko has discussed some of the reforms he wants, so that the troops can live better? An easier life, so that young men won't try to avoid their military responsibilities? Let the recruits think they know as much as their officers?"

"Our concern is with living conditions and some other problems," Yasev said.

"There are weaknesses in our military," Smilga said. "We need tighter discipline, not limp-wristed slacking off. The price of security is constant vigilance. I suggest to you that our vigilance is becoming less than it should be."

The bottle of Armagnac was nearly empty. Smilga divided the remainder between his glass and Yasev's, giving the latter rather more than half. "Well, it may not matter. I just wanted to point out to you that ministers of defense who can't control their forces are often replaced by ones that can. I wouldn't want to see that happen to you. There's a lot we have in common. Perhaps I ought to mention that Secretary Romanenko doesn't know quite all that happened in Herat. The report I submitted to him was very similar to yours." He paused. "In that I considered the event not unlike some other ones, and hardly worth mentioning."

Yasev didn't seem to be listening. He was rotating the stem of his glass slowly between his fingers. The alcohol lamp hissed and fluttered.

Abruptly, the minister of defense put his glass down and stood up. "I'm sorry, Dmitri Alexeyevitch, I didn't realize I'd been here so long. I have to return home."

Smilga had been about to put an end to the conversation in any case. "I've enjoyed the evening, Minister," he said. "We must meet again soon. Another meal, perhaps?"

"Perhaps," said Yasev. "Thank you."

When he had seen Yasev to his car, Smilga went back to the restaurant and waited until the chauffeur brought the Zil around to the front door. Instead of getting into the rear seat, however, he slid into the passenger side in front and said to the chauffeur, "Out. Leave the engine running. I won't need you until tomorrow morning. The car will be in its usual place."

The chauffeur said, "Yes, Comrade Chairman," and departed rapidly. Smilga got behind the wheel and waited. Three minutes later a tall, lanky man left the restaurant and got in beside him. Smilga accelerated away from the curb while the passenger door was still closing.

"I'll drive you home," Smilga said. "Your chauffeur can take care of your car?"

"Yes," Zarudin said. "What's the situation with Yasev?"

Smilga turned the car into Leningradsky Prospekt, heading for the center of the city. Just ahead the twin towers of the civil-aviation ministry gleamed wetly in the mist and the glow of the streetlights. "Two things," Smilga said. "First, he is now worried about Romanenko's infatuation with Libermanism. I pointed out some of the implications that had escaped him."

They were nearly at the Aeroflot Hotel and a large bus was pulling out of the long glass terminal connecting it to the civil-aviation ministry. Smilga braked abruptly and the windshield fogged with spray from the rear wheels of the vehicle.

The KGB chairman switched on the wipers and drove around the bus.

"The second?" Zarudin prompted.

"Yasev feels he may need our support if Romanenko's so-called reforms start turning the armed forces inside out. He's worried about that now, I think. What have you managed so far?"

"The government ministries will fight this decentralization scheme of his every centimeter. And I've been working indirectly on some of the less committed Central Committee members. But Romanenko isn't sitting on his heels. He has key supporters, and he's using them."

There was a silence that lasted until the Zil reached the intersection of the Prospekt and Begovaya Alleya Street, with its pair of horse statues. The mist was congealing into rain and Smilga turned on the wipers again.

"Good," he said. "Every day, just a little more rope. When the time comes, we'll hang him with it."

Herat, Afghanistan
May 15 – 16

ON HIS WAY TO WORK from his billet in the Bizhad Hotel west of the governor's mansion, Mikhailov saw the two white chalk stripes on the lamppost. They were ragged, as though they had been put there hurriedly. In the morning sun they seemed very conspicuous.

He walked across the irregularly shaped plaza in front of the mansion. Almost everyone in sight wore Russian uniform, but there were a few Heratis in Afghan robes who walked hurriedly, eager to escape the presence of the foreigners, the unbelievers. Two Afghan soldiers sauntered along the northwest edge of the plaza. In the past three years the national army had decayed to such an extent that there were only half a dozen effective units left, and these were all in Kabul, to protect the government. Herat possessed only a company of Afghan militia, which, from the Soviet point of view, was worse than useless, since they were not to be trusted; it was quite possible that they were militia by day and mujahidin by night. Politically, though, they were necessary, so that the Russians would not appear quite so much the occupying army. The Afghan military governor of Herat lived in a compound at the Soviet firebase, the only place he was reasonably safe, and did nothing. The rule of the city and its surrounding region was effectively Bachinsky's; he gave the militia company whatever orders were necessary. Sometimes they were obeyed.

How am I going to get through the day? Mikhailov wondered. He wished he hadn't seen the chalk marks so early. He had begun to wonder whether the Americans had failed to get someone into the country after all. Part of him hoped that this had happened.

Major Rosseikin was already at work in the cubicle adjoining Mikhailov's office; or he appeared to be at work. The man had a talent for furious activity that produced few results. Mikhailov had considered getting rid of him, but then had concluded that if he really were trying to subvert Russian effectiveness in Afghanistan, the more incompetence the better, as long as it didn't jeopardize his own position. Rosseikin looked through the doorway and said, "Good morning, Colonel."

"Good morning. Have Scherbitsky and Masherov gone?"

"Yes, Colonel. Just before you came in."

Scherbitsky and Masherov were the other two members of Mikhailov's staff. This morning they were at the firebase lecturing the company officers on changes in guerrilla tactics during the past few months. Both were competent, if uninspired. Training of the more senior officers was carried out by Mikhailov and Rosseikin, so that rank wouldn't get in the way.

"Is that report typed yet?" Mikhailov asked. There had been sporadic mujahidin activity during the past fourteen days; Mikhailov had collated the intelligence on it and written it up for Gordik. He had to use Bachinsky's staff clerks for office work, however, since the OSB office had none of its own. Unfortunately, the OSB was seen by Bachinsky's staff as an unwelcome intrusion from Kabul and cooperation left something to be desired.

"Not yet."

"They promised it yesterday. Light a fire under them, would you?"

"Yes, Colonel."

Mikhailov closed the door connecting the two offices and sat down. On the other side of the door he could hear Rosseikin on the phone, badgering someone about the report. He shut the voice out of his mind and got down to work.

There was definitely something going on at headquarters in Kabul. He knew that GHQ had been pestering Bachinsky and his staff for reports on troop readiness, mujahidin activity, logistics efficiency, fuel and ammunition tonnage, training, and acclimatization of new troops. Mikhailov kept a digest of this data, together with anything else he thought useful, in case the Americans did contact him. The digest in itself wasn't suspicious; he kept it quite openly in a desk drawer. If anyone asked about it — which was unlikely — it was no more than a way of keeping all pertinent information organized for Mikhailov's own work. There was nothing in it he shouldn't know.

Occasionally he wondered whether Rosseikin were Third Directorate. The man appeared so harmless that it was quite possible. There would be other Third Directorate informers in the division, but Mikhailov had no idea who they were.

He worked steadily until two o'clock, almost forgetting the visit he would have to make to the ruined minarets that evening. Shortly after two, Rosseikin tapped at his door and said, "Colonel, shall we go to lunch?"

Mikhailov considered his littered desk, said "All right," and tidied up. The more important papers he locked away, including the digest to which he had been adding material.

On the way down to the officers' mess Rosseikin said, "They finally got the report typed. But it's full of mistakes. Those clerks can read, but they can't spell."

"It's late," said Mikhailov. "Let it go anyway. After I've seen it."

"Yes, Colonel."

Rosseikin dropped much of his working-hours formality when they sat down for lunch. Today, wonder of wonders, there was roast beef, not evenly cooked but beef nonetheless. Mikhailov looked at his plate in surprise. There were peas as well, canned, but undeniably peas.

"Food's getting better," Rosseikin said. Mikhailov thought back. There *had* been a steady improvement in their rations over the past two weeks.

"Troops are eating better now too," Rosseikin went on around a mouthful of beef and peas. "I checked. They're getting meat once a week now, sometimes fish. It's dried, but it's fish. There's more of it than there used to be, too."

"Something to do with the spring?" Milhailov suggested.

Rosseikin chewed, swallowed, and said, "Partly. But I've been posted here for a year, and it was always worse than this, even in spring. Somebody's been shaking up the commissariat." He smiled slyly. "Your uncle, maybe?"

Mikhailov hadn't gone out of his way to let people know his uncle was now the country's leader, but the word had been getting around. Rosseikin had already noted an improvement in the support, poor as it was, that the clerical staff was giving the OSB. Even Bachinsky took care not to be excessively rude to Mikhailov, a care he rarely took with his own officers. "I don't know," Mikhailov said. "I know he used to worry about service conditions."

"There's even a directive that troops in a combat zone are to have no more than three hours of political education a week. That's half of what it's been. What do you think of that, eh?" prodded Rosseikin.

If Rosseikin worked for the Third Directorate, this was a loaded question. "Three hours of education properly absorbed is better than six of the other kind," Mikhailov said. "It's the quality, not the quantity, that gives the men a socialist consciousness. As Engels would say."

Rosseikin nodded sagely. Mikhailov asked, "What are they supposed to do with the extra time?"

"Depends on the unit. Tankers, they use some of it for maintenance. Infantry, more training. The rest is free time."

"Where'd you get all this?"

"Colonel Alferyev."

"What does *he* think of it?"

"He thinks it's a good idea. So did General Bachinsky, apparently. They both said the men needed more time to themselves. Although what they'll do with it in this hole, I don't know."

Mikhailov knew how directives from higher up could be ignored or "modified" by the time they reached the troops' level. "How serious is all this?"

"Very. Apparently they're going to make quite sure it's done. Severe penalties for not carrying it through. The unit political officers are supposed to inform the men about it Monday, new daily schedules, all the rest of it."

They *were* serious. Mikhailov thought he could see Romanenko's hand somewhere behind the changes. It looked as though he had finally persuaded the General Staff to do something about the miserable life of the soldiers. And it was a radical something: to tamper with the soldiers' political education was an unprecedented move.

"What do *you* think?" asked Mikhailov.

"If it's what the Party wants," Rosseikin said, "it's what we ought to do."

They left it at that. Through the interminable afternoon Mikhailov kept thinking: perhaps Uncle Vasily is going to do something after all. Perhaps at last there will be a change.

Perhaps I should not have gone to the Americans.

He went to the drop anyway, in the late evening. Bizhad Park was deserted, its pines and tanbarks gloomy in the fading light. Once, where the park now lay, there had been a *musalla*, a place of prayer. Its ruins poked here and there among the silent trees: old mausoleums, broken walls, the newer but tumbledown brick *madrasa*, the theological school, which had been in use up until the time of the invasion but now was derelict and falling into deeper ruin. Beyond the trees, ahead of Mikhailov, stood the six remaining minarets of the old mosque complex.

It was still light enough for Mikhailov to be reasonably safe, although a Russian was always at some risk in Herat. The risk was less here on the north edge of the city because of the proximity of the firebase and the headquarters in the old governor's mansion, and the fact that many of the division's officers, as well as Mikhailov, were billeted in the decayed Bizhad Hotel a block from the park. Nevertheless, Mikhailov was watchful. Several times army trucks full of soldiers had passed him as he walked from HQ toward the park and his billet, and twice there had been armored cars with the heads of the driver and commander protruding like cabbages from the hatches. He didn't want to be noticed entering the park, although officers did wander around in it from time to time, looking at the ruins and picking up odd bits of faience and blue-and-white tile as souvenirs. To be on the safe side, he hunted about until he found a fragment of an inscription. This led him well into the park, among the trees. Pocketing the fragment, he went on past the *madrasa*, past a heap of ruins that had once been an arched gallery, and around the back of the northwest minaret.

The crack was where he remembered it. He stopped, put his hand up on the wall as though to steady himself, and wiggled his boot with his right hand, as though there were a stone in it. The fingers of his left hand searched the cleft. There was a fold of paper in it. He extracted the paper (remembering momentarily another wadded note he had held in Saint George Hall), crumpled it in his hand, straightened, and went on. The light was going. In his pocket the message jostled softly against the shard of tile with its fragmentary, enigmatic inscription.

Mikhailov left the hotel the following evening just before it was dark. He walked the block north to the street that ran along the southern edge of the park and turned right, toward the governor's mansion and headquarters. The streetlights were few and dim; off in the distance he could hear the growl of a patrolling armored car. In this part of the city there were no Afghans in the streets because of the curfew, although in the Old Town the curfew was ignored. Russians did not go in there at night, and rarely during the day. The infantry patrols also kept to the New Town and the outskirts after dark; Mikhailov could see a group of four soldiers and a sergeant walking slowly ahead of him, weapons unslung. He knew the patrol pattern and had timed his departure from his billet to fall in the gap between two patrols.

In the pool of darkness between two streetlights he glanced around to make sure there was no one near and left the road. In the park under the pines it was already night, except where the pale stones of the ruins glimmered in the darkness like shadows in a negative. The air was heavy with the scent of pine pitch, tanbark, dust, and the charcoal cooking fires of the city. Mikhailov felt alien, intrusive; the park had a foreignness it had not possessed in the light of the previous evening.

He made his way past the black bulk of the *madrasa*, and on to the ruined *musalla* complex where the minarets thrust upward against the stars. At the northernmost minaret he found a block of squared stone and sat down on it, his back against the minaret's warm masonry. He began to wait. A bird twittered sleepily; then an owl called. Mikhailov heard his stomach growl. He hadn't eaten any supper. After a while he felt the stone behind him begin to grow cold and he hunched forward, elbows on knees.

Someone was standing beside him.

Mikhailov, startled, began to get to his feet. Something pricked him under his ear, then jabbed. He stopped moving abruptly. "Summer rain," he said, in his very best Pashto. The knife was removed from the line of his jaw and he stood up shakily. An indistinct figure in a gray robe materialized in front of him, and the other Afghan stepped behind. The one in front motioned Mikhailov to follow.

They went north, out of the park and toward the road that stretched away to the northeast and Iran. On the near side of the road stood the Tomb of Jami, and just short of that a group of the peculiar cylindrical Afghan windmills. At the base of the first windmill the man ahead paused and whispered something. From the ruinous doorway in its base came an answering whisper.

The man behind Mikhailov prodded him, not gently. Mikhailov went on, stumbling once on the rough ground, and through the broken doorway. Inside the windmill it was pitch black. He heard a fluttering sound, like heavy cloth unfolding. Someone had drawn a blackout curtain across the door.

A match spurted and a dim yellow light sprang into being: an oil lamp. The glow illuminated a circle no more than two meters across. Outside the circle Mikhailov sensed empty space; the mill's wooden machinery was long gone. Next to the lamp, which was standing on the beaten earth floor, sat a man in Afghan clothing. A dirty cloth with faded blue stripes was drawn across the lower half of his face, revealing only the eyes and forehead. Mikhailov looked around. There appeared to be no one else.

"They're all outside," said the man in English, "except one. He has to listen, so we'll speak English."

Mikhailov sensed movement off to his right. He didn't look around; he was still far from safe. "You're the American?"

A nod. "You're Colonel Mikhailov. Naturally." He paused, staring at Mikhailov's face as though comparing it with a photograph. "You weren't followed, we made sure of that. How long do you have and where are you supposed to be?"

"Not long. Twenty minutes. I'm supposedly at work."

"You'll go there next?"

Mikhailov nodded.

"Good," said the American. "I'm pleased to meet you, Colonel." He extended a hand. Mikhailov shook it. "I have something for you," Mikhailov said, and reached toward his tunic. He heard a sudden movement in the darkness, and stopped.

"It's all right," the American said in Pashto, and then, to Mikhailov, "go ahead." Mikhailov took the copy of the digest out of his tunic and gave it to the American. "You might as well sit down," the American said.

Mikhailov squatted. The American skimmed the documents quickly and then put them inside his robes. "Thank you," he said. "These look very good. Let's work out future contacts."

They arranged a number of drops and fallbacks. There would be no more face-to-face meetings, except in emergencies. When they finished, Mikhailov asked, "What kinds of information are you looking for?"

"These," said the American. "All information on anti-guerrilla operations. Reports on your troop morale, unit strength, training level, any administrative or logistics problems. Regional command structure and tables of organization and equipment. Third Directorate activity in the army, anything you can remember from Moscow and haven't told us. And any information about the army's political relationship with the Kabul regime. Anything else unusual."

"There's a limit to what I can write down," Mikhailov said.

The American reached inside his robes, fumbled, and brought out a Minox camera and three rolls of film. He handed them to Mikhailov. "Use these for important documents. Do you have a safe place to keep them?"

"Yes." There was a loose floorboard in his room at the billet. There was no point in hiding the camera anywhere less accessible; if it were stumbled across they would simply watch for whoever came to get it.

"There's one more thing. Maybe the most important."

"Yes?" Mikhailov was taken aback.

"The political situation in Moscow has changed since your uncle took power. We want you to arrange a posting home as soon as you can."

"Oh." It made sense. "I'll do what I can."

"It's very important for you to succeed. Use your uncle's influence if you have to. Moscow is more important to us than Herat."

"All right." The memory of Valeria tugged at him.

"Anything else?"

"No," Mikahilov said.

"They'll take you back," said the American.

When the Russian had gone, Mir stepped into the circle of light. Gray drew the striped cloth away from his face. "Well?" he asked the mujahidin leader. "Is he worth it?"

"I am not sure," Mir said. "To be anywhere near a Russian is to invite treachery. See how he betrays his own people."

"To him," said Gray, "he is not betraying his people. He is trying to stop his people from doing wicked things."

"He may be betraying us all," Mir said. "I don't like it. All Russians are treacherous. I think he should be killed. It is much safer."

"If he's killed," Gray pointed out, "Washington will be very unhappy. Perhaps they would be unhappy enough to stop the arms shipment they promised us. But I myself promise, if we find the Russian is betraying us, that you shall kill him yourself."

Mir considered this, and the possibility of losing the guns and grenades and antitank missiles the Americans were to supply. "All right," he said grudgingly. "We'll let him live."

Gray exhaled a minute sigh of relief. He had not been certain that Mir's hatred of the Russians would be balanced by clear thinking.

"His information," said Mir. "What was it?"

Gray carefully did not frown. Langley was worried about letting the Afghans know too much, but they had to be given something to repay them for the support they were giving Gray. There were the weapons, of course, those that Gray had brought and others to be delivered, but these alone would not be enough. To complicate matters, there was the communications problem. Mir had an effective courier organization to keep in touch with ANLF headquarters in Peshawar, Pakistan, but Peshawar was several days away by courier. Worse, if a messenger and his dispatches were captured, it would not be long before the KGB realized that someone was leaking high-level information.

For his own communications Gray had brought a small but powerful transmitter capable of compressing a long coded message into a split-second radio pulse. At regular intervals an ELINT satellite passed over Herat, and Gray could pass information back to the United States over this link. He could not receive any via the satellite, however, since this would require a dish antenna several meters across. For instructions he had to rely on coded messages from the US-South African electronic-intelligence installation at Silvermine, in South Africa. Unfortunately, the mountains around Herat tended to block or reflect Silvermine's transmissions, depending on atmospheric conditions. Then, of course, there was the tedious business of decoding.

And using the radio was dangerous. The Russians constantly snooped around the radio spectrum for illegal signals, and the transmitter's batteries periodically needed recharging, which made it necessary to keep the device near a power source. It was always possible that by some fluke the Soviet electronic-intelligence monitors would pick out suspicious signals originating in Herat, and the hunt would be on. He probably would not know anything about it until the KGB kicked the door in.

Gray longed for the ease of the diplomatic bag, and the simplicity of not having to share information.

He realized that Mir was waiting for an answer. "I haven't

read everything he wrote yet. When I have, we'll share the information. Some of it will be of interest only to Washington."

"I trust you as an elder brother," Mir said, meaning he wanted to. Gray put a hand on his friend's arm and said, "Mir, understand me. Some of what he will tell us we cannot send to Peshawar. If one of your couriers is caught, there must be nothing in his pouch that will point to the Russian. Otherwise we lose all. Not even everything he tells us can be put on the radio, for the same reason. Those things will have to wait until I return home. This man is too valuable to endanger needlessly. Or even just for a small need."

The mujahidin leader nodded pensively. "I understand. I will send to Peshawar only what you prepare, as we agreed. But it may mean we lose men we might have saved."

"It may," Gray said. "But not doing so will lose us many more than that."

Mir stood up. "It's time to go," he said. The lamplight threw the lines of his face into cruel relief. He's tired, Gray thought, we're all tired. It's dangerous here, too dangerous, no matter what Mikhailov has to offer us, the communications are too vulnerable.

Get him back to Moscow, Langley had ordered, twist his arm if you have to, but get him back. Never mind about the mujahidin, they can't offer us what he can. There's been no one like him since Penkovsky. He has to go back to Moscow.

Moscow
Thursday, May 20

*I*T WAS DRIZZLING AND WINDY. Mikhailov's sister, Nadia, tramped wearily along the path between the apartment towers toward the kindergarten building. Her wrist ached from the weight of the plastic bag in which she carried a quarter of a ham. She had bought the ham in the Beriozka store near the GLAVLIT building, using some of the certificate rubles her brother had left her before he went back to Afghanistan. Certificate rubles were not like ordinary rubles; you got them as part of your pay if your work put you on the *nomenklatura*, the list of privileged positions that stretched from top to bottom of the Party hierarchy. Nadia's work as a department supervisor in GLAVLIT, the state censorship bureau, was on the *nomenklatura*, but she did not receive as many certificate rubles as Andrei. Her brother seemed to get plenty, more, in fact, than she would have thought a colonel warranted. It probably had something to do with his work in Afghanistan, although he never talked about what he did there. But the certificate rubles made life much easier; they meant, for one thing, that you didn't have to scour Moscow every time you needed this or that, or have to spend three hours a day standing in line for shoddy goods that ran out just as you reached the counter. There was always enough of everything, and good stuff, in the Beriozka stores. She didn't know how she would feed Valeria properly if it weren't for the certificate rubles; her pay was adequate but what good was that if there was nothing to buy, as was usually the case in Moscow these days? By all accounts it was worse in the country and in the cities westerners weren't allowed to visit.

She hitched the bag up a little and pulled her scarf more closely around her face. The rain was light but wind-driven and had chilled her; she was afraid she was catching a cold. At the door of Valeria's classroom the teacher, a harried woman of about thirty who looked ten years older, said, "She's in the infirmary. She's not feeling well."

Nadia felt her stomach plummet. She lived in dread of something happening to Valeria while Mikhailov was away; the child's bout with pneumonia had driven her nearly frantic. "What's the matter?"

"I think it's chicken pox. She shouldn't come back until all the spots are scabbed over. Seven to ten days."

"What about her schoolwork? Should she take some home?"

"If you like," said the teacher. "But she won't feel like doing any. She's bright, she'll soon catch up."

"Thank you." Nadia hurried away to the infirmary, which was a small, overheated room in the rear of the building. There were two cots in the room, on one of which was Valeria. She was curled up under a blanket, pale and half asleep.

"Valeria, kitten. Time to go home."

She sat up. "I got chicken pox."

"I know. You have to stay home for a few days." Nadia started putting on the child's raincoat.

"Can daddy come home because I'm sick?" She looked overtired and woebegone.

"I'm sorry, kitten, he can't."

This precipitated tears. Valeria was still sniffling when they reached the apartment. Nadia put her under a blanket on the living-room couch and found a children's program for her on the television. Then she went into the kitchen to prepare supper.

As usual in the evenings she was tired, and, unusually, worried. There was a great deal of tension in the GLAVLIT offices, and had been since the rumors started. There was to be a relaxation of censorship, it was being whispered in the cafeteria. Some of the women in the typing pool Nadia supervised said that Postnikov, head of the censorship bureau, was about to lose his job because he had been resisting the new Party directives on what should be allowed into print. Nadia's own boss had been acting oddly for two weeks. Because of her uncle's position he had always been careful not to work her too hard, but since Uncle Vasily had become general secretary he was positively fawning. Her path had always been smoothed for her because she was Romanenko's niece, but not to the present extreme. People either avoided her or were unusually polite, and some, like her supervisor, were ingratiating. Most of the time this amused her; some of them were so obvious about it, hinting at the *nomenklatura* positions they'd like, as though she could call her uncle and have them bumped up the ladder two or three rungs.

Lately, though, the situation had been getting on her nerves. She liked the thought of being able to read some of the books on the forbidden list, if censorship really were relaxed, but there was more to the situation than that. To begin with, there was more *samizdat* literature floating around now, some of it really trashy and expecting its readers to think it was art simply because it was in *samizdat*, but a good deal of it was outright subversive by the standards that had prevailed under Chernenko and his predecessor, Andropov. As well, she'd heard that some of the manuscripts being considered for publication would have earned their writers a chat with the KGB five months ago.

And finally, the mood of the city was one of suppressed excitement. People seemed to be waiting for something to happen, either for a signal that they could breathe and live more freely, or that they should draw back again into the old Russian shell of silence, hypocrisy, and dissimulation.

I wish Andrei were here, she thought suddenly, the carving knife poised to slice the ham. Something either very wonderful or very dreadful is going to happen. I'd feel much safer if he were here. And Valeria's sick again, the poor child, and I'm going to be away from work for a week at least, they'll all think I'm taking advantage. I've hardly ever asked Uncle Vasily for anything. But Andrei's been in Afghanistan, except for leave, for nearly two years. I *would* be taking advantage. Andrei would hate it.

"I don't care," she said softly to an unseen, critical audience. "He's been away too long. Uncle Vasily has to bring him home."

Herat, Afghanistan
Friday, May 21

*T*HE MINOX CAMERA was at the bottom of Mikhailov's document case, which was made of soft leather and was quite capacious. Nevertheless, Mikhailov felt as though the camera bulged into a prominent and betraying lump, proclaiming him traitor.

He returned the guards' salutes and went through the front door of the HQ building. The lights in the dingy main hall were working poorly, the power voltage down again. HQ was on its own generator but this had been malfunctioning for two days and the technicians couldn't seem to repair it.

He went upstairs and unlocked his office door. Rosseikin never worked in the evenings if he could help it, which suited Mikhailov nicely. He closed the door, leaving himself in near darkness, with the office's only illumination the dim glow from the streetlights out in the square. After closing the curtains he turned on the desk light, made sure the connecting door to Rosseikin's office was locked, and sat down at the desk.

First, the digest. He brought it up to date, noting that the artillery component of the division had been reinforced with another battery of 105 mm self-propelled guns, and that a fresh draft of troops had been received to replace those lost in the mutiny. The sheaf of papers he would leave in the dead drop was getting quite thick.

Last of all he transcribed the contents of a buff-jacketed folder. It was important, however, that the Americans have an exact copy of the document it contained, so with some reluctance he had decided to use the camera. He arranged the desk lamp carefully, hoping there was enough light; one of the reasons he had gone to the trouble of writing out the folder's contents was that he didn't trust his camera technique, although the instrument was supposed to be fully automatic.

He opened the folder to the first page. At its top was the title STARLIGHT and the stamp SECRET — GAMMA. Under the title was the legend "Herat Region." The document had been distributed only to colonels and higher rank. Mikhailov had received one, although he was not in the chain of operational command in Herat; he needed it because he and his staff were to give intensive refresher courses in counterinsurgency warfare for the division's senior officers. He had received from Gordik the day previously an envelope containing a thick paperbound book entitled simply "Operations Manual F-2100-A," which was a distillation of all the Soviet army had learned about fighting the mujahidin. Mikhailov had contributed a significant percentage of it. He was to make sure Bachinsky's officers understood what was in it, because starting on 8 June they were to clear out the mujahidin in the Herat region once and for all. STARLIGHT was the code name of the operation, and it was the operational plan that Mikhailov was now beginning to photograph.

Title page. *Click*. Second page, objectives of the operation: destroy ANLF offensive ability in the region, wipe out all supporting infrastructures in the villages, farms, and countryside, establish permanent blocking positions on known supply routes, and forcibly relocate the populations of mujahidin-sympathetic villages to less mountainous parts of the country where they could be more easily controlled. This last amounted to the systematic depopulation of much of the rougher part of the countryside.

Click.

Third page. Operational strategy: several thrusts up the river valleys and along the main roads, fanning out into the more remote villages as they went.

Click.

Fourth to seventh pages: tactics to be based on combined-arms teams consisting of helicopter-borne troops, helicopter gunships, ground-attack aircraft, and motorized infantry supported by artillery. Known and potential ambush positions were to be denied the enemy by the use of persistent chemical weapons; when appropriate, concentrations of the enemy were to be attacked with gas to drive them into the open where they would be vulnerable to air and artillery attack.

Click.

Click.

Click.

Click.

To be on the safe side, Mikhailov photographed the document again before locking it up. Then he removed the film from the camera, tucked it into an envelope with the other materials he had prepared, and put everything back into the document case. He stuffed three or four innocuous files in on top, just to be on the safe side.

Footsteps thumped in the corridor. Mikhailov put the document case on the floor beside his chair, moved the lamp to its normal position, and spread some papers about the desk. He watched the doorknob. It turned slowly, then rattled. The footsteps then moved off along the corridor and he heard Rosseikin's doorknob being tested.

The ten o'clock security check, of course. He hadn't been keeping track of the time.

He tidied his desk, waiting for the security officer to finish his round and come back down the corridor. When the footsteps finally receded in the direction of the stairs he turned out the light and left the office. Downstairs he ran into Alferyev, who clearly had been drinking.

"Working late, Colonel Mikhailov?"

To Mikhailov it sounded like an accusation. "There's a lot to do," he said noncommittally.

"A lot to get ready for," Alferyev said. "This time we'll wrap the black-asses up for good, eh?"

"For good, this time."

"I hear you're trying to get a posting back home." Alferyev's sibilants were mushy.

"That's right." Mikhailov had requested a transfer back to Moscow two days after the meeting with the American. He had done this only partly because of the American's request; he was heartily sick of Afghanistan and thought he had done enough to satisfy his professional conscience. And he ached for his daughter.

"Any luck yet?"

"No answer so far."

Alferyev hiccuped. Mikhailov was hoping desperately that the man wouldn't decide to walk back to the billet with him. "Don't worry," the chief of staff said. "With your connections you won't have any trouble. I wish mine were as good. Want to celebrate? There's a real party getting started."

From the direction of the officers' mess up the corridor there was a mounting din of clinking bottles, glasses, and raucous laughter. For a moment Mikhailov badly wanted a few hours of drunken fellowship. "Not tonight, sorry. I've got a lot of work to get through tomorrow."

Alferyev weaved slightly. "Whatever you like. Afterwards, then, if any of us live through the next two weeks. All glory to the Red Army."

"Right," said Mikhailov.

He left the headquarters building and turned right along the street that led to Bizhad Park and his billet. As he went he considered the implications of STARLIGHT. Although it was not specifically stated anywhere in the documents to which he had access, he had the impression that STARLIGHT was part of a general strategy Kabul had developed to break the mujahidin for good. Some aspect of the plan — details glossed over, a general impression of haste — made him think that the operation had been put together quickly, as though GHQ Moscow were anxious for a convincing victory before something, or someone, intervened.

The Americans couldn't possibly interfere, and the Chinese had their own problems, so it had to be one of the power centers in the Kremlin that was taking a hard look at the Afghan situation. Somebody, Mikhailov thought, wants us out of here, and the General Staff wants to show they can really do what they've been promising so long, defeat the guerrillas. That's why they're going to pull out all the stops and use gas.

Soviet forces had in fact used war gases in isolated areas of the country, partly for the military effect and partly for experimentation. The substances had normally, though not always, been strengthened variants of riot gas, and not fatal except in very high concentrations. For STARLIGHT no such restrictions had been made: both GD semipermanent nerve gas and mustard gas were to be used, delivered either by artillery shells or by helicopters or aircraft, depending on the tactical situation. The mujahidin, who had absolutely no antigas equipment, would take frightful losses. Even if the field forces of the ANLF and its sister organizations were not completely destroyed, it would take years for them to regain their strength. This would be made even more difficult by the relocation of their sympathizers into military-controlled enclaves in the lowlands.

There would be a great many people killed, horribly, and often slowly. The gases were cruel.

I wonder if I'll get that posting before the beginning of STARLIGHT, Mikhailov thought. I hope so. The Americans want me back in Moscow, so do Nadia and Valeria, so do I. The Americans are right, I can be of more use in Moscow. I hope they have sense enough to use the STARLIGHT information to get everybody out of the way, let the sweeps hit nothing but air and empty villages. Our intelligence will know that the mujahidin found out somehow, but enough people know about STARLIGHT for the information to come from dozens of places. Maybe even from someone in the Afghan government; we'd have to let a few of them know about it, for political reasons.

He had reached the edge of the park. This particular drop, one of several, was just inside a grove of pines surrounding the ruined shrine of some long-forgotten Moslem saint. Moving one of the stone blocks would reveal a cavity where an envelope would be safe until the drop was serviced, which would likely be only a matter of minutes. Mikhailov had sensed more than once that he was being watched, but not by Russians.

This is another reason to go home soon, Mikhailov thought. Sooner or later someone's going to wonder why I take long walks in the evenings, spend so much time working late. Alferyev, maybe. The city's too small and we're too conspicuous for this to be safe indefinitely. Time to go home.

He was among the pines. The ruined shrine was a pale, jumbled blur in the darkness. He knelt to remove the stone block concealing the cavity.

A pebble rattled behind him.

Mikhailov threw himself sideways. Something snagged his tunic and then broke free. The document case went spinning. Off balance, Mikhailov fell heavily across the stones. His attacker, having missed with his first knife stroke, threw himself at Mikhailov, blade raised, its metal glinting momentarily in the distant glow of the streetlights. Mikhailov had time to think: this man doesn't know how to fight with a knife. He rolled sideways and kicked at his attacker's knee.

He connected only glancingly, but well enough to throw the strike off aim and bring his attacker down beside him. Mikhailov grabbed for the knife arm but missed in the dark. He rolled off the mound of stone blocks and landed heavily, partly winded. Before he could move again his attacker had straddled him, knife raised. Mikhailov managed to grab the wrist as the blade descended; the wrist was thin as a stick but the arm behind it was very strong. Mikhailov instinctively turned his face away from the blade's point.

There was a thud, a whooshing sound, and the weight left his chest. Mikhailov struggled to his feet as quickly as he could, fumbling for his Makarov.

The man who had kicked his attacker off him was standing two meters away, waving his hands warningly. The hands were empty. The attacker, stretched out on the ground, was breathing in deep gasps, trying to get his breath back.

"Russian," hissed his rescuer, "this is one of the boys from the city. He didn't know about you. Give me what you've got, and go." He stretched out his hand.

Slowly, because he had scraped one knee, a shin, and an elbow, Mikhailov searched about for the document case, found it, and extracted the envelope. The guerrilla was making hurry-up motions. Mikhailov handed him the envelope.

"Go now," whispered the man. "Quickly." Mikhailov did.

The Old Town, Herat
Sunday, May 23

IN RUSSIA a samovar is an urn for making tea; in Afghanistan the word has been imported and refers, in the vernacular, to a teahouse, replacing the older designation, "*chai khana*." The teahouse in which Mir had established Gray belonged to a man who was part of the ANLF cell organization in Herat; his name was Daud Kasim and he provided food, refuge, and information to ANLF guerrillas when they ventured into the city. Kasim treated Gray well, within the limits of Afghan poverty. He had given the American a small, bare room at the rear of the teahouse — well away from the quarters of his wife and two daughters — and furnished it with a sleeping mat, a brazier, and a couple of threadbare rugs. Gray's radio was hidden under the hearth of a disused bread oven in the kitchen. Kasim had been impressed, and a little frightened, by the radio, for it would earn him his death if it were found. But Mir had told the man it was to help rid the country of the *Rus*, and that had been enough. Kasim, because of Gray's familiarity with Afghan customs and the country's version of Islam, had also gained the impression that Gray was intending to convert to Islam when the Russians were driven out, and he occasionally engaged Gray in long theological conversations. Gray had done nothing to disabuse the teahouse-keeper of the notion.

Just now Gray was sitting on a figured orange-and-brown rug in the teahouse courtyard. In the center of the courtyard stood two ancient and enormous samovars, which steamed gently in the gathering dusk. Next to the samovars was a low table covered with a striped cloth, on which rested a dozen small blue teapots and a galvanized water pail. A boy of about twelve, Kasim's servant, was adjusting the flame under one of the samovars. Three other Heratis sat against the courtyard wall nearby; one of them was smoking a water pipe. They watched the boy gravely, not speaking. Kasim had given out that Gray was from Badakhshan province in the northeast, which accounted for his accent, and that he had left because of some unspecified trouble with a government official. It was a common enough story, and Gray had discouraged attempts at conversation by the teahouse's patrons. No one paid much attention now to the taciturn man from the northeast.

Gray was worrying. He had received the contents of the Bizhad Park drop the previous morning, and had read Mikhailov's synopsis of STARLIGHT with mounting concern. The Russians meant business this time; it was the biggest counterinsurgency operation in at least three years, perhaps the biggest since the invasion itself. He had spent most of the day encoding the information and preparing it for transmission; after it got dark he and Kasim had taken the radio to the roof and squirted the signal into the sky where, invisible and far above, the satellite was passing. The essentials of the plans of STARLIGHT were now, Gray hoped, being evaluated in Washington. The roll of film on which Mikhailov had photographed the document would be on its way to the CIA station in Peshawar by courier as soon as Gray could get it to Mir. He had sent a message off to the Afghan leader, who was up in the mountains, that he had to see him, and quickly.

Now Gray was wondering how much to tell the mujahidin leader. In a postscript to his digest Mikhailov had recommended that the mujahidin simply go to ground during STARLIGHT, withdrawing into Iran or well into the mountains, but Gray knew that possession of the STARLIGHT plans presented the guerrillas with a unique opportunity. They could launch preemptive attacks before the operation actually began, or use their knowledge to surprise and savage the Russian forces.

However, Mikhailov's safety had to be guarded. A Russian thrust that missed its target might be written off to bad luck and coincidence, but a counterattack that showed the guerrillas to be ready and waiting could not be dismissed so easily. A lot of probing questions would be asked. Gray had put this dilemma in his transmission to Washington. He hoped they would instruct him to tell Mir just enough to persuade him to get his forces out of the way, but not enough to let him plan a counterattack. He would know an hour after midnight, when the next transmission from Silvermine was due.

Mir came down from the mountains near midnight. He and Gray drank tea in Gray's room, and Mir ate bread and pickled vegetables while they waited for Silvermine to come on the air. When Mir had finished eating he burped gently and asked, "What is so urgent?"

"The Russians are planning a big operation against you. In June."

"How big?" Mir started on his third cup of tea.

"Very big. I am awaiting an evaluation from Washington. It will help you decide what to do." Gray was uncomfortable at the prevarication; emotionally he wanted to see a major Soviet defeat, but he was sure that Langley would prefer not to risk Mikhailov. In the short run, though, there would be less bloodshed.

On the other side of the world, at CIA headquarters in Langley, Virginia, Jared Blake, who had set up Gray's insertion into Afghanistan, was staring aghast at the deputy director for special operations. "They can't be serious," he said.

"They are," said the deputy director. "The President and the Secretary of State made it a direct order. They want the Russians to get a bloody nose. The transmission's already gone to Silvermine."

"They're risking the best high-level source we've had in years."

"I told them that. They want to keep the pressure on Romanenko. The State Department says that what with all the other problems he has, a defeat in Afghanistan may be just too much, and he'll decide to pull out. This situation's just what the doctor ordered. According to State."

"Jesus," Blake said. "And I persuaded Gray to go. They catch the Russian, they'll get him too. Almost certainly."

"There's a good chance they won't get on to the Russian," the deputy director said. "He's Romanenko's nephew, after all. And we'll try to plant evidence of some leaks in Kabul, make them look in the wrong place."

"Has he tried to get that posting?" Blake asked.

"He's tried. They haven't answered yet."

"It's going to be bloody, isn't it?"

"Yes," said the deputy director. "But it's out of our hands now. It all depends on what the mujahidin decide to do."

The transmission was coming in. Gray, wearing the lightweight earphones, was hunched over the radio, scribbling down the code groups. The message wasn't long. When Silvermine signed off he got to work with the one-time pad, decoding. Mir sat motionless on the sleeping mat on the other side of the room.

When Gray finished decoding he did it over again, not believing what he'd written down. It came out the same. The last sentence read:

PROVIDE ALL INFORMATION RE TAKEOVER BID TO CLIENT, SOONEST.

"Richard-jan?" said Mir.

Gray put down the pencil and turned to his friend. His mind was full of visions of poison and death.

"It's called STARLIGHT," he said. "This is what they're going to do."

Chesht-i-Sharif — Herat
June 8 — 9

OPERATION STARLIGHT's first phase was a thrust up the Herat-Quala Nau road by one regiment of General Bachinsky's division, another drive by a second regiment along the road to Shahrak, and a third, by the remaining motorized regiment, along the road that started south of Herat at the town of Shindand. Supported by helicopter and aircraft attacks using gas and high explosive, the infantry would then sweep up into the foothills to trap and destroy the mujahidin in the enclaves they had established over the winter. This phase would require ten days. When it was completed, a second offensive would be mounted south of Shindand, to clear the guerrillas out of the mountains that bordered the road to Kandahar to the southeast. Subsidiary operations would be carried out in the flatter lands west of Herat by the division's tank regiment and its attached battalion of motorized infantry.

It's a good plan, Mikhailov thought, and then, with satisfaction: but it hasn't turned up many guerrillas. He was jolting from side to side in the BRDM reconnaissance vehicle that was carrying him up the road toward Chesht-i-Sharif, the third main objective in the Herat-Shahrak thrust. By now the mujahidin would be well off into the mountains to the east, in the near-inaccessible gorges and peaks of the Siah Koh and the Band-i-Baian ranges. Even the helicopters had difficulty maneuvering up there; the valleys were no more than deep knife slashes in the ragged landscape. It was the third day of the operation, and they were well ahead of schedule, although this was not to Bachinsky's liking. His communications from battle HQ, which was back at the village of Obeh, were becoming more and more irritable as he waited for the contact with the guerrillas, which still had not come. There had been only two very minor skirmishes, both near Obeh, with a few guerrillas who probably hadn't got the order to withdraw or were simply bloody-minded. Mikhailov was relieved; it looked as though the Afghans had decided to take his advice and disappear into the landscape.

The advance guard had secured Chesht-i-Sharif by the time they reached the village, which was a small place beside the Hari Rud River. There was barely enough room on the flatlands around the village for the regiment to bivouac. Overhead, as the sun went down, helicopters ferried soldiers to the tops of the ridges near the river valley where the men would dig in as perimeter guards. One battalion of the regiment had remained at Obeh; the second would stay at Chesht-i-Sharif the next day while the third went on to Shahrak preparatory to the sweep into the mountains.

Mikhailov sat on the ground next to the BRDM and ate the dry combat rations. He had had some argument with Bachinsky to get permission to come on the operation, but had prevailed after contacting General Gordik in Kabul and getting *his* permission. Bachinsky thought he simply wanted to check up on the effectiveness of the troops, which was true; but Mikhailov also wanted to find out for himself whether the Americans had persuaded the Afghans not to fight, and what the reaction of the officers would be to that. He thought the Americans would find the information useful. There had been no communication from the CIA since he had made the drop of the STARLIGHT documents.

He spent a few minutes with the regiment's commanding colonel, who was as surprised as Bachinsky at the lack of resistance but not as irritated. This could have been reported as a "negative attitude" but Mikhailov had been among front-line soldiers more than long enough to recognize the natural relief of a man who expects to be shot at and isn't. He and the colonel drank a little vodka and then Mikhailov went off to sleep on the ground beside his vehicle. The village had been occupied by security troops but nobody wanted to bed down in it because of the risk of lice or a knife between the ribs.

He awoke to the sound of roaring engines. His driver was shaking him. "What the devil's going on?" Mikhailov said irritably, sitting up. It was still pitch dark and the cat's-eye slits of the vehicles' combat driving lights gleamed all around.

"Sir, the colonel wants you at the command post," the driver said.

Mikhailov was stiff and chilled. He made his way to the colonel's BRDM, which was parked down near the river. A hooded light was glowing over a small map table set up beside the vehicle.

"Colonel Mikhailov. Good." The regimental colonel was unshaven and had bags under his eyes. "We have to go back to Herat immediately."

This shocked Mikhailov completely awake. "What for?"

"A large force of bandits has attacked HQ and the firebase. There's been street fighting and the Old Town's full of armed insurgents. They've also overrun the airfield and blown up a lot of planes and helicopters."

"What's the Afghan militia doing?"

"Gone over the wall; in fact, they helped the bandits get into the firebase. The firebase is holding, they pushed the bandits out, but it's under pressure. General Bachinsky's started back from Obeh with the battalion there. He's stopped the tank operations west of Herat. We're going to try to catch the bandits between us and the tanks."

"What about the other two regiments?"

"They're detaching a battalion each to flank Herat on the north and south." The colonel paused, and then said furiously, "It's as though they were waiting for us to leave. How did they get so many men down into the plain?"

The question, Mikhailov knew, would be repeated many times in the weeks to come. He hoped no one would ask it of him and expect an answer.

From Chesht-i-Sharif to Herat was one hundred and fifty

kilometers by road, and the road was poor. The head of the two-battalion column left the bivouac at high speed at one-thirty in the morning and by half-past three had nearly reached Obeh. Bachinsky's headquarters and the other battalion had already left the place, and had reported by radio that they had reached Pashtun Zarghun, fifty kilometers from Herat. Neither force had time for the precautions taken on the way out, when they had been sweeping the terrain on both sides of the axis of advance, so it was not a great surprise to Mikhailov when they were ambushed five kilometers short of Obeh.

His BRDM was near the tail of the advance-guard column, just behind one of the SAU-122 self-propelled guns that provided fire support for the combat reconnaissance patrol if and when it ran into trouble. The moon had gone down and the only lights Mikhailov could see from his position in his vehicle's hatch were the stars and the dim blue light on the rear of the SP gun ahead.

Because the Russian column was bereft of its air support at night, and because the terrain was too rough to both move quickly and put out flank patrols, the mujahidin force on the rocky slopes above the road had the immediate advantage. A streak of light arced high into the air about five hundred meters ahead of Mikhailov and exploded into the hard white radiance of a parachute flare. The squat bulk of the SP gun in front was abruptly thrown into stark relief. Mikhailov saw the gun's commander, who was riding in the turret hatch, look upward in surprise.

Another streak of light, then a third. This time they were not parachute flares. The second streak hurtled at blinding speed toward the SP gun and struck it where the low turret joined the vehicle's hull. There was a tremendous bang accompanied by a great bloom of flame and the turret flew into the air, turning over and over like a thrown frying pan, and then crashed to the ground ten meters from the road. The third streak, which, like the second, was the exhaust of an antitank missile, struck the road beside the wreck. Metal fragments rang on the hull of Mikhailov's BRDM and whistled around his ears. He ducked out of the hatchway, down into the vehicle's passenger compartment. The radio, which had been silent before, was suddenly spouting a cacophony of messages, orders and counter-orders.

The road at this point was too wide for the wrecked SP gun to block it completely. Mikhailov's driver wheeled the BRDM around the burning hulk and speeded up; it was essential to keep moving until the road opened up and some, at least, of the battalion's forces could deploy. The regimental colonel's voice was now cutting through the hubbub on the radio, trying to bring some order to the chaos. Mikhailov risked a look out the hatch. Behind, at least two other fighting vehicles had been hit. Tracer and small-arms fire was flying both ways between the column and the fissured slope above it. Three more flares hung in the night sky, obliterating the stars, but it was impossible to see where the mujahidin fire was coming from. The noise was appalling, with explosions, the roar of overrevving engines, and gunfire almost covering the screams of men trapped in burning vehicles. Somewhere farther back a heavy weapon opened up, either a tank or another self-propelled gun, and shell bursts flickered on the mountainside. In the light of the flares, the shelling, and the tracer, Mikhailov could see men running from their armored personnel carriers toward the slopes bordering the road; either someone had ordered a counterattack or they were abandoning damaged vehicles.

The narrow valley in which the road lay was widening. They should have caught us farther back, Mikhailov thought, as the hatch rim of the lurching BRDM beat at his shoulders. We'll be able to maneuver half a kilometer on, and they didn't manage to block the road. Something went wrong for them, they didn't get into position in time, or we moved faster than they thought we would.

The Americans must have told the guerrillas to attack anyway. The shitheads. Staying out of the way would have been good enough, why did they have to do this? What's going on in Herat? This is disaster for both sides; Bachinsky will root every guerrilla out of the city if he has to level it. He might level it anyway, if Kabul or Moscow doesn't stop him.

The firing was dying down; no more guided missiles like

the one that had destroyed the SP gun shot out of the darkness. Either, Mikhailov thought, they used them all up or they're saving them for later.

The BRDM lurched in a pothole and he struck his jaw on the hatch rim, biting his tongue painfully. There was only one flare now, and it was guttering, but the night was still lit by flames. Somewhere behind him shells were popping off in a fire, hurling incandescent showers high into the air. The tanks would have to shove the mess off the road when the ammunition stopped going off, but Mikhailov could see that the column was still moving. It would have to stop at Obeh to reorganize, though, and give first aid to the wounded, for they could not possibly be left behind for the mujahidin. A year ago, up in the mountains near Faizabad, Mikhailov had come upon the pink-and-black remains of a Russian soldier lying at the bole of a dehydrated thorn tree. The man's skin was hanging from the tree above him.

If the mujahidin had wanted to delay the column, they were only partially successful. The colonel commanding the regiment had been in Afghanistan for three years, and was more competent than the average. By four-thirty he had his force back into order and onto the road again. It was growing light by now and because of this and the fact that the road was now more open, the danger of ambush was much diminished. There was still no air cover, though; the helicopters and fighter-bombers that had escaped the mujahidin attack on the airfield were committed to the fighting in and around Herat.

The column reached the city two and a half hours after leaving Obeh. Part of the firebase was burning, and other clouds billowed from the city itself, both the old and the new towns. The colonel's command vehicle stopped beside the road while the SP guns, armored troop carriers, and tanks shook themselves out into battle order across the parched and dusty fields. Sukhoi ground-attack aircraft and helicopters howled and clattered overhead. They seemed to be making attacks both on the city itself and on the countryside to the west. Mikhailov got out of his BRDM and walked stiffly to the colonel's vehicle, where he and his regimental staff were having a rapid consultation. Mikhailov waited until the unit commanders had received their orders and then asked, "Can I help?" He was very tired and beginning to realize that the carnage in the city and up in the mountains was at least partially his fault.

"I don't see how, at the moment," said the colonel. He was gray with fatigue. "It's all dirty work from here on in." Mikhailov winced inwardly at the implied insult; he knew the colonel was thinking, here's a man who's supposedly an expert on counter-guerrilla operations and he gets ambushed just like the rest of us.

"What's the situation?" Mikhailov asked.

"General Bachinsky's driven the bandits off the firebase into the city. A lot of them broke off just before dawn, and seem to be heading west. The planes are after them. But there are still a lot of them in the Old Town. They'll try to hold out until dark, and then get away to the west and northeast."

The mujahidin miscalculated, Mikhailov thought. They likely intended to break off the action before first light, and have everyone well away from the city by dawn. Now there would be house-to-house fighting. He wondered how many guerrillas were still in the city. "What's happened to the tanks that were supposed to block them? General Bachinsky's idea was to catch them between us and the tanks, I thought."

"The tanks were hit by missile fire as soon as they turned around, about three o'clock. Same as we were, except there were a lot more missiles. The infantry had to stop and dig the bandits out of their holes. It took about two hours. They'll be here any minute, but they're not going to find much. They were too far north." The colonel began to climb back into his BRDM.

"How many mujahidin were there?" Mikhailov asked.

"Three to four thousand. A lot of them got away to the west just before dawn. The others are still in the city or the outlying villages." The colonel disappeared into his command vehicle.

Mikhailov made his way back to his own transport. The size of the raid had shocked him, and he was certain it would shock GHQ Kabul. As far as he knew, no one had suspected there were still so many mujahidin at large in the Herat region. Some would have come over the border from their enclaves in Iran, but even so.... And they appeared to have been well-supplied with antitank missiles. STARLIGHT, which was supposed to eliminate the insurgent threat once and for all, was quickly turning into disaster. No matter how many of the guerrillas were caught or killed, it smelled like defeat.

Half an hour later the two battalions had moved up to the edge of the city on the northeast. The colonel went into the firebase with the advance guard, Mikhailov tagging along behind him in his BRDM since he didn't know what else to do. There were several fires inside the base, which were sending great clouds of oily black smoke high into the early-morning light. The razor wire outside the base's perimeter defense was cut through in several places, and the fence behind the gaps was holed. Several bodies hung on the wire, none of them Russian. The headquarters building was only slightly damaged; there had been a fire there but the garrison had managed to put it out. Mikhailov and the colonel found Bachinsky and several other officers in the operations room, leaning over a large ordnance map of Herat. Alferyev, the chief of staff, stood next to him as Bachinsky moved a blunt finger around on the street plan, organizing the counterattack. There was a smudge of ash on Alferyev's forehead and his left hand was bandaged. Both he and Bachinsky were hollow-eyed and unshaven.

"It's about time you got here," Bachinsky said to the colonel. "What did you lose in the ambush?"

The colonel told him. When he had finished, Bachinsky said, "It could have been worse. You know what's happened here?"

The colonel shook his head. "A lot of casualties?"

"Yes." Bachinsky began to grow red, rage building. "They got the *armory*," he shouted. "Half our fucking reserve-weapons stocks went through the wire. *And* ammunition. Then they started shooting at us with our own bastard guns." He stopped, breathing heavily. "I want every bandit cleared out of the Old Town by dark, or the lot of you are going to be pushing shovels in a punishment battalion. Mikhailov. You've got nothing else to do, take a squad from the guardroom and go see what shape the governor's compound is in. There was an attack near it last night but nobody's had time to go inside. Get going."

Mikhailov left hurriedly, collected the men from the guard-room — they had been resting from the night's fighting and were sullen at being disturbed — and started through the firebase streets for the governor's compound. Two of the barracks blocks were on fire and a mob of soldiers with two small pumps and a water tanker were trying to extinguish the flames. They weren't making much progress; there wouldn't be enough water from the wells the Russians had drilled to put out everything, any-way. Most of the fires would have to burn themselves out. The air reeked of explosives. It made Mikhailov's eyes water.

The governor's compound consisted of a house attached to a high-walled courtyard at the edge of the base. The house and courtyard had been there before the Russians came, and the firebase had incorporated it, originally as a headquarters build-ing. The Afghan military governor had moved into it after it had become plain that he wasn't safe in the governor's mansion in town, and he and his family had lived there ever since. The house itself was two stories high, mud-brown with narrow windows and a heavy wooden door, bound with iron, in the center of the lower story. The perimeter fence was about a hundred meters beyond it, and between the house and the fence lay a scattering of bunkers and foxholes. Mikhailov could see Russian troops around the bunkers and sitting on the rims of the holes, smoking. A squad was repairing a large break in the fence and on the other side of it more men were laying down a roll of razor wire to fill the gap the mujahidin had blown with cutting charges. There were no soldiers around the governor's compound, and the house appeared untouched except for a few bullet pocks, which might have been there for decades.

Mikhailov banged on the heavy door. It swung inward, neither locked nor latched. He stepped inside, took one look around, then staggered back out and vomited in the dust. The squad watched him in consternation, fingering their rifles nervously.

"Sir?" asked the corporal.

Mikhailov spat saliva. There hadn't been much in his stomach and acid burned in his throat. He straightened up, and said, "Come with me. We have to see if there's anyone left."

The door opened into a large room that had other doors leading off it. The furniture was undamaged but had been disarranged and there was smashed pottery on the floor, lamps perhaps. Blood was everywhere and the air was thick with the smell of it and the hum of flies. Two of the younger soldiers saw what had been done and abruptly ran outside.

The governor and his family were still gagged and in their nightclothes. The governor had been hung up by the ankles from one of the roof beams and his throat was cut, like a slaughtered sheep's. His wife, who was mercifully lying on her stomach, appeared to have been raped and disembowelled. Two of the children, boys of about six and eight, had been beheaded. Their pubescent sister's throat had been cut, like her father's.

Mikhailov hoped it hadn't taken very long. The men were standing, awaiting orders. They had all been in combat, but this was different.

"Search the rest of the house," ordered Mikhailov. "Then get some litters and take them over to the morgue."

He waited until they were finished. They found two more bodies, both women, probably servants. They had been merely hacked to death. When the men had taken the corpses away Mikhailov stood for a moment in front of the house, filling his lungs with the smoky air, as though he would never get the stink of blood out of his nostrils. Then he straightened his tunic and walked away from the house into the chaos of the firebase.

Before the Russian invasion Herat had a population of eighty thousand. This dropped to fifty thousand over the next few years, as people fled across the border to Iran or into the mountains, or were killed or executed, or died of disease and malnutrition. By the time Bachinsky's soldiers had suppressed the guerrillas in the Old Town and the outlying suburbs the morning after the attack, the population had shrunk by another fifteen thousand. Of these approximately half were casualties: burned, shot, blown up, or poisoned. Many had fled into the countryside, where the helicopters hunted them down like grouse, it being impossible to tell civilians from guerrillas from the air. To overcome the harder knots of resistance in the city Bachinsky had ordered the use of gas, and the helicopters crisscrossed the Old Town for two hours, spraying down clouds of GD and mustard gas. The gases caused most of the deaths in the city, primarily among the civilians. One hundred and sixty-two Russians died when they attacked the Old Town, both from gunfire and from gas that seeped into faulty protective suits.

At the end of it all, half the city was a tumbled and poisonous ruin.

On the northwest slope of the Koh-i-Dashakh, a two-thousand-meter-high range of crags twenty kilometers from Herat and ninety from the Iranian border, there was a deep V-shaped ravine in the mountainside. One wall of the ravine had been undercut by eons of spring runoff and now formed a shallow overhang. The deepest part of the overhang had been walled in by loose stones and mud-plastered brush to form a small bunker just above the bottom of the ravine. When the entrance was covered by a mud-caked rectangle of horsehide, the bunker was indistinguishable from a heap of rubble deposited by the runoff. At four in the morning it was completely invisible.

Mir and Richard Gray were in the bunker with two of Mir's senior commanders. Outside, a score of mujahidin lay about on the stones in postures of utter exhaustion. They were among the last to escape from the tightening Russian noose around the Old Town. If Gray listened carefully he could just make out the sound of weaponry to the east, where Bachinsky's troops were grinding out the last mujahidin resistance.

Mir was sitting on an ammunition box, his head in his hands. The Kalashnikov lay beside him, filmed with dust that looked velvety in the light of the hissing hurricane lamp. The lamp was turned very low to save fuel but it still made the bunker hot. Sweat was trickling out of Gray's armpits and down his sides.

"We broke off too late," said Mir, raising his head. "Four hundred men. We've lost four hundred men. And who would have thought the Russian pigs would use gas in the city?"

Gray shrugged helplessly. No one, not even at Langley, would have believed that the Russians would react with such savagery. Apart from all else, the diplomatic repercussions would be dreadful. "But you've won," Gray said. "Their STARLIGHT plan's in ruins. And you have many of their weapons."

Mir nodded briefly. "We could have had all of them. But their Musulman soldiers didn't help us."

"They couldn't," Gray said. "They were disarmed and sent to barracks before the sweep began."

One of Mir's commanders muttered, "*Sayyid*, many of the men in the city may have gotten away. We killed many Russians. We didn't need their soldiers, even if they were believers."

Mir said, "I gave the order to try to bring the Russian believers into the mountains, before you came here, Richard. After the fight at Karrukh their officers watched them. I should have waited."

"You couldn't have known this opportunity was coming," Gray told him. "You did what was best with the information you had. And you've given the Russians a defeat they won't forget. See it as they would. Seven years they've been in Herat, yet there were still three thousand soldiers of God to remind them whose city it is. Now they will wonder how they can ever win."

"God is great," said the commander who hadn't spoken. He spat on the ground next to the lantern. "With the weapons we took from them we will make their lives a misery until Ramadan, and on into the winter."

Mir straightened. "Yes. They won't forget STARLIGHT. Next time our planning will be better."

"*Insh'allah*," said the commander.

"Richard-jan," said Mir. He was regaining his composure after the shock of the casualty report. "What will you do now? You cannot go back to Herat. Russian patrols will be thick as lice in a beggar's beard, and the samovar you stayed at has been destroyed."

Gray opened his hands. "We didn't expect such destruction." And if Washington had, he reflected with bitterness, would it have made any difference? It was quite possible that Mikhailov was dead and with him the best agent-in-place they had had in years. "It's true I can't go back to Herat. But there are two things I must find out, if you will help me, before I'm summoned home." If they do decide to pull me out, he thought. "First, whether the Russian we met is dead. Second, whether he is going back to Moscow. I have to know."

"We will try to find out," Mir said.

Moscow
Saturday, June 12

*T*HE EMERGENCY SESSION of the Politburo was held in its Staraya Square conference room at eight in the morning. All fourteen full members were present; none of the candidate-members had been summoned to attend. The instant the red leather-padded door of the room had closed, Romanenko stood up at the head of the table, took a wad of newspaper out of his jacket, unfolded it, and slammed it down on the green-beize tabletop. Two or three of the members jumped.

"That," said Romanenko, "is the front page of yesterday's *New York Times*. This is what it says: 'Thousands Reported Dead in Soviet Attack on Afghan City.' Underneath it goes on, 'Gas Used to Crush Resistance.' That's just a sample of what's being said all over the place. We have been doing our best to convince the west that we want to ease tensions, *and now this*. Even the Syrians are berating us in the Damascus newspapers. Our Middle East strategy is dependent on goodwill in the Islamic nations; now that's knocked into a cocked hat. *Gas*, in the name of heaven. In the mountains it would have been one thing, but in a city it makes us look like Nazis. And into the bargain, Minister Yasev, and despite your assurances, the guerrillas haven't been defeated; they're probably stronger than ever with the weapons they captured, and our actions in Herat have given them a credibility they couldn't have arranged for themselves in a hundred years. Who gave the order to use gas?"

"The general commanding the Herat region," said Yasev. He was pale and his lips were compressed into a thin line.

"Who authorized his order?" The other Politburo members were watching the exchange with varying expressions, except for Smilga, whose face was unreadable.

"GHQ Kabul. For the original STARLIGHT operation."

"There was nothing forbidding the use of gas on urban targets?"

"No, Secretary."

"Why not?"

Yasev made a helpless gesture. "It wasn't considered. There were no orders about it. All the fighting was supposed to be in the countryside."

"So your Herat commander just went off on his own."

Yasev nodded.

Romanenko sat down heavily and folded the newspaper. The flush of anger was disappearing from his face. "Recall and discipline him. And anyone else who was involved in the decision. We'll have to make the best of it. Lebedev, have something put in *Pravda* to the effect that this excessive use of force will be severely punished. Make it look as if this general went out of his mind, if you like; just make sure the west realizes that this government doesn't countenance such atrocities. Orchestrate everything to disassociate this...catastrophe from our policies. Especially with the Islamic nations. The Americans will be falling over themselves to make diplomatic capital out of this. Slow them down, understand?"

Lebedev, among whose major responsibilities was supervision of the propaganda organs, made a note, nodding as he did so.

"Minister Polunin," said Romanenko, "we are going to have to buy grain from the Americans again this year. What effect will Herat have on the negotiations?"

Eduard Polunin, Minister of Foreign Affairs, carefully lined up three pencils on the notepad in front of him. "This morning the Americans informed the Ministry of Trade that they were suspending negotiations. They refused to give a reason, but said the suspension might be temporary."

"What are we going to do if it becomes permanent?" snapped Romanenko. "The Canadians might go along with another American embargo. And the Argentines are having their own crop problems; we won't be able to depend on them the way we did in 1980."

"We could arrange third-party purchases," Lebedev pointed out. "We've done that before."

"Yes, and you know what that extra transaction costs, don't you? Have you looked at the state of our foreign exchange lately?" Romanenko was becoming angry again. "We *cannot* afford another embargo. And what about the technology we need to buy? For a change, we have to look farther than the ends of our noses. We're already rationing meat and dairy products. Do you want us to have to bring in bread rationing as well? Remember what happened the last time the Russian people ran out of bread?"

They all did. The 1917 revolution began with a spontaneous bread riot in Leningrad.

Romanenko sat back in his chair, looked around the table, and said, "We have to take a diplomatic initiative. Afghanistan has sapped us for too long. We are not going to win there except at the cost of depopulating the country. We cannot afford that cost. We are going to withdraw from Afghanistan."

Pandemonium broke out around the table. Romanenko's supporters, who had been briefed on the proposal before the emergency meeting, tried to shout down the others. Smilga, noticeably, held his peace. Romanenko pounded on the table until there was silence. "This is supposed to be the Politburo of the Central Committee," he bellowed, "not a drunken meeting of the Irkutsk City Soviet. Speak one at a time. Chairman Zarudin? You're among the loudest."

"I speak for several others here," growled Zarudin. "We cannot leave Afghanistan overnight. The country would collapse into anarchy and the Americans — or worse, the Chinese — would move in. Our southern flank would be threatened."

"*Move in?*" said Romanenko. "What do you mean, *move in?* With what? An army? Do you think anyone else is going to invade Afghanistan after seeing what we've been through? As it is now, you couldn't give the country away. Let them go back to slitting each others' throats instead of Russian ones, they've been doing that happily for centuries. Minister Yasev, do you think we're going to have an Afghan army at the gates of Moscow this time next year, if we let them go?"

"Certainly not, Secretary. But an American economic and diplomatic presence there — "

"We have serious problems at home," Konstantin Tsander put in. "If we don't get our house in order soon, we may be withdrawing from more places than Afghanistan."

"Chairman Smilga," said Romanenko. "What is your opinion?"

"Konstantin Tsander is right," Smilga said. "We do have problems at home. But have you thought out the reaction of our Warsaw Pact allies to a withdrawal such as you propose? They might consider it weakness. No one here wants another Hungarian uprising, nor even a police action like the one we reluctantly carried out in Czechoslovakia."

"Minister Polunin?"

"There are considerable diplomatic gains to be had through a withdrawal from Afghanistan," Polunin admitted. "On balance, I would say that a withdrawal would be preferable. The Warsaw Pact allies are not in the same category as Afghanistan. We are much better established in Eastern Europe."

The argument went on for more than two hours. Gradually, Romanenko achieved his consensus: a third party, possibly India, would be approached to moderate a discussion on the withdrawal. The major condition would be that the country be neutralized, on the model of Austria, so that it could not become a proxy battleground between the two superpowers. Foreign Minister Polunin would add any secondary conditions, work out the presentation, and report upon progress within a week. The meeting adjourned at eleven o'clock.

As the others were gathering up their papers, Smilga gave Zarudin the faintest of satisfied nods.

Moscow
June 17 − 18

MIKHAILOV WALKED southeast along Gorki Street toward Pushkin Square. He had banged his right forearm on the door frame of the subway car as he was leaving it, and the burns still hurt fiercely despite the analgesic ointment and the bandages. He had got the burns in the horrible cleanup after the battle of Herat, and at first they had been so painful he had been unable to use his right hand at all. The antigas suit he had been issued had a flaw in the sleeve fabric, and a whiff of mustard gas had gotten inside. Fortunately it was mustard and not GD, and had been quite diluted by the time it reached his skin. Had it not been, he could very well have been dying by now, his body turning a reddish-brown except where the flesh erupted in enormous yellow blisters, the mucous membranes stripped from his bronchial tubes, his lungs filling slowly with pinkish-gray froth.

With an effort he pushed the image out of his mind. The burns had had one useful result: GHQ Kabul, apparently not wanting the general secretary's nephew to die within its jurisdiction if the gassing were more serious than it first appeared, had processed his transfer in record time. He was back in Moscow on the sixteenth of June, with orders to report to General Staff HQ for reassignment the following Monday, if his health permitted. He also had instructions from General Gordik to report to Tolbukhin before he did that. Mikhailov wasn't sure what the Third Directorate's reaction to his reassignment was going to be; he had informed Gordik when he first put the request in through the normal army channels, and Gordik had made no attempt to block it. Either they didn't mind if he went back to Moscow or they were wary of the influence Mikhailov might be able to exert through his uncle.

He crossed Strasnoi Boulevard at the lights, still favoring his arm although the pain was ebbing. It was a windy day and the sky had a broken cloud cover for the first time, so Nadia had told him, in two weeks. There hadn't been nearly as much rain as usual and Mikhailov gathered from his sister that early vegetables were almost impossible to find, except in the certificate-ruble stores.

Mikhailov hadn't intended to be walking down Gorki Street at half-past two in the afternoon. What he had wanted to do was sit in his favorite chair in front of the stereo, listen to Mozart, and drink vodka very slowly until it was time to collect Valeria from the *detsky sad*.

At nine o'clock that morning somebody had dialed a wrong number.

So here he was, nearly opposite the Armenia Shop, with Gastronom Number One just ahead of him, and right on time.

He walked the last few meters to the old czarist food emporium and went in. Before it became Gastronom Number One it had been Yeliseyev's, and unofficially still went by the name of its pre-revolutionary proprietor. It was a cavernous place, lit by enormous crystal chandeliers, pillared and pilastered, with great arched mirrors set into the walls a good six meters above the parquet floor. The walls between the mirrors were festooned with scrollwork, moldings, and carved garlands. As usual, it was crowded; if you had the money, you could get a better selection of goods here than anywhere else in Moscow outside the hard-currency and the certificate-ruble stores. Mikhailov walked nonchalantly across the diamond-and-octagon patterns of the floor and managed to squeeze up to the counter in front of a display of baked goods. He couldn't actually buy anything at this counter, since he hadn't been through the lines where you paid for your purchases in advance, but since Moscow clerks did as little as possible at the best of times, no one would ask him what he wanted. After a moment he took a handkerchief out of his pocket and blew his nose, making sure his bandaged hand was conspicuous. Then he moved along the counter a little, leaving a few centimeters of clear space to his right.

Somebody pushed into the space. In the reflection in the polished mahogany of the shelves opposite, Mikhailov glimpsed a woman in a drab cardigan. He didn't recognize her. She studied the display and then turned away.

He felt the brush of her fingers as she made the contact.

He continued to study the display for half a minute and then left the counter. As he walked idly around the rest of the store, pretending to look at the unusually sparse inventory, he thought: I don't believe she was Russian. One of their embassy people, junior enough not to interest the watchers much. The American must have picked up that last drop I made in Herat. That was risky, the city was crawling with patrols. I wonder where he is now?

He left Yeliseyev's, tried a couple of other food stores for vegetables just to cover himself, and then went to the certificate-ruble store in Gruzinskaya Street where he bought a head of lettuce, half a dozen oranges, and a kilo of tomatoes. The quality was unusually low for Beriozka goods.

The trip home took forever, but he didn't dare take the note out of his pocket to read it. Even when he was in the apartment he put the fruit and vegetables away and poured himself a sizable glass of vodka before unfolding the slip of paper.

On it was written in neat black Cyrillic script:

I'll call you this evening in case you'd like to come over for dinner tomorrow. You'll probably want to tell your boss you're going, so he can reach you in an emergency. By the way, I hear your uncle is throwing a big party this weekend. You should try to go; it might be quite something.

Mikhailov burst out laughing. Ekaterina Romanenko had already invited him, but he didn't think even the Americans had the resources to know that.

Fowler did call him that evening. Mikhailov gave an equivocal response to the invitation, in case the monitors were listening.

As instructed, Mikhailov went to see Tolbukhin the next morning. This time he didn't have to wait in the outer office.

"How's your arm?" Tolbukhin asked when they had exchanged greetings.

"Better, sir," Mikhailov said. He was staring at the picture of Vasily Romanenko over Tolbukhin's desk, where Chernenko had once hung. He had seen a few of these official portraits since he returned to Moscow, but he still wasn't used to them: he knew Uncle Vasily as a person, not an icon, and he had trouble connecting the two. "I was lucky," he added.

"Luckier than some," Tolbukhin said. "General Bachinsky's been sacked."

Mikhailov nodded, not surprised.

"What I wanted to see you about," Tolbukhin went on, "was this. You're being attached to the General Staff officer pool, aren't you?"

"Yes, General. This coming Monday."

"The arm good enough?"

"Yes, General. As long as I don't knock it on anything and keep the bandages fresh."

"That's good socialist dedication," said Tolbukhin. Mikhailov thought he detected a trace of irony in the words. "Anyway," the general continued, "we don't particularly want you back in the GRU. It's too narrow a field for someone of your abilities. Let me tell you, Andrei Sergeyevitch, I can count on the fingers of one hand the officers in our employ who have your combination of intelligence, skill, and commitment." Tolbukhin looked thoughtfully out the window, where the sun was shining brightly through a gap in the clouds.

"You're very kind, General," said Mikhailov.

"I'm not flattering you," said Tolbukhin. "You have the potential to go very far indeed. My opinion is shared by others in this directorate, and your army colleagues speak very highly of you."

Mikhailov made a deprecatory gesture.

"We'd like you to have a wider scope than a military-intelligence desk," said Tolbukhin. "Now, a few years ago, the General Staff Combat-Training Directorate established a special commission to integrate what we've learned in Afghanistan with all our army training programs. Unfortunately, there's been some difficulty with our Eastern European forces over this, they don't seem to want to take it seriously. They're not meeting the established norms."

"Oh," said Mikhailov.

"They don't want to accept the need for it. They can't see the connection between a lot of badly armed hill men and the sort of troops they'd fight if we had a full-scale counter-revolution in one of the Warsaw Pact nations, say Poland, and the Polish army went over to the counterrevolutionaries. The training directorate has its usual problems: by the time the training procedures filter down to the troop level, they're ignored except just before an inspection, and then the unit commanders dream up all sorts of ways to make it look as though they've been following orders. The inspectors are usually from another army district, and they've been doing the same things themselves, so *they* don't look too closely either."

"The result is that nothing gets done," interjected Mikhailov.

"Exactly. It makes the operations and training directorates want to tear their hair out by the roots. Anyway, they're setting up an inspection commission to monitor the training directly from Moscow, rather than rely on cross-inspection from other military people who have their own skeletons in the closet. It's called the special training inspectorate and there are positions open in it. I want you to apply for one. We'll make sure you get the one you're supposed to."

"What would I be doing, exactly?" asked Mikhailov.

"As I understand it, you'd descend on a divisional HQ like the wrath of Stalin, and demand to see all training records. Those will be hugely optimistic, of course. You then request an immediate demonstration of a randomly selected unit's skill. Their performance forms your report. You won't be popular."

"What will I be doing for the Third Directorate?"

Tolbukhin drummed his fingers on the desk for a moment. "There are some changes being made in the way officers are required to handle their troops, especially regarding the maltreatment of recruits. Also, junior officers are going to be required to take more initiative, instead of blindly following orders handed down from on high. Political training is also being reduced to what it was a few years ago. That's not all, but it's enough to start with. It may not sit well with some officers. We want to know about any grumbling. We also want you to probe for dissatisfaction. Get a few senior officers drunk, grumble yourself, see what they say. Afterwards, write everything down."

Mikhailov studied Tolbukhin. The general returned his gaze expressionlessly. After perhaps ten seconds Mikhailov looked out the window and said, "Yes, General. To whom am I to submit these reports?"

"To me," said Tolbukhin. "And to no one else. After you've got your posting, you never heard of the Third Directorate, understand?"

"Yes, General Tolbukhin."

"Good. Any problems?" The interview was clearly over.

"Actually, General, there was something I wanted you to advise me on."

Tolbukhin raised his eyebrows.

"The American, Eric Fowler," said Mikhailov. "The one —"

"I remember," Tolbukhin said.

"He telephoned me yesterday evening. He wants me to come to supper tonight, at his apartment. I didn't want to say yes or no until I reported the contact."

"That's wise," said Tolbukhin. "What does he really want?"

"I don't know, General. He may only want to renew our acquaintance. We knew each other in London."

Tolbukhin looked out the window again. "I doubt that's all

it is," he said. "Your uncle's position makes you a valuable contact for anyone. Well, you're hardly defector material; go ahead unless you hear from me before tomorrow evening. I'll have to make sure it won't interfere with anything my colleagues in the Second Directorate are planning for Fowler. Report anything to me that goes beyond the social."

"Yes, sir. Will the militia at his apartment building let me through?"

"Don't worry about the militia," said Tolbukhin. "And remember, come and see me the day you receive your Training Directorate posting and I'll give you detailed instructions on what you're to do."

Uspenskoye
Sunday, June 20

*R*OMANENKO'S DACHA was an enormous sprawling yellow-pine building tucked well back from the Moscow road and screened from it by a pine wood. In front of the house, which consisted of a central two-story block with wings on its east and west, a circular graveled driveway enclosed a patch of lawn and a green bronze fountain salvaged — or looted — from some forgotten czarist garden. To the east of the house, partly hidden in a grove of birch trees, was a set of garages built to resemble a peasant cottage. The driveway was jammed with cars, many of them bearing the distinctive white-and-black licence plates issued to foreigners. Under the pines where the driveway entered the wood, a couple of dozen chauffeurs sat listlessly in the afternoon heat.

Behind the dacha there was a deep slate-flagged patio running the building's length. It was divided from the lawn beyond it by a stone balustrade set with flower urns. Three wide flights of steps led down to the lawn, which was dotted with oak and birch trees. The lawn descended in a gentle slope to a stream running along the back of the grounds some fifty meters from the house. Beyond the stream lay a thick pine wood, which was constantly patrolled by guards.

Long tables with white cloths had been arranged under the oaks, and on them was set out a spectacular array of food and drink. The food was still covered, though, and would be until

Romanenko had finished the press conference. He was standing at a small podium at the top of the central flight of patio steps, and in front of him on the lawn was gathered nearly every journalist in Moscow, foreign and otherwise. As Romanenko spoke in his rather stilted but fluent English, all were scribbling furiously; the only tape recorders and cameras that had been permitted were those of Novosti, the Soviet press agency. Nonetheless it was a journalist's fantasy come to life: no general secretary of the Communist Party since Khrushchev had given a press conference in such informal surroundings. Moreover, he seemed to be answering their questions candidly, although most of them avoided the potentially embarrassing ones, for fear of later retribution.

Romanenko finished describing his plans for agricultural reform and said, "In a minute it will be time to eat. I don't know about you, ladies and gentlemen, but I am very hungry. So, one last question."

Threescore hands shot up. Romanenko looked through the crowd and pointed. "Yes?"

He had singled out one of the Novosti people, a young man who looked extremely nervous. "Comrade General Secretary," he said, and hesitated. Romanenko waited patiently. "Comrade Secretary," the young man blurted, "what plans are being made for the resolution of the problems presented to us by Afghanistan?"

Mikhailov, standing at the edge of the crowd among the Russian officials and the Third World and western diplomats who were the real audience for the press conference, felt his eyebrows climb toward his hairline. The crowd, which had been stirring gently in anticipation of lunch or the dash to the telephones linking the dacha to the overseas wire serices, went absolutely still. Mikhailov could hear the brook tinkling softly at the foot of the lawn.

He wanted that question asked, Mikhailov thought. No one would have dared otherwise.

Romanenko smiled. "I'm glad to say that we have made some progress. The Indian government has agreed to act as a moderator, and the Soviet Union is ready to begin talks with all interested parties to arrange the withdrawal of Soviet peace-keeping forces from Afghanistan and the establishment of a government in Kabul that will be friends with both east and west, with nothing to fear from either. To emphasize our commitment to this, we will be withdrawing twenty-five thousand troops at the end of August. For those of you who find such statements suspect, I point out that these soldiers will not be replaced by others, and that there will be a true and verifiable reduction of our forces in Afghanistan." He stopped smiling. "I also wish to remark, however, that we expect negotiations to be carried out in good faith by all concerned. Attempts to take advantage of our actions will be met with the attention they deserve." The smile returned. "Now, my throat is dry and my voice is about to stop working. Thank you all for your attention." He stepped away from the podium.

Instantly the press corps broke for the house and the telephones. Four very large men appeared out of the French doors behind Romanenko and took up positions at a discreet distance from him as he started down the steps, waving the crowd in the direction of the tables. Mikhailov began to drift in his uncle's direction. He looked around for Ekaterina but couldn't see her, which wasn't surprising. She avoided large social gatherings except when attendance was a political necessity.

Her invitation hadn't prepared Mikhailov for anything like this. From what she had said on the telephone it had sounded like no more than a small garden party. He supposed she had asked him to come simply because she thought he would enjoy it; Ekaterina did things like that from time to time, without much concern for the social niceties.

Mikhailov had found out about the press conference over dinner at Fowler's apartment on Friday evening. Even the American had expressed surprise at this turn of Soviet politics, although he had said little more in that vein because of the microphones that were an inevitable fixture of any apartment inhabited by foreigners. Fowler's four Russian guests, a pair of officials from the International Trade Center and their wives, were little more forthcoming. What saved the evening from unutterable dullness was the presence of Fowler's Australian friends, the Masons, that of a bubbly girl from the United States embassy consular section, who was related distantly to Fowler's wife, and, for Mikhailov, Chantal Mallory. Fowler carefully introduced Mikhailov to her in front of the Russians, and made sure that they, and the microphones, knew who he was. The two trade officials had been extremely deferential to Mikhailov all evening, much to Chantal Mallory's carefully veiled amusement. By the end of the evening Mikhailov had begun to feel quite sorry for them; to sit at a table with a western journalist was perturbing enough, but to have the general secretary's nephew present as well must have been thoroughly unsettling. The two officials and their wives had left early, and Mikhailov and Fowler had sat up until one in the morning, drinking and talking about London. Mikhailov had had a headache until Saturday noon.

The lawn was crowded now. By the time Mikhailov got to within twenty meters of his uncle, Romanenko was surrounded by a halo of diplomats, officials, and senior Party members, with the notable exclusion of Oleg Zarudin. His four body-guards looked distinctly nervous, eyes scanning the stands of trees that edged the lawn and minutely inspecting the guests who were trying to get a word with the general secretary, who with his shock of white hair and great height was the most prominent figure in the gathering. Romanenko appeared to be enjoying himself immensely, punctuating sentences with bites of caviar-heaped biscuits and talking with his mouth full. Mikhailov gave up on his intended conversation with his uncle — he didn't know what he would say that wouldn't be out of place in this gathering, anyway — and went to one of the other tables to eat something.

He fell into conversation with a British attaché and they discussed life in London for a few minutes, until the Englishman saw greener diplomatic fields elsewhere and drifted off. Nobody else paid much attention to Mikhailov. He began to feel decidedly out of place, and wished that Aunt Ekaterina were there. He also wished that Nadia hadn't refused to come. Mikhailov was still a little irritated at his sister. The previous evening, after much beating about the bush, she had confessed that she had asked their uncle to arrange Mikhailov's return home, for Valeria's sake mostly. He had believed that he had got the posting more or less by his own efforts. On the other hand, it explained why Gordik hadn't made any comments on the request for transfer. He must have thought that Mikhailov was exercising his unofficial right to get what he wanted through political influence. It was a common practice among the elite.

There were ranks of wine bottles on the table. Mikhailov sampled three, drinking the wine in sips between bites of smoked sturgeon and rye bread. He decided to get pleasantly but not noticeably mellow, pay his respects to his uncle, and then go home.

"Hello, Andrei."

He turned around. Chantal was standing behind him, holding a shallow glass of something effervescent. Pinned to her blouse was a card bearing her picture and the word "press" in Russian. Mikhailov swallowed his mouthful of salmon and said, "Hello, Chantal. I was beginning to think you hadn't come."

She favored him with a faint half-smile and sipped from her glass. Mikhailov thought: her eyes are the same color as the pine trees.

"I've been here for a while," she said. "After your uncle finished I joined the dash for the telephones. There were twenty of them, and a list of who was to get first crack, but journalists are pushy people."

"Oh." He didn't know what else to say. Gallantry seemed out of place.

"Isn't anybody paying any attention to you?" she asked. The idea seemed to amuse her. "You've been standing here all alone for at least ten minutes."

She had been watching him, then. "Nobody seems interested in anyone as anonymous as me."

"The general secretary's nephew is hardly a nonentity."

"I haven't mentioned it to anyone."

"Oh, I see." She turned and looked around the expanse of green lawn with its knots of elegant people, and up at the long shadows being cast on the rear of the house. The air was hot and heavy with the scent of pine pitch, and the deep blue of the morning sky had now turned a brilliant, hazy white. "How is Valeria?"

He had mentioned the child's bout with chicken pox at Fowler's. "Oh, she's been back to school for a couple of weeks. Just a few fading spots left."

"I had chicken pox when I was eight. My mother was terrified it would ruin my complexion." She touched the champagne glass to her lips. "I must say this is a pleasanter meeting than the other evening. No disrespect to Eric Fowler."

"Yes," he said, cursing himself for being so tongue-tied. The years in Afghanistan had taken away whatever knack he had had for talking to women. "Are you staying here long?"

She gave him a sideways look. "Only to finish this," she said, meaning the champagne. "Then I have to do some work at home."

"You knew I was back in Moscow," he said, dropping the pretense. "Before the dinner at Eric's."

"Yes. He was told you were coming back two days before you arrived. I didn't know about your arm, though. How is it today?"

"Better. The bandages will likely be off in two or three weeks."

"Was it a bad burn?"

"Mustard gas," he said. "We used it in Herat. The general who ordered it has been relieved."

"We'll need to know all about that," she said, "but later. We've made a start on freer contacts. Eric's dinner was groundwork, to give us a chance to meet again."

His spirits shot up. He caught the scent of her perfume. "They still won't like me associating with a western journalist," he said.

"You've only been back a few days, so you probably haven't noticed. Your authorities are noticeably less worried about contacts between Soviet citizens and westerners. There's a thaw starting. Today's a sample of what's going on. It will make it easier for us to see each other."

Two men arguing violently in some Scandinavian tongue walked up to the table and began to slosh wine into glasses. Mikhailov said, "Let's walk."

They started toward Romanenko's table, where he was still holding forth. "I've been posted to the General Staff Training Directorate," he said softly. "I'll be doing some work in Eastern Europe."

A worried look crossed her face. "Stationed there permanently?"

"No. I'm to be based in Moscow. I'll have it all for you when we meet next. When will that be?"

"Eric will arrange it. It won't be for a while. We have to let this build slowly."

They were quite close to the crowd around Romanenko now. Mikhailov's uncle was half a head taller than anyone around him, and Mikhailov could see the animation in his face quite clearly. Romanenko noticed him and waved briefly. Mikhailov waved back.

"Would you like to meet my uncle?" he asked suddenly, without thinking. The wine was having some effect.

"They said he wouldn't talk to any more journalists after the press meeting."

"You're with me." He realized as he said it that it sounded pompous. He took her forearm and towed her after him, elbowing his way through the crowd, which by now was thinning. He got within two meters of Romanenko only to hear his uncle say, "It's been very pleasant, ladies and gentlemen, but I really must return to my office. I have a great deal to do." Turning, flanked by his bodyguards, he started for the house.

"Damn," Mikhailov heard Chantal mutter.

At that point Romanenko caught sight of his nephew. "Andrei," he said, "walk along with me."

Mikhailov started forward, trailing Chantal after him. One of the bodyguards suddenly lumbered forward, looking past Mikhailov at Chantal. "No journalists," he said loudly, in Russian.

"She's with me," said Mikhailov, both to the bodyguard and to his uncle.

"Stop," said Romanenko. The bodyguard stopped instantly. Romanenko said to Mikhailov, "Fine. Both of you come."

The bodyguards fell in behind them as they walked toward the house. Romanenko said, "I don't believe I've had the pleasure."

"Sorry," Mikhailov said. "Uncle Vasily, this is Miss Chantal Mallory. She's a friend of someone I knew when I was in England."

"You're a journalist, Miss Mallory?" Romanenko asked. They were nearing the steps leading up to the patio.

"Yes, Mr. Secretary. With a Canadian magazine called *Seven Days*."

"Did you enjoy the press conference?"

"It was — illuminating," Chantal said.

Romanenko burst into laughter. At the top of the steps he said, "Very diplomatically put, Miss Mallory. I have to take my leave of you now. Do you have transportation home?"

"Yes, Mr. Secretary. Thank you very much. Andrei, do you need a ride back to the city?"

"I have a car," Mikhailov said. Ekaterina had arranged the loan of a Zhiguli the day before. "But thank you."

"Perhaps we'll meet again," Romanenko said to Chantal, presenting her with a slight bow. "Until then, good-bye."

"Good-bye, Mr. Secretary." Chantal hesitated, unsure of protocol, and then simply walked away along the patio toward the end of the house and the path to the driveway. Romanenko watched her go. Mikhailov waited uncertainly.

"Nadia couldn't come?" Romanenko asked abruptly.

"She said she'd feel out of place."

"That's too bad," Romanenko said. His face was thoughtful beneath the carefully groomed silver hair. "How long have you known Chantal Mallory?"

Mikhailov told him about Fowler and the dinner invitation. Romanenko glanced at the bodyguards to make sure they were out of earshot, and then, leaning toward Mikhailov, said quietly, "Don't lose contact with her. She could prove useful."

Startled, Mikhailov could only nod. Romanenko said in normal tones, "Be sure to come and see your aunt this week, she's looking forward to spending some time with Valeria."

"I will," said Mikhailov.

As he inexpertly maneuvered the Zhiguli down the lane toward the Moscow road, Mikhailov began to laugh. Without any particular intention of doing so, he had managed to introduce the General Secretary of the Communist Party of the Soviet Union to an operative of the Central Intelligence Agency. Even Fowler's superiors couldn't have planned *that*.

Could they?

Two kilometers farther on, it didn't seem so amusing. Vasily Romanenko was beginning to behave as though the people of the Soviet Union were more important than weapons or ideology, and if his reforms took hold, Mikhailov's reasons for going to the Americans simply evaporated.

He wondered if they would let him go.

Mlada Boleslav — Prague, Czechoslovakia
June 30 — July 3

*T*HE BASE of the Eighteenth Guards Rifle Division was several kilometers outside Mlada Boleslav; in the city itself was the headquarters of the army command to which the division belonged. There were two Soviet armies in Czechoslovakia, controlling between them five full-strength divisions and some two hundred attack aircraft. The Czech army, in its turn, included ten divisions, although three of these consisted only of the headquarters staff and some support organizations, and would be fully manned only in the event of war. Altogether the joint Soviet-Czech forces made up the exact complement of a front, the second-largest fighting organization in the Soviet-Warsaw Pact ground forces. The headquarters of this front, if war came, was in Prague; in peacetime it was known simply as HQ, Central Group of Forces.

Mikhailov was standing under a beech tree, watching a company of soldiers from the Eighteenth go through an inspection exercise. The rolling countryside of Czechoslovakia shimmered in the heat; Mikhailov could imagine how the men were sweating in their heavy uniforms. Near Mikhailov a knot of divisional officers anxiously watched the men's performance. Even General Abrashkin, the division's commander, had been careful to attend. On paper he outranked Mikhailov, but Mikhailov was from Moscow and his report could affect General Abrashkin's career, depending on how well the troops met the training norms. This particular exercise, which was based on a recent field manual of counter-guerrilla tactics, was a simulation of a company-sized attack on a tree line after an ambush from the rear.

Mikhailov had arrived from Prague at the Eighteenth's divisional headquarters that morning, requested that a company be put at his disposal for evaluation, and had revealed what the exercise was to be only at the last moment. He would repeat the technique, with different exercises and different units, for the next two days, by which time he was supposed to have a good idea of the adequacy of the division's training program. The procedure and the exercises had been laid down in Moscow, and Mikhailov was to deviate from neither by so much as a hair. Like everything else in the Soviet army, evaluations were carried out according to the plan, and only by the plan.

The soldiers were actually doing fairly well for men who had never been in combat. They avoided clumping, advanced by short rushes while being covered by the overwatch sections, and their mortar fire — simulated by smoke grenades — would have been adequate to suppress at least some of the imaginary ambushers in the tree line. Nonetheless they were using standard frontal-assault tactics; Mikhailov knew they would take heavy casualties if they behaved so in a cleft in the mountains in Afghanistan, at night, trapped and with an invisible enemy above and all around them.

Also, Mikhailov knew about troop-performance evaluations, from having been on both sides of them. One particularly scandalous affair — but only because the trick was found out — occurred when an inspecting officer became suspicious of the superb marksmanship displayed by a rifle company in the regiment Mikhailov had first served with. The officer had made a quick dash for the bushes above the observation point and had discovered a sniping specialist with a telescopic sight and a silenced rifle. The sniper had been hitting the targets for the men on the firing point, who had been intentionally missing. Several officers were severely punished, but only because the cheating was discovered. Things of that sort went on all the time, but most were undetected, not least because the officers of the unit being evaluated did their best to befuddle the inspectors with alcohol before they went out to do their work. Bribery was also not uncommon. The important thing was to avoid being downchecked, never mind how.

Mikhailov had drunk only water at lunch, much to the distress of General Abrashkin's chief of staff.

The men reached the tree line and the exercise was over. As the men began double-timing their way back to the barracks, Mikhailov put his clipboard and notes under his arm and joined the group of divisional officers. They were looking relieved; their troops hadn't disgraced them. Abrashkin looked expectantly at Mikhailov.

"A textbook frontal assault, General Abrashkin," Mikhailov said politely. "I'll give you my observations in your copy of the report."

Abrashkin didn't look particularly happy at this. "How would they have done in a combat situation? Afghanistan?"

Mikhailov didn't answer for a moment. Then he said, "I think they'd have been cut to pieces unless they had air or artillery support. Your men need more training in infiltration tactics."

Abrashkin went red, then white. Turning to his chief of staff he said, "Carry on with the tests. I'm going back to my office. Colonel Mikhailov, are you joining us for supper?"

"Certainly, General Abrashkin."

"Good." Abrashkin stalked off. Mikhailov nodded to the chief of staff, and the next exercise began.

At eleven o'clock that evening there were only four men left in the senior officers' mess, which was a small stone building adjoining the headquarters block. The four were Mikhailov, General Abrashkin, the chief of staff, and the division's *zampolit*, or political officer, who was a colonel. They were sitting around the end of a long table whose white cloth was now stained with red wine and scattered with breadcrumbs. They were all drunk, Mikhailov less than the other three. The wine had been finished and they were now drinking vodka.

Somebody, somehow, had got hold of an air conditioner for the mess and it hummed and dripped in one of the windows.

"So I got out of the training division," General Abrashkin was saying, "and got myself posted to a combat one. Best thing I ever did. Everybody thinks a training division's a soft touch, the sergeants do all the work, but let me tell you it's not like it looks from the outside." He poured more vodka for everybody. The chief of staff and the *zampolit* were looking glazed. Mikhailov guessed that they had heard about General Abrashkin's military career more than once. "Not like it looks from the outside," Abrashkin repeated, setting the bottle down heavily. "They're rough places, training divisions, there are always a few recruits who can't take it and end up killing themselves. Or worse. There was one thing that happened, fortunately not in my battalion, where this little asshole, out on the firing range one morning, turns around with his rifle and saws three sergeants in half with one burst. The whole magazine. Then he calmly puts in a new magazine and blows his own head off. You have to watch them every minute, one of them wipes himself out, you get a black mark on your fitness report that *never* goes away." He burped. "Never again. Give me a combat division any day."

The chief of staff and the *zampolit* dutifully nodded agreement.

"Colonel Mikhailov knows what I'm talking about," Abrashkin went on with heavy good-fellowship, peering at Mikhailov as though his eyes were focusing unevenly. "Good type. Might be sent out here from Moscow to breathe down our necks but at least you've been shot at, Colonel, not like some of these staff types that come trotting around here with enough papers to wipe the ass of every man in the division, never been shot at in their lives. You've got exprience." He pronounced the last word with difficulty. "And you've been wounded in combat." He waved clumsily at Mikhailov's bandaged hand. "That's resh — respected."

Mikhailov nodded, he thought graciously. His head seemed to take a long time to regain its equilibrium.

"Look here," said Abrashkin to the *zampolit* and the chief

of staff. "Colonel Mikhailov's part of the new broom, that uncle of his is going to help sweep all the shit out of the army. And the air forces, and the navy too, you watch. Things are getting better already."

"How so?" asked Mikhailov. His tongue felt wooden. He wondered fleetingly how much of this was Abrashkin's attempt to be ingratiating, and how much was sincere. It didn't seem to matter much just now.

"Well, look at discipline. Used to be you got downchecked if your men had too many disciplinary arrests. So ev'rybody ignored discipline problems except when they were already out of hand. Or you fucked the men around if they stepped out of line, nothing formal, just night marches in the rain, like. Now we've got a rule says the unit commander doesn't carry all the can if he slaps his men under arrest, unless he's a real screw-up, in which case he ought to be sacked anyway."

"What do the men think of it?" asked Mikhailov. This was the sort of thing Tolbukhin wanted to know: he tried with some effort to follow what Abrashkin was saying.

"They think it's all right. Means if a unit has a couple of bad apples, not everybody gets pissed around with. Look at it from their point of view. It's the socialist justice everybody's always telling them about."

"To each according to his crimes," said the *zampolit*, paraphrasing Marx. He laughed and poured more vodka. "Secretary Romanenko is extremely popular among the troops. We political officers make sure they know who's responsible for these improvements."

Mikhailov nodded. A good deal of propaganda was being aimed at the line soldiers, extolling the benefits of the new regime. Vasily Romanenko was a careful man; in the triad of forces holding the Soviet Union together — army, KGB, Party — the army was the one with most of the guns.

"Food's better, too," said the chief of staff, slurring. He was the drunkest of all of them and seemed poised to slide off his chair. "We're trying to stop the hazing," he said in a non sequitur.

"That's going to be a long job," said Mikhailov. The hazing

was one of the worst aspects of military service, unless you escaped it by going through officer training, which was bad enough. Raw recruits were persecuted by the six-month men, the six-month men by the one-year men, and so on up the hierarchy until demobilization after two years of service. A vicious pecking order established itself in every barracks, with the recruits having to give up their food, new uniforms, boots, and whatever else might be of value, to soldiers further along in their service. Often it went much beyond that: after lights out the new men were beaten with belts, ridden naked like horses, made to sleep in the barracks latrines; and when they stumbled out in the morning they found their beds sodden and stinking with urine and worse. The officers did nothing to stop it, for it had a purpose. It divided the soldiers among themselves and gave them an outlet for the rage they normally felt against their sergeants, and not infrequently against their commanding officers.

Abrashkin scowled. "That's going too far. You're always going to have soldiers beating the snot out of each other. We can't hold their hands every minute. Where's that other bottle? Colonel Mikhailov, drink up, have some more mushrooms, or we'll have to feed them to the pigs in the morning."

The rest of the evening dissolved into a blur.

The following Saturday Mikhailov was back in Prague, at a luncheon in the Soviet headquarters complex behind Hradcany Castle. This headquarters controlled the central group of forces, and Colonel-General Litovtsev was its commander-in-chief. Litovtsev was giving the luncheon, an elaborate and sedate affair. Around the table sat a selection of Litovtsev's staff, Mikhailov, and the nine other special training inspectorate officers Moscow had sent out to shake up the central group's training apparatus.

Colonel-General Litovtsev was quite unlike General Abrashkin. The commander-in-chief was urbane, handsome, and dignified, and appeared unworried that the inspection commission's report might cause him any undue difficulty.

Mikhailov suspected that Litovtsev had powerful friends on the General Staff.

"Colonel Mikhailov," said Litovtsev, pushing his empty wineglass aside and motioning to the uniformed waiter for a refill, "you spent some time in Prague, I believe."

"Yes, sir," Mikhailov said. "Some years ago."

"What do you think of the city now?"

Mikhailov ruminated for a moment, looking at the large photograph of his uncle hanging on the wall opposite. "I've only been here a few hours," he said. "Not long enough to really form an impression."

"It's not what it was a few years ago, or even six months back," said Litovtsev, sipping wine delicately. "Comrade General Secretary Romanenko's reforms, while certainly in the best interests of Marxist-Leninism, are being misinterpreted here. The STB is quite worried."

If the STB, the Czech equivalent to the KGB, was worried, then so was the KGB itself. Mikhailov nodded. He realized that Litovtsev wasn't saying these things for the present audience alone; Mikhailov was meant to take them back to Moscow, either to his uncle or the Third Directorate. A warning. He wondered who had put the words into Litovtsev's mouth.

"Some of the more reactionary Czechs have never gotten over their resentment for our fraternal support in 1968," Litovtsev went on. "The ill-will crops up periodically. A couple of years before Brezhnev died his official photograph started appearing in shop windows all over Prague. Everybody in the Party was delighted at first, socialist fraternity on the upswing, they thought. Then somebody noticed that the photographs were always in butcher shops, and always flanked by two pigs' heads. A stop was put to it, of course."

Nobody smiled until Litovtsev did. The commander-in-chief continued, "Do you recollect the Charter 1977 difficulties?"

"Yes, Colonel-General." The Charter was a document that had circulated in 1977, pointing out the failure of the Czech government to abide by a number of human rights that were, in fact, written into its own constitution: freedom of movement and assembly, access to foreign newspapers, and the like. It had floated about Prague for a short time until it was suppressed and its authors and supporters "normalized" — subjected to systematic persecution until they gave up their efforts in fear or frustration.

"The phrase 'Charter '77' used to appear on walls occasionally up until a couple of years ago," continued Litovtsev, "then it stopped. In the past two months it's begun again, but much more frequently. The STB has the graffiti painted over, the next morning they're there again." He smiled briefly. "It's very frustrating for the police."

"Counterrevolutionaries," suggested one of the inspection-commission officers helpfully.

Litovtsev looked at the man with a certain peevishness. "If that's so, then there are counterrevoluntionaries in the Czech government — again. They think they're taking their cues from Moscow, however. Our government has decided to move in the direction of increased socialist democracy, and Prague believes this to be a license to do whatever it likes." He glanced momentarily at Mikhailov, as if concerned that he might seem to be criticizing Romanenko. Then he looked pointedly at the general secretary's photograph and said, "It's to be hoped that no one moves too quickly in *any* direction. These things need time." He drank the contents of his wineglass at a gulp.

And who was *that* meant for, Mikhailov asked himself. Tolbukhin and the Third Directorate, or my uncle, or the General Staff? Not the last, I think; I suspect that's where it's coming from. Does it mean the army's ready to join with the KGB against my uncle and the Party, or that the KGB shouldn't push the Party to enforce a crackdown on the Czechs, or what?

Litovtsev sat up straight and pushed his chair away from the table. "Thank you for your company, gentlemen. If you'll excuse me, I have a number of things to do. Please feel free to spend whatever time you like in the officers' mess before you return to Moscow."

He stood up, imitated quickly by everyone else. Litovtsev motioned one of his aides, a major, over to him, said something inaudible in his ear, and then left the room. His guests sat down and began to talk, more noisily than before. The major walked over to Mikhailov and said quietly, "I'm Major Kapitsa. Colonel-General Litovtsev would like to know if you'd enjoy seeing a few of the sights of Prague before you go back. I'd be happy to escort you."

Litovtsev knows which side of the bread his butter's on, Mikhailov thought. He looked around the table. With Litovtsev's rather forbidding presence removed, both the talk and the alcohol were flowing more freely. He didn't care for the prospect of a drunken afternoon and a hung-over flight the next day.

"Certainly," he said. "It would be a pleasure."

"Do you have civilian clothes with you?"

"Yes." There were standing orders that *no* Red Army men, regardless of rank, were to appear in uniform in the streets of Prague. This was a legacy of the 1968 invasion, and the Kremlin's desperate efforts afterward to legitimize their intervention. Russians were to keep a low profile at all times.

"Good," Kapitsa said. "I'll change and meet you at the vehicle-park gate in fifteen minutes. It's where you came in this morning."

Kapitsa's automobile was a Czech-built Skoda with civilian license plates. "We keep a few of these cars around," he confided to Mikhailov after they left the Russian compound and were driving along the road that led along the front of Hradcany Castle. "Every so often we have to change the plates and repaint the cars; the Czechs have a nose for Russians. Try to get a beer in one of their taverns; even though you're not in uniform you'll wait a *long* time," he said. He was a blond man who would have been handsome except for a nose that had been badly broken once and poorly repaired.

"That hasn't changed much, then," said Mikhailov. "It was the same way when I was here."

"They're always sullen," Kapitsa said. "No matter what the Party says. Where would you like to go, Colonel Mikhailov?"

"I always liked the Old Town."

"We'll go over Manesuv Bridge, then, it's closest."

They were driving along Letenska Street past the Sala Terrena Gardens when Mikhailov ventured, "Colonel-General Litovtsev mentioned some problems the STB was having."

Kapitsa gave Mikhailov a sidelong glance. There were beads of sweat on his upper lip, although the car windows were wide open; it was sunny and very hot. "That's right," he said. "You haven't heard what's going on?"

"No."

"The Czech government's been easing up on things. Like at home, I'm told; I haven't been back for a while. *Literary News* has started publishing again. It's printing things that wouldn't have got past the censors six months ago. And there's supposed to be a new Charter '77 group starting up again."

"It didn't take very long, did it?" said Mikhailov. They had swung around the curve on Letenska Street and were nearing the bridge over the Vltava River, which bisected Prague. There was much more vehicle traffic than in Moscow, mostly Skodas, imported East German cars, and a few trucks.

"No. There was some trouble last night, too. A woman tried to hang a Charter '77 slogan on the base of the Hus statue over in the Old Town square. A patrol saw her and tried to pick her up. She ran and one of the idiots shot her."

"Dead?"

"Don't know. It's that kind of thing that sets off trouble; they should have let her go and picked her up later. Somebody would have informed."

They reached the bridge. Beneath it the Vltava flowed wide and blue-green, dotted with skiffs. There was a jetty a little way south of the bridge and Mikhailov could see half a dozen bathing-suited figures on it. There were swimmers in the water. It looked very peaceful.

On the other side of the bridge Kapitsa drove around the north perimeter of Krasnoarmejcu Square and turned into Kaprova Street. This was a very old district of Prague and the facades of the ancient buildings were dark with centuries of smoke. They loomed over the narrow streets, blocking out the sun.

"We'll start at the Old Town square and work outwards," Kapitsa said. "Hey. What's going on up there?"

They were nearly at the square by this time and Mikhailov could just glimpse one of the ancient mottled towers of the Tyn Church projecting into the clear blue. "There's a big crowd ahead," he said. He hadn't been watching the sidewalks particularly, and only now realized that they were crowded with people, mostly young. Almost all of them were walking toward the square, and doing so in a hurry.

Kapitsa looked in the rearview mirror. "Where in hell did they all come from?" he asked plaintively. He had slowed down and was looking worried. Three young men were crossing the street in front of the Skoda; they didn't hurry to get out of the way. As Kapitsa drove past, one of them pointed at the car and said something to his companions. All three stopped on the curb and stared fixedly at Kapitsa and Mikhailov. The one who had pointed made a gesture which wasn't quite obscene.

"They've spotted us," said Kapitsa. He drove on a few meters to where Kaprova Street debouched into the old square. The square was packed with people; at least a score were sitting on the base of the Hus statue. Somebody had draped a Czech flag over part of the statue's base. One young man was standing next to it, haranguing the crowd.

"Fuck," said Kapitsa. "They're demonstrating over that girl that was shot, I'll bet." He reached under the dash for the microphone clipped to the two-way radio, then quickly withdrew his hand. "They see the radio," he said, "they'll know we're police or Russians. Roll up your window and lock the door."

Mikhailov wound the handle. The car's internal temperature abruptly rose several degrees. Kapitsa put the Skoda into motion again, skirting the southwest edge of the square so as to leave by Melantrichova Street.

They didn't make it. There were hardly any vehicles in the square, and since theirs was moving it attracted attention. Worse, Kapitsa had to drive slowly because of the crowd flowing over the pavement toward the statue. Mikhailov was looking out the driver's window at the statue, where someone was putting up another Czech flag, when there was a tap on the glass behind him. He looked out to see the young man who had pointed at them in Kaprova Street. He had bad skin and lank yellow hair. Mikhailov nodded and smiled. The youth didn't smile back; instead he straightened up and shouted, "Russians," and then went into a stream of Czech, which Mikhailov couldn't follow. He felt his stomach turn over and the adrenalin start to flow. This was a crowd that could turn violent in seconds.

"Ah, balls," said Kapitsa, and fished under the dash for the microphone. "Yellow Control," he said into it, "this is car six. Do you know what's happening in the old square?"

"Car six, this is Yellow Control. What are you doing down there? Don't you know there's a problem in your area?"

"*Problem?*" snapped Kapitsa. "We're sitting in the middle of the problem. Why weren't we warned?"

"Please observe radio procedure, car six." The Skoda was barely moving now. The youth was still shouting and people in the nearby crowd were turning to look at Kapitsa and Mikhailov. "We only found out about it a couple of minutes ago. It's completely spontaneous. Can you get out all right?"

"Yellow Control, ask me in a minute. Keep this channel open." Kapitsa put the microphone on the seat beside him and tried to speed up. Half a dozen young men and three girls of about twenty linked arms in front of the Skoda to form a barrier. Kapitsa had to stop or run them over. Melantrichova Street was only a dozen meters away.

"Yellow Control from car six," Kapitsa said, picking up the mike. "They've formed a human chain to stop us. Were the fuck are the police?"

"Car six, they're on their way. Where are you exactly?"

Mikhailov watched the crowd while Kapitsa described their location. The young Czechs blocking the way to Malantrichova Street stared back at him, hostile and hard-faced. Outside Mikhailov's side window he could see only more of the crowd; the car was completely surrounded. A gob of spittle struck the window and rolled tiredly down the glass. Somebody began pushing up and down on the Skoda's rear bumper, rocking the small vehicle.

"They're getting nasty," Kapitsa said urgently into the microphone. "How long before the police get here?"

"We're checking, car six, Wait."

"Are you carrying a gun?" asked Kapitsa.

"No. Are you?"

"Yes. But I don't want to get it out yet. Provocative." Kapitsa engaged the clutch and edged the Skoda forward, pressing against the human chain in front. At first they resisted, then moved back a pace. One of the girls stumbled and almost fell. The mutter of the crowd swelled angrily. Kapitsa let the car stop, then moved forward again. This time the line refused to budge. Mikhailov realized that he was badly frightened; this was worse than being shot at in battle, where you could at least fight back. The violence embryonic in the mob was primeval, psychologically overwhelming.

"Yellow Control," said Kapitsa. "Where —"

A heavy stone smashed into the Skoda's hood, bounced, and struck the windshield, which starred crazily. The car began to rock violently again. The mob surrounding it roared. Another stone, a cobble likely, hit the rear window and broke clear through it.

"Where are the police?" Kapitsa yelled into the microphone. Mikhailov couldn't hear the response, if there was one. He ducked sideways as his window was smashed in by a metal bar. A hand followed the bar and groped for the door handle. Mikhailov grabbed the hand and ground the wrist across the ragged edge of the broken glass. There was a howl of pain and the arm withdrew, leaving blood behind. Kapitsa was revving the engine despite the chain blocking the way, but the car didn't move; the rear wheels were being lifted off the ground. The Skoda tilted to the left.

"They're trying to turn us over," Kapitsa shouted to Mikhailov, the microphone, or both. He fumbled in his jacket and pulled out a Makarov pistol. The mob on his side saw it and tried to back away but the crowd pressure behind them was too great. Kapitsa fired a shot upward through the shattered windshield. The human chain in front of them broke apart.

It was too late. The car lurched and turned onto its side. Mikhailov fell heavily against Kapitsa. The air was suddenly full of the smell of gasoline.

"They're going to burn us," yelled Kapitsa, panic in his voice.

Mikhailov scrambled into the back seat to get off his companion, striking his right forearm on the gearshift as he did so. The mustard-gas burn flared with pain.

The stench of gasoline was stronger in the back of the car. The shouting outside reached a new crescendo. Mikhailov twisted about and began kicking at what was left of the rear window. He could hear Kapitsa cursing steadily in the front seat, but there were no more shots.

The window was finally clear of glass. Mikhailov hesitated, not wanting to crawl out of the Skoda into the hands of the mob. He peered out at the crowd.

The young man who had pointed at them in Kaprova Street was trying to light a cluster of matches.

"Get out, Kapitsa," Mikhailov yelled and launched himself through the window. His ankle caught on the window frame and he hit the cobbles, nearly winding himself. The cobbles were wet: gasoline from the Skoda's upended tank. Mikhailov rolled and kept on rolling, right into the crowd.

Behind him there was a soft *whump* and a wave of heat struck him. He struggled to his knees and looked back. The Skoda was enveloped in flames and the crowd was surging away from it, several people with their clothes on fire. Kapitsa had got out in time; Mikhailov could see him pushing into the mob, trying for Melantrichova Street. Screaming filled the air. Somebody kicked Mikhailov in the small of the back and he went down. Another kick caught his bad arm and he nearly fainted.

This is how it ends, he thought, feeling the side of his head strike the cobbles. All through Afghanistan, and now this. Valeria. Never when you expect it.

A stream of icy water, hard as an iron bar, slammed into his side, drove him bodily into the gutter, and passed on. He raised himself on one elbow.

From Melantrichova and Zelezna streets, wedges of Czech police in riot gear and supported by water cannon were pouring into the square. Mikhailov pulled himself onto the curb, cradling his arm, and waited for it to be over.

Moscow
Wednesday, July 7

THE POLITBURO COMMITTEE ROOM seemed to reverberate in the silence that followed Lebedev's pounding on the green-baize tabletop. The thirteen Politburo members, even Smilga, were staring at him with considerable surprise. The old ideologue seldom raised his voice, much less hammered on the table with his fist.

"If the chairman of the præsidium would desist from his dramatics," said Romanenko, "we might be able to address this issue more rationally."

Lebedev pointed a withered finger at Romanenko. "Rationally?" he said in his thin voice. He was the oldest of them all, nearly ninety, and the only one among them who had survived the upheavals wrought by the revolution and the civil war and the famines, the purges, the show trials, Stalin, Beria, Vishinsky. He was an iron Marxist and as rigid as the barrel of a gun.

"Rationally?" he repeated. "Vasily Romanenko, you are threatening to light a fire here and in the Warsaw Pact that may consume us all. Look at what just happened in Prague. Do you think it will end there? Have you forgotten 1956 and the Hungarians? The political and economic changes you propose to announce to the Warsaw Pact leaders at this Leningrad meeting of yours, they're bourgeois revisionism. They will open the doors to nationalism and capitalism again. Everything the revolution stands for, everything we suffered from the

Fascists in the great Patriotic War, will have been *pointless*."
He seemed about to pound on the table again, but refrained.

"For the twentieth time," Romanenko said wearily, "I am
not calling the Warsaw Pact leaders to Leningrad to announce
the reintroduction of capitalism, either here or anywhere else.
Lenin permitted the employment of up to ten people by small
entrepreneurs during the New Economic Policy in the twenties.
I am only proposing something like that."

"That was an emergency," Lebedev snapped. "With the
NEP Lenin had to take a step back from pure Marxism because
we were about to be destroyed by bourgeois counterrevolutionaries and capitalists. He would never have done so otherwise.
That's not all, there's also the censorship —"

"I'm not going to argue with you about what Lenin *would*
have done," Romanenko broke in, suppressing an urge to shout
at the top of his voice. "We can't know what Lenin *would* have
done. The fact remains that we also have an emergency,
although we've been careful to conceal it. A quarter of a
century ago Khrushchev promised we'd achieve full communism
by 1980. In 1980 the general population was worse off than it
was when he made the promise. We haven't been able to feed
ourselves for years. Konstantin Chernenko said we were to exert
every effort to overtake the west in high technology by the turn
of the century. We're further behind than ever. Children's toys
in the United States contain electronic circuits we can't even
build. One of the promises of the revolution was that we would
overtake and outproduce capitalism, so that the superiority of
our system would be clear to everyone. It's far from clear to
anyone with eyes to see. Comrades, we have to find a better
way of achieving communism."

"What methods do you propose?" asked Zarudin. He
flicked a disdainful finger at his copy of Romanenko's proposed
political and economic policies. "These? Repeal the criminal-
code articles dealing with private employers? Let the Warsaw
Pact nations decide what products they want to send us, what
they'll keep? Let Solidarity revive in Poland, Charter '77 in
Czechoslovakia? Reduce censorship and permit every subversive
and malcontent to shriek his freakish ideas to the population at

large? Why don't you get somebody to organize a Fascist party while you're at it? It would make as much sense."

"I have explained this all before," Romanenko said tightly. "I am not going to go through it again. We cannot mouth the same exhausted slogans at the Russian people forever; we need constructive action. If we don't believe our slogans any more, why should they? I am trying to offer us all a fresh start."

"We don't need fresh starts of this kind," Lebedev growled. "The people need better indoctrination and political instruction, that's what they need. If we've failed, it's in not keeping the spirit of the revolution alive, the spirit of sacrifice. I call for more ideological vigilance, not this milk-and-water slop that's not communism but doesn't have the nerve to call itself bourgeois-revisionist capitalism either."

"In the name of Lenin and holy Mother Russia," Romanenko exploded, finally, and momentarily, losing his temper, "we've had seventy years of indoctrination and sacrifice and it's not working." He paused and unclenched his hands. "We need indoctrination, yes, and there will still be sacrifices to be made, but let's turn the indoctrination into education, let's show some confidence that the people can see what needs to be done, and will help do it. The Party and the people are supposed to be one, or had you forgotten that? The Russian people don't want western political systems anyway, they want a Party and leadership that don't lie to them and don't make them stand in line two hours for a kilo of bread."

"You're digging the grave of communism," Lebedev snarled. "The day after the Warsaw Pact leaders get home from this precious Leningrad summit of yours, the first shovelful of earth will be turned."

"What would you prefer?" Romanenko snarled back. "Simultaneous revolts in Poland, Hungary, East Germany, Czechoslovakia? We tried to mobilize to invade Poland over Solidarity; remember what happened? Nothing worked. Minister Yasev, what would happen if all four of those countries went up in flames tomorrow? Could we handle them?"

Yasev looked unhappy. "We could," he said, "but it would take time."

Konstantin Tsander spoke for the first time since Lebedev banged on the table. "Prolonged mobilization would cause severe dislocation in industry and agriculture. We would have to buy even more grain from the Americans. If they would sell it to us. That is to say nothing of the political and diplomatic embarrassment."

"Tighter control is the answer," Lebedev said. "We can forestall any counterrevolution if we are vigilant."

"Perhaps," Tsander said. "But—"

Smilga raised a hand. "I would like to speak to that."

There was a fractional pause in the room, while alliances were reexamined. "Go ahead," said Romanenko.

"It is certainly possible to increase our vigilance," said the KGB chairman, "and that of the Warsaw Pact security forces as well. But I am not certain that that is wise at the moment. We are gaining considerable goodwill in the west, or so Foreign Minister Polunin has told us, with the general secretary's decision to leave Afghanistan to its own devices. We would not want to jeopardize that, surely, with rigorous measures against malcontents." Smilga looked into Romanenko's eyes for a moment. "And it is clear that we need the goodwill of the west, if we are in such a precarious position as the general secretary suggests. I believe that we should give Comrade Vasily Romanenko's new policies a chance to prove themselves."

He ceased talking and sat back in his chair. A long silence ensued.

"Have you lost your mind?" Lebedev said at last. "When the KGB will have to pick up the pieces afterwards?"

Smilga adjusted his shoulders against the back of the chair, in a movement that was not quite a shrug.

"Vote," said Konstantin Tsander.

Vasily Romanenko's policy paper was adopted, eight to five. To the consternation of some members present, Smilga voted with Romanenko.

"Why in the name of all the devils of hell did you do that?" Zarudin raged. He was standing in the middle of his living room, waving a large tumbler of vodka in the air. Some of the vodka had spilled onto his shirt, leaving semitransparent patches. The Politburo meeting had been over for two hours.

Smilga was sitting on the couch under the window. Zarudin hadn't given him anything to drink. "I had to," he said.

"Why? What for?"

"Romanenko was going to get his policies adopted anyway," said Smilga. "If I had not supported him, he would have begun looking harder than he already is for ways of removing me. We cannot afford that. I have consolidated my position, and in doing so strengthened yours."

"You've helped give him the opportunity to have his Leningrad summit this month," Zarudin said angrily. "We needed more time."

"There is no way to delay the summit," Smilga pointed out. "So we must take the opportunity it offers. Moving against Romanenko now carries considerable risk for us, but if we wait he may become stronger yet. He also is taking a risk, in convoking his meeting this summer. I believe he would have preferred to delay it, until he has consolidated his position more. I think we must act now, while he's still vulnerable."

"Romanenko," said Zarudin. "How did we ever come to be saddled with Romanenko?"

"There are always enemies of the revolution," Smilga said. "May I have something to drink?"

Zarudin handed him the vodka bottle and let him find his own glass.

"Didn't it go well?" asked Ekaterina. She was curled up at the end of the big velvet settee in the flat's living room. The lamp on the end table threw a pool of yellow light over her lap and the ball of yarn in it. She was knitting.

"No," Romanenko said. "It didn't. Lebedev thinks I'm digging Russia's grave."

"He's almost in the grave himself," she said, counting stitches with an index finger. "He wants everyone else to join him. Especially you."

"He has a good deal of company," said Romanenko.

"You got the policy paper through," she pointed out. "It's a start. What did Dmitri Smilga think of that?"

"He voted for it," Romanenko said.

She dropped a stitch and put her needles down. "He what?"

"He voted for it," said Romanenko. "It doesn't mean he's in favor of it, only that he's securing his position a little. He knows I daren't force the removal of someone who's voting for me. It would look too arbitrary. It's the sort of thing Stalin used to do."

"What are you going to do with him?"

"I don't know yet," Romanenko said. He ruminated while his wife's knitting needles clicked.

I have to protect my flanks, he thought. While I'm busy here I need to convince the west, especially the Americans, that I'm no threat to them, that I'm in control, that I'm exactly the sort of Soviet leader Washington has always wanted to deal with: liberal, pragmatic, unaggressive. Novosti and Tass and *Pravda* won't do for that message, I need a channel to the west the Americans will believe, or at least pay attention to. I need my very own propaganda organ.

He had been thinking about this for some weeks, but the opportunity of achieving it had only recently presented itself. Romanenko made a decision.

"Ekaterina," he said, "I want you to do something for me."

Uspenskoye
Sunday, July 11

IT WAS EARLY AFTERNOON. On the shaded terrace behind Romanenko's dacha the air was pleasantly cool; a weather front had passed over in the night, taking with it the damp heat of the previous three days. On the terrace, sitting on white wrought-iron chairs around a table on which lay the remains of an excellent lunch, were Mikhailov, Nadia, Romanenko, and Ekaterina. Chantal Mallory was leaning on the stone balustrade, watching Valeria chase butterflies on the lawn.

"It must be a relief to have those bandages off, Andrei," Ekaterina said. "Does it still hurt?"

"Not much," Mikhailov said. The mustard-gas burns were nearly healed, but there was still an angry brownish-red scar across the back of his hand and up his arm. The bandages had come off the previous Wednesday, two days after he returned from Prague. "I just have to be careful not to hit it on anything."

Chantal came back from the balustrade and sat down again. She was wearing a pleated white dress and a single fine gold chain. Mikhailov, watching the grace of her movements, felt a curious constricting sensation in his chest; he had noticed it for the first time the day before, when Beth and Eric Fowler took them both on a picnic in Gorki Park.

"You were lucky you weren't killed," said Ekaterina. "Not in Afghanistan, in Prague I mean. Mobs in Prague! Why can't they wait for things to happen normally?"

Chantal nodded. "There was a demonstration in Prague," she said. Mikhailov knew she was wondering why she was at Uspenskoye; Ekaterina had telephoned the evening before to ask Mikhailov and his household to lunch, and then she had added, apparently as an afterthought, "And bring that Canadian girl your uncle was so impressed with." They had all driven down to the dacha in Mikhailov's borrowed Zhiguli.

"Prague was the most overt display of discontent," Romanenko said. "There are similar undercurrents in Poland, East Germany, and Hungary."

They were all silent. Mikhailov stole a glance at Chantal. She seemed to be listening to something, perhaps the distant murmur of the brook in the wood at the end of the lawn.

Romanenko sipped at his coffee. "Miss Mallory, I confess I have done some extensive checking into your background."

Mikhailov thought his heart would stop. The KGB are in the house, he thought, they'll take both of us at once.

"May I ask why?" Chantal asked, interested but unconcerned.

"Certainly. You're an excellent journalist. And Canadian, rather than American. Your magazine has always been reasonably objective about Soviet problems and behavior. Your articles have given me personally less irritation than those of a number of your colleagues. I think that is something that should be rewarded. Now, I know what you are thinking: you're thinking that if you accept this reward your journalistic integrity will be called into question. You are also thinking that if I am so comfortable with your portrayal of Soviet society, perhaps you had better be more critical in future. Please don't leap to such assumptions. What I want to offer you is simply first access — what do you call it? — to some important news."

"A scoop," supplied Chantal. Mikhailov felt himself emerging from the momentary nightmare.

"Yes, a scoop, very apt. Miss Mallory — "

"Chantal, please."

"Chantal," Romanenko went on. "Tomorrow I am going to hold a press conference, at Saint George Hall. At this conference I will announce that the leaders of the Warsaw Treaty nations and I are going to meet in Leningrad to resolve the long-standing differences between Moscow and the treaty governments. The Council for Mutual Economic Assistance will be given new priorities, some of the most rigorous forms of press censorship will be lifted, and our Warsaw Treaty allies will be allowed to pursue a more independent line of internal development. In short, if the Czechs want to indulge in another 'Prague Spring,' as they called it, Moscow won't stop them. We cannot afford to be so rigid in our ideology any more, or we will strangle ourselves."

Chantal's mouth had dropped open with an astonishment that was probably real. Nadia put her cup down with a clatter. "But... Uncle Vasily, what if everyone is allowed to do just as they like? What if the Warsaw Pact countries side with the Americans against us? What if the Hungarians revolt again?"

Romanenko put up a hand. "There are restrictions. Membership in the Warsaw Pact is not voluntary. We will keep our armed forces in the Pact countries as long as the Americans keep theirs in Europe. We won't permit the dismantling of socialist parties or governments or reversion to capitalist economies. What we want to develop is socialism with a human face." He lowered his hand. "That's all I can tell you just now. The Politburo, the government, and the Party are all in full agreement with this policy, so I can't be accused of either going off on my own path or of betraying state secrets." He smiled faintly. "I would ask, however, Chantal, that you not file your story before the end of the press conference."

"Thank you, Secretary," Chantal said. "I promise I won't use it before the conference. May I ask why..."

"Why I decided to give you the information? It's very simple. You're beautiful, competent, and a friend of Andrei's. And you have the inestimable advantage of not being an American, and so have fewer obvious axes to grind." Romanenko was getting up. "Could you excuse Andrei and myself for a few minutes?" he said. "I have a matter to discuss with him."

Ekaterina busied herself with coffee cups. Romanenko and Mikhailov walked down the steps onto the lawn.

"Let's go on down to the stream," said Romanenko. "The sun's very strong."

It was cool and fresh under the birches and the oaks. The stream was two meters across, running clear over a stony bed between banks of emerald turf. At this point the streambed formed a small, noisy cascade half a meter high, and there was a grassy slope beside it. The two men sat down on the grass.

"Cigarette?" asked Romanenko, offering a packet. Mikhailov accepted. They smoked and watched the water flow.

"There won't be any microphones here," Romanenko said. "I don't believe there are any on the terrace, either, but I can't be sure." He stopped. Mikhailov waited.

"The meeting I referred to will take place in Leningrad two weeks from tomorrow," Romanenko resumed. "I'm having it in Leningrad so the atmosphere will be freer; there are too many bloody memories associated with Moscow. Andrei, the political situation is not at all settled. Not at all. There is a tremendous resistance to what I'm trying to do." He took a deep drag on his cigarette and turned to look at his nephew. "There is a significant chance that my career won't survive the next few months. I originally intended to have the Leningrad summit next spring, but my opponents have been more vigorous than I'd hoped, so I've decided to move it up. It's a calculated risk. Our European allies are powder kegs with short fuses at the moment, and even with our old techniques of military force and political terror we couldn't handle all of them at once, if they exploded simultaneously. We have to get more willing cooperation from the Warsaw Pact allies so that we can concentrate on solving our problems at home. That's partly why I've started negotiations on Afghanistan. I hope to have us out of there by the spring."

Mikhailov nodded. Romanenko flipped his cigarette into the water above the cascade. The tiny white chip spun in an eddy and then slid over the brink of the waterfall into the white foam at its foot. Mikhailov watched for the butt to surface, but it didn't reappear. He threw his own cigarette end after it.

"You won't be going back to the training directorate," Romanenko said abruptly.

"I won't? Why not? I've only just been assigned there."

"That was necessary," said Romanenko. "It was a plausible

reason to return you to Moscow permanently, rather than keep you in Afghanistan where you're of more obvious and immediate use. Now that you're here, no one will pay any particular attention to another reassignment."

Mikhailov felt a wash of irritation. He was being moved around like a chess piece by too many people: first Gordik, then Tolbukhin, then the Americans, and now his uncle.

"I wouldn't do this," Romanenko went on, "but I may need you soon. The major power behind my position is the armed forces, particularly the army. Not all officers agree with what I'm doing. I need someone I can trust in a responsible military position in Leningrad. I've arranged for you to be posted as deputy commander of the Thirty-seventh Guards Rifle Division there. Unfortunately I can't make you full commander, as the incumbent has too much seniority and there's no plausible reason to relieve him. Once he does move along, however, you'll take over the command. From there you'll be in a good position to move into the operations directorate on the General Staff in Moscow. Until then, however, you'll be where I need you. I know it's a good deal to ask."

Mikhailov's reactions were mixed. Deputy divisional commander was a substantial appointment, but it was a step away from the General Staff and could be seen as a demotion, from a political point of view. It would be some time before he started up into the higher echelons of the military hierarchy. That wouldn't please the Americans. But then it might cause them to lose some of their interest in him, which would be a step toward freeing himself from them completely. Uncle Vasily's doing all the right things, Mikhailov thought, my reasons for working with the Americans have all but disappeared. I should tell Chantal it's over. . . . How can I go on seeing her if I do that?

"Andrei? How do you feel about it?"

"I — well, it's all right. I've been away from Valeria so much, that's all."

"Oh, you'll have to take her with you. Nadia as well, if she wants to go. I'll arrange a decent apartment, you won't have any problems there. One of my aides can arrange to have your belongings moved."

Shit, Mikhailov thought. Tolbukhin. What's he going to think about this? Although even the KGB won't be able be block the posting if Uncle Vasily exerts himself. But I'll have some explaining to do, they'll think I arranged it for some reason of my own.

Romanenko said, "If what's worrying you is your other employer, don't worry. There will be no trouble from General Tolbukhin."

Several apparently unrelated events arranged themselves into a pattern in Mikhailov's head. Gordik, who hadn't cared about Mikhailov's recall. Tolbukhin's concern, the first time they met, about the army's attitudes to the regime. Litovtsev's obtuse comments in Prague, directed not against Romanenko's reforms but against KGB interference with them. The posting, unresisted, to the division in Leningrad. Tolbukhin was working not for the KGB but for Romanenko.

"You knew," said Mikhailov. "How long?"

"For a long time," said Romanenko. "Not all the KGB supports Chairman Smilga and the neo-Stalinists. Just as not all the Party, nor the military, support what I'm trying to accomplish."

"Chantal?" asked Mikhailov. "Where does she fit into all this?"

"I may need an unofficial communications link with the west," said Romanenko. "The west doesn't trust our press, with good reason. Through her I can speak clearly, if need be."

"It could be dangerous for her," said Mikhailov, aware as he spoke of the irony of his words. "She might be asked to leave the country."

"She'll be protected," said Romanenko. "As long as I'm capable of it."

Ekaterina was calling their names from the house. The voice was very faint, obscured by the rustle and splash of the stream.

"We'd better go back," Mikhailov said. "They'll think we've fallen in and drifted away."

He was surprised at the strength of his uncle's grip on his arm. "Andrei," Romanenko said, "if it goes wrong, in Leningrad or anywhere else, get out. Forget everything else, get yourself and Valeria and Nadia out of the country. In Lengingrad you're close to the border, you'll have a better chance. If I lose, and the Berias and the Stalins come back, they'll try to kill us all. It will be the Great Purges over again. For my sake, for all of them, promise me, *get them out*."

"I will," said Mikhailov. "I promise."

"Good," said Romanenko, releasing his arm. "Let's go back and have a cognac before you leave."

KGB CHAIRMAN DMITRI SMILGA had an earache and the pain was making him even more irritable than usual. His driver had the misfortune to let the Zil limousine jerk to a stop in the courtyard of Lefortovo Prison, and the sudden movement drove what felt like a hot nail through Smilga's right eardrum. He swore violently. The driver hunched lower in the front seat, as though ducking a stream of bullets. Smilga got out of the car, slamming the door violently — which made his ear hurt even more — and searched in his pocket for the vial of painkillers. He had avoided taking any all morning, since he needed a clear head for the business at hand, but he gave in now and put two tablets into his mouth. As he crunched them, dry and bitter, he looked up at the courtyard walls. They were a dirty mustard color, with peeling patches under the windowsills. The windows were barred and blank. Lefortovo was the main KGB prison in Moscow now; with the organization's expansion in the 1970s the old headquarters at the Lubianka in Dzerzhinsky Square could no longer provide the luxury of cells on the premises. The basements of the Lubianka were needed for offices, and so the dark cellars of the old building had been cleaned, painted, brightened, and furnished, leaving not a trace of the agonies of their former occupants; KGB men were not, fortunately, susceptible to hauntings. Now ideological heretics were confined here at Lefortovo, or in camps outside the city, or in carefully specialized mental hospitals.

The pills left a bitter aftertaste. Smilga, observed nervously by the two guards beside the double doors, walked toward the entrance to the administration wing. He was two meters from the doors when one of them opened and Semyon Yegrov came out. Yegrov gave a slight formal bow and said, "Chairman, I'm sorry I didn't meet your car. The questioning is still going on."

"Where is he?" asked Smilga. The two men entered the building, much to the relief of the guards.

"The west block," said Yegrov. Yegrov was head of the special-investigations department of the KGB, which handled cases of suspected treason or high-level espionage, as well as major penetrations of the KGB or military intelligence, the GRU.

"What have you got?" Smilga asked.

"Apart from the photographs, very little. The man was no more than a courier."

"So you think," Smilga observed snappishly. "If you've got so little out of him, how can you be sure?"

"Quite so, Comrade Chairman. I spoke too quickly. Certainly there is more to be discovered."

They walked through the corridors, which were painted a pale muddy green and whose floors were covered with frayed red carpeting, until they reached the interrogation cells. Yegrov unlocked the fourth one in the row and he and Smilga went inside. A naked man was lying on a wooden table, secured by straps at his ankles, knees, belly, wrists, and neck. Two men in prison-warders' uniforms stood at the head off the table, talking quietly to each other. They broke off quickly at the sight of Yegrov and Smilga and snapped to attention.

"Anything?" asked Yegrov.

"No, I'm sorry, Investigator," said the taller of the two. "We really haven't had enough time yet."

"Work faster," Smilga said. The man on the table was an Afghan. He had been wounded, trailed, and eventually captured by border guards at the north end of the Bolan Pass. He had clearly been making for Pakistan. The fact that he was a mujahidin courier hadn't been suspected until the border guards found the remnants of a package of documents he had tried to burn. Most of it had been reduced to ash but there were a few scraps left, and a roll of film. The courier had tried to expose the film but hadn't remained conscious long enough to complete the job; there remained one full frame and two partials that the light hadn't reached. The courier had been captured on 18 June, but in the chaotic aftermath of the STARLIGHT debacle no one had bothered to question him for another twelve days. Three days after that, military intelligence in Kabul finally remembered to get the film developed. They were so horrified by what it contained that they sat on the film for another week before they reluctantly, and only because General Gordik of the Kabul Third Directorate had found out about the film, released it to the KGB counterintelligence section in Kabul.

The film appeared to have contained the full operational plans for STARLIGHT. The courier had been whisked out of his Kabul prison cell and flown to Moscow, where the Lefortovo specialists had been interrogating him for twelve hours without apparent result. Smilga had decided, that morning, to take a hand in the situation himself.

"Yes, Comrade Chairman," said one of the specialists. We — "

"Don't explain," said Smilga. "Just do it." He turned to Yegrov. "Do either of these officers speak the prisoner's language?"

"Both of them, Chairman. I made sure."

Smilga went over to the table and stared down into the man's face. The courier's eyes were glazed, pupils contracted, and he was sweating, although it was cold and damp in the cell. "Drugs?" asked Smilga.

"Yes, Chairman. Aminazin and sulfazin. We're going to administer Ataryl-Q as soon as they've taken full effect."

Ataryl-Q was a refinement of scopalamine; it loosened inhibitions and lowered psychological resistance, especially when combined with the extreme physical discomfort produced by the other two drugs.

"Drain him dry," said Smilga. "But don't kill him doing it. I'll have all your heads if you do."

"We'll use extreme caution," one of the interrogation specialists assured him.

"I don't care whether you use caution or clubs," Smilga snapped. "Don't kill him, and find out where and when he got that film. I want to know by tomorrow at this time." Privately he didn't think the courier would be much help, but it was necessary to cover all eventualities. In any case, a special-investigations team was already on its way to Kabul; they had been instructed to find the leak but not to take any action on their findings without orders from Smilga himself. In a way, the STARLIGHT leak was a powerful weapon in Smilga's hands; he almost wished he had arranged it himself. It would embarrass the army and strengthen his hold on Defense Minister Yasev, which would help undercut Romanenko's power base. In addition, since Tolbukhin's people hadn't spotted it, the leak would be another stick with which to beat the Third Directorate chief. Tolbukhin was entirely too sympathetic to the military's problems for Smilga's taste, but his experience and skill made him indispensable, to a point. When Romanenko was disposed of there would be a reckoning, in the shape of a thorough purge of the military command structure and of the Party itself. If Tolbukhin went along wholeheartedly with the purge, well and good; if he didn't, he could join it as one of the purged. It was past time, in Smilga's opinion, for the Party, the government, and the military to be cleansed of all revisionists and heretics, potential and real. And if Oleg Zarudin interfered, he could be retired. Smilga had no particular desire to be general secretary himself, but he had every intention of controlling whoever held that dangerous post.

"There's somebody meeting me," he told Yegrov. "Take me back to the courtyard. I'm leaving shortly but my car is to stay here until I get back."

In the courtyard a yellow Zhiguli was drawn up beside Smilga's Zil. There was only one man it it, dressed in civilian clothes. Smilga got into the car and the driver turned around while the guards opened the courtyard gates. Only when they were through the gates and into the street did Smilga realize, with some relief, that the painkiller was taking hold. His eardrum was now only a sullen throb.

"Drive out Gofkovskoye Schosse," he said. "We have to be there in thirty minutes."

The driver nodded. He was a tall man, barely fitting the Zhiguli's seat, and possessed a seamed, weatherbeaten face. A long, thin scar ran from his right cheekbone down to the line of his jaw. His name was Leonid Kinyapin. He was a lieutenant-general and head of the KGB Ninth Guards Directorate, which was charged with the protection of the senior members of the Party and government. He was also a person who thought very much like Smilga. The two men had known each other for nineteen years.

They drove for several minutes before Kinyapin asked, "They're expecting us, Dmitri Alexeyevitch?" He geared down for the turn onto Entusiastov Schosse, the road leading out of the city.

"Naturally," Smilga said. "You took precautions yourself?"

"My staff doesn't ask me where I'm going."

"Good."

They drove past Izmaylovsky Park, on out of the city and past the Ring Motorway. The area was still built up to their right, but on the left of the road the buildings gave way to fields and occasional patches of woodland.

Several kilometers farther on, buildings began to appear again on the left. These were part of the outlying suburb of Balashikha. Just past the suburb Kinyapin turned right, onto a paved lane that led into a stand of pines. Bordering the pines was a chain-link fence, topped with barbed wire, and a gate with a wooden guardhouse. Two KGB guards with blue lapel flashes and trouser stripes were stationed at the gate. They inspected both Smilga's and Kinyapin's identification minutely, and then respectfully waved the Zhiguli through.

Beyond the fence the road continued through another pine wood, a deeper one than the first. On the other side of this wood lay the complex of buildings the KGB referred to simply as "Balashikha." They were constructed of grayish-yellow brick in an uninspired style: flat roofs, tall, narrow windows, poured-concrete steps and porches. The area was dotted with trees and there were flower beds with petunias in them. The plants were wilted; it had been very dry for the past week.

Kinyapin stopped the car outside a long two-story building and he and Smilga got out. Inside the front door they were met by an immaculate KGB captain who inspected their identification again and then requested them — politely — to follow. He led them through the building and out a back door. Behind the first building stood a much smaller one, which had more flower beds in front of it. These were well watered, a blaze of white and pink petunias. On the sun porch attached to the front of the building, which was the home of the Balashikha complex's commandant, sat the commandant himself. His name was Vladimir Lazarev, and he was head of Department Eight of Subdirectorate S of the KGB First Directorate. Subdirectorate S controlled KGB illegal agents throughout the world, and in 1972 had absorbed what had hitherto been Department V, the independent KGB organ specializing in what was euphemistically referred to as "executive action." Colonel Lazarev was Department Eight's second commandant, the first having been retired by Smilga shortly after he became head of the KGB. Balashikha, as well as being Department Eight's headquarters, was a school for the training of terrorists. Here also was carried out the detailed planning and organization of "executive action:" assassination, kidnapping, sabotage, and extortion with violence.

Lazarev stood up and the three men exchanged greetings. Smilga asked, "Can we find a quiet place? We have some important planning to do."

Colonel Lazarev nodded and led them upstairs to his office. It was a utilitarian place with white walls, a large desk with two telephones on it, a settee covered in green corduroy, and a pair of armchairs upholstered in a rough, grayish fabric. On a small table between the two chairs sat an ice bucket from which protruded the neck of a vodka bottle, and between the chairs and the couch was a low coffee table bearing a selection of *zakuski*, appetizers: cold sturgeon, bread, deep-fried cheese, butter. Smilga looked at the ice bucket with some relief. His ear was beginning to hurt again. He and Kinyapin sat on the chairs while Colonel Lazarev busied himself with the bottle and glasses. Outside the window Smilga could see more buildings and a line of woods beyond them. Lazarev saw his look, handed his guests their vodka, and closed the venetian blinds. Sitting down on the couch, he raised his glass in a silent toast. The three men drank.

"Let's get down to business," said Smilga. Lazarev refilled their glasses. "There's agreement," the KGB chairman went on, "that the general secretary's insane behavior can't be allowed to continue. That is the consensus of the responsible senior members of the Party." This was not true, Smilga reflected, but Kinyapin and Lazarev didn't know it, nor would it make any difference to them if they did; they owed their careers to Smilga and would follow his orders without question. "It's sooner than I wanted to execute the operation, but this Leningrad summit of his has left us no choice. If Romanenko's harebrained schemes are endorsed by counterrevolutionary elements in the Warsaw Pact governments our job will be made even more difficult. We have to cut off the head of this snake of counter-revolution, if you take my meaning, and the head will be in Leningrad on the twenty-sixth. As soon as the summit opens but before the delegates and Romanenko have a chance to start talking, we'll arrest the lot of them. They're going to be meeting in the Mariinsky Palace on Saint Isaac's Square starting at half-past one. Kinyapin, your Guards Directorate will seal off the palace and hold it against all comers, not that we need expect any particular resistance. They will also take the Warsaw Pact delegates into custody. Colonel Lazarev, I want a select team of your best people to carry out the arrest of Romanenko himself. All of them are to be taken out of the city as quickly as possible. Have them flown immediately to Kirov and held in the KGB barracks there; I want them out of the way while the Central Committee convenes in Moscow to select a legitimate Party leadership. There will be a number of Central Committee members and members of the Secretariat to be detained as well, but the Second Directorate staff will deal with that. Within thirty-six hours I want detailed plans of how you intend to carry out these assignments." He took a sheaf of papers out of his jacket. "This is a preliminary agenda, a list of where the delegates will be staying, and a number of other things you'll need to know. See me at Dzerzhinsky Square at nine o'clock the day after tomorrow, and bring your operations plans. Don't make any mistakes, and *don't* involve any of your staff at this point. Do the work yourselves. You may select personnel but don't give them any orders until I've gone over everything with you. Is that quite clear?"

The two men nodded. "What about the army?" asked Kinyapin. "Romanenko's done a lot for them in the past few months. Misguided though his actions are," he added hastily.

"Don't worry about the army," Smilga said. "If you do your job properly, it'll all be over too fast for them to react. And there are long-term plans for ensuring that they don't interfere later on."

Kinyapin nodded again. Although Smilga intended Kinyapin's Guards Directorate — which included the full-scale and well-equipped Dzerzhinsky Division, based just outside Moscow — to provide for the central government's safety during the purge of the armed forces and the Party, it would be poor security to disclose the breadth of his plans before Romanenko's overthrow. The purge itself would be carried out by the Second Directorate, which was responsible for political control of the general population and would arrest civilian targets, and the Third Directorate, which would detain key military personnel. Smilga estimated that he could comfortably eliminate any military resistance to the purge before the officers could react effectively; after all, he had at his disposal, besides the Dzerzhinksy Division and the KGB Guards Directorate, the MVD militia and police, the KGB internal-security troops, and the tens of thousands of men of the Border Guards Directorate. As well, Defense Minister Yasev's support of Romanenko was far from wholehearted. Yasev would dither, hoping that his influence might mitigate the extent of the purge and that, by remaining uncommitted, he might retain his political and military position. If he failed to take action for even a few hours, it would be too late. Too late, particularly, for Yasev. Smilga had no use for a man whose allegiances could be shifted so easily.

He stood up. Despite the vodka, his earache had returned. "You have thirty-six hours," he said. "You can imagine how important this is to your careers."

Moscow
Friday, July 16

MIKHAILOV LEFT THE METRO and walked over to the Berezovskaya Embankment and the ferry dock on the river. One of the ferryboats that served as both public transit and excursion vessel was about to cast off. Mikhailov paid his twenty kopecks — the fare hadn't changed in years — and went up to the second level. It was glass-enclosed, except over the stern where there was an open deck area. As he walked out of the cabin a raindrop stuck his cheek, cool and fresh.

She was there. He went and leaned on the rail beside her. Beneath them the ferry's engines rumbled, its propellors kicking up muddy water and bits of flotsam, and a gap appeared between the boat's side and the dock. When they were a meter away from the land Mikhailov said, "Hello, Chantal."

"Hello, Andrei. How are you?"

"Busy." He had invited her on the ferry ride as they were leaving Uspenskoye the previous Sunday, but he hadn't told her about his transfer to Leningrad. He had also been debating all week whether to tell the Americans he could no longer work for them. He had made one drop of information about the Prague riot and everything he could safely find out about the General Staff Training Directorate, but even as he was doing so he felt like a traitor. It was an experience he hadn't had in Afghanistan, nor when he first contacted the Americans. If Vasily Romanenko were like the rest of them in the Party, Mikhailov thought as he watched the dock recede, I wouldn't be feeling this way. How can I work against a man who really is trying to solve my country's problems? I should be concentrating on helping him, not the Americans. They can't do nearly as much as he can.

He glanced around. There was no one else on the fantail. There was not much point in hiding his association with Chantal anyway; the KGB would be well aware of it by now. As long as the Second Directorate's suspicions weren't raised by accident or clumsiness on his or her part they were safe enough. With the system of drops now in place he didn't need to pass her any documentary information.

"Have they been watching you lately?" he asked.

"No. Unless it's from a great distance." She was looking off to the right, where the tower of the foreign ministry jabbed into the low gray sky. There was a breeze now, caused by the ferry's movement, and it blew a few strands of black hair across her mouth. She brushed them away and went on, "The militia at my apartment building has been unusually polite, though. And the Novosti people can't do enough to help me all of a sudden."

He decided to tell her part at least of what had happened at Uspenskoye. "My uncle's behind it. He's likely given orders that you're not to be interfered with."

She looked at him, eyes large and green. "Why?"

"He says he wants an unofficial link, a voice in the west. He's selected you."

"That will make my people very happy," she said. "You've done well. Better than Washington hoped."

Mikhailov frowned. "I have some not-so-good news," he said. "My posting's being changed again."

"Again? Hell and damnation. We wanted you here in the General Staff. Where are you going?"

"I'm being assigned as a deputy divisional commander in Leningrad."

She frowned. "That's not so good. Is it permanent?"

"I don't know. My uncle wants me there in case of trouble." He told her what Romanenko had said in the birch wood. When he had finished, she remained silent, her lower lip caught between her teeth. Off to their right a northbound ferry swished and rumbled past, heading for the Kievskaya River terminal. The other boat's wake rocked theirs rhythmically; her shoulder touched his. It was several seconds before she drew away.

"The situation's that fragile, is it?" she said. On the riverbank the Novodevichy Convent was slipping by, the colors of its walls and domes subdued under the gray sky. "To all appearances, Vasily Romanenko has no problems."

"It's deceiving. He is very worried. He's made arrangements for Nadia and Valeria to come to Leningrad as well. He needs all the help I can give him. Listen..." He stopped. A gull swooped low over the boat's wake, searching for garbage.

"Yes?"

"I can't work for your people any longer."

He thought she had been expecting it. She looked at him. The strands of black hair were blowing against her mouth again; she didn't brush them away. "Why not?"

"I just told you. My uncle's trying to do the things that should have been done long ago, after the revolution. How can I work against him?"

"You're not working against him. The KGB is still there; that's what you're working against."

"If I were ever caught my uncle would suffer. If he were in a precarious position, it might be all the butchers needed."

"That's true," she said, "but — "

"There's another thing," Mikhailov said. "You wouldn't be able to work in Leningrad, they'd never let you. And my uncle wants you here. You couldn't act as my principal any more."

"I'd be replaced," she said.

The river was about to enter Gorki Park. There was another ferry landing just south of the Krasnoluzhsky Bridge and as the vessel passed under the span it began to turn for the north bank of the river.

"I know," Mikhailov said. The boat slowed, edging toward the dock. Then he said, "I don't want you to be replaced."

She studied him. A gust of wind once again blew her hair across her mouth. Mikhailov reached up and brushed the strands away from her lips. Her skin was very smooth. She regarded him gravely.

"I can't do it any more," he said. "Not even for you."

She let her head fall against him then, forehead against the white cotton of his shirt. Her perfume smelled a little like apple blossoms. The ferry bumped the dock and the gangway rattled. She raised her head and said, "I'll have to tell control. Look, you shouldn't decide just yet. I'm one of the press delegates to the Leningrad summit; I can see you there. Where are you going to be living?"

"Housing Estate Number One. It's on the west side of Vasilevsky Island."

"I'm staying at the Astoria. Novosti's booked a block of rooms for the non-communist press there. Your uncle's determined to make diplomatic capital out of his internal liberalization. I'll try to be in my room in the Astoria between eight and nine every evening, starting Friday. Will you be able to call me if that's all the arrangements we can make?"

"I'll try."

"Andrei," she said, "you know how these arrangements work. You're a KGB officer. You've committed yourself. Don't forget it."

They went down to the dock without speaking. It had finally begun to rain.

Shortly after six that evening Chantal placed a coded-phrase telephone call to the American embassy. Two hours later she was in the embassy's Marine Bar. The bar was on the ground floor of the twelve-story chancery building, which stood at the center of the new embassy compound, which had been completed only a few years previously. The perimeter of the compound was formed by a continuous block of apartments, which faced inward to the chancery and a grassy, treed quadrangle. It was a vast improvement over the old mustard-yellow embassy building, although so many microphones had been incorporated into its fabric that its residents sometimes referred to it as "the Bughouse," an epithet which could be understood in more than one way.

There was no worry about microphones in the Marine Bar, which was a Friday-nights-only establishment run by the embassy's marine-guard contingent to provide westerners with a few hours of relief from the gray rigidities of Moscow life. Microphones there probably were, but any listeners would be deafened by the music. Chantal picked her way among the crowded tables and dancing couples to the back of the bar.

Fowler had installed himself at a table at the very back of the room. Reflections from the revolving mirror-globe over the dance floor shifted erratically over the wall behind him and over the blue sweater he was wearing. The chancery building was always over air-conditioned. He nodded as she sat down.

"Drink?"

"Please."

He signaled for a waiter. She ordered beer. Fowler didn't say anything until it came, only stirred his half-finished drink with the plastic swizzle stick, which was shaped like a cavalry saber. When she had taken a grateful pull at the beer — it was still dreadfully hot out, the rain hadn't cooled the air at all — he asked:

"What's the matter?"

The music stopped. Chantal grimaced and drank more beer. After a moment the sound system came to life again, this time with Abba playing "Should I Laugh or Cry." Nostalgia night at the Marine Bar.

"Andrei wants out," she said.

"Oh, shit," Fowler said. "Why?"

"He feels he's working against his uncle. Crisis of conscience. We might have expected it."

"When did he tell you?"

"This afternoon, on the ferry." She told him the rest of it. At the end she noticed with some surprise that her beer was gone. She ordered another while Fowler thought.

"He's right about your being unable to handle him in Leningrad," he said finally. "We'll have to find someone else. Deputy divisional commander, dammit. That's hardly a step straight up the ladder. More sideways. He'd be much more useful here at the General Staff. He won't be nearly as good to us in a combat command."

She hadn't thought they'd let him go. "Suppose he refuses outright to cooperate any more?"

Fowler grimaced. "He's hardly in a position to do *that*. He's an intelligence officer; he's aware of the realities of his position."

"He's not the sort of person you threaten," Chantal said. At a nearby table a bearded young embassy staffer was holding hands with a blond girl in a blue dress. They were tapping their linked hands in time to the music. "I know him reasonably well by now. Threats would have to be a last resort."

"There's no way he can get out of the Leningrad posting?"

"I don't think so," she said. "Not without going against his uncle's wishes, and he won't do that. We'll have to be careful, if we want to keep him."

"I'll have to talk to some other people on this. You're going to Leningrad for the summit, aren't you?"

"That's right. They're putting the western press contingent up at the Astoria."

"It's going to be hard to put you in touch with him," Fowler said. "Especially if he's tucked away in a divisional headquarters. This may be our last chance at a secure contact for some time. Did you make any arrangements to meet?"

"I told him my hotel. He's told me where he's going to be living. I pressured him to contact me."

Fowler's face assumed a look of relief. "That's all right, then. I — wait a minute. That must mean he wants to keep in contact. Why do that? If he wanted to get away from you he could have just gone, not told you a thing. We might not have found out where he was for months. What's he up to?"

Chantal looked out at the dance floor, which was becoming crowded. The globe flung wedges and quadrilaterals of colored light across the dancers. The air was smoky and the air conditioning was finally beginning to lose ground. "He didn't say he wouldn't see me again," she said. "He said he wouldn't go on working against his uncle."

Fowler watched her steadily. "Oh," he said.

"Eric," said Chantal, "find somebody else. Pull me out."

"It's mutual, is it?" he asked. "I'm sorry."

She didn't answer, only stared down into the depths of her glass where the bubbles danced.

"I'll take this a few steps farther," Fowler said. "We'll see what needs to be done. I'd better get onto it. Are you going to stay?"

She nodded. Fowler finished his drink and left. Chantal got mildly intoxicated before going home.

Later still, high up in the chancery, Lasenby said to Fowler, "We can't possibly let him go. There's no question about that. Too many people have invested too much in this. Politically as well as otherwise."

"How are we going to keep him?" Fowler nearly snapped. He liked Chantal, and he was tired and worried. "He can guess, if he hasn't by now, that we can't coerce him. We can't jeopardize Romanenko by blowing his nephew. Romanenko's too much to Washington's liking, compared to who we'd get if he went down the drain. Mikhailov's as safe as if he'd never approached us."

"He's vulnerable in at least one fundamental way, though," the CIA station chief said. "He's gotten attached to Chantal Mallory."

"She's gotten attached to him," said Fowler. "That's a lousy state of affairs. If she were just bait, I wouldn't worry. But with her feelings involved she may not remember to act professionally. We ought to pull her out. She could screw things up."

"We can't pull her out," Lasenby said. "She's got to secure him for us. He's Romanenko's nephew. If Romanenko survives, Mikhailov won't stay in Leningrad forever. We've got to look forward to that day."

"And if Romanenko doesn't survive?"

"Look, Eric," Lasenby said, "there's more going on here than the CIA having a mole in the Soviet General Staff, or wherever. Washington's looking at the alternative to Romanenko, which is a government run by Zarudin and Smilga, in other words the same pack of fanatics and butchers this benighted country had to put up with under Stalin. If Romanenko needs help from the west, he may need to ask for it unofficially. *That's* why we can't lose contact with Mikhailov. Washington isn't trying to pull the rug out from under Romanenko, for Christ's sake. He's the best hope we've ever had for taking some of the warheads out of the missiles and dumping them in a very deep hole. Romanenko's no democrat, but he understands the west a Jesus sight better than the rest of them." Lasenby finally remembered to lower his voice, although the office was sound-proofed. "Chantal Mallory's emotional problems come a very distant second."

"All right," Fowler said tiredly. His eyelids felt gritty. "How do we do it? What does she say to him so he won't pull out?"

"There are any number of arguments," Lasenby said. "She'll have to know them all before she goes to Leningrad. She'll have to believe them herself. That's your job, friend. Make her believe." He looked at his watch. "I'll talk to Washington tonight. Let's get together at eleven tomorrow morning. We'll work out the best way to handle the pair of them."

Moscow — Leningrad
Friday, July 23

THE THIRTY-SEVENTH GUARDS Rifle division's head-quarters lay on the eastern edge of Leningrad, just outside the city boundaries near the road to the Rzhevka airport. The Thirty-seventh was a class-A division, meaning that it had a full complement of twelve thousand troops and a reasonable allotment of vehicles although, like almost all Soviet formations except the Taman and Kantemirov show divisions in Moscow and the front-line units in central Europe, it was woefully short of BMP armored personnel carriers. In the event of a mobilization, two of its three infantry regiments would travel in trucks requisitioned from the civilian sector. The tanks that equipped the division's armored regiment were in storage sheds on the western edge of the base, except for two dozen vehicles kept active for training purposes.

The streets of the base were laid out in a grid, with barracks and mess halls on the east side and the vehicle parks and maintenance shops on the west. To the south was a partially wooded area of about one square kilometer, which was used as a training ground for small-scale exercises. The head-quarters block, the parade square, and the junior-officers' quarters and mess were on the north side, just inside the main gate, which was at the end of a lane about two hundred meters from the airport road.

It was five-fifteen in the afternoon. Mikhailov was sitting

behind his desk in his office in the HQ block, having a drink with Lieutenant-General Yuri Zarkitch, who commanded the division. In the five days of his settling-in period, Mikhailov had formed an assessment of this officer: fairly competent, a climber who would very much like a posting to the staff of the Leningrad military district, but who was hampered in this by a lack of political connections. Lieutenant-General Zarkitch, Mikhailov thought, would follow anyone who promised to give him a good push up the promotion ladder, and no questions asked. He had welcomed Mikhailov last Monday with literally open arms, seeing in his new deputy commander the kind of influential person he needed to release him from the Thirty-Seventh Guards Rifle Division. Mikhailov, mindful of his uncle's need for support, had since his arrival cultivated Zarkitch's good will. The vodka, which was the best (and Mikhailov's), was an essential ingredient in this exercise; the divisional commander liked to drink, and to do so often.

"Got yourself all organized, eh?" asked Zarkitch, pushing his glass at Mikhailov for a refill. Zarkitch had a very wide face and a double chin, which bulged over his tunic collar. His nose accentuated the roundness of his features, being almost as wide as it was long.

"Everything's coming well," Mikhailov said absently, refilling both their glasses. He was thinking about getting back to Leningrad and trying to bring some order to the apartment, which was in a state of post-move chaos.

"No particular problems, then?" Zarkitch asked, as though he wished there were, so that he could help with them. "If there's anything I can do —"

It was sometimes difficult to tell who outranked whom in these conversations. In any case, Mikhailov didn't need Zarkitch's help. He had found the division in good order, with the men in reasonable spirits, and he had taken over the unit's administration without much hardship. His predecessor, who had gone to a divisional command in the Kiev district — a step up, that — had obviously been the officer who kept the division running on a day-to-day basis. He had also, apparently, seen that Romanenko's reforms were administered to the letter. The officers, particularly the junior ones, who had the thankless task of controlling and training the men, appeared cheerful and fairly enthusiastic, which in Mikhailov's experience wasn't all that common. As well, the incidence of drunkenness had fallen in the past three months. There were still difficulties with the variety of the food, but there was more of it and the men looked fit and they tackled their assignments with renewed vigor.

"Everything's fine, sir," Mikhailov said. "I'm impressed with the quality of the men," he added. Zarkitch beamed. Mikhailov pushed the bottle at him. "Why don't you finish this?" he suggested. "With the General's permission, I'd like to go on home. My quarters are a terrible mess."

"Of course, of course," Zarkitch said, picking up the half-full bottle and weighing it thoughtfully. "Is everything all set for Monday?"

"The new training schedules will be posted tomorrow," Mikhailov told him. "The clerks typed them up this afternoon." Like the divisions in Czechoslovakia, the Thirty-seventh was now required to upgrade its training programs to meet the new norms. This had been the job that Mikhailov saw to first on his arrival.

"It's a great advantage," Zarkitch said, standing up, "to have someone with your combat experience on my staff." He clapped Mikhailov heavily on the shoulder. "We'll make this the best division in the Leningrad district, eh? Better even than those spit-and-polish toy soldiers in Moscow. See you Monday."

Mikhailov reached the apartment at a few minutes after six. Housing Estate Number One covered half a square kilometer on the western side of Vasilevsky Island, and consisted of a complex of nine- and twelve-story blocks separated by avenues of poplar trees and flower beds. There were also a kindergarten, two schools, a shopping complex, and playgrounds. It was a much more pleasant place to live than the spartan housing development in Moscow; from the window of Mikhailov's two-bedroom apartment on the twelfth floor of one of the towers he could see well out into the Gulf of Finland and southwest to the deep-sea port where the big merchant ships and excursion liners moored.

He ate supper from the top of a packing case and then puttered around the apartment, halfheartedly trying to bring some order to it. At ten past eight he gave up and went down to the shopping complex to find a pay telephone. After some difficulty he got the Astoria switchboard and asked, in his least-accented English, for Chantal Mallory. She answered on the second ring.

"Chantal? It's me."

"Ah." The hesitation was only momentary. "How are you?"

"Very well. Can you spare a little time this evening?"

"I'm rather tied up, if you can understand what I mean."

"Why don't I drop over there, then?"

"All right. How about the main-floor restaurant. It's pretty noisy now with all the press, but..."

"That's okay," said Mikhailov, and rang off.

He went back to the apartment and unearthed a suit, the same one he had worn to Saint George Hall. It needed pressing. No time for that. He went to his bedroom, rummaged about in his kit, and found his KGB identity card. For security reasons he rarely carried it, but he might need it at the Astoria.

He took the trolley and the metro instead of the Zhiguli, which he had driven up from the capital; with its Moscow-coded licence plates the car was a little too conspicuous. Although, he thought as he left the Nevsky Prospekt station, my KGB brethren will know by now that I'm in fairly regular contact with a western journalist. I hope Tolbukhin and Uncle Vasily have put words in the right ears.

He walked the three blocks to the Astoria Hotel. It was still broad daylight; there would actually be little night at all. For most of the normal hours of darkness Leningrad, lying so far north, would be bathed in a pale, pearly radiance: the "white nights" of the city's summer.

At the corner of Moika and Dzerzhinskovo streets he spotted the first security: black Moskvitch sedans containing two men each. There were also a lot of KGB Guards soldiers, with their blue shoulder straps, pacing steadily up and down the sidewalks.

The policemen and guards became more numerous until,

by the time he reached Saint Isaac's Square, there seemed to be more of them in the street than civilians. Just ahead on his left Mikhailov could see the object of the security: the old czarist Mariinsky Palace, now the Leningrad City Soviet building. It was in this relic of the Romanovs that the Leningrad summit was to begin on Monday.

Mikhailov turned right, into the square, past the big Academy of Sciences building. Out in the square the equestrian statue of Nicholas I reared on its drum-shaped pedestal. Ahead and to the left rose the great domed and columned mass of Saint Isaac's Cathedral, looming above the trapezoidal park on its southern side. The Astoria Hotel, which hailed back in its faded opulence to the last days of the czars, stood on the east side of the square, at an angle to the cathedral. There were four uniformed guards outside its entrance.

Mikhailov decided to trust to his western clothing. He walked past the two security men on the south side of the hotel's glass doors and turned to enter.

"Hey. You."

This blasted military haircut, Mikhailov thought. No journalist anywhere, not even here, wears his hair this short. He turned around. "What?" he said in English, trying to look both surprised and aggrieved.

One of the guards hurried toward him. There were dark semicircles of sweat at the armpits of his green uniform. "Where do you think you're going?"

"Inside," Mikhailov said.

"Let me see your identification. This hotel is restricted."

"Asshole," Mikhailov said in Russian. "Are you *trying* to draw attention to me?"

The guard stopped, taken aback. From a few meters away his partner interestedly watched the exchange. Then the first man said, "It's restricted. I need to see some identification." His tone was distinctly less arrogant.

Mikhailov shrugged and pulled out the pink-bordered KGB card. The guard studied it for a moment. A look of consternation spread over his face.

"That good enough for you?" Mikhailov asked. "Are you happy now?"

The guard backed away, nodding rapidly. "Yes, Colonel, of course, I'm sorry —" his right arm twitched.

"Don't salute, .you idiot," Mikhailov snapped. "You've done enough damage already. Keep your mouth shut about this. Understand?"

The guard nodded rapidly. Mikhailov turned on his heel and went into the hotel while the guard beat a hasty retreat down the sidewalk.

The doorman inside the hotel paid him no attention: if he had got past the guards outside he obviously had business in the Astoria. The lobby retained a dimming czarist grandeur: high ceilings, brocade, open elevator cages, spiraling grand staircase. Adjoining the lobby was the restaurant. Mikhailov ignored the signs that said "Guests Only" — which meant foreigners or Russians with hard currency — and went in.

It looked more like an extremely rowdy press club than a restaurant, packed with journalists of all shapes, sizes, political persuasions, and nationalities. Nearly every non-communist newsman and woman in the country, and more than a few from outside it, seemed to have maneuvered themselves into the Astoria. Mikhailov couldn't see Chantal anywhere. He looked around in confusion. The air was thick with cigarette smoke, alcohol fumes, and the din of conversation. The few waiters he could see looked harried and despairing, their usual lethargy bludgeoned out of them by the energetic mob. Stacks of western television equipment stood on chairs and were piled against the brocaded walls.

An arm protruded itself, waving, from the crowd around one of the nearer tables. Mikhailov caught a glimpse of Chantal's face behind a screen of gesticulating hands. He started toward her. The noise disoriented him, the half-heard phrases and babel of accents somehow representative of the apparently planless, disorganized western way of life in which everything seemed, to Mikhailov, to happen at the whim of chance or fancy. He had never gotten used to it, even in England.

She was jammed into a chair between two men who were arguing belligerently in English about the proposed Soviet withdrawal from Afghanistan. Mikhailov looked down at her and said hello. He felt the smothering sensation under his breastbone again. After a moment it went away.

"Hello," she said. The two men who were squabbling over Afghanistan stopped talking and looked up. Mikhailov nodded politely at them. The man on Chantal's right was thin and tanned and wore a small, neat beard at the bottom of a triangular face. The other was graying but without distinction; he was overweight and jowly.

"This is Andrei," she said raising her voice to be heard above the din. "Andrei, these two characters are Len Cathcart, the one with the beard, and Henry Cole, the one without. Henry's with Reuters, Len's with the Canadian Broadcasting Corporation."

"Pleased to meet you," Cathcart said. "I'm the CBC one. Don't bother talking to Reuters here, he can never file a story the way it was told anyway."

"What Leonard hasn't mentioned," said Cole in an accent that was much more elegant than his appearance, "is that he never listens to what he's told at all. He just talks into a microphone and points a camera and sometimes the pictures turn themselves into a story. Then he sends it off to Canada. They don't know any better over there, so they broadcast it."

"Shut up, you two," Chantal said. She was flushed, enjoying herself. Mikhailov had never seen her working in her other profession and he felt faintly jealous. "Let me introduce you properly, Henry, since you're so bloody British. This is Andrei Mikhailov, a good friend of mine from Moscow."

Cole's eyes narrowed. "Would you by any chance be Secretary Romanenko's nephew?" His speech was slurred by the effect of a little too much alcohol.

"Yes," Mikhailov answered. Without being able to do anything about it, he realized what she was doing: drawing him into her circle, so that no matter how innocent he might be in reality, to the KGB he would appear suspect. It was a dangerous technique, but she was clearly willing to use it, taking out insurance against his defection from her.

"Jesus Christ," Cathcart said to Chantal. "So *that's* how you got that nicely polished piece off to *Seven Days* while we were still pissing around after Romanenko's press conference. The old inside contact. I'm going to file a complaint." He sounded put out. "I don't suppose you could drop any scraps my way while you're here?" he said to Mikhailov.

"I was just going," Chantal said, shoving her chair back and standing up abruptly.

"Give Andrei your seat, then. Otherwise some asshole from AP will grab it."

"Sorry," Mikhailov said. "I'm on my way too."

"Don't tell her anything," Cole called to Mikhailov as they left. He was barely audible over the drunken din. "She'll just get it wrong trying to write it up in the dark."

"There's one in every crowd," said Chantal, as they were passing through the lobby. "Henry's the one in this crowd."

"I couldn't follow his English," Mikhailov said. "Something about writing in the dark?"

"Let's go for a walk," she said, ignoring the question. "We need some time together."

The KGB guards didn't bother them as they left the hotel. They might have stopped Chantal had she been alone, but neither of them wanted to face Mikhailov's irritation. Chantal and he walked north along Mayorsky Avenue to Admiralteysky Prospekt and crossed the road to the walk that ran along the Gorki Gardens bordering the south side of the old czarist Admiralty Building.

"There's a lot of security around," she said as they started east. "Everybody's been put in rooms at the back of the Astoria. Nobody in the front ones that overlook the square. They don't want anybody taking shots at the leadership."

"They'd rather do it themselves," said Mikhailov, with some bitterness.

"This may be the last chance we'll have to talk, for a while," she said. "I'm going back to Moscow after the summit."

"Will you be able to come back to Leningrad sometimes?"

"I suppose so." She sounded dispirited. "Your uncle's favor permits me a lot I wouldn't be able to to do otherwise. I had VIP treatment coming up from Moscow. It made some of the other journalists furious. I don't know if you can understand this, but your uncle's interest is causing me some professional problems. Some of my colleagues don't like it if you get sources that are really good; they say you're selling out."

"I know about — what did you call it? — selling out," Mikhailov said. "If anybody does."

They were approaching the end of the Gorki Gardens. Ahead of them, expanding slowly as they walked, lay Palace Square and the Alexander Column piercing the pale sky. It was nearly as dark as it was going to become; the sky's mother-of-pearl light lay luminous along the great facades of the old czarist guards headquarters building far away on the square's eastern side.

"I know you want to stop," she said in a rush, "but think first. You said yourself your uncle's in trouble. He needs help, even help from the west. Suppose something goes wrong soon? The Americans don't want the Stalinists to come back, your uncle's the best chance we've ever had for a real peace between east and west. Don't you think you'd do better to keep in contact with us, so that we won't make mistakes about the situation here? You know how political and military actions can be misinterpreted."

"I know," said Mikhailov. They were on the west edge of Palace Square now, with the Winter Palace on the left: the Winter Palace, where the old czars and then Kerensky's provisional government had fallen to Lenin and the Bolsheviks in 1917. The revolution, Mikhailov thought. The lost revolution.

"The Americans aren't supporting my uncle because they love Mother Russia," Mikhailov said. "They're doing it for their own interests."

"For Christ's sake, Andrei, what did you expect?" she said. "They are far more frightened of your uncle failing and being deposed than they are of him staying on. Think, Andrei. You can't help him if you pull out now."

"The Americans want us to become like they are," he said accusingly. "Everyone for himself, dog eat dog. Like it was under the czars. You don't understand what we have to face. Russia is chaos, always has been chaos. Conquered, overrun, the Mongols, the Tartars, the Germans. You can't know what it's like. How would you feel if you'd had to rebuild Chicago from a ruin? How would you feel if two million people had starved to death in a blockade of Boston? If you couldn't feed yourselves, if you couldn't make your factories work properly, if even your allies hated you, how would you feel? The Americans don't understand that. They think if we just decided to be exactly like them, all our problems would disappear. They're wrong; we're easterners, not westerners."

"Andrei," she said sharply, "lower your voice."

He rubbed his eyes. He was very tired. They started along the east edge of the gardens toward the vast gray frontage of the Winter Palace.

"It's true," he mumbled. "We've always felt we were no good, beside you. Beside the west. You can always do what you want; for you there's always enough."

"Not true," she said. "And you know it."

"All right," he said, shrugging. "Have it your way."

She stopped, turning on him. "*My* way? You stupid bloody Russian, can't you see I'm trying to help you? You came to us in the first place, wanted a reason for living. If we hadn't given you that, you'd have ended up one more vodka-soaked officer with his eye on the next rank up, nothing more, a leech. Andrei Sergeyevitch Mikhailov, let me give you some hard truths. First of all, Washington wants you. They'll do almost anything to keep you, and keep you safe. Second, President Hayes wants Romanenko to stay in power, and Hayes needs to know when and how your uncle's threatened so he can exert pressures in your uncle's favor. We need you to tell us about those threats. Third, when the summit's over, as soon as you reasonably can, we want you to exert yourself to get back to Moscow and into the General Staff. That's not a request, that's an order. Fourth, and last, I've been instructed to tell you this: we can't prevent you from pulling out. But if you do, and if you're ever found out and need help, we won't provide it. We won't turn you in, but if you back out on us now don't be surprised if Langley does the same later on. Think about that for a moment before you say anything. I like you a great deal, Andrei, and I don't want to see you and Valeria abandoned. That was from me, not Langley."

Was it? he wondered. Had she been ordered to seduce his

◆

emotions, and later his body? How far would Langley go, how far would Chantal go, to keep him? Langley was indeed giving him a choice, more than most agents were given. But he had gone a long way down the traitor's road, and the chance always remained that ill luck could expose him, not now, not next year even, but sometime. Then he would need the Americans, and they would not be there.

Furthermore, it was conceivable that he could, in fact, help Romanenko more if he kept in touch with the Americans.

"All right," he said, taking her shoulder. "I'll go on." She turned and looked at him, still angry. "We're on the same side," he went on clumsily, "after all."

"Yes," she said, taking his arm, "we are."

They walked along the front of the Winter Palace. At its east end Mikhailov stopped and said, "Here's where the revolution began. Now we have to complete it."

"None too soon," she said dryly. They turned south at the czarist guards headquarters and started along the sidewalk bordering the front of the old General Staff building. They were still arm in arm. Mikhailov could feel the rhythmic pressure of her left breast against his forearm as they walked.

"What did Cole mean?" he asked suddenly.

"Cole? What did he say?"

"That you'd have to write in the dark."

She didn't answer for a long time. He waited. Then, as they were entering Admiralteysky Prospekt again, she said, "He meant he thought I was getting my information by sleeping with you." She let go of his arm.

"What kind of a colleague is he?"

"That's how some of their minds work, if a woman outdoes them professionally."

"I'm sorry," Mikhailov said.

"Doesn't matter," she said.

His desire for her swept over him so suddenly and intensely that it made him feel weak. "Chantal," he said, "I do want you."

"Yes," she said. "I know." A breeze was rising and the trees in the Gorki Gardens had begun to stir. "I want you too. But we can't. Not now."

He had to think about something else, so he thought about Afghanistan, the cold mountains, the dreadful ruins of Herat. It helped.

"Someday," he said. "When all this has quietened down."

"I hope so," she said. "If it ever does. Look, we'd better do some business. We're going to try to put somebody into Leningrad to act as your principal. It may take a while, we may not be able to do it at all. If that happens, can you manage to get to Moscow periodically?"

"Probably," Mikhailov said. "My aunt and uncle like to see Valeria, it'll be a good reason to go there. What kind of information do you want while I'm here?"

"Everything you can supply about attitudes to your uncle's regime. We want to evaluate his chances of staying in power."

"I don't know what the higher echelons are thinking," he said.

"Don't worry about that. Give us what you know."

"All right."

They were nearly to Saint Isaac's Square. "I'd better go back in now," she said. "Memorize this telephone number. If you need to contact us urgently, use it." She told him the number. When he had it, he asked, "What about your people contacting me? There's nothing arranged —"

"There's a slip of paper in your pocket," she said.

Moscow — Uspenskoye
July 23 — 24

TOLBUKHIN'S HANDS WERE STILL SHAKING. When Smilga had called him up to the office on the top floor he had been certain there was going to be trouble, and there had been. Not outright disaster, but building toward it, like the quiver in the air before a lightning strike.

Smilga had wanted to know about Andrei Mikhailov. He particularly wanted to know why Tolbukhin hadn't told him that the general secretary's nephew was the officer who filed the report on the Herat mutiny, and why Mikhailov had been posted to a division near Leningrad precisely at this time.

"Colonel Mikhailov has been with the Third Directorate for seventeen years," Tolbukhin had said. "He is extremely competent. He also has unusual courage when facing unpleasant tasks. This is evident in his report on the mutiny. His loyalty to Marxist-Leninism is unquestioned."

"No doubt. Exactly what led you to arrange his posting to Leningrad?"

"We eventually want to move him into the General Staff," Tolbukhin had said. "For that he needs experience in a large combat formation. The Leningrad posting was the only one suitable at the time."

Tolbukhin had hoped this was convincing. Smilga had always been more interested in First and Second Directorate operations than in the relatively dull and routine operations of the Third; consequently the KGB chairman had only a superficial knowledge of the work of Tolbukhin's directorate. The KGB was so vast that no one person could hope to be well acquainted with more than a fraction of it.

"You want him on the General Staff, eh?" Smilga had said, apparently satisfied. "Very clever of you. A Third Directorate man as a marshal of the Soviet Union; that *would* be an achievement." A pause. "Very well," he had continued, "you know what you're doing. Or you'd better. At the moment I have a special assignment I want you to give your full attention to."

Tolbukhin had listened to the KGB chairman and then returned to his office to start carrying out his orders. Instead of beginning immediately, however, he sat for some time with his head in his hands, staring down at the green blotter. His desk clock ticked gently; it was a quarter past ten in the evening.

Smilga wanted a list of names. To be exact, he wanted a list of names divided into two sections. The first was to identify all military officers of general's rank or higher who were known to approve of Romanenko's reforms. The second part was to be a list of those generals known to disapprove. Smilga wanted the list by Sunday midnight, without fail.

He wants to purge the officers again, Tolbukhin thought, just as Stalin did in 1938. He thinks I'll believe the hard-line officers are the ones to be eliminated, but I know, as surely as if I could read his mind, that it's the others he's after. And if he's going to purge the generals and marshals, he's going to have to get rid of Romanenko. When is he going to do it? Monday? I can't believe that, it's too public, it'd be all over the western press, there'd be all kinds of repercussions in Moscow. After the summit, that's likely when. Everybody will have gone home, he'll just quietly dispose of Romanenko and then sort out the Warsaw Pact leadership once he knows who was keen on the reforms.

He looked at the telephones on his desk. He didn't dare use them. Worse, he couldn't leave the office yet; Smilga might find out about it and wonder why he had gone out so soon after their meeting. And the work would take a long time, at least until the deadline. He had better start deciding which files he'd need, and what clerical help would be required to collate the hundreds upon hundreds of loyalty reports. Smilga had expressly warned Tolbukhin not to delegate the job to any of his deputies. The clerical staff were to be warned to keep their mouths shut, on pain of penalties unspecified but understood to be dreadful.

He'd work suitably late, to show his zeal, and then leave. That should satisfy Smilga. Tolbukhin took his head out of his hands and pulled a pad of paper toward him.

In fact he did not lay down his pen until a quarter to one in the morning. He had made a preliminary list, from memory, of the fifty or so senior officers who were for or against Romanenko; these files he would pull himself first thing in the morning. He now wrote out a copy of the list, put it in his pocket, and locked the rest of the papers in his desk safe. After that he left the office and the building, logging out as usual with the duty officer. He did not, however, summon a staff car to take him home. Instead he walked five blocks from Dzerzhinsky Square and flagged a taxi. The cab took him out Mozhavskoye Schosse and deposited him where Mozhavskoye crossed Kubinka Street. From there he walked back two blocks, almost to Grishina Street. Near the intersection he entered a telephone booth and made a call. Five minutes after that he was waiting in the shadows across the street from a large apartment building two hundred meters northwest of the booth. A figure strolled out of the apartment entrance, nodded to the guards at the door, and walked away up the street. Tolbukhin followed him, keeping to the other side. When they were well away from the apartment, the man stopped. Tolbukhin crossed the road.

"Good evening, General," Konstantin Tsander said. "What brings you here so urgently?"

They started walking on. "Smilga's working on something," Tolbukhin said. He described the meeting in the KGB chairman's office. When he had finished, Tsander asked, "Will he move in the next few days?"

"I don't know," Tolbukhin said. "But he wants those lists

by Sunday night. I've brought a copy of the preliminary one. The names in the left column are the ones he's after. I'll try to get a copy of the complete list to you, but I'm not sure I'll be able to do that by Monday morning."

"All right," Tsander said. "You'd better go on home. I'll see the others as soon as I can."

When Tolbukhin had disappeared into the darkness, Tsander stood on the pavement, thinking. He had to get Tolbukhin's information to Romanenko as soon as possible. At two in the morning, however, any direct contact would draw too much attention, and he didn't want to use the telephone; most senior Party members' phones were untapped, but with Smilga it was never possible to be sure that there weren't monitors on the line from time to time. Tolbukhin's approach had been risky enough, although he had probably gotten away with it. They would have to assume he had, anyway; if they considered themselves always under surveillance, they'd never get anything done.

He'd try to arrange breakfast with Romanenko. That would have to do. The general secretary was due to leave for Leningrad Saturday evening; there would be enough time — barely — to take countermeasures if they seemed necessary.

He would also have to get to the chief of the General Staff, Marshal Paul Osipov. Romanenko still seemed to think that Defense Minister Yasev was committed to him, but Tsander didn't trust Yasev. Osipov was another matter; he had been quietly agitating for military reforms for years.

If only Osipov had had the seniority to become defense minister, rather than Yasev, Tsander thought as he retraced his steps to the apartment block, our worries would be somewhat fewer. Maybe I can come up with a reason to take Osipov to see Romanenko with me tomorrow.

He did, and called Osipov early the next morning. There was a problem with underallocation of trucks in the Byelorussian military district that was causing Tsander, who among other things supervised the armaments industry, some difficulties. There were questions of influence-peddling involved, he told

Osipov, but there was no reason to trouble Defense Minister Yasev with such matters. Could the marshal spend some time discussing the problem over breakfast?

The marshal could. Excellent, said Tsander. He would pick the marshal up in half an hour.

Then he called Romanenko's apartment. Ekaterina answered; Romanenko had not slept well and had gone out to Uspenskoye very early, to rest before what promised to be several hectic days.

Shit, Tsander thought, replacing the receiver. With a moment's consideration, though, he felt less irritated. At Uspenskoye there would be less likelihood of microphones. He'd take Osipov there.

Romanenko was sitting on the terrace when Tsander and the chief of staff were announced by the major-domo. Tsander didn't want the major-domo, who would inevitably be a KGB guards officer, anywhere within earshot. He waited until the man was gone and then sat down, followed by Osipov, who had taken care to wear civilian clothes. Romanenko appeared mildly surprised, and a little annoyed, to see them.

"Good morning, Kosti, Marshal Osipov. What brings you out here?"

The table was glass-topped, but there was no telling what might be hidden in its filigreed iron legs. The same with the apparently solid stone balustrade, the flower urns overflowing with petunias, the yellow pine siding of the dacha with its hundreds of wooden pegs, some of which might not be pegs.

"It's about this procurement investigation in the Byelorussian military district," said Tsander. He began to describe it. Osipov added a helpful word here and there, although he was clearly mystified about the need to bother the general secretary with these details, if they were too minor for the minister of defense. Romanenko, approximately two minutes after the conversation began, realized that Tsander was afraid of microphones, and joined in the charade. Finally he said, "It's a matter for the General Department and the Party control committee. This sort of corruption has to be weeded out as soon as it is detected. Now, I've been sitting down too long and I need a walk. Join me?"

They walked halfway down the lawn. The dew on the grass dampened the cuffs of their trousers. The air was warming quickly; the day would be hot.

"What's the matter?" Romanenko asked.

Tsander told him. Osipov's face took on an extremely worried expression, reasonably enough, as his was one of the first names on Tolbukhin's list. At the end, Romanenko asked, "When will Smilga move?".

"He has to set it up with Zarudin," Tsander said. "To preserve legitimacy, there'd have to be a Central Committee plenum right after they arrested you. Arrested us."

"Zarudin's not going to Leningrad," Romanenko said thoughtfully. "I made a mistake there, keeping him out of it. But I wanted to present this as purely Party business, not the government's. I shouldn't have tried to undermine his position so quickly."

Tsander had also thought it to be a mistake, but hadn't said so. He regretted it now. "I don't think Smilga and Zarudin can move in the immediate future," Romanenko went on. "I think Smilga would want to see how the Warsaw Pact leaders reacted at the summit; then he'd know who to cut down first. But it would have been better for me to have Zarudin in Leningrad. It would have reduced the chances of a surprise move on his and Smilga's part. Too late to change now, too suspicious."

"Have you noticed anything unusual?" Tsander asked Osipov.

"Nothing, Secretary. Defense Minister Yasev's behaving normally. Everything seems routine." Osipov's voice rose. "The KGB's going to do it again. Gut the General Staff and the officer corps. When Stalin did it, he nearly cost us the war. We hadn't any good officers left to fight the Germans."

"Can you do anything to help?" Romanenko asked him. They had walked nearly to the edge of the wood. The noise of the stream was almost inaudible: it usually shrank to a trickle in midsummer.

"Not a great deal. Not with Yasev leaning over my

shoulder. There's a full General Staff meeting Monday afternoon; I can't get out of that. And there are no reasons to declare any sort of alert, even a practice one."

"Let's go and look at the stream, what there is of it," Romanenko said. They went into the wood. "Who called the General Staff meeting?" Romanenko asked.

"Yasev," said Osipov. "It's about the August exercises in Czechoslovakia."

"That's normal," Romanenko said. "Those were planned in the spring."

"It's convenient, though," Tsander said. "Leningrad security for the summit is being handled by the KGB Guards Directorate. That's also convenient. Smilga would have all the senior General Staff officers at that staff conference, in one neat package, ready for the plucking, and you and the Warsaw Pact leaders in Leningrad the same way, with the KGB guards protecting you. Talk about setting the fox to watch the chickens."

"It's absolutely normal for the KGB guards to deal with security on this big a meeting," Romanenko pointed out.

"Absolutely," Tsander said. "And, as I said, convenient." He turned to Osipov. "What strength of army forces could you dispose in Leningrad?" he asked Osipov.

"There's the Thirty-seventh Guards Rifle Division," said Osipov. "It's a class-A unit. Twelve thousand men."

"I know," Romanenko said dryly. "I arranged for my nephew to become its deputy commander. He's up there now."

"You did?" asked Tsander, stopping. The air was still cool under the trees. They were only a couple of meters from the brook, a thread of clear water running among dry white stones.

"Yes. A precaution, nothing more. I'm surprised Tolbukhin didn't mention it. He's certainly aware of it. My nephew had to report it to him before he took the posting."

"Your nephew's —" said Osipov, and left the sentence hanging.

"In the KGB," Romanenko finished for him. "Don't worry about that just now. Look, I don't think Smilga can move just yet. How could he get away with a purge of the officer corps?

His position's not nearly as strong as Stalin's was in 1938; it might backfire and bring him down. And the Americans would be delighted. It could turn into a disaster, even Smilga and Zarudin can see that."

"But why the list?" asked Tsander.

"I don't say they're not thinking about a purge," Romanenko said. He sat down on the grassy bank by the little waterfall where he and Mikhailov had smoked cigarettes together. The cascade was now no more than a trickle. "I am saying that it wouldn't be sensible just now. Anyway, two things stand out. First, I can't delay the summit. Second, I can't replace the KGB security in Leningrad with army troops. That might precipitate a confrontation with Smilga and Zarudin, which I can't afford politically at this point. Third, if they are planning something in Leningrad, I have a very loyal nephew in a position to help me. Even the KGB guards can't stand up to a class-A division."

"But he's only deputy commander," protested Osipov. "What about —"

Romanenko put up a hand. "Marshal Osipov, I *am* going to take some extra precautions. I want you to arrange for my nephew's divisional commander to take some leave, starting no later than Monday morning. How you do that, I don't care. But arrange it, and be sure my nephew has command of the division when his superior leaves. Can you manage that?"

"Yes, Secretary."

"Could he move his troops fast enough?" asked Tsander. "If Smilga did decide to act?"

"I'll have to risk it," said Romanenko. "See if you can get back to Tolbukhin. Tell him to feel the pulse at Dzerzhinsky Square and try to keep in touch with you. If it appears there's going to be trouble, contact me in Leningrad on the scrambler. You've got a timetable of my movements. Preface your warning with an inquiry about Ekaterina. Then give me the time and place I should expect hostile action, pretend you're checking on my itinerary. I'll have to try to manage the situation from my end after that."

"You'll be watched," said Tsander. "Your telephones may

be tapped. How will you be able to contact your nephew?"

"I may have to use Ekaterina; she'll have more freedom of movement."

"You're assuming you'll have enough warning," said Tsander. "You might not."

"Be reasonable, Konstantin," said Romanenko. "Smilga's a careful man. If he takes action against us, he'll have to deal with the army more or less simultaneously. He can't do that without Tolbukhin's involvement. That will give us a few hours. Marshal Osipov, you must have sufficient forces near Leningrad to deal with the KGB."

Osipov nodded. "Given enough warning. But I couldn't make any major preparations without them being noticed."

Romanenko glanced at Tsander. Both men knew that Tolbukhin couldn't keep news of such preparations from reaching Smilga. Romanenko said finally, "We still have no definite evidence that Smilga intends a coup in Leningrad. I don't want to provoke him into one. Later, perhaps, but not now."

"All right," Tsander said unwillingly. "But I still think you're putting yourself at risk."

"There are always risks," said Romanenko. "This one is acceptable. Now you had better go back to Moscow."

When they had gone, Romanenko sat on the iron chair on the terrace, watching the motionless trees. There was so little wind that the birch leaves, where he could see them among the pines, hung straight down without a quiver.

The KGB, Romanenko thought, the sword and shield of socialism. The sword is a knife at our throats, the shield a weight to crush us, all of it a nightmare visited on us by Stalin, yes, and Lenin too, whatever the histories say. Viler than anything the Romanovs ever dreamed of, a cesspool.

I have to break the KGB. It will be difficult, very difficult, but as soon as the Leningrad summit is over, I will begin.

Leningrad — Moscow
9 A.M. — 1:46 P.M., Monday, July 26

IT WAS RAINING. From the window in his office in the HQ block Mikhailov could see the main gate of the divisional base, its red-and-white-striped barrier dripping dismally in the downpour. The drops pattered steadily on the roof and rivulets of water trickled slowly down the windowpane. In the divisional commander's office next door, General Zarkitch was berating an orderly for failing to have the car around when he wanted it. After a moment the voices stopped and Zarkitch came into Mikhailov's office.

"Well, Andrei Sergeyevitch," said Zarkitch. "You've got everything under control, right?"

"Right," said Mikhailov. He left the window and sat down behind his desk. He had come in to work this morning to find Zarkitch preparing to go on an unexpected leave, granted by no less than GHQ Moscow for "exhibition of the highest qualities of military leadership," or so Zarkitch had said. The general was off to the Sochi resort on the Black Sea for a week. He thought Mikhailov had arranged the trip for him, in one of those exchanges that formed the subterranean currency of the Soviet elite. Mikhailov hadn't disabused him, only smiled and shrugged. The two men had spent the past hour on the details of the temporary handing over of command. As of ten o'clock, Mikhailov was in charge of the Thirty-seventh Guards Rifle Division.

Zarkitch walked over to the window and looked out at the rain. "Where the devil's that car? Oh, well, I'll be out of this lousy weather in a couple of hours. You'll have a chance to run your own show for a while, eh, Andrei? Find out what a big command feels like. You'll do well, I'm sure."

"With you as an example I could hardly do otherwise," Mikhailov said.

Zarkitch waved dismissively. "We've all heard about your talents," he said. "Now, there are a few around who think you've done so well because you're the general secretary's nephew, but I'm not one of them, although I could name names, but I won't. You'd be where you are no matter who your — There's the car. About time. Say, look, you haven't got a drink handy, have you? It's damp out there."

Mikhailov got the vodka and a glass out of his desk and poured the general a stiff drink. Zarkitch downed it in one gulp. "None yourself?"

"On duty, General Zarkitch."

Zarkitch laughed and put the glass down. "You're a good professional, Andrei Sergeyevitch. I'll think of you while I'm on the beach at Sochi. Without my wife, fortunately." He laughed again. "She thinks I'm off to a staff conference in Moscow; very boring. If she calls to check up, that's where I am, right?"

"Right," Mikhailov said, smiling back in cheerful complicity. He wanted nothing so much as to see Zarkitch's plump behind disappearing out the door. Finally Zarkitch said, "I'd better be off. Would you mind —"

"Not at all. Take it."

Zarkitch put the vodka bottle, which was an export brand with a reusable cap, into his briefcase and gave a mock salute. "See you in about a week."

"Enjoy yourself, General Zarkitch," Mikhailov said.

When his commanding officer had gone Mikhailov walked to the window and watched until the staff car had rolled under the red-and-white barrier and turned up the road toward the airport. Then he went back to the desk. Zarkitch had taken this opportunity to unload a mountain of paperwork onto Mikhailov: schedule revisions for training and for political indoctrination meetings, vehicle maintenance requirements, combat readiness assessments, and a thick wad of personnel fitness reports to be completed and forwarded to the Leningrad military district headquarters in the city. One of the reasons our combat readiness is so poor, Mikhailov thought as he stared resentfully at the stack of documents and forms on his desk, is that we officers are up to our necks in paper. We spend so much time on reports that we haven't the time to take care of our men.

He pulled the stack toward him and started trying to organize it, but he found concentration difficult. Zarkitch's abrupt leave was unsettling. There could be only one reason for it: Romanenko was taking precautions and wanted Mikhailov in charge of the combat unit nearest Leningrad. Mikhailov knew that his uncle must already be in the city, but Romanenko had made no contact. That at least was a good sign: the arrangements were a precaution, not a preparation.

A typewriter began to clack in the outer office, where the divisional clerks worked. Mikhailov wondered whether he ought to bring some of his troops to alert, on the pretext of training. They wouldn't like it, in this weather. He looked at the wall clock. It was twenty minutes past ten. The first of the summit meetings was to begin at one-thirty that afternoon.

No panic yet, Mikhailov thought. He wondered what Chantal was doing.

Chantal pulled the rain hood closer around her face and peered past the chain of guards lining the sidewalk in front of the Astoria Hotel. She could see a double row of them — KGB guardsmen, Chantal guessed, brushing a drop of rain from the bridge of her nose — standing in front of the Mariinsky Palace. All Saint Isaac's Square had been cordoned off with wooden barriers, leaving only the sidewalks for the spectators, who were now beginning to gather despite the rain and the fact that the men they had come to see were to arrive at the palace nearly three hours hence.

There's certainly more than enough security, Chantal thought. I hope Romanenko gets back to Moscow in one piece.

A voice behind her said, in English, "Checking out the opposition?" She turned around. Cathcart was standing behind her, squinting through the rain at the front of the Mariinsky Palace. He was rather short and had to stand on tiptoe to look over the guard cordon in front of the Astoria. He looked a little the worse for wear; too much Russian hospitality.

"Yes," she said. "Too bad about the rain."

"I hope the goddam minicams work properly," Cathcart said, settling back onto his heels. "The Russians haven't come out in the open like this since...I can't remember when. Not until Romanenko. You know his nephew. What are they up to?"

"Who knows with Russians?" Chantal said. She thought one of the guards along the curb had turned his head slightly, to improve his hearing. "Just be glad you've got a chance to get a camera near them."

"Ah, shit," Cathcart said. "You know what they'll do with it back home. Thirty-five seconds on the national news the first night, twenty the second, ten the next, then forget it. Nobody in North America gives a good goddamn about internal Russian politics. For this I had to bring my own toilet paper to Leningrad?"

"They'd better start paying attention," Chantal said, meaning North America. "If Romanenko does what he looks like he's doing, things are going to change. Fast."

"Balls," said Cathcart. His hair was getting wet and beads of water had collected in his beard. "Nobody wants anything to change. You know what the Americans think? Thank God the Russians are communists, because if they had a sensible political system they'd walk all over us. The Americans *want* the Russians to go on screwing things up."

"Maybe," Chantal said.

"They're all politicians," Cathcart said, brushing rain out of his beard. "They're the same everywhere." He turned abruptly and went back into the hotel.

Cathcart may be right, she reflected, watching the guards standing motionless and glum in the drizzle. Maybe the Americans don't want Romanenko to work it all out. Maybe they want the Soviet Union to stay in its ideological trap, always on the edge of ruin and collapse. What would these people be able to do if they were set free?

She turned and hurried back into the hotel, unnerved by her momentary vision of a liberated Russia.

Smilga telephoned Zarudin at eleven-twenty in the morning. The chairman of the council of ministers answered on the first ring.

"It's Dmitri," Smilga said. "Everything is in order. Contact Pripoltsev and have him prepare to call an emergency plenum of the Central Committee. Yasev doesn't know anything about it, so this time we don't have to worry about you-know-who's friends being flown in from all over the union. You've got your speech ready?"

"Yes." Zarudin was to announce to the Central Committee that Romanenko and a number of his clique had been arrested on charges of treason: attempting to subvert the Marxist-Leninist principles of the revolution. Further charges were pending. The Central Committee would then be required to elect replacements for the arrested men to the Secretariat and the Politburo. Zarudin was to be the new general secretary. Smilga was content to remain as he was. "Romanenko is not to be harmed," Zarudin said.

"He won't be," Smilga promised. Privately he would have preferred a quick death for Romanenko, Tsander, and the rest of the liberalizing cabal, but Zarudin had insisted on trials for all of them, to preserve socialist legality. The Warsaw Pact leaders meeting with Romanenko would also be detained until it was certain that their national Parties would obey the new discipline exerted by Moscow. "There will be a lot of cleanup work to do," Smilga added.

"Don't trouble me with the details," Zarudin snapped. Smilga knew the man didn't want to be associated with the nastier side of the purges that were to come; he'd benefit, but he didn't want to carry any of the responsibility.

"As you wish, Secretary," Smilga said formally. "I'll keep in touch."

"Do that," said Zarudin, and rang off.

Smilga picked up the internal phone and dialed Tolbukhin's local.

When the phone buzzed Tolbukhin was rereading the list of officers who would be arrested in the first wave of the purge. "Yes?"

"Smilga here. Come up and see me immediately, please. Bring those lists of yours."

Tolbukhin replaced the receiver, shocked. Not until now had he believed that Smilga would go through with his attack on the military, but it looked as though it were about to begin. He would have to warn Tsander as soon as he could. Not now, though, not with Smilga waiting.

He made his way to the chairman's office. Sun beamed cheerfully in through the tall windows; the rain had stopped half an hour ago. Smilga was sitting behind his desk, hands clasped behind his head.

"Well, General Tolbukhin. You've done a good job on those lists; they separate the sheep from the wolves quite nicely. Now we have to act." He unclasped his hands and leaned on the desk where the originals of Tolbukhin's lists lay in a buff folder. "Starting at twelve-thirty," the KGB chairman said, "I want you to deal personally with the first thirty-seven names on the list you've marked one-A. Make arrangements by telephone to have them all detained at one-thirty exactly. I presume you have Third Directorate personnel in position to do so in each case?"

Tolbukhin nodded. The names were those of very senior officers who held sensitive commands in the armed forces, and who were known for their vigorous support of Romanenko. They were to be arrested by Third Directorate officers working in their own staffs. These thirty-seven arrests alone would be tremendously demoralizing to the senior officer corps.

"See to it, then," Smilga ordered. "The other lists you can turn over to your deputies, since there are so many names on them, but I want you to deal with the first list personally. Understand?"

"Yes, Chairman Smilga." Tolbukhin's stomach had clenched itself into a hard knot. He had to get a message to Tsander. One of the first names on the list was Paul Osipov, chief of the General Staff. "May I ask why this is being done at this time?"

Smilga regarded him with narrowed eyes. "Yes. You may. It's time we put our house in order. For the past twenty years the Party has been growing lax; you can see the results all around us. Disaffected young people, western influences, inefficiency, shortages, patronage. It's time to end it. Russians need discipline to make them behave, to remind them of what they owe Mother Russia. Influences that soften us have to be weeded out, especially in the military."

Tolbukhin waited, then he realized that Smilga wasn't going to continue. The KGB chairman was gazing thoughtfully out the window, into the golden summer sunlight.

"Have I the Chairman's leave to go?" he asked finally.

"Yes. Contact me as soon as you've made those calls, and inform me when the arrests have been confirmed."

"Yes, Chairman," Tolbukhin said.

Outside Smilga's door he wiped his forehead with the back of his hand. It came away wet. As he went down to his office he thought: I could simply go along with this, not contact Tsander, save my own skin. Tempting. But I can't be part of this slaughter. Anyway, sooner or later Smilga will find out I worked for Romanenko, and that'll be the end of me. If I act now Romanenko may be able to stop the purge. I might even survive.

I should kill Dmitri Smilga, he thought, closing his office door behind him. Cut off one head of the monster. If Romanenko wins, he'll have to turn the KGB inside out. But I don't think his purge would be as bloody as Smilga's is going to be.

He sat down at his desk and looked at the clock. It was eleven-forty-five. His thoughts passed momentarily over his wife, a quiet, graying woman who had followed him patiently around the many postings he had held while he rose in the KGB. If he indeed sabotaged Smilga's intentions, he was condemning her to death as surely as he was himself. They had had no children. Tolbukhin had always looked upon this as a misfortune, but it now appeared a blessing; fewer people to worry about.

With a sudden decisive movement Tolbukhin unlocked the

bottom drawer of his desk and took out the Makarov pistol. He stripped it, checked it, and then reassembled it and shoved in an ammunition clip.

There was a telephone booth two blocks away. If he hurried, he could be back at his desk in fifteen minutes, just in time to start issuing the arrest orders; except that he would do something quite different from that.

Konstantin Tsander was drinking a glass of tea. It was freshly poured and too hot; he burned his lips on the first sip. Grimacing, he put the glass down. Vera, his dictation clerk, looked at him sympathetically, pencil poised. She was a pretty young brunette with strong wrists and large hands.

"Where was I?" asked Tsander. His mind kept wandering this morning; it was ten minutes to twelve.

"'In regard to the new high-grade steel allocations,'" Vera said.

"Oh, yes. 'We should —'"

The telephone rang, the high-priority line that bypassed the switchboard. Tsander frowned and picked it up. "Tsander."

"Secretary, the other evening we were discussing an urgent matter you probably recollect."

Tsander recognized Tolbukhin's voice. He waved at Vera to leave. "Yes," Tsander said as the door closed behind her. "I remember that."

"We didn't expect the decision so early, but it is to go into effect at about half-past one this afternoon. I thought you ought to know."

"Yes," Tsander said. His voice cracked dryly. "Yes, that's very useful."

"I hope you can take appropriate action. Good-bye."

"Good-bye," Tsander said into a dead line. God in heaven, he thought, Smilga and Zarudin are going to risk it. I have to warn Vasily, anyone else I can. Paul Osipov. Not Minister Yasev, he may be in this up to his neck.

He hated using his office telephone, but he had no choice. Tolbukhin had taken a fearful risk, despite doing his best to obscure his message. Time. There was so little time.

He called the switchboard and got them to patch him

through to Romanenko on the scrambler. The general secretary was staying at the Alexander Palace in the village of Pushkin, twenty-five kilometers south of Leningrad. Tsander hoped desperately that Romanenko hadn't yet left for the city.

He hadn't.

"This is Konstantin," Tsander said. "How is Ekaterina?"

"Well, thank you." Romanenko's voice was easy, relaxed.

"I wanted to verify part of your itinerary. I left my copy at home and the idiots here can't locate another one. You're going to be at the Mariinsky Palace at one-thirty today?"

"That's right."

"Good, that was all. I wish you the best of success."

"Thank you, Kosti. Good-bye."

Tsander replaced the receiver. It was slippery with perspiration. Now for Osipov. Then he could start thinking about his own safety.

Contacting Osipov from here was going to be dangerous. He had no legitimate reason to do so, no code ready. If the phone were indeed tapped...

There might be another way. He pressed a button on his intercom and ordered his car brought around. Then he summoned Vera. She bustled in, pencil and pad at the ready.

"I have to go out for a while," said Tsander, "but I want to finish this dictation. You come along in the car. Get anything you need. I'll be back in a minute."

With an expression of faint surprise she said, "I just need these."

"Wait here," Tsander said.

He went along the corridor to Azovkin's office. Azovkin was secretary for heavy industry, one of Tsander's subordinates and also loyal to Romanenko. Azovkin looked up from a sheaf of papers. Tsander grabbed the pen out of his hand and wrote on a memo pad:

SMILGA IS STARTING A PURGE AGAINST ROMANENKO.
GET OUT OF MOSCOW IF YOU CAN.

Azovkin looked at the note in momentary disbelief. Then he nodded quickly and stood up, reaching for his suit jacket.

Tsander tore the slip of paper off the pad and went in search of others to warn.

Five minutes later he was back in his own office, frustrated and frightened. He had only been able to find Voroshilov, secretary for the lower Party apparatus. The other pro-Romanenko secretaries had already gone out to lunch and were unlocatable. There was no more to be done here.

Tsander and Vera went downstairs to the side entrance of the Central Committee building. Instead of getting into the car immediately, he said, "Vera, who is at home in your apartment right now?"

She was startled. "Only my mother." He could see the suspicion and fear in her eyes, although he had never made the slightest of sexual advances toward her.

"Where is the apartment?"

"Podzozensky Street. Number fifty-one."

It wasn't very far away. How much time did he have? "We're going there. Don't worry, this has nothing to do with you."

She nodded, mystified. They got into the Zil and the chauffeur pulled out into the traffic on Staraya Square. If he was surprised at their destination he didn't show it. When they reached Podzozensky Street, Tsander got out with Vera and said to the driver, "Come back in two hours. Then wait. In the meantime go and have some lunch." He stuffed a wad of rubles into the man's tunic pocket, seeing in the man's eyes what he wanted to see: belief in an afternoon affair between the secretary and his dictation clerk.

They went up to the third floor. Vera's family's apartment, which overlooked the street, was an ordinary Moscow one: cramped, dingy, smelling of cabbage, a brown oilcloth on the kitchen table. Vera's mother wasn't home; so much the better. Vera said she was probably out shopping.

Tsander looked out the window into the street. The Zil was gone. "Is there a public telephone near here?"

"Around the corner, turn right when you leave the building. You can use ours."

He shook his head. A clerk in the Central Committee

offices would be subject to intermittent telephone surveillance, to see whether any gossip were being passed along. He took his jacket off and rolled up his sleeves. A minimal change of appearance was the best he could manage. "I'll be back in a minute," he said.

Outside the day's heat was building up and the recent rain had left the air humid and sticky. There were large puddles on the sidewalk and broad damp patches still blotched the asphalt of the road. Tsander rounded the corner and spotted the pay phone up ahead, no one in it, a small mercy. He fished a two-kopeck coin out of his trousers. Wouldn't it be amusing, he thought, if disaster came because I didn't have change for the telephone.

It took some time to get through to Osipov. Tsander finally broke the bureaucratic logjam by identifying himself as Secretary Lebedev, one of Zarudin's clique. He hoped fleetingly that this would make trouble for Lebedev later on.

"Yes, Secretary?" Osipov's voice was neutral. He had little use for Lebedev.

"Marshal Osipov," Tsander said, "you probably remember the last conversation we had, near the little waterfall."

"Ah, yes," Osipov said, his tone changing fractionally, "I do remember."

"We really ought to continue the discussion. At your earliest convenience."

"All right," Osipov said. "Where are you?"

"Podzozensky Street, number fifty-one."

"I'll pick you up in a few minutes," Osipov said.

Now, Tsander thought as he walked back to Vera's apartment building, *if* they aren't watching Osipov too closely yet, and *if* Tolbukhin can do something, anything, to head off Smilga, and *if* Vasily Romanenko can stay out of the claws of the KGB, I may live to see another morning.

Ekaterina flicked the intercom switch to talk to the chauffeur in the front seat of the Chaika limousine. "Driver."

"Yes, madam?"

"I've decided I don't want to go into Leningrad after all.

There's somebody I want to visit. Just drive where I tell you to."

"Yes, madam. I should report our destination, for your security." He reached for the microphone clipped to the dashboard.

"Never mind that," Ekaterina snapped. "You can tell them when we get there, if you like. Don't you think everyone has enough to do today, looking after my husband?"

The driver released the microphone as though it had bitten him. "Yes, madam, but I —"

"Don't worry. I'll see that you don't get into trouble. Turn right on Slavy Ivanovskaya Prospekt and go across the river. Then turn north on Dolnevostochny. And don't waste any time." She tried, without much success, to keep her hands from trembling. Just before noon Vasily had received that phone call, in the big bedroom in the Alexander Palace. He hadn't said anything at first, simply replaced the receiver carefully and stared at it for several seconds. Then he said, "Ekaterina, it's going to be boring for you to wait around here all day. Why don't you arrange a car and go into Leningrad for a few hours? We can meet at the Mariinsky Palace for the evening reception."

She looked at him with sudden understanding. "All right," she said. "I'll just put on some more lipstick."

He returned to the final draft of the speech, which he had laid out in neat piles on the desk. She could hear his pen scratching, a flutter of pages. She finished her makeup and went to stand beside him. On a sheet of paper he had written:

> Andrei. Come immediately to the
> Mariinsky Palace with all the men you
> can mobilize. Secure the palace and re-
> move all KGB personnel. Locate me.
> Use any necessary force. Make arrange-
> ments for Ekaterina's safety.

Underneath he sketched a map of the route to Mikhailov's base and then folded the paper and handed it to Ekaterina. She put it in her purse.

"I'm off now," she had said. "I'll see you tonight."

"Have a good time," her husband had answered. "Don't waste any of it."

Ekaterina looked out the Chaika's window. The suburbs of Leningrad lay ahead, smoky-gray in the rain. She wondered whether they intended to take Vasily alive, or simply put him against the nearest wall and shoot him.

Tolbukhin was working against time, and he saw by his desk clock that there was simply not going to be enough of it. Instead of telephoning the Third Directorate officers who were to make the arrests, he had been calling the targets and trying to persuade them to take preemptive action themselves. Several of the contacts he had made so far had sounded unconvinced. Why should a high Third Directorate officer — Tolbukhin had not identified himself by name — be giving them such a warning? It smelled of a KGB provocation.

Worse, he had been unable to locate several of the men he wanted to warn. And in half an hour Smilga would want to know that the arrests had begun. Many of them would, in fact, be carried out successfully; Tolbukhin had had to turn the long lists of lower-ranking officers over to his two deputy chiefs, and there was no possibility that *that* pair would commit what amounted to treason. But if Tolbukhin could manage to get the major combat commanders out of harm's way, Romanenko would still have a chance.... Osipov, at least, seemed to have gotten away. He had been the first contact Tolbukhin tried to make; one of his aides had informed Tolbukhin that the marshal had just left for an urgent appointment. Tsander must have reached him in time.

At the moment Tolbukhin's major worry was that he couldn't reach the generals commanding the Taman and the Kantemirov divisions, the two most powerful army units based near Moscow. Without those two formations there was no hope of holding the capital for Romanenko.

Maybe Osipov warned them, Tolbukhin thought, passing a hand over his sweaty forehead. He picked up the phone again and ordered a connection to Marshal Georgi Pervishin, who commanded the Western Strategic Direction and controlled all Soviet and Warsaw Pact troops in Poland, Germany, Czechoslovakia, and the Byelorussian military district. He had already tried to contact the commander of the Southwest Strategic Direction — Hungary, Romania, Bulgaria, and the Kiev and Carpathian military districts — but the marshal was on an inspection tour and it could take as much as two hours to locate him.

Tolbukhin didn't have an hour, much less two. He still hadn't managed to reach the commander-in-chief of the Leningrad military district, and if the KGB got control of that district's forces, Romanenko's chances of survival diminished to the vanishing point.

Tolbukhin watched the second hand rotate around the face of his desk clock while the line to Germany clicked, beeped, and tinkled. Finally:

"Zossen HQ. Marshal Pervishin's office, Colonel Alipov speaking."

"This is Moscow Center," said Tolbukhin. "Get me the marshal, and be quick about it."

A short, worried silence in East Germany. Then, "Yes. May I inform the marshal who's calling?"

"You may not. Put him on immediately."

A thud as the receiver at the other end was placed roughly on a hard surface. It was four minutes past one. Finally a gruff voice said, "Pervishin. What is it?"

"Marshal, I won't tell you who I am, for obvious reasons. Within the next hour a Third Directorate colonel on your staff, his name is Turasov, will receive orders to arrest you. He will be supported by other KGB operatives in your headquarters. They are to fly you to Moscow, where you will be imprisoned, at the very least, because you favor Vasily Romanenko. I suggest you take immediate precautions."

A long silence. Finally Pervishin said, "Who are you? On what authority are you doing this?"

He *had* to convince Pervishin. The man commanded the largest combat force in the Soviet military machine. "I am General Tolbukhin, chief of the Third Directorate. I urge you to take action immediately to protect yourself."

Another lengthy silence, while the wires hissed. "All right," Pervishin said at last. "I'll take measures. Good-bye."

Tolbukhin exhaled a great sigh of relief and put down the receiver. Then he called the Leningrad military district again, only to be told that the general was expected in half an hour or less. Tolbukhin cursed inwardly and said he'd try again.

Mikhailov looked from his uncle's note to his aunt's anguished face as she sat on the chair beside his desk. "Where's Uncle Vasily right now?"

"Partway from Pushkin to Leningrad. The motorcade's to arrive at the place at exactly one-forty. He starts his introductory speech at ten to two. Andrei, can you help him?"

"Yes," Mikhailov said, getting up. He put his head out the office door and said to one of the clerks, "Get the chief of staff to my office *instantly*. And have all regimental commanders report as well. I don't care what they're doing, get them here inside three minutes." He closed the door and went and looked out the window. It was raining again, a steady drizzle. "Ekaterina, do they know you're here?"

"I don't think so. I wouldn't let the chauffeur report where we were going, so the KGB thinks I'm in Leningrad. When we got here I made him carry my umbrella for me and told him to wait inside the front door until I was finished. I think he's still there."

"I'll have him kept here," said Mikhailov. "Look, this is what I'm going to do. I can start moving my troops in fifteen minutes. It will take another thirty to get into the city. If the KGB holds on the arrests until everybody's settled in the conference hall we'll just make it."

There was a rap on the door and the chief of staff entered, followed by the four regimental colonels of the division. They looked at Ekaterina with some surprise.

"This is General Secretary Romanenko's wife," Mikhailov said. "She's brought word from the secretary that reactionaries are attempting a counterrevolution in Leningrad. I want three battalions of troops on their way to Saint Isaac's Square within ten minutes. Secure the Mariinsky Palace and the surrounding area. Follow the infantry with a tank battalion. I will ride with the lead elements. Get the commander's BRDM here immediately. The rest of the division will follow within twenty minutes. Also," he went on, emphasizing the words heavily, "there's evidence that the plot has supporters in Moscow. You are to take orders only from me; ignore any that may reach you from anyone else. These are the general secretary's wishes. I will have anyone who disobeys them shot immediately. Is this understood?"

"Yes, Colonel Mikhailov," said the chief of staff. The other four men nodded vigorously.

"Good," Mikhailov said. "Now *move*." They began to troop out. "Colonel Utkin," Mikhailov said to the chief of staff, "wait one moment. Close the door."

Utkin shut it and waited expectantly. "I didn't want to mention this in front of the others," Mikhailov said, "but there's evidence that some elements of the KGB are involved in this affair. I want you personally to lead a battalion from the 349th Regiment and take over the Leningrad KGB headquarters. Cut off all their communications with Moscow. Understand?"

Confusion and doubt warred in Utkin's expression. Finally they cleared away; it was simplest and best to follow orders. "Understood, Colonel."

"I want your troops hot on the heels of the others. There will be great rewards for protecting the leader of the Party. Go, quickly."

When he had left, Ekaterina said, "I'm coming too."

"You can't," Mikhailov said. "What if —"

"Andrei, you won't keep me here except by locking me up."

"Aunt Ekaterina," Mikhailov said desperately, "you're the wife of the general secretary. I can't let you put yourself in that kind of danger. If you were taken hostage..."

"Andrei," she said sharply, "I'm the wife of the general secretary; exactly. I have to be willing to take the same risks he does. I order you to take me with you. If you still refuse, I'll drive the car I came in and follow. I am *not* going to remain here. I hope that's clear. Now get on with your business; we have no time for arguing."

She was right, there was no time. "All right," he said.

"You can come with me in the BRDM. It won't be comfortable."

"It will be much less comfortable out here, not knowing what's happening. And don't forget," she added practically, "to arrest that chauffeur."

The line to Kabul was very bad. Tolbukhin had to strain to hear General Gordik's voice at the other end.

"Stepan? It's me, Tolbukhin.... Yes, I'm calling from Moscow. Can you hear? Good. Shortly you may get orders to pick up several of the Kabul headquarters staff. I advise you not to do it. The situation here is very fluid." He paused, sweating. The devil only knew who might be listening in, even with the scrambler on. He had gotten away with all his calls so far, but Smilga would soon be requesting confirmation of the first arrests. Gordik, fortunately, was a long-time colleague of Tolbukhin's and owed much of his rise in the KGB to Tolbukhin's influence. The two men shared similar views on Smilga's direction of the KGB; Tolbukhin was gambling that Gordik would delay any action in Kabul until the situation at home was resolved.

"What exactly do you mean?" asked Gordik. The caution in his voice was evident even over the bad line.

"Smilga's trying to start a purge of the armed forces," Tolbukhin said bluntly, "without the general secretary's knowledge. It's treason."

"What are his chances?"

"Bad," said Tolbuhin, and added untruthfully, "most of his targets have been alerted. I urge you to support me in this. Warn the Kabul GHQ."

A considering silence. Then Gordik said, "All right. It may cost me my head, but I agree with you. We don't want any more of that kind of purge. Good luck."

Tolbukhin broke the connection by pressing the cradle of the telephone. He had to make one more try for the Leningrad military district commander.

The office interphone buzzed. Tolbukhin snatched it up with his free hand. "Tolbukhin."

"Smilga. Have you completed the calls? And have action confirmations started to come in?"

"I have one more call," Tolbukhin said. "There are no confirmations as yet. I expect the first within minutes."

"Call me," Smilga said, and hung up.

Tolbukhin put down the interphone and tried Leningrad again.

Upstairs, Dmitri Smilga frowned at the wall. Tolbukhin should have completed his contacts by now. The KGB chairman picked up the interphone again and dialed the switchboard. "This is Chairman Smilga. Is General Tolbukhin's long-distance line busy?"

"Yes, Chairman. He placed a call about a minute ago."

"Patch me in. Without him noticing."

The operator did so. Forty seconds later Smilga put the receiver down. He had gone white except for two red splotches, one over each cheekbone.

Tolbukhin wiped his palms on his trouser legs; they were so sweaty that he had almost dropped the receiver before hanging up. But the Leningrad military district had been warned. Now, if the man would only take it seriously... Better try Budapest again. He was being graced with more time than he had expected.

Buzz.

"Tolbukhin," he said into the receiver.

"Be so good as to come up here immediately," Smilga ordered. "Order any calls to your office to be routed here."

"Yes, Chairman," Tolbukhin said. He stood up slowly. There would be no time to call Budapest after all, nor anywhere else. Think. He could make a run for it... but if Smilga knew what he'd been doing, he'd never get out of the Lubianka. And if Smilga didn't know, to attempt flight would be immediate self-betrayal.

Tolbukhin took the Makarov out of his tunic, slipped off the safety catch, put the pistol back, and left his office for the last time.

Smilga's secretary looked up as Tolbukhin entered the outer

office. "The chairman is expecting you," she said, with a bright smile. "Go right in." Tolbukhin nodded briefly, thinking: that's the last time I'm likely to see that smile.

Smilga's office door, which opened inwards to the left, was slightly ajar. Tolbukhin pushed it open with his left hand and walked in. His right hand remained in his jacket pocket, grasping the Makarov.

Smilga looked up from a stack of papers. His face was devoid of expression.

"Take him," he said.

Just inside the door on Tolbukhin's right stood a Ninth Directorate guard. Smilga had given strict orders that the Third Directorate chief was to be taken alive and without serious injury. This reminder slowed the guard a little, just enough for Tolbukhin to evade him for perhaps two seconds. It was not enough time for him to get the Makarov out of his pocket, but it was enough to allow him to point the gun roughly through the cloth and squeeze the trigger.

The 9mm bullet struck Smilga's desk at a shallow angle, gouged out a spray of wood splinters, and ricocheted up to strike the KGB chairman in the left forearm. Deformed by its impact with the desktop, the bullet narrowly missed the bone of the arm and then passed upwards out of Smilga's body to bury itself in the wall above and behind his desk.

The guardsman grappled desperately for the pistol, which went off once more, harmlessly. His partner, who had been on the blind side of the door, didn't waste time with the gun; he kicked Tolbukhin hard in the testicles. Tolbukhin by this time had given up trying to shoot Smilga, and was attempting to turn the weapon on himself. The blinding pain from the guardsman's kick put an end to this, although in reflex Tolbukhin got off one more round, which grazed his right thigh, leaving powder burns and a superficial flesh wound.

It was over. Tolbukhin lay bleeding and groaning on the carpet. The secretary was standing in the office doorway, eyes round as coins.

"Bastard," snarled the guardsman who had kicked Tolbukhin. "Don't stand there with your finger up it," he yelled at the secretary. "Call a doctor." He unbuckled his pistol belt, ripped off the holster, and began to put a tourniquet on Smilga's upper arm. The desk was puddled with blood. Smilga's eyes were slightly glazed; he was in mild shock and struggling to remain in control.

"Tolbukhin," he said. "Tolbukhin. I want..."

"Yes, Chairman?"

"Take him to Lefortovo. Turn him over to Inspector Yegrov. I want to know everything. Everything."

"Immediately, Chairman. As soon as you're taken care of. Can you move your fingers?"

Smilga could. "The bone is all right, then," said the guard shakily. He was very frightened; he and his partner were likely going to end up in the camps for dereliction of duty. He wished momentarily that he had shot Tolbukhin, and then retracted the wish: what would happen to Tolbukhin in Lefortovo was far worse than a dignified death by gunshot.

Smilga was regaining his color. "Loosen this fucking belt," he snarled to the guardsman. "I don't want gangrene." The man complied hurriedly.

May all the devils of hell fry Tolbukhin when I've finished with him, Smilga thought. How many targets did he reach? No way of knowing until we go over his list again. I never suspected him. I should have. No drawing back now; we'll have to be even more ruthless, no mercy.

The other guardsman was now dragging Tolbukhin by his heels through the doorway. There was a clock above the door. Smilga looked at the clock. Its hands stood at one-forty-six.

*R*OMANENKO WALKED ACROSS THE DAIS at the front of the Hall of the Leningrad City Soviet to the podium. Before him, flanked by advisors and functionaries of their various national Parties, sat the leaders of the Warsaw Pact nations: Poland, East Germany, Czechoslovakia, Hungary, Bulgaria. Even the Rumanians, who had a Yugoslav-like tendency to go their separate way, had consented to attend.

Romanenko would have felt more satisfaction at this gathering had it not been for the worry at the back of his mind that a violent reaction to the summit was impending, if not actually underway. Tsander's phone call from Moscow had shaken him; he could hardly believe that Smilga and Zarudin would act so soon. Tsander had once told him that he thought too rationally, and worse, believed that most other human beings did the same; that he ignored too much the emotional drives underlying men's behavior. This could be one of the times he had miscalculated.

It's going to be a very embarrassing scene, he thought as he arranged his papers on the podium, if Andrei's soldiers come roaring into Saint Isaac's Square to rescue me from a mirage. How I'd handle *that* politically, I don't know. Endangering Ekaterina too.

But Tsander is sure it's happening. Unless, of course, he's joined the other side, and is stage-managing a political disaster for me.

He smiled wryly at the idea. His audience misinterpreted the expression and broke into prolonged applause. After half a minute of clapping he had to put up a hand for silence; it had begun to look like one of Stalin's Party congresses where no one dared be first to stop banging his palms together.

He adjusted his glasses, cleared his throat, and said, "Comrades. Comrades of the Warsaw Treaty nations. We have all had experiences of historic events. Perhaps too many historic events, for those of us who are older."

A whisper of laughter, nods. "This event, however," Romanenko continued, "is —"

He stopped and looked up. A minor commotion had broken out at the back of the hall. The delegates at the front were craning their necks to see what was happening. The lights illuminating Romanenko made it hard for him to see the hall's rear, but he could make out uniforms. Army? KGB?

Motion on the dais to his left flickered in his peripheral vision. He turned to look. Four men in gray suits were walking along the platform toward him, and they all carried pistols.

Military vehicles and men in uniform were a common sight in Leningrad, but the dense column of trucks and BMP armored personnel carriers roaring along the Palace Embankment on the south side of the Neva River produced considerable astonishment among the pedestrians, who stopped to gawk, and consternation among the drivers, who had to get out of the way or risk being rammed. In the command BRDM at the head of the column Mikhailov dashed rain out of his eyes and watched the Winter Palace draw closer on his left. Two more blocks and they would be in Saint Isaac's Square, and they would probably have to fight.

"Are we nearly there?" Ekaterina called from the interior of the BRDM, over the engine's roar.

"Nearly. Don't leave the vehicle when we arrive. There's going to be shooting. And keep low on the floor."

"All right."

Mikhailov was worrying about his troops. There had been time to give them only the sketchiest of plans, and they might be reluctant to fire on the KGB. He wasn't sure they would follow their orders without hesitation, and any hesitation might be fatal to Romanenko. The KGB might have orders to kill him instantly if it appeared he might be rescued.

The column reached the intersection of Nevsky Prospekt and the embankment and swung left, past the Winter Palace's west facade and south to Admiralteysky Avenue, where the line of vehicles turned right. Ahead the dome of Saint Isaac's Cathedral and the great gray spire of the Admiralty rose against the slate-colored sky. They were nearly there.

"This is Colonel Mikhailov," he said into the battalion communications network. "Deploy."

The BRDM turned down Mayorov Avenue, toward Saint Isaac's Square and the Mariinsky Palace. There were two more columns in Mikhailov's force; one was proceeding southwest along Plekhanov Street, and another along the parallel road running behind the palace. Mikhailov had planned the operation as a hammer-and-anvil attack: his column and the one from Plekhanov Street formed the hammer and would strike the KGB front-ally at Saint Isaac's Square, and the forces behind the Mariinsky Palace, the anvil, would prevent them from retreating.

It would also prevent them from escaping with Romanenko, if the KGB had already committed itself to action.

The rain was slackening. Just ahead, where Gogol Street ran along the south side of the cathedral, Mikhailov could see the crowd-control barricades the KGB had set up. A scattering of spectators who had braved the weather to watch the start of the summit stood along the wooden rails. Beyond them patrolled the KGB guardsmen in their green uniforms with blue shoulder flashes and trouser stripes.

Some of the spectators were looking over their shoulders now, at the fighting vehicles roaring three abreast toward them. They scattered toward the sidewalks. Out in the square by the statue of Nicholas were half a dozen trucks, around which stood more guardsmen, looking drenched and miserable in the rain. On the south side of the square was a solid line of KGB troops arrayed across the front of the Mariinsky Palace.

The BRDM carrying Mikhailov, and the two tracked BMPs

flanking it, crashed through the wooden barricades. The KGB men threw themselves out of the way, too startled to unsling their assault rifles. The guards by the trucks and in front of the Mariinsky had more time. After a moment's hesitation they began to drop into firing positions.

"Dismount," Mikhailov yelled into the common radio network. Ten more BMPs, followed by half a dozen trucks, fanned out into the square and slammed to a halt. Troops began to spill out of the hatches and over the tailboards, weapons at the ready.

If the KGB troops had held their fire, Mikhailov's worry about his men's hesitancy might have been justified, but they did not. The damp air was split by the rip of AKMS rifles on full automatic; bullets hammered on the armor of the BRDM and the BMPs. Mikhailov's troops shot back, although they were not very effective since they were still bunched up from dismounting. Then the heavy machine guns in the BMP turrets opened up, giving covering fire. The KGB guards, caught in the open and lightly armed, began to take casualties. A tracer bullet struck the fuel tank of one of the trucks by the Nicholas statue and the vehicle exploded into a sphere of bright flame, incinerating the guardsmen who had taken shelter behind it. Two more of the trucks by the statue caught fire, driving the KGB men into the open, where the BMP machine guns and Mikhailov's troops mowed them down. The KGB fighting line in front of the palace began to melt away, the surviving men trying to retreat down the side streets flanking the building. Firing broke out behind them, from the column Mikhailov had sent into their rear. Caught in a crossfire, they began to throw down their weapons and raise their hands. It was no use. The soldiers shot them down indiscriminately.

Mikhailov didn't try to stop them. "Get me over to the entrance," he yelled at his driver, and the BRDM lurched into motion. Four BMPs followed; the rest were busy moving about the square, supporting the infantry as they winkled the last of their opponents out of cover. The BRDM drew up to the arched portico of the palace and Mikhailov jumped out, dragging his assault rifle behind him. "Lieutenant," he shouted at a young officer leading a skirmish line of about thirty soldiers toward the building. "Follow me. Secure the inside."

This was not what he had planned. There should have been three platoons, about sixty men, already penetrating the palace. What had happened to them he couldn't tell; smoke from the burning trucks had obscured half the square. As he searched for the missing men one of the truck's fuel tanks exploded, adding to the confusion.

Shit. We'll have to go in anyway, Mikhailov thought. Followed by the lieutenant and the soldiers, he plunged into the Mariinsky Palace.

As the four men walked across the dais toward him, Romanenko thought: Well, it's over. I should have paid more attention to Konstantin. I should have taken action against Smilga. I should have.... I hope Ekaterina's safe.

He turned to face them. His own bodyguards were nowhere to be seen: thorough betrayal. The men who had come to take him were all ordinary, even nondescript, but professional, disinterested in everything but the work at hand. Romanenko spared a glance for the hall itself. A cordon of KGB guardsmen had formed around the delegates, most of whom were now standing up, muttering in consternation.

"What do you want?" he asked the leading man of the four. "We are in no danger here. Go back where you came from, and get those other men out of here."

"We are to take you into protective custody," the man said, without emotion, as though he were stating the diameter of the earth. "You will come with us immediately, please."

"Not until I know the reason for this 'protective custody,'" Romanenko said. Without much hope, he had decided to delay. There was always the chance that Andrei would come. "I am the elected general secretary of the Party. I want your names and ranks and your authority in this."

"Certainly," said the man. "I'm Captain Ivanov, of Department Eight, Directorate S." He smiled. His teeth were badly tobacco-stained. "I'm following my orders. Everything will be explained, I'm sure."

"No doubt," said Romanenko, standing his ground. Out in the hall faces were beginning to turn toward him, to see what was going to happen. The hall was very still.

From outside there came the sound of machine-gun fire, like ripping cloth.

"Shit," said the Department S man. "Grab him." Two of the others seized Romanenko under the arms and began to drag him off the dais. Pandemonium broke out among the rows of seats as the guards tried to drive the delegates out the side exits. There was more shooting outside the rear of the hall, much louder this time.

He's just barely too late, Romanenko thought despairingly. They have me, Smilga's won.

In the corridor leading to the Hall of the Soviet there was carnage. The guards posted there had fought hard, and their bodies mingled on the bloody marble floor with those of unlucky civilians of the delegation staffs and several of Mikhailov's men.

The ornate carved doors to the hall were locked. From their far side Mikhailov could hear shots, curses, and the sounds of blows.

"Shoot the locks off," he told the lieutenant. He looked behind. Now that the KGB forces in the square had been suppressed, more of his men were storming into the palace. "Down the side corridors," Mikhailov shouted. "Cut them off!"

The lieutenant's AKMS banged, a single shot. He kicked at the doors, but they opened outward and wouldn't budge. Mikhailov grabbed a projecting splinter where the locks had been shot away and dragged the right-hand leaf open. In the hall the delegates were all by the side doors, where the KGB guards had driven them in an attempt to get them out of the building. Mikhailov's troops had stopped any further movement. Mercifully, no one in the hall had opened fire.

"You're trapped," he shouted at them. "Put down your weapons." The east doors boomed open and half a dozen army men ran through the opening in a fighting crouch. They stopped at the first file of seats, weapons sighted, waiting.

For perhaps five seconds everyone in the hall remained

motionless, as though posing for a photograph. Then Mikhailov called out, "You've been betrayed. Your orders don't have the authority of the Politburo. You're acting for counter-revolutionaries. Comrades! Put down your weapons."

The guardsman nearest the soldiers at the east door let his rifle slip from his fingers. It made a heavy thud as it struck the red carpeting of the floor. Another guard dropped his gun, then another.

"Disarm them, separate them from the civilians," Mikhailov said to the lieutenant as he scanned the hall. He couldn't see Romanenko anywhere. "You six," he said to the nearest soldiers, "follow me."

One of the delegates shouted in heavily accented Russian, "They took the secretary out to your right. There were four of them. To your right."

Mikhailov vaulted onto the dais and ran to the door leading off it. The door had an ornate frame and a carved plaster cornice. On its other side was a narrow corridor leading toward the rear of the building. The corridor was lined with offices. None of Mikhailov's men had penetrated this far yet.

Hoping the soldiers in their heavy combat gear would keep up, he pelted down the corridor. It ended at a big iron-bound wooden door, which was ajar. Somebody was still fighting near the rear of the building; he could hear sporadic shots. Carefully he pushed the door open a few centimeters and, taking a considerable risk, peeped out.

There was an alley behind the building. In the alley was a big Chaika limousine, facing toward Mikhailov. Two men were shoving Romanenko into the back seat. In the front Mikhailov could see two more men.

"Stop!" Mikhailov shouted. Startled, the two men by the car door looked up. Romanenko kicked one of them violently, broke free, and threw himself flat on the ground.

Momentarily the two men couldn't decide whether to pursue Romanenko or deal with Mikhailov. The moment was too long. Mikhailov shot them both in the chest with two short bursts of automatic fire; the impact of the bullets threw them backward, one of them landing neatly on top of Romanenko.

The Chaika's driver decided to cut his losses, and jammed

the accelerator to the floor. With a whine of tires spinning on wet asphalt, the big car leaped forward and hurtled past Mikhailov. The two men in the front seat were keeping low, although the windows were bullet-proof. Mikhailov emptied his magazine at the car without effect. The Chaika was nearly out of the alley into the street when one of Mikhailov's soldiers stepped calmly past him and shot out both of the limousine's rear tires. The Chaika slewed, struck the alley wall with a great screeching and tearing of metal, and slid to a halt, steam hissing from its burst radiator.

Mikhailov ran to Romanenko, who was pushing the KGB man's body off so he could sit up. He looked dazed and his suit was drenched with blood.

"Uncle Vasily?" said Romanenko.

"Not my blood," Romanenko said. "His." He pushed the KGB man's legs off his own and stood up shakily. Mikhailov slung his rifle and threw his arms around his uncle. They embraced tightly for a few seconds. Then Romanenko said, "Only Russians would hug each other in the middle of a palace revolution. Andrei, come on, we've got work to do. What's happening?"

"We've secured the square and the palace. As far as I know all the delegates are safe. I sent a battalion to the KGB headquarters and another one to the military district HQ. We're all right for a while."

"Ekaterina?"

"She's in my BRDM." Mikhailov looked guiltily at his boots. "She wouldn't stay behind."

"I'm not surprised," said Romanenko. "Come, quickly. This can't be all Smilga and Zarudin have planned. I have to get as much of the military under my control as I can. We have to crush the KGB once and for all. If we can do it quickly, we've won."

"If not?" Mikhailov asked. There was a dull boom from Saint Isaac's Square; another truck exploding.

Romanenko said, with profound sadness, "Then there will be another civil war."

When the fighting began in Saint Isaac's Square, Chantal had been drinking with Cathcart in the Astoria's restaurant. Most of the other journalists in the hotel were doing the same thing; there wouldn't be much to report before the press briefing that Romanenko had promised for the evening. The sound of shooting precipitated an immediate stampede for the lobby, whose glass doors provided a view of most of the square. Before her view was blocked by a pushing, cursing mob of newspeople trying to get outside, Chantal saw three uniformed bodies lying on the sidewalk, all with the blue shoulderboards of the KGB guards. At that point several wildly aimed bullets smashed in through the glass of the doors, fortunately too high to hit anyone, and the crowd dropped flat on its collective face. After that nobody tried to get outside; most retired to the restaurant, keeping low. There was no rush for the telephones, either; it was possible to make international calls only from the branch post office on Nevsky Prospekt. A few correspondents from the larger papers tried the hotel phones to contact their bureaus in Moscow, but there was something wrong with the lines and none of them succeeded.

Half a dozen braver souls, Chantal among them, had stayed prone on the lobby floor, peering out through the shattered glass doors. Chantal knew enough about the Soviet military to identify the KGB's attackers as army troops.

Smilga tried it, she thought as a stray bullet whined overhead and struck the elevator cage with a clang. But Romanenko's putting up a fight.

She waited. After a while the firing died down and stopped. A group of soldiers appeared in front of the hotel doors and took up positions on the sidewalk, using the fallen KGB men as rifle rests. Chantal, trying to avoid the broken glass, crawled to the door and peeped out. An instant later she found herself looking into the bore of an assault rifle. One of the soldiers had turned around.

"Get back inside, you fool," he snarled at her.

Badly frightened, she scuttled back into the lobby.

For the next twenty-five minutes the journalists remained in the Astoria, becoming steadily more restless, until most of the soldiers and fighting vehicles left the square and the situation seemed to be approaching normal, except for the bodies and the smoldering trucks. Then there was a concerted rush for the branch post office and the overseas phone lines.

No luck. There were soldiers outside the post office, and they were letting no one in. It was still drizzling, and knots of worried tourists were mingling with the newspeople. One American father accompanied by his wife and two small boys asked Chantal plaintively, "What's going on? How come there's soldiers all over the place? Somebody declared war?"

"I'm sure I don't know," Chantal said hastily and hurried away. God only knew what was going on in Moscow. The odds were good that nobody in the United States embassy there knew what had happened in Leningrad.

There was no point in trying to call the embassy from the Astoria; the other attempts had proven that. Chantal walked quickly toward the Gostinny Dvor metro station, carefully observing her surroundings. Away from the post office and Saint Isaac's Square the city seemed to be going about its business as usual, except that there were army trucks full of soldiers at every other street corner. The MVD militia — the police — weren't paying much attention to the soldiers, although twice on her way to the metro Chantal saw army lieutenants in heated conversation with policemen. There was no sign of the blue flashes and trouser stripes of the KGB Guards Directorate.

She left the metro at Chernyshevskaya Station and walked the block north to the United States consulate. Two soldiers had replaced the militiamen who normally guarded the consulate. They didn't want to let her in until she showed them her passport and convinced them she was a westerner. One of them grinned then and said, "Canada, hockey, very good, yes?"

"Very good, hockey," Chantal said. "Yes."

Bloody Russians, she thought as she entered the lobby. In the middle of a coup they want to talk about hockey. To the young man at the security desk she said, "I'd like to see Mr. Gregory Clarke, please."

"Do you have an appointment?"

"No. It's urgent. Tell him it's Chantal Mallory, from *Seven Days*. He'll see me."

The man looked doubtful but buzzed Clarke anyway.

With some surprise he said, "Mr. Clarke will be here in a minute."

Clarke was fortyish and prematurely gray. Chantal had been told by Fowler to go to him in an emergency, so he was something other than the middle-level consular official he appeared to be. He took Chantal up to his office and leaned against the desk, studying her with an air of faint hostility. He didn't ask her to sit down. "What's the matter?" he asked.

"Have you noticed you've got army troops on your doorstep instead of militia?" she asked.

"Oh, that," he said, looking pained. "Apparently there was some fuss over at the Leningrad summit meeting a while ago. They've merely beefed up the regular security with some troops."

"Who told you that?" she demanded.

"We received a call half an hour ago from one of Romanenko's aides."

"Jesus," she said, and stopped. Romanenko was trying to keep the situation quiet until he had it under control. But Fowler had to know.

"Jesus, what?" said Clarke irritably.

"There's been a full-scale battle in Saint Isaac's Square," she said. "Army against KGB Guards Directorate. The army won, I counted at least forty bodies. The square's full of troops, or was, and there are some trucks on fire. You can probably see the smoke if you'd bother to go and look out a widow. There are trucks full of soldiers all up and down Nevsky Prospekt. Somebody's tried a coup, and Romanenko's called out the army."

"You can't be serious," Clarke said. But the irritation was being replaced by a look of concern. "Are you sure?"

"Take a drive over to Saint Isaac's if you don't believe me. Have you got a line to Moscow? The ones at the hotel weren't working, somebody's cut them off."

"I'll check," he said, hurriedly getting behind his desk. Chantal turned to leave. "Miss Mallory, can you stay — "

"I've told you everything I know," she said. "I'm a journalist; I've got to get back to work."

The Antonov light transport whined over the dull green

landscape at minimum altitude and maximum speed, dragged through the misty air by its twin turboprop engines. It was holding a course for Leningrad, and flying low to avoid radar. In the cabin were Marshal Paul Osipov, Secretary Konstantin Tsander, and Colonel-General Sergei Istomin, commander-in-chief of frontal aviation, the air arm responsible for supporting the ground forces.

The three men were lucky to be in the Antonov. Osipov knew Istomin as a favorer of Romanenko, and had brought Istomin along when he collected Tsander outside Vera's apartment at twenty-five minutes to one. The three men had driven around randomly for five minutes while Tsander explained what seemed to be happening. Osipov then tried to contact the generals of the Taman and Kantemirov divisions, but Smilga's people must have reached them first: the two officers were not available, but if the caller would like to leave his name and present location...?

That decided them. Osipov took a long chance and drove to Kubinka airbase to the west of the city. He was gambling that the KGB would be too busy with events in Moscow and Leningrad and at military district headquarters to seal off every airbase in at country. He was proven right. Istomin commandeered the Antonov transport, and they were in the air at half past one.

Osipov now looked out the round porthole at the ground flashing past. "I wish I could have warned Shokolov and some of the others," he said, partly to himself. "But I didn't think I had time. Sergei, you were lucky you were in my office when Secretary Tsander phoned."

Istomin nodded. He hadn't known anything of the impending purge until Tsander had told him about it in the car, and he was visibly shaken. "What chance have we got?" he asked plaintively. "If the KGB controls Moscow — "

"They need to control more than that," Tsander said. He winced as the Antonov surged abruptly upward to clear a hill and then dropped again. "If Secretary Romanenko's still free, and if my colleagues at Staraya Square managed to get away, and if Tolbukhin was able to warn at least some of the officers on that list of his, Smilga won't have it all his own way. There is also the question of whether the men themselves will follow officers put in command by the KGB. Romanenko is popular among the enlisted men."

"A remarkable achievement," said Osipov thoughtfully. "None of the enlistees ever had much use for Andropov or Chernenko."

Tsander shrugged. "Romanenko improved the way they lived. That was long overdue, and they won't forget it."

"No," said Osipov. He looked out the porthole to where a small gray lake was sliding past and rubbed his eyes.

"What are the military problems we have to face immediately?" asked Tsander. He laughed without humor. "To save time, just give me the major ones."

"There are several," Osipov said, as though he were beginning a staff briefing. "To begin with, I'm fairly sure Smilga's going to get control of the strategic rocket forces. Marshal Abramov never approved of Romanenko, and I think he'll turn his long-range missiles over to the KGB. This leads to the whole question of our nuclear weapons, and whether they'll be used if there's serious fighting. There is also the question of the American reaction if we don't get our house in order soon. Then there are the Chinese, and the Warsaw Pact armed forces to worry about.... But I am most concerned with the Americans."

"Secretary Romanenko will have to arrange some kind of accommodation with them," Tsander said, adding to himself, *if Vasily's still alive and free.* "We can't deal properly with Smilga and his thugs if we have to keep looking over our shoulders at the west. But you've overlooked a more significant problem."

"What?"

"If there's heavy fighting, both we and Zarudin's faction are going to have to mobilize. That means requisitioning vehicles. Civilian vehicles."

He needed to say no more. Every truck and car in the Soviet Union had two registrations, one civilian, one military. If they were carrying soldiers and ammunition and war supplies they would not be carrying food or clothing or anything else for the civilian population. And there would be no soldiers to help bring in the harvest, as they always did.

There would be not only war, but famine.

It was four o'clock in the afternoon. Smilga had known of Romanenko's escape for slightly less than two hours.

The KGB chairman had sent General Kinyapin, head of the Guards Directorate, to Leningrad to oversee the action against Romanenko. The man had telephoned at nine minutes past two. He had sounded out of breath and worried.

"Chairman Smilga? Kinyapin."

"Have you got him?" Smilga had asked.

"Chairman, no I — "

"*What?*" Smilga exploded. "Where are you?"

"At the Leningrad KGB headquarters," Kinyapin had said desperately. "Chairman, I haven't much time; please listen. I was in continuous radio contact with the assault team and the Department Eight executives. They had just moved into the meeting when they were attacked by soldiers, I think from the Thirty-seventh Guards Rifle Division. They took a lot of casualties. The target got away, and the Department Eight team hasn't reported in."

"Get back here immediately!" Smilga roared into the phone.

"Chairman, I can't. The army's also surrounded the headquarters here. They're already in the building. I — "

And the line had gone dead.

The whole operation's a shambles, Smilga thought as the limousine rolled through the Kremlin's Nikolsky Gate and drew up to the big triangular senate building. Osipov's slipped away, Tsander as well, two more of the Secretariat are in hiding, Tolbukhin managed to warn at least a third of the people he should have arrested. At least we've still got Yasev; he gives what's left of the General Staff some authority. Bugger, bugger, I wish I'd got Osipov and Tsander; they're dangerous.

Moscow's secure anyway, he thought as he walked with his bodyguard under the senate's west portico into the courtyard. Tolbukhin nearly killed me, holy Mother Russia my arm hurts,

but we have the Taman and Kantemirov Divisions and the KGB
Dzerzhinsky Division to keep them obedient. We'll just kick
Romanenko and his cronies out of their Party positions, get
some reliable people in, and he'll evaporate like a bad dream.
He can't put up much resistance from Leningrad.

The Central Committee plenum was being held in Sverdlov
Hall in the east corner of the senate. Inside the round blue-and-
white hall with its Corinthian columns and bas-reliefs, a
hundred-odd members of the Central Committee had gathered,
in a buzz of agitated conversation. There should have been
many more, but Romanenko's faction was noticeably absent;
Zarudin and the Party control-committee executive had made
sure there would be little opposition to the selection of a new
Politburo and Secretariat.

Smilga made his way to the front row of seats. At a long,
polished table on the dais ahead of him were sitting the four
Secretariat members loyal to Zarudin, with Zarudin himself at
the center of the table and Lebedev, chairman of the Præsidium
of the Supreme Soviet, on his right. The six secretaries who
normally supported Romanenko were conspicuous by their
absence. Tsander and two others had escaped, and the remaining
three were being held outside Moscow at Balashikha.

That will also deal nicely with the Politburo election,
Smilga thought, as he settled his injured arm carefully across
his lap. We just won't replace the members we arrested, and
we'll dump Amelin and Demichev. No more revisionists in the
Politburo.

Zarudin, who had been reading some papers, looked up
and saw the KGB chairman. He got up hurriedly and left the
dais.

Now what? Smilga thought as Zarudin approached.
Zarudin leaned over him and whispered hoarsely into Smilga's
ear, "Yasev's dead."

"What? How?"

"He shot himself in his office. Your people found him five
minutes ago. They tried to get you on the car phone but you
must have just arrived and left the car. Now what do we do?"

"Elect a new defense minister, of course. We would have

had to get rid of him anyway. He's saved us the trouble. Did he leave a note?"

"Something about having betrayed the armed forces to another Beria."

"He must have lost his nerve when the purge started. He's no loss. Can we get this procedure under way? I have work to do."

Zarudin went back to the dais and called the plenum to order. He then gave a detailed description of Romanenko's political and economic crimes, and followed this with a request for the Central Committee's advice on how to deal with a Party leader who failed to carry out his ideological obligations. As arranged, the head of the Moscow Party committee got to his feet and demanded Romanenko's immediate ouster from the Party, and the stripping of all his ranks, honors, and privileges. Somebody else seconded the motion, adding that criminal charges of treason and sabotage should be considered.

"We will now vote on the motion," Zarudin stated. With this packed Central Committee plenum, there would be no need for a debate. The few allies of Romanenko who were in the hall wouldn't dare open their mouths.

"Just a minute," called a voice from the rear of the hall. Smilga turned around abruptly, banging his arm on the seat next to his. The pain made his eyes water. He blinked away the tears and saw Pavel Amelin, Party secretary for Kazakhstan and one of the lesser Politburo members, standing truculently in front of one of the Corinthian columns. Amelin had been a favorite of Romanenko's but had no power base in the political *apparat*, which was why Smilga hadn't bothered to have him arrested. He wished now he had.

"This is illegal," Amelin shouted. His voice echoed in the dome above him. "This is not a full plenum of the Committee. Where are the other secretaries? And where is Vasily Romanenko? Are you all idiots, to bring this down on our heads again? Oleg Zarudin, where is the general secretary, and what have you done with the rest of the Secretariat?"

"Vasily Romanenko is in Leningrad," answered Zarudin.

"Is he under arrest?" demanded Amelin. "Or not?"

Smilga got to his feet. Zarudin was going to mess it up, he'd have to improvise. "Vasily Romanenko was taken into protective custody this afternoon," Smilga said easily, "to protect him from the Leningrad proletarian workers, who had found out how he was betraying their revolution. Unfortunately, with the help of a revisionist clique of army officers, he escaped, after murdering several of the men sent to protect him. He is still in Leningrad, and attempting — vainly, I should add — to continue his counterrevolution. He intends to do this with the misguided assistance of some of the members of the Secretariat, the Politburo, and, I regret to say, some people of this very Central Committee. You will know them all by their absence; they are afraid to show their faces to us. I urge this body to take immediate action and select a new Politburo and Secretariat to defeat the forces of Romanenko's counterrevolution."

"You're full of cowshit, Dmitri Smilga," shouted Amelin. "The only counterrevolution here is the one you're trying on for size." His voice was anguished. "Vasily Romanenko is a better Communist than anyone in this room."

"Remove that member," Zarudin called out. "He's a disgrace to the Committee."

Four other members began hustling Amelin toward the doors at the rear of the hall. He was silent until he reached the exit. Then he shouted: "When they knock at five o'clock in the morning, it'll be too late to change your minds. You'd better act now, you'll never be able to again."

That was a weak exit, Smilga thought as the doors banged shut behind Amelin. But we'd better pick him up as soon as this meeting's over.

"Let's have that vote," said Zarudin.

It went unanimously against Romanenko. In short order six new Secretariat members were elected by acclamation, and the Politburo was reorganized to exclude any of Romanenko's faction.

As the meeting was breaking up Zarudin whispered to Smilga, "Amelin was quite right, you know. This is illegal under Party rules. A full plenum is required. When the local Party organs hear about it, if they like Romanenko, they could cause trouble."

"So what? We're as legal as we need to be at the moment.

This was an emergency. And Romanenko's stuck in Leningrad with a few thousand troops; none of his clique will stay with him when they find out we control the General Staff and the Party and the central government. Russians will always obey authority, if it appears strong enough. How do you think the czars lasted so long?"

A KGB guards colonel appeared out of the rapidly dispersing crowd of members. "Chairman Smilga, please excuse me."

"What is it?"

"Chairman, it's regarding Marshal Pervishin." The colonel's eyes flicked toward Zarudin, and then back to Smilga. Smilga, for the first time since the coup began, felt a tremor of unease.

"What about Marshal Pervishin?" he asked.

"Chairman, he's mobilizing the Western Strategic Direction. And he's arrested every KGB man he's been able to get his hands on."

Smilga and Zarudin looked at each other in appalled silence. Sverdlov Hall was nearly empty.

"Now what?" said Zarudin.

Leningrad
Tuesday, July 27

BY THE TIME dawn had swept over Leningrad on the day following the battle at the Mariinsky Palace, Romanenko still had only the sketchiest picture of the political and military balance. Severed from the communicatins resources of Moscow, and from the intelligence-gathering and analysis apparatus of the General Staff, he was at a considerable disadvantage. When Marshal Osipov finally collated what information they possessed — he had been on the telephone all night — it was past six in the morning. Romanenko was looking out a window in the Leningrad military district headquarters, in the eastern part of the city, when Osipov and Konstantin Tsander brought the assessment in. The large office was normally used by the commander of the district; he had turned it over to Romanenko and Osipov as a central command post.

My very own General Staff office, Romanenko thought as he turned to Osipov. The marshal's face had the gray-blue pallor of fatigue; even Tsander's dark skin was sallow and pale. None of the three men had slept for twenty-four hours.

"What have we got?" asked Romanenko.

"It would be easier to read it than hear it," said Osipov.

Romanenko nodded and adjusted his glasses. He began to skim the typewritten sheets Osipov handed him.

After perhaps five minutes he looked up. The early-morning light was flooding in through the tall windows. Osipov stood at the northernmost one, looking down into the street as Romanenko had a few minutes earlier.

"In short," said Romanenko, "Pervishin has brought the bulk of the first-line divisions in central Europe to our side, and we hold the Baltic and Leningrad military districts." He looked down at the last page of the assessment. "And the nuclear missiles of the northern fleet's submarines."

"Yes," Tsander said. "Fortunately."

Romanenko rubbed a hand over his forehead. So close, it had been so close. If Tolbukhin's warning hadn't secured the northern fleet for him, Romanenko would have had no political or military counter to Smilga's control of the intercontinental missiles in their silos east of the Ural Mountains. The short- and medium-range nuclear weapons with Pervishin's forces, despite their destructiveness, were no substitute for the ICBMs. The faction that controlled the missiles could very well claim to be the legitimate leadership of the Soviet Union, if by no other argument than that of might. Washington would have had to recognize Zarudin....

It hadn't happened.

"Is there anything on the forces in Afghanistan since this was prepared?" asked Romanenko, tapping the assessment.

"No," Osipov said. "We still don't know whether Tolbukhin was able to warn GHQ Kabul. Same with the central Asian and far-east military districts, and the Pacific fleet."

Smilga might have the Vladivostok-based nuclear-missile submarines, then. Too bad. "How are we for air power?"

"Reasonably well off. We were also fortunate that the bulk of the airborne assault troops was in the loyal districts. As far as I can tell, we also have most of the military air transport. A lot of it was in central Europe for the Warsaw Pact exercises. Which, needless to say, have been canceled."

"Needless to say," repeated Romanenko dryly. "On balance, where do we stand?"

"The forces are too evenly matched," said Osipov gloomily. "The KGB has seventy-five thousand troops on the western frontier and Smilga's people grabbed control of the army units in Hungary and the Carpathian military district. He's also got the KGB border divisions out on the Chinese frontier, if he dares bring them west. And we can't trust the Warsaw Pact allies not to stab us in the back, so Pervishin will have to leave some units in Poland, Germany, and Czechoslovakia. Moreover, even if half the soldiers and airmen and sailors won't fight for the KGB, Moscow's communication and intelligence facilities are still in

KGB hands. We outnumber them on the ground and in the air, but their central position is worth a lot of men."

"How long could the fighting last," asked Romanenko, "if there's no other solution?"

"Heavy fighting for three to four weeks," Tsander said. "Then it will drop off quickly as stocks are used up and the industrial and transport infrastructures start to fall apart. After that there will be civil disorder and famine."

Romanenko put his head in his hands. "That's an impossible path to follow. We have to find another solution."

"We could surrender," Tsander said. "For the good of Russia."

Osipov glared at him. "They'd kill us all. Do you call that a solution?"

"There's another solution at the other end of the scale," Tsander went on. "Nuclear strikes on Moscow and the supreme command center at Zhiguli. Cut off the head of the counterrevolution."

"Not possible," said Osipov. "It would weaken us too much. There would always be the danger of retaliation. Also, the Americans might find the temptation to attack us irresistible. They might do so out of self-defense, thinking we would lash out at them before they could strike. There are too many uncertainties."

"No nuclear weapons," said Romanenko. "No matter whether we lose or win. That's final."

"Not even battlefield tactical ones?" asked Tsander. "Do you think Smilga will hold back from using them if he's losing?"

"I don't know whether he will or not," Romanenko said. "I don't want to cross that bridge yet. Look, it's only sixteen hours since this all began. We still have room for political maneuver. Konstantin, make sure the videotape I made last night gets onto all the stations under our control. Jam Moscow's transmissions wherever possible. We have to use all the propaganda tools we can, shortwave radio, radio, local newspapers, everything. Find the secretary of the Leningrad Party committee, Demichev, and turn him loose on it. Get him to supply whatever resources you need, personnel, equipment."

Tsander nodded. Demichev was a member of the Politburo,

or at least of the Politburo as it had existed until yesterday, and a longtime ally.

"Then," said Romanenko, "we must establish ourselves as the legitimate government and Party leadership. If we can persuade the Party rank and file that Zarudin is a traitor and usurper, he may lose his support in the middle and lower Party organs. It will strengthen us."

"General Secretary Romanenko," Osipov said formally, "I think you're making a mistake. We should strike now with our conventional forces, as hard as we can, while the military in Moscow is off-balance from Smilga's purge. You can't win by political action alone. We've already mobilized Pervishin. Use him. There is going to be fighting. Strike first."

"We have to try a political solution," said Romanenko. "We must try to get the Central Committee to oust Zarudin. We have to avoid a civil war if we possibly can."

Unfortunately, Osipov was right. By nine o'clock on the morning of the twenty-seventh, Smilga had concluded that Pervishin's threatening movement eastward wasn't going to be easily stopped by the KGB Border Guards Divisions and ordered military action of his own. In the late afternoon the reconnaissance elements of the Second and Fifth Tank Divisions, originally based near Budapest, made contact with Pervishin's Sixty-sixth Division near Kosice, just west of the Czech-Soviet border. The news of Romanenko's apparent fall had not yet filtered down to the tank soldiers, and they had been told they were attacking a renegade division subverted by the CIA. This didn't seem fantastic to them, as they had been well indoctrinated about the perfidy and deviousness of the Americans, and they went into battle dutifully if not enthusiastically. The fighting continued well into the night.

Washington, not surprisingly, had been caught totally unawares by the events in Leningrad. For a dreadful two hours in the late afternoon of 26 July, it had appeared to President Hayes and his staff that Pervishin's sudden mobilization presaged a violent conventional attack on West Germany. The intelligence that

Pervishin's divisions were moving eastward, toward the Soviet Union, was greeted with intense suspicion, which changed to stunned disbelief when the Leningrad television station broadcast Romanenko's appeal to the armed forces to help suppress a KGB counterrevolution. Shortly after that President Hayes received a telephone call — routed through Helsinki — from Romanenko himself. The Soviet leader requested that the west not misinterpret the troop movements in Europe, that they were intended to deal only with a transitory internal disturbance. Hayes said he would watch the situation but would undertake no unusual political or diplomatic actions.

When Moscow television burst into a diatribe against Romanenko, and Zarudin also telephoned Hayes with a strongly worded request for noninterference, it became clear that the Soviet difficulties were far from transitory. And with the news of the fighting in Czechoslvakia, Hayes's secretary of state was moved to utter, somewhat crassly, the essence of the situation as the Americans were beginning to perceive it:

"Jesus Christ," he said. "The poor bastards are going to tear themselves to pieces. All we have to do is wait."

Moscow
Wednesday, August 18

SMILGA WAS LOOKING at the large map of western Russia and central Europe that hung on the wall opposite his desk. His left arm, still bandaged, lay across the green desk pad. The wound Tolbukhin had given him wouldn't heal; the doctors muttered at it, dressed and redressed it, laced it with antibiotics, but still it suppurated. Occasionally Smilga worried about gangrene.

His arm troubled him less than the map. The plastic overlays showed much the same situation as did the bigger map at STAVKA HQ, the military-command headquarters up in the Kremlin. Most of the situation was bad. Since the fighting began in July the Soviet military machine on both sides of the civil war had begun to unravel at the edges, first slowly and then with increasing speed. Pervishin's forces from Poland, Germany, and Czechoslovakia had rapidly driven off the attack from Hungary, and then rumbled ponderously into the northern part of the Carpathian military district. Zarudin had then ordered full mobilization of all forces under Moscow's control west of the Urals, but the mobilization had gone very badly indeed. Large numbers of reservists had simply failed to appear at the collection points, and when the KGB and MVD searched for them something like half were nowhere to be found. It was even worse than the aborted preparations for the invasion of Poland in 1979, when twenty percent of the men called up were found to have moved. Most of the men the KGB finally dragged into the units were years past their training and had forgotten nearly everything they had learned. As well, there was not nearly enough motor transport, and the civilian vehicles that were requisitioned to make up the difference were too few and in dismal mechanical condition; the breakdown rate was astronomical, and there were no spare parts. Pervishin, by contrast, was well equipped. By 12 August he had moved the bulk of his forces into the Byelorussian and Baltic military districts, pinned down what was left of the partially mobilized units in the Carpathians, and was obviously preparing for a drive from the north and west on Moscow itself.

The only consolation was that Pervishin was clearly having his own difficulties, what with lack of planning — what Soviet marshal in his right mind would have planned for a civil war? — and the inevitable toll that a large-scale military movement takes of men, tanks, guns, transport vehicles, and supplies. The KGB Border Guards had fought viciously but there were not enough of them, and the Moscow-controlled army units had given a very poor account of themselves, even when threatened with mass executions by KGB troops. Large numbers had deserted to Romanenko. Air power was treacherous to use, since both sides flew the same types of aircraft, and the pilots had difficulty telling which ground targets were friendly and which were hostile. Too many pilots had attacked KGB units they were supposed to support and then flown to the west, if their planes had the range, or defected to Romanenko, if they did not.

Smilga stood up heavily and walked to the map, where he traced with a blunt forefinger the main positions of both sides. The forefinger passed over Smolensk, lost now to Pervishin. There had been typhoid in that city before its fall. Everywhere industrial activity was starting to slow, transport was crippled because of the mobilization of vehicles, and shortages of food and medical supplies were approaching the crisis point in some areas. Smilga had hoped at first that the Warsaw Pact nations would revolt in Pervishin's rear, but that had not happened. The old marshal had been very careful, leaving enough Russian units behind him to control the allies. And Romanenko's promises to Warsaw, Berlin, Prague and Budapest had something to do with it. He would have promised them the moon to keep them neutral. Romanenko. Smilga suppressed an urge to smash his fist against the red blotch of Leningrad on the map.

As if that would help, he thought. At least the Americans are sitting on their hands; not much wonder, they don't want to commit suicide. Now if we can only keep the Chinese from our throats until the country's back under control.

The intercom buzzed. Smilga went back to the desk and swiped at the switch, almost breaking it. "Yes?"

"Special Investigator Yegrov is here, Chairman."

"Send him in."

Yegrov stepped tentatively into the office. Smilga waved him to a chair. "What is it?" he asked irritably. "I already received your report on General Gordik. He can't do anything in Termez."

Two days into August, and after some confused fighting in Kabul, Gordik had taken over command of the Soviet forces in Afghanistan. The day after that, to Smilga's consternation and fury, he had declared for Romanenko. Nobody in Moscow had had time to pay much attention to events in the south for the next ten days; Gordik only had five divisions and they were a long, long way from the capital. Then had come the news that the renegade KGB general had pulled most of his troops out of Afghanistan and captured Termez, the big Russian supply base on the Soviet-Afghan border. It still didn't matter; Termez was thirty-six hundred kilometers from Moscow. Gordik might as well have been in Australia for all the good he could do Romanenko.

Yegrov shifted uncomfortably on the very edge of the chair. A file folder was resting on his knees. "If the chairman would give me just a few minutes to explain, it may be very important."

"Shit. All right, go ahead."

Yegrov spoke rapidly, not opening the file. "The team investigating the STARLIGHT leak left Kabul — fortunately — just before the traitor Gordik began his coup. However, there was a good deal of information for them to collate. The Second Directorate has been very busy with subversives lately and the assessment wasn't completed until this morning. I didn't want to trouble you with the investigation as it was proceeding, but the results are startling."

"Get to the point."

Yegrov opened the file. "We were certain fairly early on that the leak originated in the divisional headquarters in Herat. The STARLIGHT phase in that region was the one that ran into the most opposition. Now, there was never any leakage from Herat prior to that operation so we began looking for staff transfers. There were four new officers put into the division during the period immediately preceding STARLIGHT. None of them had access to the plans as a whole, only their own parts in it. So we looked farther afield."

"You found the leak in the operational studies bureau," said Smilga. "The traitor was in Gordik's organization. Wasn't he?"

Surprise flitted across Yegrov's features. "Yes. There was only one personnel move in the appropriate time frame. Colonel Andrei Sergeyevitch Mikhailov, Vasily Romanenko's nephew, replaced the OSB chief in Herat."

"Are you *certain* Mikhailov was the leak?" Smilga was leaning forward over the desk.

"His Herat office was searched and his colleagues interviewed. There was no physical evidence. But his deputy, a Major Rosseikin, recalled that Mikhailov often worked late when there was no obvious need to do so. We also discovered that he was occasionally absent from both his office and his billet for extended periods of time, always in the late evening after dark. My team finished up in Herat and went back to Kabul to see whether the pattern of Mikhailov's conduct was similar while he was serving there. It wasn't. Then we discovered that just before he was posted to Herat he was on leave here in Moscow."

"What did he do here?"

"Unfortunately, there was no reason at that time to keep him under surveillance, so we know little about his movements during his leave. But we think he kept very much to himself. There is only one known instance of his contacting a westerner. Mikhailov was assigned temporarily to the Second Directorate to introduce one of their operatives to an American embassy official named Eric Fowler. Mikhailov was once on a GRU posting in England and knew Fowler there."

"That's when the bastard did it," Smilga said. "Fowler was Mikhailov's initial contact. Is Fowler CIA?"

"We don't know. There's been no evidence of it."

Pull Fowler in? wondered Smilga. No. Not worth the risk of offending the Americans. Later, perhaps. "Then what happened?"

"Mikhailov went back to Herat. After the battle there he was posted home. Then Fowler introduced him to a female Canadian journalist named Chantal Mallory. No evidence of intelligence work by her, either. Mikhailov introduced Mallory to his uncle. Romanenko took a liking to Mallory, apparently, because he issued orders that she was not to be interfered with and that all but spot surveillance was to be ended."

"I know," Smilga said with annoyance. "That was reported to me." Stupid, stupid, he thought, I should have disobeyed. But I didn't want to annoy Romanenko then. Calculated risk; failed. "Go on."

"Mikhailov then went to Czechoslovakia for the General Staff Training Directorate. We haven't been able to follow his movements there, because of the counterrevolution. But he was posted, after Czechoslovakia, to Leningrad, where he prevented Romanenko's arrest. Chantal Mallory was also in Leningrad, for what Romanenko was pleased to call the summit. Since then we have had no word of Mikhailov."

"That's all?"

Yegrov put the file on Smilga's desk. "There is a lot of detail in the file I haven't bothered you with. But if I were to make an arrest over STARLIGHT, I would start with Mikhailov and the journalist."

Smilga gently stroked the buff file with his fingertips. "Yegrov, you did well to bring me this. You have no idea how useful it may be."

"May I respectfully ask the chairman in what manner?" Yegrov asked, both pleased and relieved.

"It's quite simple. Mikhailov is a CIA agent. His control is Chantal Mallory. Romanenko has been protecting both of them. We have been calling Romanenko a subversive and a traitor. Now we have something concrete. Suppose Romanenko *knew* what his nephew was, what Chantal Mallory was, and didn't order their arrests? What does that make Vasily Romanenko?"

"Ah," Yegrov said. "I see."

Moscow
Saturday, August 21

LIKE AN INJURED SNAKE the line crawled painfully along the sidewalk in the suffocating heat. Maya was now only twenty places from the entrance to the bread shop. In her string bag she carried six onions, which was all she had been able to find in the open-air market where the peasants came to sell the vegetables they grew in their private plots. But half the peasants had stopped coming after Moscow radio and television announced the new leadership. Shortly thereafter, when rumors began to spread that Romanenko was alive in Leningrad and that there was fighting between the army and the KGB in the west, the peasants had disappeared altogether, except for a few of the very oldest women. Maya had been lucky to get the onions.

The peasants are hoarding, she thought as the line shuffled forward another pace. They know by smelling the wind when there's trouble coming. If only it weren't so hot. I should have gone to the bread store first, I wasn't thinking. Six onions. What good are onions without bread? I wonder if we'll ever have another meal like the one we gave Chantal; I wonder what's happened to her? There's not a foreigner on the street any more; just as well, there's nothing for them to eat anyway.

Food shipments into Moscow had declined even in the past two days. Maya had spent four hours in line on Friday for two loaves of bread, half a kilo of very poor sausage, and two hundred grams of moldy cheese. Volodya had ducked out of work for two hours to try his luck, but had left it too late and come home depressed and empty-handed. It was at that point that the two of them had begun to worry seriously about going hungry.

It must be terrible for people with children, she thought. Four hours I've spent in line already, and all I have to show for it are six onions. Maybe Volodya's found something.

The copy of *Pravda*, which she had brought with her to wrap the bread in — it was dangerous to carry food openly these days — was sticking damply to the inside of her arm. Idly, she unrolled the newspaper and glanced over the front page. As usual, it was dedicated to venomous attacks on Romanenko and his faction. The major headline read, "Defeat Inevitable for Arch-Criminal Personality-Cult Clique." Farther down, another one, almost as big: "Counter-revolutionary Gangs Smashed at Smolensk."

The newspapers almost never referred to Romanenko by name, nor did Moscow radio or television. If you knew what was good for you, you followed their example; to refer to the previous general secretary in even the most vaguely favorable terms was to invite a pounding on the door at five o'clock in the morning. You didn't even have to do that, in fact; several of Volodya's colleagues from the institute had simply disappeared with their families, for what reasons no one knew or dared ask.

Thank heavens Volodya's always kept out of politics, Maya thought. If he had let Chantal take those stories of his to the west and they'd got published... I wish he'd burn them.

She looked behind. The line stretched down Ostrovskogo Street for nearly a block. There was next to no traffic because all civilian trucks and cars had been requisitioned for military use — except those belonging to Party members, of course. Most of the vehicles on the streets these days were official limousines or trucks carrying loads of cold-faced KGB troops or MVD militia. Public transit was running as usual, although some bus routes had been cut, to save on fuel, it was said. There were also rumors that all staples were going to be rationed soon. Vodka and other spirits had simply disappeared, to be bartered later for food, if necessary. If there was no food you could always drink.

She was the tenth person from the door of the bread shop when a scuffle broke out at the head of the line. A young woman, who had been next to enter, was shouting:

"You can't close now, you have to have more, what about my children — "

"There's no more, I tell you," the clerk shouted back from behind the door he was trying to close. The woman must have put her foot in the opening, because he was having trouble. "There was only one truck this morning. What am I supposed to do about it? Try somewhere else, take yourself off."

"Let us see for ourselves," a man shouted somewhere farther back in the line. "What've you got under the counter?" The line was beginning to lose its definition and was forming into a crowd around the bread shop's door.

"Nothing, it's all gone," shouted the clerk. "Go somewhere else."

"They've got more in there for themselves and their friends," somebody yelled, "or they'd let us in to see."

The clerk had managed to pry the woman's foot out of the doorway and was pushing it closed against the pressure of the crowd. "What about my children?" screamed the woman.

"To hell with 'em," the enraged clerk yelled back. "Feed them grass."

It was the wrong thing to say. A stone or fragment of paving shot through the air and struck the shop window, which starred and shattered. The crowd surged forward, carrying Maya with it. Somebody started kicking the shards of glass out of the window frame to get inside.

This is going to end badly, Maya thought. She turned and pushed away from the shop toward the curb, nearly losing her onions. Beyond the heads of what was now a mob she could see the high cab and canvas top of a military truck coming rapidly down the street. At the curb, free of the worst of the crush, she began to trot quickly southeast toward Kropotkinskaya Street. Behind her she heard the truck rumble to a halt. She was far enough away by this time to risk a look back. MVD men were tumbling out of the truck and wading into the crowd with truncheons. Somebody was brandishing two loaves of bread in the air.

So they did have more, she thought as she turned for home. The bastards. Now what? I'll go back to the apartment, get a drink of water, leave the onions, and go out again. Oh, my heaven, I'm hungry. What am I going to feed Volodya tonight?

Wearily she climbed the stairs to the apartment, fumbling with her key. About to insert it into the lock, she stopped. The door was off the latch and slightly ajar.

She pushed hesitantly at the door. It swung inward ten centimeters, creaking.

Without warning the door flew open the rest of the way. An arm in a KGB-green sleeve shot around the jamb, grabbed her wrist, and pulled her into the apartment. She stumbled on the edge of the worn carpet and fell to her knees as the door slammed shut behind her.

A man in a dirty gray suit was sitting at Volodya's desk. The KGB soldier moved to stand behind Maya, against the door. Volodya was on the settee, elbows on knees, head in his hands.

"This your wife?" asked the civilian.

Volodya looked up, nodded, and then put his head in his hands again.

"Papers," said the man, snapping his fingers, arm extended. Maya got to her feet, retrieved her purse from where it had fallen, and got out her internal passport. Her knees smarted from the rough contact with the carpet.

"All right," said the civilian, putting the passport in his pocket. "Let's go."

Maya was regaining some of her courage. "Just a minute," she said. "Go where? What do you want us for? You've got no right — "

"Shut your mouth," said the man. "We found your husband's little stories. Fine things for a man in his position to write. You should have kept away from that Canadian journalist, now you're in for it." He stood up. "Let's go, I haven't got all day."

"Where are you taking us?" Maya asked. The quaver in her voice would not stop.

"You'll see when you get there. You'll have lots of company."

The KGB trooper shoved Maya and Volodya out the door. The man in the gray suit picked up the six onions in their string bag, stuffed them into his pocket, and followed.

"Riots," said Zarudin. "Food riots already. There are going to be more."

He and Smilga were talking in Smilga's office at Dzerzhinsky Square. It was one of the few places Zarudin felt safe these days. The others were Staraya Square, which was cordoned off and stiff with KGB, and the Kremlin Arsenal, where STAVKA, the high command, was situated.

"Let them riot," Smilga said. "We have more serious problems at the moment." Over the past week the dominant role in the partnership had shifted from Zarudin to Smilga. Zarudin had seemed almost glad to let this happen; he was well aware that his power was now founded on the KGB, since the military was untrustworthy and the Party had been split by Romanenko's survival. Smilga still needed Zarudin to maintain the appearance of legality, but for all practical purposes the ruler in Moscow was Dmitri Alexeyevitch Smilga.

Smilga leaned back in his chair and clasped his hands behind his head. The afternoon sun poured in a great golden bar through the window. Small dust particles swam in it like fish undersea. Ironic that with the excellent mix of sun and rain in the past month the harvest was going to be the best in years. Unfortunately at least half of it would rot in the ground and many people would be starving to death before spring. This did not entirely displease Smilga. He had already begun to ensure that the best proportion of the food available would go to the cities of the Russian Soviet Socialist Republic, with its Slav population. For several years Soviet demographers and the government had worried about the high population growth of the non-Slav ethnic groups, which would eventually turn the Russians into a minority in the Union. If enough of the non-Russians died it would redress the balance, perhaps significantly. A famine might also shock the people out of their lethargy, make them willing to work again for Leninism and the Revolution.

If, of course, the bourgeois revisionist and tràitor Romanenko could .be beaten. Smilga had reactivated STAVKA, the Soviet high command, and established it with an elaborate communications center on the top floor of the Kremlin Arsenal. Despite the fact that STAVKA had been thoroughly purged of all supporters of Romanenko, Smilga still didn't trust its officers. They couldn't seem to control the military situation. At the morning's situation conference they had stood around the map table with long faces, trying to decide which army and air units would be least likely to dissolve if ordered to fight Pervishin's divisions.

Tolbukhin did well, Smilga thought, fury rising in him as it always did when he remembered the erstwhile head of the Third Directorate. If it hadn't been for him, Romanenko would be locked up in Kirov; Osipov and Pervishin would be in Lefortovo; we wouldn't be at a nuclear standoff with the northern fleet; we wouldn't be having a — yes, say it — a civil war, with the Americans rubbing their hands with delight in Washington. At least *they've* had the sense to keep their meddling fingers to themselves. But the Chinese are still hanging over us out there on the Issuri. I need those borderguards divisions, can't move them or the Pacific fleet, even if it stays loyal, that bastard General Guyanov out there in Vladivostok, he's just waiting to see which way the wind will blow. And the United States still refuses to say whether they recognize us or Romanenko.

"Romanenko," he said aloud.

"What?" said Zarudin, with a start. Smilga realized that the two of them had been sitting there wordlessly for several minutes.

"Romanenko. It all hinges on Romanenko. He's the strength of this rebellion."

"You've said that before," Zarudin pointed out irritably.

"If we could be sure of eliminating him," Smilga said, "it might be worth any price we had to pay."

"So?" asked Zarudin. He was studying Smilga with apprehension.

"Pervishin will be here by mid-September if the military

situation continues to deteriorate. The KGB can't check him indefinitely unless we use tactical nuclear weapons. He would then respond. We would then respond in kind. Neither side can afford that level of devastation; it would set us back to 1945, and it could escalate. But one swift blow to remove Vasily Romanenko and the spirit would be gone out of the rebellion. If it slowed Pervishin down even for a couple of weeks, the autumn rains would have begun and we'd have time to regroup. If we can survive long enough, Romanenko's army will wither on the vine. But only if he's dead."

"What kind of decisive blow are you thinking of?" Zarudin's face was turned away, into the sunlight, but Smilga knew he understood.

"Five megatons on Leningrad ought to do it," the KGB chairman said, "if we could be sure Romanenko were there."

Tolbukhin was certain he was dying.

He lay naked on the wooden bench, the only furniture in his cell. His body didn't hurt much except deep in his abdomen and where his bones pressed his flesh against the bench. There were a few bruises over his kidneys but the interrogators had done that more for form's sake than in any conviction that physical torture would make him talk. They had relied on the drugs for that. Tolbukhin sensed that he had told them everything, although not immediately, not while he was trying to give everyone he had warned just a little more time to get away. He hadn't really broken completely until they brought his wife in and got down to work with the electrodes. He wasn't sure she was still alive when they carried her out.

He turned his head to one side and retched. Nothing came up. The nausea was perhaps the hardest to bear, now that the interrogations seemed to be over. He looked at the skin of his forearm. The yellowish cast was more pronounced now.

Hepatitis-induced jaundice, he thought, having seen it more than once in his career. One of their needles must have been dirty. I must have lost ten kilos in here. Not been so slim since I was thirty. I wonder if they're going to put me through a trial. Not likely, or they'd be trying to patch me up.

I wonder if Romanenko got away.

He dozed, then, despite the nausea and the fever from the jaundice.

When he woke to the cell door banging open he was shivering uncontrollably. Two guards and a KGB major he had never seen were in the doorway.

"Bring him out," said the major.

Tolbukhin tried to preserve some dignity by sitting up but he was too weak. The guards pulled him roughly to his feet. He staggered. They had to grab him under the armpits to keep him from falling.

"You're not much use to anybody, are you?" said the major. He had a wide, flat face and black eyes: not a Slav. He was enjoying himself.

Tolbukhin tried to shrug but nothing happened.

"Let's go," the major said.

Tolbukhin wasn't sure where in Lefortovo he was, or even if he were still in the prison. They dragged him along a corridor lined with cell doors and then down a narrow stairway to a subbasement. It was cooler down here; the chill made Tolbukhin shiver even harder.

"Try to show a little courage, old man," the major said from behind. Tolbukhin saved his breath; the nausea was coming again.

"In here," the major said. The guards pushed a thick door open. It didn't have a peephole. Inside was a small room lit by a single low-wattage bulb in the ceiling. A pipe ran down one wall, ending in a faucet. Attached to the faucet was a length of canvas hose, coiled untidily on the cement floor. Near the back wall of the room was a round hole about twenty centimeters across, some kind of drain.

"Kneel," said the major. The guards lowered Tolbukhin to the floor. They had to hold him up to keep him from sprawling on his face. Tolbukhin heard the snap of a holster flap being unfastened and then a small whisper of metal on leather.

"Anything you want to add to your confession?" asked the major from behind Tolbukhin.

It might be a mock execution. Tolbukhin, swimming in nausea and fever, didn't care much. He couldn't remember what he had or hadn't told them, anyway.

"Get on with it," he said. To his self-disgust, he spoke with a slur.

"Sure?" Mockingly.

Tolbukhin tried not to say it, not to give them the satisfaction, but the words came out of him anyway.

"What has happened to Vasily Romanenko?"

One of the guards snickered. Tolbukhin felt a small, firm pressure at the base of his skull.

"He's dead, old man, and so are the rest of them."

Tolbukhin started to cry, but before they noticed the major shot him in the back of the neck, twice. After the major left, the two guards used the hose to wash the mess down the drain, and then took Tolbukhin's body up to the morgue. He was so light they didn't have to bother with a cart.

Captain Ilitsev stood at attention with the soldiers of his rifle company at the edge of the parade square, part of the Taman Division's base, which lay five kilometers south of the Moscow ring road. On all sides of the square except the north were arrayed selected battalions of the division's four regiments.

At the center of the north side of the square stood a two-meter-high wooden post. Its supports were sandbagged to hold it steady. The post threw a shadow its own length; the sun was westering. A light breeze had sprung up in midafternoon and a scrap of yellow paper was blowing erratically across the square's asphalt. Ilitsev watched it as it lifted, came to rest, lifted, came to rest. Sweat was trickling town the right side of his nose.

He heard a command shouted from behind. They were bringing the deserter out. The man, blinking in the sunlight, walked unsteadily into the square in front of the other soldiers. On his feet were light canvas shoes; he wore a pair of army trousers and a regulation shirt without badges or tie. The MVD had caught him on the outskirts of Moscow as he tried to hitch a ride toward the north and Leningrad. It was stupid, of course; he hadn't the slightest chance of getting away like that; he should have taken to the fields and traveled by night.

That's what I'd do, Ilitsev thought as he watched the

punishment detail bind the young deserter to the post. I'd go east first, though, they expect you to head west or north. The peasants might help. They liked Romanenko. How much longer are we going to put up with this? All the good senior officers taken away and replaced with KGB idiots, punishment details if you so much as mention Romanenko's name, rotten food and little of it, five men shot for desertion in the past week, and three they haven't caught yet. I hope they don't catch them. And they've put KGB security troops outside the base, too. The high command in Moscow is scared stiff of what might happen if we got loose. Nobody swallows their lies any more, and they know it.

They were blindfolding the deserter now. He had blond hair and was short: a tank crewman. One of the punishment detail pinned a disk of white paper over his heart. The execution squad was doubling out into the parade square. They halted in rank ten meters away from the condemned man.

The major in charge of the execution marched over to the squad and stood at its left. He was one of the KGB replacements and had been on the divisional staff — as an informer, everybody knew that now — in the personnel office. He had been in operations before that, but had been so bad at his job that the divisional commander had moved him. Now he was a deputy regimental commander and was loathed by the men and the junior officers alike.

The major shouted. The squad raised and aimed rifles.

"Fire!"

A ragged volley. Ilitsev gaped in disbelief. The soldier bound to the post hadn't even twitched. He should have been slammed back against the post by the bullets.

A moment later Ilitsev understood. Every man of the execution squad had deliberately missed. They were going to be in trouble over this, especially if the major could prove they arranged it beforehand.

The major was screaming at them. The soldier at the post seemed to have fainted; he was hanging limp against the ropes. The members of the execution squad remained standing in their firing positions. Ilitsev thought he saw one of the rifle muzzles twitch minutely toward the major. He wondered if the major knew how much danger he was in.

The thought must have occurred to the major at the same time, because he stopped shouting and gave some orders. Slowly, almost insolently, the squad shouldered arms. A captain trotted up from one of the rear ranks and began marching the squad away. The major walked to the deserter, drew his pistol, placed the muzzle five centimeters from the man's forehead, and shot him.

There was an almost inaudible stirring in the ranks of the onlookers.

Ilitsev wasn't the only one to notice it. The deputy divisional commander, another of the KGB creatures, hurriedly called out,

"Diiss*miss*."

As he marched his company away, Ilitsev thought, That was close, too close for them. I don't think they'll have any more public executions. Today was almost too much.

It's probably only a matter of time until they decide to disarm us. I wonder what we'll do then?

SMILGA'S WOUND was flaring up again. The doctors had given him a new antibiotic and it was making him nauseated; or perhaps the nausea was caused by strain and fatigue.

The KGB chairman was in his temporary office on the top floor of the Kremlin Arsenal, where the Politburo had taken up residence two days previously, when Kalinin, a hundred and twenty kilometers northwest of Moscow, fell to Romanenko's troops. Smilga had been sleeping in the office; a military cot with rumpled sheets stood in one corner. Sleeping on the cot made his back ache.

They'll have him here soon, Smilga thought. He lowered himself gingerly into the big leather armchair facing the door. Despite his care, the movement sent a sharp stab all the way to his shoulder. The pain raised the anger, which was always with him now, to a savage heat.

The past two days had seen disaster piled on disaster. The loss of Kalinin was likely the preliminary to a major assault on the capital itself, and there were hardly any reserves. The army units could not be trusted, and the KGB and MVD troops had been bled white. Three KGB Border Guards Divisions were on their way from the Chinese frontier, but rail transport was breaking down and there was no predicting when the men would arrive. Smilga would not even have dared move these three formations had the Chinese been the least provocative, but Peking appeared to be waiting on events, content to scavenge after the Russians had exhausted themselves.

I should have moved those divisions earlier, Smilga thought, but those assholes in STAVKA said Kalinin would hold. So I waited. Fool. Maybe it's time to get out, go to Zhiguli...

No. To leave the capital now would be to court political, if not military, defeat. And Pervishin's and Romanenko's troops would be tired too, short of ammunition, supplies, and vehicles. They might not be able to attack immediately. And if they could be slowed down some more, until the eastern divisions arrive and the autumn rains come...the Nazis were stopped and turned back in 1941 from the very suburbs of Moscow. It could happen again.

Smilga fingered the dossier on his lap. It was Mikhailov's, and the key to possible victory. The truths it contained were damaging enough, but the painstakingly added forgeries made it appear that Romanenko had known of, even abetted, his nephew's treachery. In the right hands it could cause enough suspicion of Romanenko to undermine his leadership of the counterrevolution, perhaps even bring him down. And if that failed, if Moscow were about to fall, there was always Zhiguli, the great command center deep in the still-loyal Volga military district. The battle could go on from there, if it had to. And there was still the other, final solution.

There was a sharp rap at the door.

"Come in," Smilga said.

Two guards brought Foreign Minister Polunin into the room. He was unshaven, bedraggled, and his knees were muddy. He was plainly terrified. Smilga waved the guards out and got up.

"Sit down," he said, motioning to the chair. Polunin sat, as though his knees had given away.

After a short silence Smilga said, "I see you didn't make it through the lines."

"Dmitri Alexeyevitch, it wasn't what you think."

"Be quiet. It was exactly what I think. You were trying to desert, to get to Romanenko. You ought to be shot. Why shouldn't I have you shot?"

Somewhere, Polunin found some courage. "All right. Go ahead. Do so. What good would it do? We've lost; Romanenko will be in Moscow in two weeks. What good will it do to stay here to die? We should capitulate, now, before everything's in ruins."

"Shooting's entirely too good for you," Smilga said mildly. "I would really prefer to turn you and your wife and daughter over to a specialist unit."

Polunin's already pale face turned paler still. For a moment Smilga thought the man was going to vomit.

"However," Smilga went on, "I'm not going to do either of those things. I'm going to send you to Leningrad, since that's what you want so badly. You are going to take this with you." Smilga picked up the dossier, pushed it into a heavy brown envelope, and sealed it. "I advise you not to read this, for your own safety. When you reach Leningrad, see that it reaches either Paul Osipov or Konstantin Tsander. I have people in Leningrad. If you fail to do this, they'll find you." He extended the envelope to the foreign minister, who stood up unsteadily and took it.

"Get out," Smilga said. "The men outside will take you where you want to go. Don't get shot going through the lines; I suppose you've figured out how to manage that. If you want to stay alive for any length of time, get that envelope to Osipov or Tsander by tomorrow."

When Polunin had gone, Smilga went to the window and looked out into the heart of the Kremlin: the senate, the cathedral spires, the great palaces. Off to the north the invaders were coming, as they had come so often before, from every point of the compass. Moscow would hold out for perhaps fourteen days, and then there would be street fighting as the last of the KGB was hunted down.

Unless, thought Smilga, I destroy Romanenko. One way or another.

He came to a decision.

Zhiguli is a granite rock forty kilometers wide, eighty kilometers long, and several hundred meters thick. Inside it is the supreme command post, prepared for the Soviet leadership in time of nuclear war. It is also the command center for the hundreds of intercontinental missiles of the strategic rocket forces.

When the commander-in-chief of the rocket forces received Smilga's telephoned instructions, he obeyed without question, uncomfortably aware that his life and rank both depended upon his caller's pleasure. He gave certain orders to the commander of one of his missile regiments, which controlled four SS19 missiles in silos some two hundred kilometers east of the Zhiguli complex. Soviet missile-launch installations are manned by four men: two regular officers and a pair of KGB guard-technicians who actually arm and target the weapons. The KGB men changed the targeting information of all four SS19s.

Leningrad
Saturday, August 28

IT WAS HALF PAST ONE in the morning. Mikhailov slumped in the rear of the staff car as it slid through the pale northern light that illuminated the sleeping city. He was exhausted. After the fighting began in earnest in early August, Romanenko had ordered him to establish a security force for the city and the new Politburo and Secretariat; this entailed disarming the KGB and MVD throughout the military district, and partially dismantling their organization. Once the KGB Third Directorate agents had been weeded out of the military, the soldiers had gone to work with a will, but the KGB had so infiltrated every organ of the Party and government that it sometimes seemed to Mikhailov that half the population, in one capacity or another, had worked for Dzerzhinsky Square. Inevitably, many known KGB people had to be left in their posts, simply because there was no one to replace them. Mikhailov had beheaded the apparatus as best he could in the time available, but if Romanenko lost the war it would grow many new heads, each bent on vengeance. Only a few of the senior KGB men had been shot; the rest had been sent to camps in the north, where they appropriately replaced the political prisoners Romanenko had seen fit to release.

But we still have the camps, Mikhailov thought as the staff car turned into the street leading to Romanenko's headquarters. Necessity dictates their existence. Dmitri Smilga could claim as much. Is there to be no end to it? Even my uncle is trapped by our history.

The car drew up at the HQ building. Its tall windows gleamed with rectangles of yellow light, warm under the cold, pale sky. The driver held the door for Mikhailov as he got out.

"Wait," said Mikhailov. "I probably won't be long."

He was still puzzling over Romanenko's summons, which had come just as Mikhailov was about to leave for the apartment on Vasilevsky Island. He had managed to pass a total of eight hours — he had counted them one evening — with Valeria since the beginning of the civil war. In a way it was worse for her than his being away for months at a time; too many departures. Nadia said the child was troubled by nightmares.

I hope she isn't getting sick, he thought, as he showed his identification to the guards at the HQ entrance. One more problem. Don't worry about it now. What does Uncle Vasily want? He would only ask me here for something important. Smilga gave up? Hardly.

Inside, in what had been the lobby of the district headquarters, a communications exchange had been established. Staff officers were everywhere and the air was full of the sound of ringing telephones, radio transmissions, conversation, and the odor of boiled cabbage and unwashed soldiers.

A major wearing guards-tank badges appeared at Mikhailov's elbow. "Colonel A.S. Mikhailov?"

"Yes."

"May I see your identification, please?"

Mikhailov produced his papers. After inspecting them carefully the major handed them back and gave Mikhailov a green badge to clip to his tunic.

"If the colonel would be so good as to follow me."

They went up several flights of stairs and along a corridor whose floor was covered with faded green carpet. The lighting was very dim. At the end of the corridor was a door, on either side of which stood a guard. Both the major and Mikhailov showed their identification. The guards inspected the papers minutely and then gave them back. The major knocked.

"Come in."

It was Romanenko's voice. Mikhailov went in and closed the door quietly. The major didn't follow.

The room was quite large. Mikhailov had never been in it, but guessed that this was where Romanenko's high command planned strategy. In the center of the room stood a long trestle table on which were strewn sheaves of maps. One very large one was spread out, an army survey map of the Moscow region. It was overlaid with clear plastic, and red and blue arrows in grease pencil had been marked here and there on it. Leaning over the table was Vasily Romanenko, and next to him Marshal Paul Osipov.

"Andrei," Romanenko said. "You came."

The customary warmth seemed lacking. Fatigue, Mikhailov thought. We're all so tired. "As ordered," he said.

"Marshal Osipov, please excuse us for a while," said Romanenko formally.

"There's no time to lose if we're going to take advantage of the revolt," Osipov said warningly.

"This won't take long," said Romanenko. He led Mikhailov through a connecting door into an adjoining room. There was a bed in this one, and a nondescript battered desk. On the desk stood a small china lamp with a translucent red shade. It cast a dim, pinkish light. The curtains at the windows were closed. Romanenko sat down at the desk and motioned Mikhailov to sit on the bed.

"Andrei," said Romanenko, "Foreign Minister Polunin escaped from Moscow two days ago. He gave a certain document to Konstantin Tsander. Konstantin, because he is loyal and no fool, gave it to me. The document was prepared by Dmitri Smilga. It could be dismissed as a forgery."

Mikhailov sat quite still. Romanenko studied him for a moment. Then he opened a desk drawer and drew out a file folder bound with pale pink ribbon. "Read it," he said. "I could not believe it either at first, I also thought it was a deception. But it is very convincing. Times, dates, places, means of contact. Take it."

Mikhailov opened the folder. The typescript danced on the paper, obscure in the dim light, but readable. In a little while he closed the folder and looked up.

"Well?" said Romanenko.

"I — " said Mikhailov. He thought: the time for lies is over. I need to tell him. "Yes," he said.

"Why?" There was no anger in the voice, only grief, disappointment, and resignation.

"Because I had to kill a child in Afghanistan. Because the Party was corrupt, a tyranny. Because I wanted to weaken it so that it would have to keep the promises it has always made and always broken. Because it betrayed Russia and the revolution. You cannot call me a traitor."

"Did you believe I would do no more than continue the old ways?"

"No. When you began changing things, I told the Americans I wouldn't work for them any longer. They said you might need help, that I might be needed to help them help you. It was true."

"Yes. That much could have been true, to some degree. But as it has turned out, I haven't needed their help, except inasmuch as they haven't attacked us. They will also, I think, try to keep us all from starving to death. But, Andrei, although what you say about the Party's corruption is true, nevertheless you took matters into your own hands. You thought you knew better than anyone else, what was good for Russia. You forgot the underlying principle of the Party: even when it appears most misguided, *the Party is always right*. There is always the core of correctness at its center, in its ideology, in its concern for the welfare of human beings. That is what I represent. No Party member has the right to attack the foundation of the Party itself, which is what you did in going to the Americans. They have always been the enemies of the Party, no matter how political realities force them to cooperate with us or support us. Andrei Sergeyevitch Mikhailov, if you are not a traitor, than you are at the least foolish, naive, and ignorant."

It was like a slap in the face. Mikhailov tried to think of something to say, of some reasoned answer, but could not.

Romanenko took the folder back and put it on the desk. "Your guilt does not end there. Do you know why I called the Leningrad summit on such short notice?"

Mikhailov shook his head.

"I had decided we must leave Afghanistan as soon as possible. That was unpopular with the various factions opposing me within the Party, government, and army, and gave them something of a common cause. I could not afford, on top of that, any widespread and overt discontent in the Warsaw Pact nations. It was clear, from many sources, that they were moving into another period of unrest. I judged that by relieving them of some of the weight of Moscow they would remain quiet until I had strengthened my position at home. I was even willing to risk some disturbances, such as the one you saw in Prague, to achieve this. But I had not intended to call the Leningrad summit until the spring. It was the decision to leave Afghanistan that made that necessary. Do you know why I decided to leave with so little political preparation?"

Again, Mikhailov shook his head.

"Because of the defeat we suffered at Herat. It was a defeat, no matter who held the city in the end. And that defeat resulted from your passing information to the Americans. Had you not done that, I would not have felt driven to act so quickly. The Leningrad summit could have been delayed."

He paused, looking down at his hands resting one atop the other in the dim pool of yellow light beneath the lamp. "There might have been no civil war."

Mikhailov heard the words, accepted them, but they carried no emotional weight; not yet. He thought: When I can feel again, how will I bear this? "Some of it is forgery," he said. "You never knew what I was doing."

"If some of it is true," Romanenko said, "all of it may be true. You have put me and the revolution in an unenviable position."

Mikhailov nodded; there was nothing else to do.

"You cannot stay in Russia," Romanenko said slowly, as though the words were being pressed out of him by some great weight. "You are too much of a political liability to me. When Moscow falls, I will be the only one who can hold this unhappy country together. If you are not here, I can deal with the charges that I knew what you were doing. If you stay, you may have to answer questions, which I cannot afford. There will be other copies of this dossier. I am giving you a choice. First, you

may go to the west, and disappear. Your friends in the CIA wi
be glad to help you do that." He fell silent.

"And second?" said Mikhailov.

"I think you know what that is," said Romanenko. "Ther
is still much fighting to be done."

Mikhailov looked at the counterpane in the bed. It wa
patterned in large red-and-white squares, like a chess board
There were wrinkles in it, betraying where Romanenko ha
lain. The lamplight cast ridges of shadow across the cloth.

I cannot go to the west, he thought. I knew I never could
even when Chantal asked me. I'm a Russian. I can't go. Uncl
Vasily was right. Traitor.

"I can't go," he said.

"Go, Andrei. I cannot predict what I'll have to do if yo
stay."

"There will be nothing you need to do."

"All right," Romanenko said without inflection. "Matter
are reaching a crisis point. Yesterday morning the Guard
Taman Division revolted in Moscow. Apparently the KGB trie
to disarm them and they resisted. The junior officers killed th
KGB men Smilga put in command and the division has attacke
the city from the south. It is trying to take Domedovo Airport
If and when it does, we will attempt to airlift troops in t
support the revolt. Unfortunately we cannot spare more than
regiment for that purpose."

Mikhailov dragged his gaze away from the dossier where i
lay under Romanenko's folded hands, trying to concentrate o
the immediate. "I thought we had most of the airborne forces."

"We do," said Romanenko. "They are to sieze the Zhigul
supreme command complex by airborne assault a few day
from now."

"*Zhiguli?*" said Mikhailov. "But there's a full KGB divisio
there. And an air-defense division."

"Osipov has studied it," Romanenko said. "He believes i
to be possible. There are two prongs to the attack. Th
strongest one will be launched from Kirov, from the north. Th
second, using the airborne division that was in Afghanistan
will start from Termez. That is why Gordik was ordered t

take the city. We must end this war quickly. If we can take Moscow with a ground attack from the direction of Kalinin, and the Zhiguli command complex from the air, Smilga and Zarudin will lose. But if our attack on Zhiguli fails, those two will have a bolt-hole even if we take Moscow. The war could go on into the autumn, with results no one can foresee. But we have to move very soon, if we are to take advantage of the Taman Division's revolt. If the Taman draws off enough troops from the Moscow garrison we will also try to drop a battalion onto the Moscow central airfield. The battalion will try to take the Kremlin by surprise. But that is a long and slender reed to support us."

Mikhailov thought hard, taking refuge from his shame and despair in the demands of his profession. The Moscow central airfield was a great empty space near the Aeroport metro station, on the edge of the central city. Despite its great value for development, no one, not even the KGB, had ever been allowed to build there. The airfield was the departure point for the leadership in time of crisis, and was only fifteen minutes from the Kremlin.

"It should be possible," he said slowly. He looked up from the red-and-white counterpane. His uncle was telling him these things to some purpose. "What do you want me to do?"

"We need a liaison with Gordik's forces. I am sending you to Termez. You will leave tomorrow evening. One of the TU26 supersonic bombers will take you south. The chances of it being intercepted are very small. Be here tomorrow at noon for your briefing. Order your deputy commander to assume your duties. You will also give certain information to Chantal Mallory. Tell her, for her control, that we are regrouping for a major attack on Moscow, and that we expect to be in control of the country within two weeks. You may also tell her about the Taman Division's revolt. But tell her nothing of Zhiguli. If you do, you will never go to Termez."

Mikhailov nodded and stood up. His knees felt as though they were to float away from him. "What will you do with her?"

"Miss Mallory? Nothing. Now that we know about her,

she is neutralized. Also we need her to tell the Americans what we wish them to know."

There was a pause. At the end of it Mikhailov said, "Yes, Uncle Vasily."

"Please go."

Mikhailov's hand was on the doorknob. "Andrei," said Romanenko, "if it had been anyone else, I would have had him shot. You were my son."

"I know," Mikhailov said.

When he had gone Romanenko smoothed the cover of the dossier carefully, running his fingertips over it as though it were something fragile and precious. Unforeseen consequences, he had said to Andrei. Some were already much too easy to foresee. The civilian population west of the Urals was facing catastrophe. Even the west could not feed all of Russia if the war were not over by autumn, if the harvest lay ungathered.

We have to succeed, Romanenko thought. If we fail, there will be chaos and death. Years and years of disaster on disaster.

He folded his hands on the dossier that had condemned his nephew. He thought: No matter what happens to Andrei, I must make sure that Nadia and Valeria are out of harm's way. If Smilga wins, he will kill both of them, simply because they are of my blood. Vyborg, I'll send them to Vyborg. If it all goes wrong they can get to Finland; the border's only sixty-five kilometers away.

Should I send Ekaterina? Smilga would kill her too.

No, he thought finally. For her to leave would be to imply that I feared defeat. In any case, she wouldn't go.

He took the dossier and burned its contents in the big pottery ashtray from the windowsill. Then he went back to the adjoining room, to Osipov and the maps.

"I'm being sent to the south," Mikhailov said. He and Chantal were walking along the Palace Embankment. It was nearly noon, and cloudy. The sky above them glowed a soft gray-white, casting light without distinct shadows. Across the Neva the Peter and Paul Fortress lay on its island, its low, grim bastions and ravelins gray and forbidding. Above the fortress walls rose the great spire of the Cathedral of Saint Peter and Saint Paul. There was no wind and the surface of the Neva barely rippled.

"When?" she asked, taking his arm.

"This evening."

"When will you be back?"

"I don't know." He told her what Romanenko had instructed him to say. There was a certain relief in it, as though in deceiving the Americans he was redeeming himself a little. Chantal listened intently. She was among the few foreigners still in Leningrad, and one of a handful of journalists Romanenko had permitted to remain. Her acquaintance with the Russian leader had served her well, professionally. She had filed three pieces on the events of 26 July and after, one of them an informal interview with Romanenko himself. Excepting diplomatic and intelligence channels, her writing had become the primary source of western knowledge about the disaster that had befallen the Soviet Union.

"Why are they sending you?" she asked. They were more than halfway along the Palace Embankment now. On the far side of the Neva Mikhailov could see the eastern tip of Vasilevsky Island; farther west, out by the Gulf of Finland, Valeria slept in her bedroom in the great housing estate.

"Liaison with General Gordik's forces, to develop our southern strategy. That's all I've been told. They're sending me straight from the briefing to the airport."

"I'm going to be out of Leningrad shortly," she said. "I've got permission to go to Riga, to do a story on the human effects of the war. Your uncle is laying groundwork to ask for economic aid, I think."

"Good," he said.

She studied him intently. "Andrei," she asked, "what's the matter?"

"I'm tired, that's all. For a Russian this is like the end of the world."

She stopped and looked away, across the Neva. "You'll never come over, will you? No matter what happens, you'll never come to the west."

"No," he said. "I can't." He almost added, *Not now*.

She sensed the words, or seemed to. "You're going to be away for a long time?"

They were standing very close together. Beyond them the river flowed silent and cold toward the Baltic Sea.

"Yes," he said. "It's quite likely."

"I wish," she said, "that we had had one day to ourselves. Just one day."

"Perhaps when I get back."

"Yes."

He looked at his watch. "I have to go."

"Try to be careful," she said.

Zhiguli-Moscow
Dawn, Tuesday, August 31

THE ANTONOV-12 TROOP TRANSPORTS boomed through the night, low over the invisible landscapes of northern Kazakhstan. They had been in the air for three and a half hours. Following them at a slightly greater altitude flew four enormous Antonov-22 strategic transports. Farther back still, because of their greater speed, was a pair of Ilyushin-76 turbofan jets carrying between them six BMD armored personnel carriers, their crews, and the headquarters staff of the 352nd Regiment of the 103rd Guards Airborne Division.

Mikhailov was sitting on the port side of the leading Ilyushin, his feet braced against the heavy cable securing one of the BMDs. He was half asleep, but even in this state he was examining and reexamining their prospects of success.

Their chances were fifty-fifty, perhaps sixty-forty in favor. There hadn't been enough aircraft to lift all the regiment's support vehicles, so the men would have limited mobility when they reached the ground. This was more worrisome than the lack of heavy weapons; if they were unable to achieve surprise and move quickly at the command-complex airfield, the KGB defenders might wipe them out before the big Antonov-22s and the Ilyushins could return from Termez with the second lift. The smaller Antonov-12s, without the range to go back to Termez, would have to fly on to Kirov in the north, if they had dropped paratroops, or land at the complex with their loads of infantrymen if they had not.

There was no chance that a single airborne regiment could defeat a KGB division and overrun the Zhiguli command center in any case. The reaction of the regiment's officers, when the plan was first explained to them, had been dismay and disbelief. Only the division's senior officers and the 352nd's regimental commander had been told that they were not the only formation to attack Zhiguli. Up north, at the big airbase at Kirov, Romanenko's staff had been collecting every transport aircraft they could lay hands on, and had managed to accumulate enough planes to lift two of the three regiments of the 106th Guards Airborne Division and half their support arms into Zhiguli. Across the Volga River and just a few kilometers away, another two battalions of the northern force would drop onto the airfield at Kubyshev and sieze that as a staging base so the rest of the third regiment could land on the next lift. This force would drive into Kubyshev in captured vehicles plus whatever they could bring with them, and overrun the Volga military district headquarters. It would then cross the river to support the attack on the command complex.

Two regiments dropped onto Zhiguli, with surprise and air support, might just succeed in taking the complex, especially with the diversion provided by the attack on Kubyshev. The defending KGB division would have to react to two threats at once, with corresponding confusion and dispersion of forces. The confusion would not likely be all on the side of the KGB, unfortunately; coordinating an airborne attack from two widely separated bases was chancy at the best of times, and the Mig-23 fighters that were to provide air support from Kirov wouldn't be available until daybreak. Plans had been made for the sophisticated and heavily armed Tu-26 bombers to hit the KGB base a kilometer from Zhiguli just before dawn, but this was a calculated risk. The bombs might miss, perhaps hit the airfield and alert the defenders, or worst of all crater the runway so the Ilyushins and Antonovs couldn't land. The paratroops would be quickly overrun if the planes carrying the bulk of the men couldn't get down.

On top of everything else were the antiaircraft defenses around Kubyshev and the command complex. These had to be suppressed or the planes would be shot out of the air before they were anywhere near the landing zones. The attack transports were flying low to deceive enemy radar, but they would be reported from the ground. Their main defense lay in several electronic-countermeasures aircraft; they were out there somewhere monitoring the targeting radars of the guns and the missile emplacements. There had also been intense radio and radar jamming for the past day, to make life difficult for the defenders without implying an imminent attack.

The objective of the assault was the underground command complex itself. The first wave of planes was to try to drop one battalion right at the mouth of the main access tunnel. These three hundred men were to capture the enormous blast doors that sealed the complex against thermonuclear attack, and destroy the huge electric motors that opened and closed the doors. If the doors were already closed, or if the defenders managed to seal themselves inside before the doors were disabled, the raid would be a failure no matter who won on the airfield.

But it was worth the risk. With Zhiguli in Romanenko's hands Smilga and Zarudin would have lost not only their most destructive strategic weapons, but also what credibility their government had left. The Americans might recognize Leningrad, undecided members of the Party would desert Moscow, and the civil war would be nearly over. The last major risk lay in the ballistic missiles of the Pacific fleet, but with Zhiguli gone and the collapse of Zarudin's government the guardedly pro-Moscow commander of the far-east district could do little but capitulate.

That, at least, was the theory. There was always the possibility of a last-ditch Armageddon precipitated by Smilga or Zarudin from Moscow, but that risk had to be accepted. The war had to end before the autumn rains.

Mikhailov opened his eyes in the dim red light of the Ilyushin's cargo hold and looked at his watch. Twenty-five minutes to the landing. He unbuckled his safety belt and made his way over the outstretched legs of the HQ officers up to the cockpit. Outside the windows to the north the sky was still pitch-black, but off to the east there was the faintest of gray light over the horizon, so faint that it might have been a trick of the eyes.

The regimental commander was sitting in the jump seat behind the pilot, studying a map in the light of a pencil torch. He looked up at Mikhailov.

"Any time now," Mikhailov said, "if they're on schedule." He was respnsible for ensuring that the attack on the control complex went forward as planned, and for reporting to the Kirov and Termez headquarters the success of the operation. Far away to the north and west the battle for Moscow had already begun; the twelve divisions of Pervishin's and Osipov's ground forces were grinding slowly toward the capital. The fate of the Taman Division, still fighting in the southern part of the city, was uncertain. At last report it had still been unable to take the Domedovo Airport so that Osipov could airlift troops to its support.

"There," said the pilot.

Far ahead there were pale flickerings on the horizon, like heat lightning. But it was not lightning; it was bombs falling on the KGB barracks and antiaircraft emplacements on the great rock of Zhiguli.

"Ten minutes of that," said the regimental commander, "then the paratroops start dropping."

At least the air bombardment had started on time. In a few minutes the paratroops should be on the airfield, and the battalion dropped at the access tunnel at the start of the bombing should have reached the blast doors. If the Antonovs are not shot down, if they find the drop zones in the dark, if the commander of the complex hasn't ordered the blast doors closed at the first sound of engines...

After a few minutes the flickerings stopped. The gray line in the east was now distinct and the sky above it was paling. The Ilyushins would be over the airfield in ten minutes. Mikhailov hoped there would be no collisions in the air or on the ground. Zhiguli's airstrip was not large.

There was a sudden reddish glow in the sky to the north. A plane had been hit. The glow sustained itself for twenty seconds and then faded, but there was still an orange light ahead: fires.

The trees below were resolving themselves from the dark landscape, like a photograph developing. A road flashed by under the Ilyushin's nose.

"I've got the ground-control officer," the pilot said. "The runway's clear. They've got half the first wave down. Light resistance at the north end; he wants us to come in from the southwest."

"That's convenient," said the colonel.

"They hit one of the planes in the first wave," the pilot added. "It went down by the river."

Neither Mikhailov nor the colonel spoke.

The Ilyushin banked steeply. The horizon, discernible now even in the north, tilted bodily.

"It's just ahead," said the pilot.

At the northern latitude of Moscow it was already fairly light, despite a patchy cloud cover at eight hundred meters. South of the river pillars of smoke rose where the Taman's tired soldiers were trying to push forward against the grim resistance of the KGB troops of the Dzerzhinsky Division. Although still bitter here and there, the fighting had dropped in intensity during the past eighteen hours as both sides began to run low on ammunition. The Taman's commander had hoped to take both Domedovo Airport and the Kremlin before this happened, but he had been able to do neither. On the other hand, the KGB troops hadn't succeeded in driving the Taman out of the city, and were at least as exhausted as the army men. It was a temporary stalemate; the winner would be the side to first receive support and reinforcement.

And that won't likely be us, thought Captain Ilitsev. Romanenko won't reach Moscow before the KGB finds some fresh troops. If only we had been able to grab the airport.

Ilitsev was crouched behind a barricade a hundred meters from the end of the Kammenyi Bridge. Across the Moscow River, at the bridge's northern end, rose the rust-colored walls of the Kremlin's southwest corner. Ilitsev's men had got farther than anyone else, but it was unlikely that they would get across the bridge; it was too well-defended. They had tried to rush it during the night but had been driven off with nasty losses.

Through his binoculars Ilitsev could see the Kremlin towers quite clearly.

They might as well be on the moon, he thought.

"What the devil's that?" said the lieutenant squatting next to him.

Ilitsev was slightly deaf from a shell that had exploded near him during the attack on the bridge. "What's what?"

"That noise. From the north. Listen."

Ilitsev raised the binoculars, searching. Multitudes of black specks, scattered among the clouds, danced into view. Planes and helicopters, scores of them.

"It's fucking well about time," he said.

"There," said the colonel to Mikhailov. The airfield was in sight ahead, a pale stripe leading away into the dawn light in the east. Away to its north rose a great cloud of smoke underlit by flames; the KGB base was on fire. There were also fires at the far end of the runway, where the paratroops were fighting for the control tower and the hangars.

Half a kilometer ahead of them flew one of the Antonov-12s, likely the last of the first wave. The waves were getting mixed up; just settling onto the runway ahead of the Antonov-12 was one of the enormous Antonov-22s, carrying three hundred and fifty men. The smaller plane behind it was too high.

"He's going to hit the lower one," said the pilot.

"Shit," said Mikhailov. There were three more of the big Antonov-22s and their own and the other Ilyushin. If the runway were blocked by a crash the attack would peter out and fail.

A string of orange and red balls, garish in the pale early light, erupted from a gun emplacement far up the runway, probably aimed at the Antonov-22. The gunners fired too high. The tracers passed over the Antonov-22 and several of them disappeared into the nose and wings of the Antonov-12 behind it. The transport seemed to pause in midair. Then an engine exploded, shredding the starboard wing. The Antonov turned half over, stalled, plummeted into the ground two hundred meters from the edge of the runway, and blew up.

"*Look out!*" screamed the copilot.

The underside of an enormous fuselage was suddenly visible through the Ilyushin's windshield. It was close enough for Mikhailov to make out dirt streaks and bright scratches in the metal skin. It was the other Ilyushin, and it was about to land on top of them.

Mikhailov's pilot had just enough altitude, and just enough power on the engines. He pushed the transport's nose down to clear the plane above, and carefully slid the big jet away to the south, banking as little as possible, but losing even more height. The engines howled. The underside of the other aircraft, visible now back to the twenty huge tires of the landing gear, slipped away to the left. Mikhailov's pilot banked a little more. Mikhailov looked out the cockpit window at the ground; he thought he could see a bird's nest in the treetops. They waited for the shudder of the port wingtip striking the other aircraft, or the jolt of the starboard one ramming a treetop.

Nothing happened. The pilot straightened the Ilyushin and began to gain height.

"Fuck," he said shakily after a moment. "That asshole. We'd better go around again."

Mikhailov found that he was quivering all over. He willed his body to stop, but it wouldn't.

Somebody was shooting at them from the ground. The tracers slid past above the cockpit and then stopped. A delta shape flashed by to starboard, waggled its wings, and climbed steeply away. The air support from Kirov had arrived.

It would be a short respite. The Migs had only enough fuel for ten minutes over the airfield before they had to return to base. Mikhailov looked at his watch.

"We've got to get down," he said urgently. "The northern support group will be here in five minutes."

"I'm doing my best, Colonel," the pilot said snappishly. Mikhailov let it pass. They had all been frightened out of their wits.

The airfield slid into sight again. In the light of the transport burning beside the runway, Mikhailov could see that the other Ilyushin and the three remaining Antonov-22s had managed to land and were rolling toward the control tower at the runway's far end. Two Migs were carrying out strafing runs on the airfield's northern side, suppressing ground fire. Moving slowly on the ground, the transports and the men inside them were at their most vulnerable.

The landing gear thumped violently onto the concrete. The pilot was putting them down fast, trying to get to the unloading point with the least exposure. The burning Antonov-12 shot past on the left and the Ilyushin's engines screamed in reverse thrust. Ahead, the other planes of the assault force grew rapidly larger. Most had their cargo ramps down and from the bays of the Antonov-22s troops were spilling in a dark mass.

There was a space left on the concrete apron in front of the control tower. The pilot swung the Ilyushin into it and tramped on the brakes. The big plane shuddered and screeched to a halt, accompanied by the loud bang of a burst tire. A grinding noise and a clang signaled the lowering of the cargo ramp. Engines burst into life in the hold: the BMD drivers were starting up.

"Let's go," the colonel said.

"We've got to get the assault guns moving toward the access tunnel," Mikhailov yelled over the din.

"I know, I know," the colonel shouted back. "Radio first; organize."

"All right."

The three BMDs were clattering out onto the apron. Mikhailov and the HQ staff swung aboard. The light was growing rapidly. From around the corner of one of the hangars a truck roared, leaning crazily in the turn. The BMDs rolled over to it, the colonel leaning out of the hatch of the lead vehicle. A major jumped out of the cab and ran to the BMD.

"We've taken the control tower for the command post," he called. "Everything's down except the two planes we lost. The assault guns are ready."

"Trucks?" asked the colonel. He had to yell as a Mig shrieked overhead.

"We captured eight. There are others but they're damaged. We'll have four more in an hour when we can fix them."

"What's happening at the access tunnel?" Mikhailov asked.

"We've got the doors but our men are under pressure. We

don't know exactly how much, we lost radio contact five minutes ago. Their communications section's probably been forced into the tunnel."

"Tell Lieutenant-Colonel Agayan to get a move on. Take all the trucks, the assault guns, put men on top of the guns. What are you waiting for?"

"Sir, Colonel Agayan was on one of the Antonovs that went down. He had all the maps."

The colonel swore, but the words were lost in a mounting rumble from the northwest. The planes of the northern support group were approaching.

"Where's Agayan's deputy, then?" bellowed the colonel.

"We don't know, Colonel, sir."

Mikhailov had to intervene. "What are your communications with Kirov and Termez like?"

"Terrible, Colonel. The jamming — "

"I'll have to go to the tunnel," Mikhailov said. He wasn't supposed to be involved directly in combat; he was supposed to insure that Agayan or his deputy carried out the planned attack. But with one of them dead and the other lost, he had no choice. "Major, go back to the assault guns and get them ready to move. Colonel, I'll need one of your BMDs with the radio in the regimental net."

The briefest of hesitation. "All right, take mine."

"Go on," Mikhailov yelled at the major. "Get going."

The BMD clanked away in pursuit of the major's truck, to the rear of the control-tower building. A clutch of sullen men in KGB uniforms sat against the wall, watched by three soldiers. On the stretch of tarmac that served as a vehicle park stood eight KrAz-214 trucks and four ASU-85 airportable assault guns. The trucks were jammed with troops, far more than their normal capacity of thirty, and more men were clinging to the backs of the ASU-85s.

Mikhailov got out of the BMD and joined the major, who was talking hurriedly to three worried officers. "Colonel — " said one of the men.

"Mikhailov," said Mikhailov. "You're the rest of the battalion HQ?"

"Sir, yes," one of them said. "I'm Captain Spassky."

"You're the ranking officer?" There was more gunfire from the airfield, mixed with the roar of descending troop transports. The KGB from the base to the north must be pulling themselves together for a counterattack.

"Yes, Colonel."

"All right. Did Colonel Agayan brief you?"

"Yes, sir, and the company commanders also. Before we left Termez."

And here he is standing around with his thumb up it, Mikhailov thought, waiting for someone to tell him what to do. If it isn't in the plan, or you don't get an order, don't do anything.

"I'm commanding you now. Get your men moving east along the road. I'll be on your heels in the BMD."

The men moved out quickly. Mikhailov said to the major, "I'll send some of the trucks back. Find whatever other transport you can and send another battalion to the access tunnel as soon as the northern support group is down and organized. I'm going to need every man I can get. If your colonel doesn't like it, tell him it's on my orders and I'll have his rank and his balls if he doesn't obey. Have you got that?"

The major nodded hastily. A shell screeched overhead, destined to fall somewhere in the forest to the south. Planes were still coming in. An Antonov howled by, low in the sky, its port wing streaming flame. Black bundles were tumbling from it, but no parachutes opened: men choosing an easier death than burning.

Sickened, Mikhailov waved his arm and the trucks and assault guns began to move.

The minister of defense looked nervously from Smilga to Zarudin and then back to the KGB chairman. "There are simply too many of them," he said. "We can't shoot them all down. They have tremendous fighter and helicopter-gunship support. Half our antiaircraft batteries on the north perimeter of Moscow were put out of action in the first five minutes of the attack."

"Are you trying to tell me," Smilga asked, "that you've lost the Moscow central airfield?"

"Not exactly, Chairman. We're preparing a counterattack. But we've committed so many men to fighting the Taman Division — "

"Let me put it another way," Smilga interrupted. "How many men has Romanenko got on the ground?"

The minister swallowed audibly and looked sidelong at his stony-faced deputy minister. No help there. "Approximately two battalions. Some transport and light assault guns. They've... captured the KGB vehicle park next to the main hangars."

"Holy Mother Russia," said Smilga. "If I didn't know better I'd swear you were working for Vasily Romanenko." He raised his voice. "Get in here!"

The office door opened abruptly and a pair of KGB men entered. Smilga pointed at the defense minister. "Take this idiot down to the courtyard," he said, "put him against a wall, and shoot him. Right now."

"*Chairman*," cried the minister. "I didn't — "

"*Get him out of here!*" screamed Smilga at the top of his lungs.

The door slammed, cutting off the minister's horrified protests. "You," Smilga told the deputy minister. "Take over. Get back to the communications center and get those troops off the airfield. Don't make any mistakes."

The new minister made a hurried exit. Smilga looked at Zarudin, who was standing against the wall chewing at a fingernail. In the past week the man had nibbled all ten of them to the quick. The habit irritated Smilga almost to distraction. "What's the matter with you?" he said.

"You didn't have to shoot him. You could have — "

"I should have had more people shot earlier. Ninety percent of STAVKA is incompetent. If they don't get those paratroops off the airfield we'll have to go to Zhiguli. What a pile of shit. Is that helicopter ready?"

Zarudin nodded. A Mil-24 gunship was on standby in the paved area in the center of the Kremlin. "It's there, warmed up. Have you been in contact with Zhiguli?" Zarudin looked at the orange telephone on Smilga's desk. It was the direct line to the command complex.

"Late last night. I — "

One of the telephones began to ring. It was the orange one.

The access tunnel's entrance was no more than two kilometers from the airfield. Mikhailov's column came under fire at the halfway point. Even before the first bullets came whipping past, Mikhailov had heard gunfire from ahead. The rear guard of the battalion dropped at the access tunnel must still be holding out, although they had to be running short of ammunition by now. They would also be under attack from inside the complex.

Men were tumbling out of the trucks ahead and leaping off the assault guns, scrambling for the protection of the ditches and trees on both sides of the road. The assault guns began pumping high-explosive shells into the forest ahead. The enemy fire slackened and stopped. The soldiers got out of the ditches and their officers waved them ahead, forming them into a firing line based on the assault guns. The trucks fell back to the column's rear and the advance continued, Mikhailov riding behind the guns in the BMD.

We're too bunched up, he thought as the BMD crested a small rise. Not enough room between the tree lines to deploy properly. We'll be shit out of luck if they've had the sense to put out an ambush.

They hadn't. From the top of the rise Mikhailov could see, five hundred meters away, the black oval of the access tunnel and the roadway leading into it. The sun had put one edge above the horizon and the rosy light fell on bodies on the asphalt, a lot of bodies. Two wrecked trucks lay in the ditch near the double fence and the pair of guard towers that formed part of the control complex's outer perimeter. On this side of the rise the forest had been cleared to give a free field of fire along the line of the fence. The KGB had thrown together some makeshift strongpoints of logs, bodies, and other wreckage and were firing at the tunnel mouth from behind them. They had tried more than one frontal attack, to judge from the number of motionless forms between the tree line and the tunnel mouth. About twenty of them, alerted by the firing to their rear, were running for the trees to take Mikhailov's small force in the flank.

They were too late. The paratroops were seasoned combat soldiers, far more experienced than the green troops — KGB or not — they faced, and they had already infiltrated the forest. One by one the KGB men went down. The assault guns formed into a wedge and charged, followed by the rest of the battalion. Thrown into confusion by the assault from behind them, the green-clad men began to throw down their weapons and raise their hands. Mikhailov's men shot them anyway.

The lead assault gun, engine screaming in low gear, rolled over a log barricade and through the broken gates of the perimeter fence. Its left-front corner hit one of the stilts supporting the north guard tower; the structure leaned tiredly and toppled across the roadway in a jumble of broken timbers. The other ASU-85s lurched around the wreckage and rolled over the fence, the soldiers following at a run across the crushed wire.

One of the trucks bounced to a stop ten meters away from the BMD. Major Spassky jumped out of the cab as the battalion HQ radioman scrambled out of the truck's rear, a big portable transceiver strapped to his back.

"Major!" shouted Mikhailov. "Can you radio the men in the tunnel?" He didn't want to send anyone in until they had done so; the paratroops holding the blast doors would assume anyone coming at them from outside to be an enemy.

"Trying now," yelled Spassky. The radioman was busy with his set. After perhaps two minutes, during which Mikhailov listened to the racket of the fighting back at the airfield and watched the road and the trees for signs of KGB activity, Spassky called, "We've got them. They're down to sixty men. They're expecting us."

"Set up a perimeter with two of the guns," Mikhailov ordered. "I'm going in with the other two and I want one infantry company. Get them together for me. Then contact Regiment and tell them what's happening."

An Antonov thundered low overhead, climbing steeply.

Spassky shouted something, Mikhailov couldn't tell what, and then waved and nodded vigorously. Mikhailov ordered his BMD forward, toward the assault guns, to help Spassky organize the attack.

Ten minutes later the blast doors, still open, were in Mikhailov's hands, and the paratroops burst into the control complex itself.

In his mezzanine office overlooking the big central control room, where the ranks of video displays and great electronic wall maps threw a multicolored glow over the rows of technicians monitoring the Soviet Union's land-based missile fleet, Marshal Oleg Abramov, commander of the strategic rocket forces, called Moscow for the second and last time that morning.

The orange telephone was ringing again. Thirty minutes had passed since Marshal Abramov had first called to report that he was under heavy attack, and that he had been unable to contact the KGB base. For that half hour, while they waited to see if the Zhiguli complex would hold or not, Zarudin had continued to bite at his fingernails until two of them bled. Smilga, apparently calm, had merely stared out the window at the old czarist senate building across from the arsenal. There was a sandbagged machine-gun emplacement on the senate's parapet, like the one on the arsenal roof directly above Smilga's office.

Smilga walked unhurriedly from the window and picked up the jangling telephone. "What is your situation?" he asked, without inflection.

"We can't hold," Abramov said. The scrambling made the words sound as though they had been uttered by a computer. "They have seized the blast doors and are inside the inner complex." He paused. "We have the command-center doors sealed but I can hear gunfire outside."

"Very well," Smilga said. "You are to execute TAMERLANE. The authorization is — "

"*What?*" shouted Zarudin. "Now? Give me that phone. I countermand that order." He lunged for the receiver. Smilga grabbed him by the shirt collar and thrust him violently away. "You cretin," Smilga hissed, "it's our only chance. No

Romanenko, no rebellion." He put the receiver back to his ear.

"You can't be sure he's in Leningrad," Zarudin snarled. "Stop. Dmitri, you fucking maniac, *stop*. Guards! Guards!"

Smilga yanked open a desk drawer. The Makarov was there. He snapped the safety off one-handed and raised the pistol.

Zarudin saw the weapon and began to fumble in his pocket.

Fool, Smilga thought, and shot the general secretary neatly between the eyes.

Abramov listened to the commotion at the Moscow end of the line with some consternation. He thought momentarily that he heard gunshots, but that was impossible. The sounds must have been out in the corridor; the attackers were getting closer. Chairman Smilga was back on the line.

"You there?"

"Yes, Chairman."

"TAMERLANE. The authorization code is as follows. A. X. One. One. Seven. Six. Two. One. One. C. B. Verify."

Abramov punched the code into the computer terminal on his desk. The screen lit up:

VERIFIED: ZARUDIN
FIELD: 21
COMPLEX: 40
PAD: 2

"Verified," Abramov said.

"Give the order immediately," Smilga said. "I will wait for your confirmation of the launch. As soon as you give it to me, shut down all power to your communications systems. I want no last-minute defense measures taken at the target, if you are overrun."

"Yes, Chairman." Abramov knew only that four missiles had been retargetted. As he picked up the blue telephone he wondered briefly what the targets were.

Seventy seconds later, in the missile-control cab buried deep under the earth two hundred kilometers east of Zhiguli, the two launch-control officers twisted their ignition keys under the watchful eyes of the KGB technicians. The silo covers blew off and the missile-ignition sequences began.

Soviet missiles, like American ones, are not very reliable unless carefully tested beforehand and fired from specially prepared silos. Of the four SS19s controlled by the cab, one failed to start its engines at all. The second had risen eighty meters in the air when a microscopic crack in its solid-fuel core caused a violent explosion that blew the missile and its warhead to fragments. The third developed a very small malfunction in its guidance mechanism, which caused it to impact in the sea, without exploding, one hundred kilometers off Novaya Zemlya twenty minutes later.

The fourth missile, obeying the realiability statistics, was right on course. It was about three kilometers north of its launch site when Mikhailov's men blew in the control center's door with demolition charges and captured the installation without further bloodshed.

Smilga sat looking at the telephone for perhaps two minutes after he received Abramov's confirmation of the launch and heard the attackers break into the control room. It was done.

Now the airfield, Smilga thought. Gas. Nobody's dared use it yet, but if there were ever a time for gas, it is now. A few hundred kilos of GD on the airfield and nobody will dare land. But quickly, quickly.

He got up from the chair where he had waited for Marshal Abramov's launch confirmation and started for the door. Zarudin could be removed later.

There was a clattering outside, from the southeast. Smilga looked out the window.

Just crossing the Kremlin wall, flying very low and fast to the right of the Konstantin Tower, were two Mil-24 helicopter gunships. Behind them bobbed at least a dozen more. The lead helicopter's nose turret was twinkling.

No, Smilga thought. Not now. He turned for the door, stumbling against Zarudin's body, knowing, as he ran, that it was hopeless; that he would never get away, that it was over.

Far above Zhiguli and somewhat to the east, an American surveillance satellite had detected the three successful missile launches. It transmitted its information to a military-communications satellite in geosynchronous orbit above North America, which then bounced it to the NORAD control center under Cheyenne Mountain in Colorado. Of the two missiles that survived their first few seconds of flight, only the one with the guidance malfunction was judged by the computers to be a potential threat to North America; the other was too far from a transpolar track. For several minutes the world was at the edge of the long-dreaded, if unintentional, holocaust. When it was noted by the computers that no other launchings had taken place, however, Cheyenne Mountain concluded that no attack was probable. The various American surveillance systems continued to track the missiles with great interest, however, and the men at the display screens under the mountain watched the trajectories lengthen with horrified fascination.

Mikhailov clung to the rear deck of the lurching assault gun as it roared toward the tunnel entrance. The circle of light expanded rapidly beyond the gun commander's helmet as the man turned in his hatch and grinned widely at Mikhailov.

We did it, he thought. Victory. Report it as quickly as possible. My uncle is waiting.

He felt no elation.

What am I going to do now? Go back to Leningrad? What then? The west, after all?

In the furious preparations for the raid and during the raid itself, he had been able to put his uncle's words out of his mind, like a burden laid down but inevitably having to be taken up again.

If you are not a traitor, then you are at the least foolish, naive, and ignorant.

It would have been better if the planes had collided after all, Mikhailov thought.

He was worried about the scene that had met them when

they broke into the command center: the screens dead, the maps dark, only the emergency lighting on. But the consoles were still warm.

They must have lost their power when we blew the door, he thought. Where were their backup generators? Maybe we got them too.

The assault gun was rolling out into the sunlight. "Over there," Mikhailov yelled to the gun captain. "The radio's over there." He knelt at the edge of the gun's deck, ready to leap off as it slowed.

Mikhailov's troops had not had time to clear the woods thoroughly. The KGB sniper up in the tree line had been watching the men around the tunnel entrance for some time, waiting, as standing orders dictated, to catch sight of a senior officer. The man on the back of the assault gun wore colonel's badges; he would do. The sniper put his eye to the telescopic sight, took careful aim, and fired.

Mikhailov was at the point of jumping from the assault gun when the bullet struck him in the left shoulder, smashed the shoulder blade, and knocked him violently onto the rutted earth. His wind was gone; he tried to draw breath to shout or scream, he didn't know which.

I have to move, he thought. Take cover.

The second bullet caught him in the throat. Blood sucked into his lungs. He tried to sit up, but he couldn't find his arms. The sky seemed to be darkening oddly.

That's not right, he thought, it can't be evening yet. Not yet.

Valeria, Valeria.

Vyborg
Tuesday, August 31, 6:23 A.M.

VALERIA WAS CRYING. Nadia struggled out of a deep sleep and looked at the bedside clock. She groaned. It was too early to get up and too late to go back to sleep. The child must be having a nightmare.

She got out of bed, pulled her green robe around her, and crossed the hall to Valeria's room. Valeria was sitting up in bed, rubbing her eyes with her fists. Nadia sat down on the bedside and put her arm around her.

"It's all right, kitten. What's the matter? Bad dream?"

The child was slowly waking up from whatever had frightened her. She nodded.

"What about? Can you remember?"

Valeria nodded. "I dreamed daddy was here, but he went away again. Where is he?"

Nadia frowned above Valeria's head, where the child couldn't see her expression. This was the fourth time in six nights she'd had the same dream. The sudden move from Leningrad to the old apartment building on Vyborg's suburban waterfront had upset her badly; the child was being uprooted too often. "He's away helping Uncle Vasily," Nadia said. "He's just fine, and he'll be home as soon as he and Uncle Vasily get rid of all the bad men."

Valeria had heard about the fighting from older children around the apartment complex in Leningrad, and Nadia had given her a child's version of the civil war, which, thank heaven, appeared to be nearly over, although the winter would be terrible unless the Americans sent food and clothing.

"Will daddy and Uncle Vasily put them all in prison so they can't hurt anybody?"

"That's *exactly* what they'll do," Nadia said. "And then everything will be nice again and daddy will come home. Now snuggle down, it's too early for you to get up yet."

"All right." Valeria lay down on her stomach, pushing her arms under the pillow, her preferred sleeping position. "Bad dreams aren't really real."

"No, love, they're just —"

The light did not grow, it was simply *there*, outside the apartment window to the southeast, with an intensity that made the very walls seem transparent. The flash lasted for no more than two seconds, but when it was gone Nadia felt as though her eyes had been exposed to a very powerful photographic flashbulb. The room seemed darkened and bluish shapes superimposed themselves on her vision. Puzzled and alarmed, she went to the window and pushed the curtain back a little.

Far away on the southeast horizon, in the direction of Leningrad, was rising the bright curve of a monstrous fireball.

Uspenskoye
Tuesday, September 14

BEYOND THE LAWN the leaves of the birches and oaks, accentuated by the dark green feathers of the pines, were a luminous gold. Above the trees the sky hung a fathomless blue, without a trace of cloud.

Romanenko, sitting on the terrace, drew the thick brown sweater closer around him. In the shadow of the dacha even the noon breeze had an autumnal edge. It carried faint scents of woodsmoke and burning leaves, as it always did out here in the fall.

Too much smoke, Romanenko thought. Too much burning. What a long road we have had to follow to go where we should have gone in the beginning. So much death on the way, Leningrad a poisoned cinder, a million dead there alone. And more to die, what do you do with a hundred thousand people whose skins have been burned away and who still live? Peter the Great's gray city on the Neva, gone forever; we will not even be able to rebuild there for a hundred years. How could Smilga have done it?

He had been able to ask Smilga that. The KGB chairman had been caught by the paratroops as he tried to escape from the Kremlin, pointlessly; resistance in Moscow was already collapsing. He had been brought to Kalinin, where Romanenko had gone to be near the front.

Asked why he had done it, Smilga had only shrugged and said: "The preservation of the Revolution is worth any price."

Romanenko had looked at Osipov, and then at Konstantin Tsander, one of the few members of the government lucky enough to be out of Leningrad when the bomb came. Tsander said, "You admit that you ordered this?"

"Why should I deny it?"

Osipov and Tsander waited to see what Romanenko would do. Romanenko looked at Smilga, who stood defiantly, his face bruised and scraped from his capture.

"I sentence you to death," Romanenko had said. "By hanging."

There was an apple tree in the rear garden of the hotel that was serving as Romanenko's headquarters. Some of Osipov's soldiers put Smilga on that. He had taken quite a long time to die.

Romanenko shook his head briefly to clear away the memory. A movement out on the lawn caught his eye. Valeria was walking slowly toward the terrace from the direction of the birch wood. She often spent time there now, as though searching for the ghost of her dead father.

Oh, lucky that I sent them to Vyborg, Romanenko thought. She would be ash, now, gone as though she had never been.

The child trailed slowly up the steps to the terrace. Her small face was wan and pinched, the spark all but extinguished. Romanenko wondered how long she would mourn.

"Hello, Uncle Vasily."

"Hello, kitten."

She sat on the chair next to his, pale and motionless. "Valeria," he said with an effort, "you're getting cold. Go find Aunt Nadia and ask her to give you something hot to drink."

"I'm not thirsty. Or cold."

"Go, kitten. We don't want you to get sick."

"All right."

He watched her go in by the French doors, and then looked out to the birch wood again. She was far too acquiescent; he would have been happier if she had argued.

The French doors behind Romanenko creaked; an army major stood in the opening.

"Secretary, the journalist is here."

"Let her come out by herself," Romanenko said. "And have more coffee sent. Also something for her to eat."

The major nodded and disappeared. Romanenko returned to his contemplation of the wood. In an hour he had to return to Moscow and the long task of rebuilding the Party and the country, but he had wanted to speak with her one last time.

She was standing in the doorway, wearing a gray dress. Beneath her eyes there were blue semicircles, prominent against the paleness of her skin. For a moment Romanenko thought they had beaten her, against his orders; then he realized that she was only exhausted.

"Come and sit down, Miss Mallory," he said. "There will be coffee and food in a moment. Have you eaten this morning?"

She shook her head absently and came to sit on one of the white iron chairs facing him. She was shivering a little. Romanenko took the jacket off the back of his chair and passed it to her. She drew it around her shoulders and sat, hands clasped in her lap, looking down at the table, not speaking.

A corporal brought hot bread, butter, jam, coffee. "Eat," Romanenko said. "You'll feel better."

She obeyed. Romanenko drank more coffee himself. It was very quiet. Most of the birds had gone south. The great house was as still as if deserted. There was security, a great deal of it, but it was unobtrusive.

She seemed to have finished eating. Romanenko poured her more coffee. She drank, for the first time looking directly at him.

"Why did your men arrest me in Riga?" she asked, setting her cup down. "The trip to Riga was approved. I was there with permission. I didn't talk to anyone I shouldn't have."

Romanenko studied her for a long moment. Andrei was in love with this woman, he thought. Did he betray me because of her?

"Miss Mallory," he said, "I know that you are an operative of the Central Intelligence Agency. You were Andrei's control in Moscow and Leningrad." Despite what he had implied to Mikhailov, he could not risk having the woman free. But he had delayed her detention until she went to Riga; it would be less noticeable there than in Leningrad. He wanted questions about her from neither the American consulate nor his own people.

"That's absurd," she said. Somewhere she found the energy to look shocked. "We were friends, Nothing more."

Romanenko shrugged. "Be that as it may. You were more than friends, I think. I saw the way he looked at you when you were together here."

"Talk to Andrei," she said. "He'll tell you I'm not a spy."

"Miss Mallory, you are either very naive or very professional. I believe the latter. I have already talked to Andrei. There were documents. He admitted that he was in contact with the Americans. He also told me why. I could not but sympathize with him. But he has cost his country a great deal of blood."

"I don't understand you."

Romanenko sighed. "I won't press you." He paused. "You were very lucky not to be in Leningrad."

She nodded dully, the defiance gone. "I couldn't believe it. I thought it was a rumor, at first."

Romanenko felt another dreadful stab of grief, and then put it away. There was no time. "My wife Ekaterina died there," he said. "I escaped only because I had gone to Kalinin."

Chantal brushed a hand over her eyes as though the light had become too bright, although the terrace was in shadow. On the lawn a sparrow bobbed, hunting.

"May I see Andrei?" she asked.

"Andrei is also dead." Romanenko's voice broke momentarily, despite his control. He looked away to the gold birch trees among the pines. "He was killed in the fighting in the south, toward the end."

Chantal nodded, as though she had known. At last she said: "What are you going to do with me?"

"I am going to send you home. There is no damage you can do that is important beside what has already been done. If things had been different —" He shrugged. "Andrei loved you."

"I know," she said. Her voice was quiet and very distant.

Romanenko studied the birch trees. The wind had dropped and the golden leaves hung motionless. He seemed to gather himself together. "It's time you went home," he said.

When she was gone he remained for a while on the terrace. Now that the breeze was gone he could hear the brook rustling beneath the birches and firs and oaks, the water noisily free these last autumn days before the frost bound it under a roof of ice, where it would run silent until the spring.